I0614360

UNDER THE RUSHES

AMY LANE

Dreamspinner Press

Published by
Dreamspinner Press
5032 Capital Circle SW
Ste 2, PMB# 279
Tallahassee, FL 32305-7886
USA
http://www.dreamspinnerpress.com/

Under the Rushes

Cover Art by Anne Cain
annecain.art@gmail.com

ISBN: 978-1-62380-244-8

Printed in the United States of America
First Edition
December 2012

eBook edition available
eBook ISBN: 978-1-62380-245-5

As always, this one goes to Mate because he loves me, and I'm not always sure why. But it also goes to Mary, who believes in my worlds and understands my craving for fantasy; and to Lynn, who likes all angst; and to Gin, who edited this one and didn't, not once, threaten to throw me in a black and brackish quarry with a granite boulder necklace to commune with the muck at the bottom.

Under the Rushes

THE boy should not have been there.

Dorjan almost stopped short, but the phalanx behind him was wearing steam-enhanced walking armor, and the subsequent crash-up and bottleneck would literally cripple the army. Still, the boy was not supposed to be there.

Dorjan was nineteen. He'd enlisted two years earlier, because the age of consent was sixteen, and he'd wanted to finish his university studies before he joined to serve his province. He was young, brilliant, and well trained. He'd also practiced for hours while using the steam-enhanced walking armor, and he had a few tricks the commanding officers were not aware of.

Fluidly, using some well-honed muscles he was justly proud of, he stepped *sideways*, taking all of the forward inertia of the steam system to propel both his armor and his body and redirect it. After two smooth steps, he disconnected the main copper tube tugging at the back of his neck, sending the steam into the frosty autumn evening. His armor suddenly drooped around him, pulling him down like weights in a quagmire. Of course, part of that might have had to do with the spongy ground and the tricky bits of gravity that rolled through the Karanos province.

The gravity was, in fact, one of the reasons Dorjan's government, the Forum of Biemansland, had refused to quell this threat of usurpation until the steam armor was perfected. Dorjan's friend Areau had participated in that development—in the development of most of the army's new technology—and was justly proud of his creation.

The gravity was behaving at the moment, and that was good, because the steam armor without the steam weighed a bloody ton... but still.

The boy was not supposed to be there.

He was young—nine at the most—and Dorjan wouldn't have noticed him, except his hair was blacker than sin-stained pitch, and he was hiding in some rushes that had gone brown with the chill of the season. The off color had caught Dorjan's attention first, but as they'd made to pass, he'd seen the eyes—almost that same black, he thought, but then they glinted midnight blue.

And that was when Dorjan broke formation.

He squatted down next to the rushes and looked curiously into them. The boy had reached that age where his arms and legs were too long in proportion to his body, and his hands and feet were even longer still. But in spite of that protuberance of limbs and predominance of elbows and knees, he seemed small for his age, and quick, and the look he cast Dorjan was unfriendly and cautious but not frightened.

"What're you doing here, boy?" Dorjan asked before he grimaced and lifted his visor so the boy could see his face. Bimuit, what a disaster. "There were to be no people here. We're destroying a building, that is all."

The boy's eyes grew huge. "A building? The only building is mine!"

Dorjan frowned and tried to speak nine-year-old boy. "Yours—you mean you have a hut around here?"

The boy's mouth pulled up in a sneer, and too late Dorjan recognized the fineness of his clothes: small-weave linen with leather patches at the elbows, and boots that were supple and had two buckles on the sides. "A hut? I'm not a bloody peasant, you prat bastard! You're heading for Kiamath Keep—I *live* there. That's the only place this road leads!"

"Lokargo!"

Dorjan swore to himself and looked up at his lokogos. "Yes, Lokogos Dre!"

"What are you doing out of ranks? Your battalion has gone on without you!"

Dorjan frowned at the man and gestured to the boy. "He says we're not heading to a weapon stockpile," he told the man, feeling lost. The stratego had been most clear—Dorjan had been in the room when he'd briefed Dorjan's superiors. He'd said they were eliminating a weapons stockpile and that there should be no civilian casualties. It would be a righteous victory, Stratego Alum Septra had proclaimed, one they could be proud of.

It was, Dorjan knew, the only reason Areau had agreed to work so many sleepless nights on the armor. He wanted peace. Hell, *all* of the citizen soldiers wanted peace. It was the banner under which they'd enlisted. As young as he'd been, Dorjan had plowed through his studies like he was being ridden by a steam-powered nisket so he could enlist in the damned army and fight for peace.

The lokogos swung down off his mechanized cricket and flat-handed the spot right behind the creature's ear. "Not a stockpile?"

To his credit, he sounded stunned.

"That's my home!" the boy shouted, and Dorjan was right—he wasn't stupid. "You're taking all these scary people to my home? And the company that went before?"

Dorjan blinked at him, the full horror of the situation descending. His company was supposed to ride cleanup. Areau was probably approaching the compound now with the stratego, the better to simply destroy the place so Dorjan's company could put out the fire and keep destruction to the surrounding marshland to a minimum.

"Lokogos!" Dorjan said, suddenly fearing.

"Connect your armor," the lokogos muttered. "Connect it. Now. Get on the cricket—I said *get on*!"

Dorjan looked at the boy. "Boy," he muttered numbly, "stay here." He looked at the lokogos, who nodded. "Stay hidden. I'm going to try and stop a disaster, you hear me?"

The boy's face had frozen, and for the first time, Dorjan saw fear. "My mum?" he said, sounding shocked. "My da? My wee baby sisters—there's three of them! You monsters wouldn't hurt the wee babies, would you?"

Dorjan didn't know how to answer that. Two minutes ago he would have said no, but now? They'd been told no casualties. They'd been told a bloodless exercise—a warning shot. How could this intelligence they'd been given be so wrong?

He reconnected the steam pipe at the back of his neck and threw his leg over the cricket. He lifted his arse just *so*, plopped his bottom down, and felt the steam jack of the cricket fit into the port in the armor, and suddenly the generator that made the armor so heavy was now powering them both.

"Hide, boy," he shouted and pointed the cricket toward the south, where Areau's regiment had been heading. He rubbed his hands flat down the back of the cricket's head. The legs—useful for hopping among the burdocks of weeds in the swamp—suddenly folded behind the cricket's metal body, and the big rubber-gum covered wheels descended and began to whirr.

The lokogos shouted through his amplifier for the entire battalion to adjust right, and a corridor opened down the road on the left. Dorjan closed his eyes, said a prayer, and thumped twice on the cricket's head to ride at full speed ahead.

It was a nightmarish ride, made worse by the cricket's speed and its tendency to leap whenever an obstacle appeared. If Dorjan hadn't been jacked into the generator port, he would have been thrown, and sometimes, in his worst moments afterward, he wished he had been. But that night, hurtling across the dirt road and through space, he still believed in honor and that this entire debacle was just an honest mistake.

The cricket arrived at Kiamath Keep after a particularly hairy bound. Dorjan actually had to close his eyes at the sight of battalion after battalion marching upon what he could see clearly from this vantage point was exactly what the boy had said: a compound, a simple keep, much like the one Dorjan had been brought up in. It wasn't an armory, it was a country town house designed to cater to the farmers who were supported by the landholders, who did their duty in the Forums and Triaris of town.

It was a large farm with perhaps ten to twenty families. From the cricket's terrible height, Dorjan had seen the people huddled against the walls of the compound, the better for the metal arrows of the infantry to miss them. He looked down at the beginning of the cricket's descent and quickly surveyed the chaos of the night. It was war, filled with the magnesium flares of soldiers preparing to launch munitions, the shouts of the techs performing maintenance on their armor, and the scream of metal and gears as the machines of war defied inertia and began the slow hurtle to murderous momentum. Dorjan landed directly in front of the other crickets in the battalion, pretty sure of what he'd find: the three lokogos as well as Stratego Alum Septra, the man who had brought wars to the borders of Biemansland.

"*Stop!*" Dorjan screamed, ripping off his visor so they could see not just the insignia of lokargo on his uniform but the human behind it, and the commanding officers all stopped in what looked to be a last-minute conference and stared at the boy wearing lokargo insignia and riding a lokogos's cricket.

"Boy, you'd better have some explanation as for what in the hell—"

"It's not a munitions warehouse!" Dorjan cried, gesturing to the castle walls, especially the fortifications with very worried-looking people on the ramparts. "Aren't you people looking? I could see it myself from the cricket—it's a keep! There are women and children in there!"

Dorjan would remember that moment. The three lokogos, they looked surprised and skeptical, their faces frozen in the glare and flicker of the magnesium torches and the arc-welding that was going on in the chaos of setting up for battle.

But Stratego Alum Septra? Dorjan saw his face, saw the way his mouth quirked up at the corners, saw the calculation in his eyes.

"You *know*!" Dorjan shouted, and Alum drew twenty years as stratego and counselor around his shoulders and lied.

"I know nothing of the sort, and I don't believe you either."

The three lokogos all jerked back, stunned, because now they were fucked. They could either believe the raw young lokargo or they could believe their stratego. What were they to do?

"Who gave you permission to ride a cricket?" the youngest lokogos demanded. Even Dorjan could tell he was dodging the point.

"My lokogos!" Dorjan snapped. "Even *he* felt this was important information!"

"Who told you this?" the stratego asked. "Why would you break formation, *Lokargo*, to learn intelligence that is *obviously* above your pay grade?"

Dorjan's jaw hardened. "A child," he said, making sure his eyes never left Septra's. "A child who was afraid we were going to slaughter his family, because *his family* occupied the only dwelling within walking distance of the damned army! Now are you people too damned lazy to even get on your lousy crickets and look? Or are you so sure of your souls that you'll risk demolishing innocent people for politics?"

The lokogos looked at each other uneasily, and for a moment Dorjan thought he might actually have their attention. And that's when he saw Stratego Alum Septra push a button on the side of his cricket while the lokogos were all looking at each other in confusion. Suddenly the chaos of the battlefield was silenced as a single massive flare launched up in the eerie quiet. It was burning so brightly that its shallow arc—designed to descend a mere half klick away—could hardly be seen.

Dorjan gazed at Alum Septra in horror, seeing him for the first time. A handsome man with a long jaw and silver hair pulled back into a smooth queue, he wore his dress uniform trappings over his armor for what was supposed to be nothing more than a training exercise.

He looked, Dorjan thought in shock, like a man dressed for the copper glyph that would make him famous.

"Oh dear," Septra said urbanely. "It seems that even if you're right, you arrived a moment too la—"

Dorjan didn't hear what else he said, because he had launched his own cricket straight up into the air, preparing the same flare Septra had launched—but preparing it to fire at the flare that was still gracefully arcing toward the innocent civilians in the compound.

"Can you do this?" he asked the cricket. The machine, which knew only what it had been programmed with, circled the probability dial slowly, even as they hovered in the air.

Dorjan looked at the dial and swallowed: 15 percent probability.

"Then do it," he muttered and pushed the same panel Septra had.

The magnesium bomb traveled a lot faster and a lot straighter than Septra's, and it connected, but not solidly, sending both projectiles spinning wildly into the brush beyond the castle.

There was an explosion so bright he closed his eyes behind the tinted goggles of his visor and barely had time to open them again to sight the cricket's landing plane.

By the time the cricket touched down, the fire sparked by the magnesium bombs in the dry grasses of the autumn bogland had turned the horizon a fiery bronze-blood red.

The cricket landed hard and Dorjan was tossed off, his armor disengaging and pummeling his body as he landed. Without the steam to provide a cushion and protection, he knocked about inside the metal plating like a plum in a steel box. Odds were good he'd be the same color the next day, but it didn't matter. He was running on adrenaline now, and he'd actually pulled himself up off the ground and was looking wildly around before the golden-haired god of his childhood intruded on his tinted vision.

"Bimuit and Karanos!" Areau thunked a wide-palmed hand on Dorjan's shoulder and was hauling him around—probably to tackle him and pummel him some more, knowing Areau's temper.

Dorjan yanked off his visor and goggles before he could try, and fought for breath. "People!" he gasped. "There are people in the keep!"

Areau stopped with his fist hauled back behind his ear and became a focused beam of stillness in the mayhem of the night. "People?"

"It's a *keep*, Areau! There're families in there, probably ten or so—they're huddled away from the safety arrows—"

Areau looked up to see the blood-bronze flare of light, and a sudden new wave of bedlam washed over the battlefield. "Bimuit! Dorjan, the fire is heading right for them!"

They locked eyes, a lifetime of understanding between them. Dorjan's father, Kyon, ruled the keep, but Areau's father was his right-hand man. Their keep had been one of the most productive of Biemansland until the war had forced them to strip away most of their gain in the form of taxes, and there was nothing—horses, lessons, their first girl, Dorjan's first kiss with a boy—that the two of them had not shared in their hearts.

They shared this too, without even a word.

Dorjan vaulted to the back of the battered cricket and made sure his port was securely attached. It was difficult to get in—the port had been bent with the fall—but he wiggled in and offered Areau his hand.

"I'll vault the children out," he called as Areau swung his leg up over the cricket. "You get the officers near the gate to help you with the others."

"Deal!" Areau's arms tightened around Dorjan's middle, and for a moment Dorjan was reminded of the helpless, useless torch he'd carried for his best friend since he'd first kissed a boy and decided they were more fun than girls. Areau had undergone no such revelation, and Dorjan closed his eyes and hoped it wasn't the guilt, Areau's ever-present fear that Dorjan's disappointment would sever their two hearts that so often beat together.

The cricket bounded up into the aether and landed solidly square in the middle of the courtyard.

Oh God. They were terrified. Without knowing what he was searching for, Dorjan found three girls, their hair as black as pitch and night sky, and thought of the boy, the scrappy, arrogant kid on the side of the road. He lifted up his visor as Areau scrambled down off the cricket, and called out to them.

"There's a magnesium fire on its way! Give me the children—I'll lift them out. Areau will try to get the adults out through the gate. We're sorry—we thought this place was empty. Please… please let us help you."

The mother had the same black hair and midnight eyes in the pale face, and the father was whippet thin and brown haired, so his blue eyes were surprising. They came up together with their daughters and about half a score of other children under twelve gathered before them.

"Please," the mother whispered. "Please—can you?"

Dorjan nodded. Areau had slid off and was herding the adults under the ramparts, where the first wave of infantry had been stationed. Dorjan could hear his voice, commanding, strong, thundering over the objections of the lokogos there, but that was not his job. He had to trust in Areau as Areau had trusted in him from the moment they'd first enrolled in the academy.

"We have a son!" the father protested as the mother shoved her girls up behind Dorjan. Dorjan pulled at leather harnesses attached to the exoskeleton of the cricket. The harnesses were hidden under the top plate of armor but could be pulled out for passengers, and the mother and father used them to secure the girls.

"Make the attachment logical!" he warned. "I need to let them off so I can come back for the rest of the children!"

The father nodded, and he seemed an able man. "About our son—"

"He's the one who told us your keep was occupied," Dorjan said. "When I left him, he was safe." His mouth quirked up, because that could have been the only bright spot in what was surely career suicide even if he and Areau survived. "Angry, but safe."

The parents nodded, and Dorjan looked behind him. "Hold tight!" he ordered tersely, hoping the girls were secure. He wasn't sure if it was the heat from the fire or his own fractured imagination, but he was sweating inside his armor, and the fire-illuminated faces of the girls seemed flushed as well. "One, two, *three!*"—and with that, the cricket took its biggest leap yet.

The girls didn't scream. He checked twice in flight behind them, and they were wide-eyed and looking past the brutal wind at their surroundings. The steam armor had served his battalion well, and Dorjan saw his own men, led by the lokogos who had given him the cricket, racing down the road as if to help. He aimed for them and landed in front of his surprised lokogos before he turned to help the girls slide off the cricket in his hurry to get back.

"What in the furry asscrack of Bieman…." Lokogos Dre stopped his swearing when he realized there were children on board, and Dorjan was so grimly determined to finish out his task he didn't even smile.

"The stratego tried to blow the place after I told him," Dorjan snapped tersely. "I kept the mag-bomb from landing, but the whole bloody bogland is on fire. Where's the boy?"

Dre grimaced. "Wriggled out of my grasp as soon as you took off! Said he couldn't trust you to do the job right."

Dorjan found he was growling, mostly because it was true. "These are his sisters. I'll be back with more. This could end badly for us, you understand?"

Lokogos Dre nodded. "I didn't sign on to slaughter children," he said. "You neither, even though you are one. You get them here; I'll keep 'em safe. Their parents?"

Dorjan looked toward the keep and shuddered. "Lokargo Areau—with munitions. He's getting the parents out. Ready?"

"Bimuit's luck!" the lokogos wished, and Dorjan thumped his closed fist against his chest even as he bade the cricket to jump.

His next visit to the keep, it wasn't his imagination—the fire was moving quickly and it was moving mercilessly. He'd seen the tech battalions hosing down their own environs with flame retardant, but he wasn't a fool. They were staying carefully beyond the keep. Alum Septra was going to let those people burn, and take credit for the kill.

Not if Dorjan could help it.

The second time at the keep, the parents must have been as frantic as Dorjan—they shoved even more children up on the cricket's back—five this time, two of them hanging precariously over the sides. "You can hold on?" he asked, and he believed their frantic nods because he had to. Up, up, and away he bounded, giving thanks under his breath when the little ones proved good to their word. He stared at the keep and the closing flames, not even speaking to Lokogos Dre as the man unharnessed the frightened children. (They had held on, but this batch had screamed, and two of the girls, tiny and terrified, were screaming still when he lifted off again.)

He landed in the courtyard, feeling his armor heat so badly his skin blistered beneath it, and saw that the children were drooping, semiconscious, in their parents' arms.

"Where's Areau!" he called, wincing as one of the smallest screamed upon touching the heated metal of the stressed cricket. Without a word, the lady of the keep ripped off her nightdress and stood, fat and middle-aged and bare in the center of the courtyard, so she could swaddle the boy from the heat. Her husband was not far behind with his own sleep tunic.

"Is that all?" Dorjan called, lifting his visor so they could talk.

The adults nodded, and two people came from the shadows with lengths of wet muslin in buckets that were already beginning to steam. "Areau!" he called. "Areau! What's your status!"

He heard a hacking and Areau stumbled from the doorway. "We're using a blow torch to get through the gate. They won't help us open it, the fucking gits, but they've promised not to kill us if we get through!" Pained voices cheered beyond the ramparts, and Areau looked up and nodded. "Go—*go*, Dori! I'll be there! I swear! We'll face the Triari together, you and I, Bimuit's luck!"

Dorjan reached down, seized Areau's hand, and pulled him close with their clasped hands between them. They touched foreheads and Dorjan muttered, "Bimuit's luck!" before he straightened and bounded upward one more time.

He barely avoided the magnesium missile that had been aimed and waiting for his exit from the keep. He pulled the steering stick to the right frantically, then pounded at the two stabilizer wheels on either side of the board to keep the thing from rolling in midair. The children screamed as the magnesium seared their skin and the heat choked their lungs. His armor protected him to an extent, but the five children bound to the back of the great metal beast—

He cried out as one of them slipped off and went tumbling down, and then another. Bimuit, oh hells! Two of them, and then a third, but she didn't even scream, and he wondered if she hadn't been dead or unconscious before she fell.

"No!" he cried. "No! Hells, Bimuit! Hold on! Oh hold on!" The cricket hurtled downward, preparing its legs for landing, and he saw that one of them was frozen, unable to support weight. He had just enough time to scream, "Jump!" as the cricket tumbled to the ground.

The children landed painfully on the soft bogland, but he was attached to the cricket. It thudded hard, throwing him against the windscreen before rolling over him twice, the force so great he felt his bones give and his skin split. He screamed in pain, and the cries of the children answered him, so for a moment he felt relieved—at least some had survived. The cricket twitched, rolling off of him, and he screamed again. With the cricket gone, he had a clear view of the keep, and now he screamed in rage.

He saw the final magnesium bomb arc gracefully into the air and fall and hit the keep, and he was still screaming as the inferno destroyed it all.

WHEN he stood before the Triari, he stood alone.

He'd been scooped off the battlefield in fractured pieces and had spent a month in recovery. Lokogos Dre was his first visitor.

"Lokargo," the lokogos said tentatively, "it's good to see you're recovering." He looked both ways in the infirmary, but Dorjan was the only one there. He'd been removed to a special ward for military criminals, and the gauze sheets separated him from... nobody. Not even nurses and doctors, whom he saw when it was necessary, but not enough to know them as people.

"The children?" Dorjan mouthed, because he was not sure how much anybody knew. Nobody would tell him.

Dre looked left and right and removed his cap, revealing blond hair cut short but not shaved. "Smuggled to my father's keep," he murmured. "Before we could get to you, Septra's personal battalion ran in, calling you a war criminal and saying you were responsible for the deaths of our men." Dre glared about him again. "This is the only military hospital anywhere near the Biemansland-Karanos border, and Bimuit, boy, I swear the only other person besides you is a boy with diarrhea. It's a ruse, sure enough, to explain why we were trying to take out that keep."

"Why *were* we trying to take out that keep?" Dorjan asked before the one thing he really wanted answered superseded the strategy of the people falsely accusing him. "And where the hell is Areau?"

He saw the tentative look of sorrow on Dre's face and knew his heart was about to fail.

"He's not—"

"No!" Dre muttered, and again, that fearful look about the place. "He suffered wounds—he was trying to drag the last of the people out when the mag-bomb hit. I heard him screaming as they carried him away, but he was still alive. As far as I know, they've taken him into the asylum in Thenis."

Dorjan tried to scowl through the pounding in his head. "Thenis? Bimuit! Why there? That place is… it's bedlam! Are they healing him, if he was hurt? Why would they shove him in that place?" His whole body ached and his soul most of all, but this… oh, God, Areau, who had followed him out of the same sense of duty Dorjan had been instilled with. "Why? Why would they shove him there?"

Dre leaned closer. "Don't you see? They don't think he has people—they think you're it. Now see, I've been to your father's hold. I know how it works there. You all have the mines, and the niskets, and that alone is a bond there, and you share that with the miners and the farmers and everybody. Areau's yours, like kin, and I've sent word to your father, so he's probably working on it, but he's working on it legal."

Dorjan remembered Lokogos Dre, back when the man was a young lokargo, seeking shelter at his parents' keep on his way to his own keep, which was even farther out from Thenis, the principal city. "Why is that wrong?" he asked, and Dre's look of pity would haunt him for the rest of his life.

"Don't you see? What they were doing? That wasn't legal. Septra got found out—he's not going to be happy, and he's going to pin it on you and on your friend there, and on me—"

"No." Dorjan looked at him and shook his head, his heart pattering against his ribs. "We can't allow them to pin it on you, Dre. We'll lie first to keep you there. We need an honest man in the army. Did this… this hieterfuck do it for Septra? Was he promoted to Triari?"

"No—which probably steamed him right through his armor plates, if you ask me. He had a reporter with a copper glyph and a wax mold for his phonograph, all ready to make a talking head for his announcement. He's putting it about that two young cadets committed treason on his watch—which sends your credibility into the privy, but it's not looking so great for him either. He's not Triari, not yet. In fact, I think it put him down on the list. The other rumor is that he led us into an ambush, and there's even another, that's the truth, that has civilians in that keep." Dre had pulled up a chair, his crisp brown uniform practically bending like pasteboard as he sat. He had gold braid at his shoulders, but he was, as far as Dorjan could tell, missing some of an officer's treasured pins at his breast. No, Dre had not done well by this, but he hadn't complained of it either.

Dorjan nodded. "We need you," he said quietly, his brain churning steadily ahead. When Areau had been working on the steam armor with the other military alchemists, Dorjan had told him once that he wished someone could connect a steam pipe to his brain so it could move in those lovely, fitful leaps and bounds, like the soldiers in their armor and the transpo crickets. Areau had laughed and cuffed him in the ear. *Your brain works fine and solid as it is. No leaping about for Dori's brain—need to keep it on the true way and have it steamroll any shite that lies in the path before it.* "We need you," he repeated, his thoughts finding their purchase in the uneven ground of maybe.

"For what?" Dre asked, but he asked it eagerly.

Dorjan wished his head would stop pounding, and the breaks in both arms and legs and his ribs and his chest, but he began to form a plan around the pain. "We need to stop him," Dorjan said. "If he's not losing his commission for this, sooner or later, he *will* be the Triari—that must be it! The power, the money—"

"The way out of harm's way," Dre grumbled, and Dorjan remembered the man's cowardly act of launching the mag-bomb.

"That too," he agreed. "So he wants on the Triari, and we need to stop him, and to do that, we need information."

Dre nodded. "So what's your plan?"

Dorjan sighed. "Well, I'll tell them I rescued the children and gave them to a soldier—a deserter. If you can fabricate a name for me, that would help. But I'll sell them that pile of slop and tell them I stole your cricket—"

"Didn't you already tell them I gave it to you?" Dre asked, upset, and Dorjan barely managed to tilt his bandaged head sideways.

"Do you think they'll gainsay me?" he asked crossly. "If they try it, they'll have to admit I told them civilians were in the keep, and at the moment, I think they're trying to ignore that part altogether. So I saved the children, gave them to someone untrustworthy, and I have no idea where they are. I knocked you cold after we found the boy—what happened to the boy?"

Dre snorted. "I told you—he ran off. I've had soldiers looking for him too, but no luck. Not in Karanos, not in Biemansland—I don't know if he'd manage to make it to any of the other provinces. He was only a wee boy."

Dorjan remembered the boy's assurance, his pride, and would have shrugged if his wounds had let him. "I'll have to believe he made it," he said, not wanting to think about the three of the five children who hadn't made that last trip on the cricket. "I have to." And it was nothing less than the truth.

"So we save your job, and then my father and I, we'll have to find out where Areau is, and get him back and—"

They both stopped. They heard footsteps coming, purposeful and impersonal. A doctor, shrouded in white, with a white cloth helmet and white cloth mask, peered around the corner. "Your time is up, Lokogos. The... *lokargo* is resting." The man's contempt was unmistakable.

Dre stood up and leaned forward. "We'll find your friend, boy. You save my job, I'll make myself useful, worry not." With that, he turned to the contemptuous doctor. "That boy has saved more people in one act than you have in your entire life, you quack—you treat him right or I'll have you transferred to the Thenis asylum, you hear me?"

And with that, Dre was gone, and Dorjan was left to wonder how long until someone who could help him write a letter would visit.

A MONTH later he stood in his basic lokargo's uniform—pressed brown pants, burnt-umber jacket, silver braid at the shoulders, and a hexagonal cap with a stiff brim—and gave testimony to the three governing Triari of the Biemansland province.

To say it was a travesty of justice was to say mag-bombs burned hot.

The three Triari were elected from the rulers of the individual keeps, and occasionally from someone who had distinguished him or herself in the military. In this case there were two men and a woman, all landowners, in their late middle age, who all wore the traditional togas (the woman deferred to the late fall by wearing a white sweater beneath hers) and crowns of oak. All three surveyed Dorjan dispassionately as he stood, with aid of a cane, and answered their questions without pause, without a chair, and without even a glass of water offered as a courtesy.

His father would say later that he'd never been prouder of Dorjan than on the day he destroyed his life.

"So, Dorjan, son of Kyon, what do you have to say for yourself?"

It felt like the sixth time (his father said it was the twelfth) that the question had been asked.

"There were civilians in the keep—"

"That's never been verified."

"Nobody wanted to verify it," Dorjan snapped bitterly. "And you've successfully buried the other lokargo who would have." He was aching and exhausted and tired of courtesy and worried for Areau. They had located him—and Dorjan's father had smuggled an honest-to-aether healer into the ward to make sure he didn't die of infection (or a lead pipe to the head)—but so far they hadn't been able to smuggle him out.

The healer said Areau needed to come out. His wounds had healed, but they'd been mishandled and had scarred terribly. The healer danced around Areau's state of mind, but Dorjan knew—without even seeing him again—that the playful, brilliant friend of his boyhood was never going to smile into Dorjan's eyes again.

"We are aware of Lokargo Areau's difficulties," the woman said, and she lowered her voice gently. "We understand that the disaster that killed so many of your men had a terrible effect on his mental health."

"None of our men died," Dorjan responded crossly. "I don't know where they've been reassigned, but before my cricket crashed, they'd effectively sprayed the fire-retardant bubble. Those battalions were going to be *fine*! But the civilians in the keep—they were going to die!"

"Are you saying the stratego and three lokogos all *lied* about the casualties of Kiamath Keep?"

"I'm saying I landed that cricket, told them there were civilians in the keep, and the stratego fired a magnesium charge at the keep without even resolving the issue!"

There was a breathless silence because this had not been part of the questioning.

"That's impossible," the oldest Triari stated. "If that charge had gone off, there wouldn't have been any children to rescue!"

"I shot the charge out of the air, Triari—how do you think the fire started?"

That airless, motionless void again, and then the youngest Triari—the other man—cried out in amazement. "That's *impossible*!"

There was a murmur in the Council Forum, and Dorjan's face heated. "The cricket set the probability at 15 percent," he mumbled.

That silence grew weighted and unhappy, and he looked up into the faces of the Triari and saw three people caught in a sudden agonizing conundrum.

"Why would he do that?" the youngest Triari mumbled. "Why would he fire on an occupied keep?"

The other two looked at him, and the oldest spoke next, his jaw hardening—but not with resolve. As Dorjan grew in wisdom and politics, he recognized that look more and more. He was a man who feared something he believed was too big for his own comprehension.

"He wouldn't," the man said, and even though his voice lacked conviction, the other two nodded in agreement.

Dorjan let out a wordless bark of a laugh, and the three Triari were suddenly a united front.

"Is there anything funny about this, young man?"

Dorjan shook his head and let the fury shake in his voice. "There is nothing funny about people who fear the truth so badly that they paint a thin lie on a flame bubble and pretend it's a steel wall."

He watched their mouths open and close in shock and indignation, and suddenly the only thing he could hear was a burbling, hearty laughter. The laugher was joined by another, and another, and when Dorjan looked up, his father was wiping tears from his eyes and the battalion of men Dorjan had led—who had not been allowed to testify, not even Lokogos Dre, who had sent him missives all week saying that he would come out and tell the truth, planning be damned—were all barking bitter, angry laughter at the Triari.

The lead Triari smashed his gavel on the marble stone several times, demanding order, and finally he snapped, "Bimuit's balls, Kyon, what in the name of steel and stone are you laughing at?"

Dorjan's father sobered abruptly. "You, Archon! You're going to rob my boy of his commission and his good name on pretense, and the whole Forum—the entire lot of us—saw when you realized it was a lie. I'm laughing because you'll carry it through out of false pride. I'm laughing because when this country is plunged into warfare and ruin in ten years, only the people in this room will know you could have saved us."

The Triari blushed. "You do *not* own so much land that we can't remove you from council," he thundered.

Kyon stood. "Try it," he said softly, "and see how fat your coffers grow without your sulfur and your bronze and your lumium and coal all mined from a rolling gravity rock tethered in the aether. My blood and I know the secrets to the asteroid mines, and nobody in this room will get it from us. I dare you to remove us and see how bloated your precious state grows when you're deprived of our resources. If you don't have the stones for that, I suggest you make sure me and mine always have a seat." Kyon bowed low and deeply. "I'm sorry, my son. I will not watch you be tortured at the whim of fools. I'm going to go do something about the one thing that causes you the most pain. Your men will bear you to the town house—I have a rabbit ready."

Kyon bowed again, and Dorjan took several deep breaths and battled the heat behind his eyes. His father loved him—of that there had never been in doubt, not when he'd been found in the pantry kissing Areau's cousin and not when he'd joined the military. There had been some surprise on both occasions, some fear for him in his chosen path, but no disgust and no ultimatums. His father had said it was a good thing he had Dorjan's older sister to keep up the niskety blood, and, in the case of the kissing, had looked meaningfully at Areau's cousin and told him he might need to come by another day. After that, he and Dorjan had spent a quiet afternoon baking pies of all things. Pie was, after all, why his father had come to the pantry in the first place. Eventually the pie had been eaten, and his father had talked gently of politics and of things Dorjan must not reveal except to a chosen few.

"Like Areau?" Dorjan had asked anxiously.

Kyon had nodded and wiped more flour across his broad-cheeked, perspiring face. Dorjan had his father's bull chest, square jaw, and almond-shaped brown eyes but his mother's narrow cheekbones and small, even nose—this combination was pleasing, he had realized early, even to young men. His father, too, was handsome, and although he was broad and heavy with age, Dorjan had always thought of him as vital. The laugh in the Forum had been like him, and the blunt speech had too.

His allusion to getting Areau out of the asylum was as subtle as he got, and Dorjan was grateful. He had felt the power of his father's support, and now he could do without it. As long as Areau could come home.

AREAU did not come home that night. The men of Dorjan's battalion helped him into the rabbit when the Triari were done with him, and one climbed inside with him. The interior of the mechanical palanquin was fitted with cushions and a nice supportive chair, all in dark navy and tan, and it enclosed the two of them in a comforting, gauze-covered shell. There was barely a quiver to the palanquin as the rabbit lowered its mechanical back legs to the ground, and the two in-line rubber wheels, much like the cricket's, made contact with the rail. Dorjan allowed his junior officer to key in their destination. The Triari had done pretty much what his father had predicted, and he was weary beyond words.

He fell asleep as the rabbit bore him to his family's Thenis town house, and was not aware of the chair folding out to a couch and lowering into a bank of pillows. He awoke when his father entered the rabbit with a steaming bowl of sweetened grain mixed with fruit, and rolled him gently awake.

"Dori—Dori, son, I need you to wake up."

Dorjan rolled over and groaned, cursing the damned bones and joints, which were still sore after a month. He'd visited the niskets briefly after his stay in the hospital, but he certainly couldn't bring them from Kyon's Gate to the city. The tiny, secret beings were exceptional healers, even if sometimes their idea of healing was harrying a body out of bed before said body felt truly rested. At least when they did that, they flickered and buzzed around the offending muscles and rubbed the stiffness out. This was just his father with breakfast, and most likely unwelcome news as well.

"What do we have to do?" he asked, startling fully awake and taking the sweet-grain because he was soldier enough to know his body needed fuel.

Kyon's jaw was set grimly, and he shook his head. "Something's happening with Areau—either tonight or tomorrow. They're moving him, doing some sort of radical treatment on him—something. Did I miss anything yesterday?"

"They kicked me out of the military," Dorjan said brightly, even though it had stung at that moment and ached now like an amputated limb. He had wanted to serve people. He'd been born to position, but his father never let him forget he needed to honor that. *That's* why he'd gone into the military when the government had talked about the threat from the west. After the derision of his peers over his father's refusal to overmine the asteroids, he had wanted to serve. Now it felt as though the privilege had been cut from his future like a leg with a festering wound.

"But…," Kyon said, and Dorjan had to remind himself that his father was, had always been, smarter. Not just smarter than Dorjan but smarter than the politicians, smarter than the businessmen—just smarter. He was a good man—a jovial man—but very often he stated the truth of things when the less astute preferred not to see it. As Dorjan grew older, he realized his father made enemies because of that. The floundering, the incompetent, the entitled—a man like his father, a fat, jolly man who had gotten his hands dirty in his own mines, was beneath them.

How dare he know more about the world?

"But what?" Dorjan asked carefully.

"Did they take you out of the succession, boy?"

Dorjan's eyes widened. "No! No. Why would they?" Dorjan wouldn't be the first disgraced landowner's son to inherit his legacy regardless.

Kyon nodded thoughtfully. "Because they think they can use Areau to control you. They know you want him, and they want you to dance to their tune. But they can't keep him there without a reason. It's... it's a bad moment for your friend, Dori, make no mistake."

Dorjan shoveled a spoonful of fuel into his mouth and swallowed. "Fine, Da. What do we need to do?"

THEY wore white robes with the cloth helmet that covered the face, and snuck in through the back, where some of the staff would sit outside, smoke their *chinkly* pipes, and relax during shifts. Not a soul watched or cared as Dorjan, his father, and the mercenary physician they'd hired strode in through the kitchen while meal preparation was in full swing.

Of course, if they were working half as hard at keeping their gullets from rising in their throats as Dorjan had to, they wouldn't have much left in them to notice. *Feaugh!* What a stench! Dorjan thought of Areau, locked in here for the last month, eating the slop he saw prepared in the kitchen, and wanted to cry. Unfortunately the kitchen wasn't the worst part.

Rats, cockroaches—yes, and the cockroaches were bigger than niskets, that was the truth—but as they walked the bare concrete floors in rooms with painted steel walls, those weren't the worst of the asylum, not by a long shot.

The worst part was the inmates—women laughing hysterically, banging on the bars of square metal cages, or men whimpering in corners, systematically plucking the hairs from their heads one by one. There was screaming and sobbing and the stink of urine left to corrode through the floor of a cast-iron platform, and walls painted and scrubbed a blinding antiseptic white, with no other color anywhere except the blood the inmates had shed to decorate on their own.

Oh Areau—how could you exist in this terrible place!

They found Areau in the infirmary, strapped down to the table with cast-iron restraints and chains. He thrashed about and moaned when they first walked in. Dorjan ripped off his cloth helmet and bent down before his friend, lowered his face to Areau's, and stroked back his wild, sweat-stained yellow hair.

"You'll be fine," he murmured, but he had to work hard not to howl. Oh, Areau... what had they done...

Or not done, as the case was. Areau *had* been burned in the battle, but his wounds—oh, Bimuit! A week with the niskets at Kyon's Gate and they would have had him cleaned up with minimal scarring, but here...

They were festering, *blistering*, with the lack of care.

"What in core's depth have you been doing!" he snarled at the physician, who was currently applying balm to the oozing chafes on Areau's wrists. Areau's grimace was twisting, almost orgasmic, at the pressure to the bloody sores. "How can you call yourself a healer if he looks like this!"

"It wasn't my fault!" The physician was a slight older man, with a fringe of white hair and a small, bitter face. "I came in and tended to his wounds, and the next day, all my work was undone and the... the *filth* they'd rub into them...." He shuddered, and Dorjan glared at him.

"Tend to them now," he muttered and sank back down to Areau, putting his face close so Areau would see him through the pain.

"We'll care for you, Ari. We'll take care of you. We'll fix this."

"You came," Areau breathed out. "You came for me. They told me you'd forget about me, that you didn't care."

Dorjan shuddered and pulled the neck of his white cocoon open to the navel so Areau could see, see the stitches from the operations where even the niskets wouldn't have been able to heal him, see the still fading bruises and the paleness and the ruin.

"I could barely stand," he whispered. "And we had to find you first. Oh, Ari, did you think I'd ever leave you behind?"

Areau's good hand was free now, and he reached out and traced the scars, his touch tentative enough to tickle. Dorjan endured it without flinching. Areau had earned the right to touch him with impunity.

"I… I need to hold on to something," he muttered, and Dorjan gave him his hand.

"Hold on to me."

His father and the physician had the restraints uncoupled by then, and they threw a clean gauze robe over his skinny, ravaged body and a gauze helmet over his once-bright hair. Dorjan supported one side of him and his father the other, and together they walked back out the doors of the asylum. They had just cleared the kitchen when someone noticed.

"What's with him?"

"Stomach ailment," Kyon supplied. "Caught from one of the patients—very contagious!"

Dorjan shook Areau gently. "Barf, Ari?"

Areau startled but, after seeing Dorjan wink over his mask, started making horrible retching noises, and whoever it was backed off.

It was a good moment, and it cheered them, all four, as they made their way to the rabbit Kyon had secreted in a nearby stable. They rounded the corner toward comparative safety, and there was a sudden motion, a man in black coming near them and flitting away, and just that suddenly, Dorjan's father went down in a blur of white and scarlet.

Dorjan grunted as all of Areau's weight sagged into his arms, and he shoved his friend at the physician. Areau barely stirred from his trance, staring and whimpering as he looked at Kyon's heavy body on the ground. Dorjan fell to his knees and saw that—oh, core's depth—his father's throat lay slashed open, the blood pooling, and his father's eyes closing just that quickly. Only that? Only a knife flashing in the fading sunlight? Was that all it took to end a man's life?

"Bimuit!" Dorjan turned toward the physician. "Get him to the rabbit and wait there!" he ordered, and military or not, something of those years studying for command must have held, because Areau and the physician struggled on. Dorjan gently slipped his father's silver pendant through the slowing pump of blood and over his head. The pendant was an unspoken part of the landowning in Kyon's Gate, and he would need it later. Once it was in his pocket, he glanced quickly over his shoulder to make sure they were gone. His last look at them showed them walking through the stable toward his father's rabbit.

Dorjan was hurtling down the street by then.

He shed his disguise as he ran, leaving it on the concrete and the rabbit rail as he leapt. The knife man had been quick, there was no denying it, but he'd hit Kyon's jugular, and he'd spattered a lot of blood on himself. His first footsteps, his direction, were all written in Kyon's blood, and once Dorjan started to run... well, before his injuries, he'd been practicing in steam armor and gravity simulations with the thought that he'd be fighting in Karanos.

Thenis—Biemansland as a whole—had none of the gravity difficulties brought about by overmining, and Dorjan had been nisket healed after he'd been allowed to leave the hospital. His sprint wasn't at its fastest, but it was still faster than the man who'd killed his father.

The people of Thenis prided themselves on clean, orderly streets, with trees planted in holes in the concrete and the rails that kept the steam-powered centipedes and the rabbits in line, which managed to keep the streets uncluttered by rickeys or hexahorses or any of the usual urban detritus. Dorjan was lucky—he had a straight enough shot to gain sight of the man.

But he followed the man to a part of the city he didn't recognize, and even as the buildings went from stone to unpainted wood, he was surprised. The change was so complete—from soaring skyscrapers to two-story storefronts, to ramshackle tenements, to pasteboard roofs between the walls of an alley.

And still Dorjan ran. His lungs burned, his heart screamed painfully in his chest, but as long as he could see—

His target turned right and ducked under the pasteboard roofs of the mock-up ghetto, and Dorjan leapt and ran atop those roofs, grateful that his usually bulky muscles had leaned this last month in recovery. He spotted the frames of the tenements under the pasteboard, and ran on those. He heard his target's progress as he went, and he had a moment to wonder: how was it that they were in the stewing seams of the city, but directionwise it seemed as though they should have turned a full circle, right back to the glittering, clean heart of it?

The alleyway opened up, and Dorjan, by whatever instinct, rolled to use his momentum and sank to a crouch in the shadows of the alley as he listened to the chaos underneath his feet.

In front of him, at the end of the alley, was a courtyard. It was lovely. Trees soared up between pale buildings that sported moldings carved intricately with animals and other symbols of luck, all glistening with bronze frames and brilliant flames of windows in the fire of sunset.

In the center of the courtyard sat the Triari, Alum Septra, and a number of other landowners. Septra was talking and the others were sitting, gathered like herd animals, and even from his position, Dorjan could see it: Septra was the tiger in their pen, not the breeding bull at all. He didn't want to lead them, he wanted to *devour* them, and it was too late for the sheep to lock Septra out, now that he'd started his first course.

The murderer emerged from what appeared to be the façade of a door, and although Dorjan couldn't see it clearly from this side, he could imagine—a bright doorway in the building, one that seemed to lead to nowhere.

And it did. None of those sheep or gazelles or deer wanted to know that right next to their graceful courtyard, with the fountain of clean water, was a hell of poverty so singularly filthy that Dorjan could smell excrement from where he crouched.

The murderer emerged and Dorjan saw the back of his head—black hair past his shoulders, curling at the ends, and efficient black trousers and boots, coupled with a black tunic belted close to his waist with a black utility belt.

Dorjan never saw his face, but he saw the man bow to Septra, and then stand, and even from a distance, he could see Septra's smug grin. Alum Septra, the man who would murder innocent children and destroy Dorjan's life and loved ones, stood up.

"Kyon of Kyon's Gate is dead. Shall we have another vote, then, about continuing the war?"

"What about his son?" said the youngest Triari. "Dorjan of Kyon's Gate is *not* a man to be ignored!"

"He's a child," Septra dismissed. "And a disgraced one. And now his father is dead, and we have a country to run. Once again. Who here favors the war?"

As Dorjan watched, horrified, grief stricken, and helpless, the Triari who ruled all of Biemansland, who ministered justice and civilization to all its citizens, stood and bowed.

In the Clutches of Darkness

Ten Years Later

DORJAN woke up and spared himself ten seconds for the dream.

It was his favorite dream, the one where he was lying next to a warm man whose identity he hadn't discovered yet. The sun was streaming through the gauze curtains of his room at Kyon's Gate, there was a cool morning breeze through the open shutters, and he could hear the children of the keep outside, playing. In the distance, above the horizon, the asteroids hovered, tied to the earth by their umbilical cords of woven cellulose, and the niskets, which looked like metallic blue, green, and gold butterflies or rose-and-silver flowers from far away, darted around them like the breeze in the clouds. He would listen to those sounds, smell the herb garden his mother planted every year and the giant climbing rosebush she'd planted to honor his father, and he'd roll over and nuzzle his companion, begging for some more time to touch skin on skin, cleanly, without metal hooks of regret gouging his heart with every breath.

He held the dream and rolled over, and even as he did so, he knew exactly when Areau would flinch and bound out of bed.

"I don't like—" Areau stammered, his voice thready and panicked, and Dorjan rolled over with his eyes still closed and nodded.

"I know," he said gruffly. "I'm sorry. I knew that."

"You know this," Areau said, upset, and oh, Bimuit, we didn't want Areau upset, did we! "I beg you… I beg you, and I touch you, and you're lonely…."

"I still know better." Dorjan's voice was flat, and he still didn't want to open his eyes and confront the thing he had done the night before. Several nights before. Bimuit! He didn't want to know how many nights they had done this, because every one felt dirtier, right down to the first one, when they'd both been lonely and torn and had needed… oh, they had needed.

But not each other.

Areau had needed a woman, one with soft hands and kindness, who would understand his need for pain and give him what he needed but not disparage him as she gave it.

Dorjan had needed succor in that time. A body, a man, someone who would love him unconditionally in spite of the thing he had done that night, with Areau's help. They had needed, and....

Bimuit!

It had been ugly, and tainted, and painful.

DORJAN had inherited the keep and his father's succession. Dorjan and Areau took Kyon's body back to the keep and mourned him in a service before having the niskets scatter his ashes on the surface of the asteroids, a thing that eased the niskets' grieving considerably and kept the keep healthy in the process. The keep was just as lovely and bucolic as Dorjan's dream—he and Areau had been back since and he knew it was truth—but he couldn't stay more than one fortnight, sometimes two. Areau was shamed by his scars, by his instability, by the way he screamed in his sleep and shuddered in ecstasy whenever he so much as stubbed his toe. And, of course, Dorjan didn't want anyone to know the thing he and Areau had become. Especially in the mines, when they blooded with the niskets and ecstasy overcame them both—after those times, the thing they really were was so much more of an abomination.

But that thing hadn't happened yet—not during that first visit, the grieving visit. During that time, Dorjan was heartsick, saddened by his father's absence, his mother's depression. Even the niskets were sad, their bright rainbow panoply muting to a solid gray-sky pewter. And in the midst of all that sadness smoldered Dorjan's burning, barely banked anger, and that alone was enough to drive him from the sanctuary of home back to the house in the city, Areau at his side. His friend hated travelling by millipede rail, and he sat, body taut like a clock spring, twitching with every clack of the millipede's legs.

They arrived back at the town house, which had been freshened and tended to by the housekeeper, Mrs. Wrinkle (who was barely in her forties that year), and sat moodily at the kitchen table over an impromptu meal of bread and fruit, waiting for the tension of the journey to fade before they took their baths and went to bed.

"I want to hurt something," Dorjan muttered out of the blue. Dinner had been silent anyway. "I'm so angry. Home isn't sanctuary, food isn't food—I want to hurt something. I want to take steam armor in their midst and lay about with a scimitar until the walls of that quad run thick with blood. It's a compulsion… it's… it's…." The plum in his hand burst with the tension in his fingers, and he hurled it at the wall. "Bimuit!" he shouted. He threw another plum against the wall, liking the explosion of muscle and bone, and another, and when the plums were gone, he reached to his plate and came back with bread.

It was light and wouldn't throw well at all, and he looked at it, feeling absurd and useless.

Areau thrust a nectarine in his hand with a bit of maniacal glee. "It's ripe, brother," he said, honestly excited. "It will make a prodigious splat!"

Dorjan's laughter was bitter and hard, but it was laughter, and Areau was right. The nectarine exploded against the wall in a satisfying thunk of pulp, and his laughter as he watched it drip to the floor cleansed itself, became almost a child's laugh. He sank to his chair, giggling helplessly, absolutely sure that tears would come.

Before they did, Areau spoke again. "There is no law," he said, his voice as calm as Dorjan had heard it since he'd seen his scarred face and body after the niskets had done their best to correct his healing.

Dorjan looked up. "You're right," he said, surprised. It was true. Since Kyon had died, the Triari and Forum had elected to have a military force instead of a civilian peacekeeping force. The military was gone, waging a war that was at best wrong and at worst plunging the province into a sort of voluntary oppression of the people. The word had been spread that the disaster at Kiamath Keep had been brought about by enemy misinformation. The conclusion was that poor Dorjan had been beguiled into treason by an enemy agent. It was a silly story, an insulting one, and Dorjan wanted to lay waste to more than fruit when he heard it repeated as he stalked about the polluted streets of what had once been a lovely city.

But there was no real civilian peacekeeping force—those left to serve in it were wounded, too old, too young, unthrifty, or barely functional. No competent peacekeepers, no community service for offenders, no one to tend prisons. The justice on the streets was quick, dirty, and violent. Gangs were emerging, even then, a scant month after Kyon's death, and the common laborer had no choice but to rely on the crazy, the immoral, and the power hungry, and hope that the man who emerged on the top of the dog pile was worthy enough to lead men.

Sometimes he was. Often he wasn't.

"There is no law, like we learned about in lessons," Areau repeated. "There is no law, and without law, your father will get no justice."

Dorjan closed his eyes. He looked to the vast sink and saw that there were ragged lengths of linen, so he walked there and wet some down. He was surprised when Areau showed up at his shoulder to help.

"I put the mess in your hand," Areau said with a faint smile. The barely there smiles only lightly stretched the scarring left by the final mag-bomb, the one that killed the boy's parents and the stragglers in the keep. From what Areau could remember, the rest of the keep's population hadn't trusted in the kindness of the battalion—they'd scurried off into the margins of the retardant bubble and waited for the fire to wash over it, and disappeared when it was safe. Dorjan had exchanged missives with Lokogos Dre, who confirmed that—but he'd also let Dorjan know, slyly and with care, that many of the people who fled into the night had made their way to Dre's own hold, and Dorjan was grateful. He'd told his mother to open the gates to any refugee from Karanos, Kiamath Keep in particular.

But the fact that some of them survived didn't help Areau. He dreamt of the ones who didn't. He screamed for the ones who had screamed for his help, and every morning he woke up and stretched his lame, scarred leg and rubbed his hand over the shiny lumps of tissue on his stomach, chest, and shoulder, and looked in the mirror at the ruin of what had once been the most beautiful face in Biemansland, and remembered that his sacrifice was just not enough.

So when Areau could smile just a little and say he'd helped Dorjan with the mess, that was amazing. Dorjan would do anything to get Areau to smile like that again.

"We could make a bigger mess," Dorjan proposed, looking his friend in his bitter blue eyes.

Those eyes widened and brightened at the thought. "What sort of mess?"

Dorjan's smile was as bitter as Areau's eyes. "The red kind. I want his blood, Ari. All it would take would be some training—a few months, I'll be as fit as I was before Kiamath Keep, you think?"

Areau smiled again, and this time it was a dreamy, wormwood smile too. "I could make you such things," he said, shivering. "Things that would help you draw blood, that would protect you better than steam armor. I tried to tell them," he rambled—but Dorjan was hanging to his every word. "I tried to tell them that the armor wasn't necessary. I couldn't tell them about the niskets, of course"—and Dorjan shuddered, because they were his keep's greatest secret—"but I knew I could have them weave the elements together to create such armor... it would be light and lumium powered...." Areau turned that dreamy, bitter smile on Dorjan. "They feared it, but you wouldn't."

Dorjan returned that smile, but with fierceness and a lion's share of rage. "No," he murmured. "I wouldn't fear it. And I'm on the Forum now. They don't trust me, but I hear things...."

"Useful things?" Areau asked with innuendo, and Dorjan nodded, so eager he could taste the blood of his father's murderer dripping on his tongue.

"Seductive things," Dorjan said, shaking with excitement. "And I know where the door is and where it leads. I pass through that square every day. Your armor, weapons, my father's nisket as eyes...."

Areau nodded and turned abruptly and started scrubbing at the walls. Dorjan did too, waiting for Areau to finish his thought. Areau had been brilliant as a child—that's why he'd been developing the armor for the exercise on Kiamath Keep. Dorjan had long learned to give him room, let his mind work like a finely tuned clock or the gears on a millipede transport.   Click-patter-click-patter-click-patter-click-patter...   Areau's brain practically made the sound as they worked.

At last the walls were clean and the towels tossed into the hamper, and Areau turned to Dorjan as they walked to their beds.

"You will start training tomorrow. I will start making your armor. In a week we will meet and see what a weapon we can forge, you think, Dori?"

Of course he did. Their plan to kill Kyon's murderer was the sweetest thing he'd heard since the breezes at his father's keep had carried the laughter of the niskets through his window, the last morning before he'd left home and come back to Thenis.

AREAU was a harsh taskmaster—he was. He set up an obstacle course for Dorjan in the courtyard, complete with targets and stunners and giant sandbags that would fall or hurtle out of nowhere to take Dorjan out. Once he was so busy throwing a knife at a target that he got thumped with a sandbag. He awakened ten minutes later with Areau weeping over him, as inconsolable as a child.

"You can't do that!" he screamed as Dorjan rolled to his knees and tried to get his bearings. "You can't! We can only do this if you promise me you'll live!"

So Dorjan promised, and training continued, and in the meantime? Oh, in the meantime, Dorjan strode the halls of the Forum, listening, smiling, arguing the ethics of hiring a street gang to pick up trash or legalizing brothels, and pretending he didn't know the government was a lie.

He found he could be extra convincing if he pretended to be stupid.

Well, why not? The rumor being spread about him wasn't exactly flattering to his intelligence, right? He practiced wandering around the halls of the Forum with a vapid smile on his face, getting along with everyone and never expressing an opinion.

It was hard. There were still some Forum members who longed for the old days without wanting to go through the hard work of changing or confronting the true evils that had insinuated themselves into Biemansland. Dorjan stood in a corner once and listened for nearly half an hour as a friend of his father's harangued him on why he wasn't standing up and arguing for a more stringent penalty against murderers, and Dorjan managed a reasonably vacuous smile.

"Oh? Someone would carry that out?" he asked, keeping his voice disingenuous. He finished with, "I didn't know anyone carried those out." And while the Forum member struggled for words, Dorjan walked away.

That same day, he snuck out the secret door from the courtyard to the stews and slipped three credits to a child who claimed she could find anyone he wanted. He had a name by then, an occupation, some of the assassin's hangouts. He gave her five more credits and asked her for secrecy. Her eyes were enormous, and he believed her when she said not even the gods would hear a nisket's peep from her.

The training continued.

Areau would shout in Dorjan's face, screaming until spittle flew out, as Dorjan assaulted a practice dummy with a sword. "Run, Dorjan—run, you bugger! I'll fuckin' lay you up, you don't move faster!"

Dorjan's back and shoulder muscles screamed in protest. He'd been up all night doing accounts for his father's keep, and he was fighting exhaustion, and he'd been running, not walking but packing his Forum robes in a satchel and running, full speed, to and from the Forum to increase his pace.

And he'd been grief stricken and angry and hiding his real identity from the world.

He wasn't sure which part of that made him snap, but one minute he was shoving the steel into the practice dummy with all of his strength, and the next he'd left the sword there, vibrating, as he hauled off and clocked Areau on the jaw.

His whole body screeched to a halt. They'd never fought. Even as small children, they had never fought, and now his knuckles were laid open and Areau was bleeding from a split down his lip and sitting in the courtyard, gazing up at Dorjan with a terrible mix of ecstasy and hunger.

"That was marvelous," he said, the unscarred portion of his face assuming a luminous peace Dorjan hadn't seen since they'd been adolescents, when his torch for his friend had burned brightest. It was during that time that he'd watched Areau fall asleep just to see him look dreamy and soft and young, and *that* was the expression gazing out at Dorjan now.

Dorjan fought against his rising gorge.

"I'm sorry," Dorjan said, looking at his knuckles absently. "I—I shouldn't have done that."

"Oh, you should have," Areau purred. He stood up and stepped closer to Dorjan, into the sweating space of his chest as he fought for breath. "I've been hoping… God, praying, you'd do it for weeks."

Dorjan couldn't look him in the eyes. "Areau… look… I know the things they did to you—"

"*Don't speak of them!*" Areau screamed, practically monkey-scuttling back from Dorjan as he stood.

"But they… you think I don't notice? You think I don't see? The cuts on your arms? The way you tear your healing scabs? They made you love it… I don't know how…."

"You don't know how?" Areau giggled. "It was simple. What's the thing the people on the streets are dying for, Dori? Do you think they didn't have plenty of that?"

Dorjan's stomach went cold. "Dust?" he asked thinly. People died of that addiction. The only way *out* of that addiction was to die.

"I know what you're thinking," Areau said, nodding. "I know it. They came, they rubbed it into my sores, and then they stopped. I should be dead!"

"Ari!"

"I should be. But I didn't die. No, no, no, no, no, no... I'm from Kyon's Gate, you know, home of the fey and secret niskets, and I didn't die. But the pain...." Areau closed his eyes and wiped a mixture of drool and blood from his chin. "Oh, the beautiful pain...."

Dorjan dropped his gaze to the ground. "You had to have been in some terrible pain," he mumbled. "I'm sorry... I'm so sor—"

"Don't be!" Areau snapped, standing up straighter and walking closer. He glared at Dorjan from blazing eyes. "Don't be sorry. You were hurt too. You were in pain, and you pulled yourself together to get me out, and that's good. But now... here we are. I want it... I want the pain. I want to shiver with it, *climax* with it! And I know... I know you're too squeamish. I know you don't want to hurt me. I know you still desire me—*use* it, Dori. Hurt me and then fuck me and let me...." Areau's voice broke a little, and Dorjan closed his eyes. "Let me feel joy again. Bimuit. Let me feel joy."

"I love you, Ari," Dorjan muttered, still not looking at him. "I'd rather find you a woman who can show you how to love softly than fuck you because you crave the hurt."

Areau turned and spat blood. "I'll go get ice for your knuckles. That girl you paid last week stopped by. We have an address in the stews, Dori. You can kill that festering turd of hexashite tonight if you've got the stones for it. Do you?"

Dorjan shuddered hard. "Yes, Ari. *That* I've got the stones to do."

Ari turned and stalked toward kitchen entrance before looking over his shoulder. "I'll get you a dressing and ice for your wound, precious. Wouldn't do to bleed on the dead man."

Dorjan winced as Areau turned the doorknob. The bitterness hadn't been there when they were children. The fierce intelligence, the contagious enthusiasm—*that* had been Areau. Tonight... yes, tonight, they would kill Kyon's murderer. But their job wasn't done. The Triari was cowed and the Forum ineffectual, but Alum Septra and the criminals he'd paid to take over the city while he was trying to conquer Kiamath and the rest of the known world had yet to pay. Even then, before that first step in their plan, Dorjan knew. Dorjan knew that they were far, far away from the end.

HE'D been sprinting through the city for a month. He was good at it. And Areau's armor was everything he'd promised—lightweight, mimicking his body contours, and filled with little gifts from Areau's still fine, if twisted, mind.

He knew his way around the stews by now. In fact, he wore ragged clothes, clean but frayed, under his Forum robes, and had spent an hour nearly every day wandering around the winding, jumbled paths of the pasteboards and tents and storied tenement buildings until he knew which gang ruled where.

He knew where the children huddled to escape the brothels, and he knew where the growing boys hid to escape being pressed into service. If it wasn't the gangs, it was the military, and if it wasn't the military, it was the pickpocket with an eye for easy cash or easy brothel meat. The stews of Thenis were no place to grow up. Very few of its children did.

So he ran, a shadow in gray/black armor, his dark hair caught in a queue and hidden under a helmet, his dark eyes hidden by the giant hexagonal glasses Areau had fashioned to help him see in the dark. He had formfitting gauntlets on his hands and boots that would grip tight, even to the side of a building, but which allowed him to run as quickly as a rubber gum-soled boot like boys in boarding schools used during athletics.

He had a belt with *things*, gadgets, gizmos, things. Areau had been shoving them at him for months: "Here, Dori—aim this at a wall and shoot, and the hook will help you haul yourself up and scale a wall!" "Here, Dori—a knife that slides right out of your gauntlet and stays attached, in case you lose your grip during a fight!" "Look… Dori, can you see this? Throw it at the ground—you'll have enough smoke to hide an escape." "Be careful with this one, Dori. The smoke from this bright lemon-colored one will cause everyone to sleep. You'll need to breathe through your cowl for this one."

The list went on, and Dorjan had concentrated hard and studied, training with the gadgets through Areau's increasingly detailed obstacle courses until he could reach for a gizmo easily at any given time.

He already had a mental map for when he'd need them.

Exit his house through the stables, patting the bronze rabbit on the nose for luck. Run silently in the shadows, through the alleyways, until the pale concrete and clean façades of the Forum member quarters faded into the streets behind him and the screams and raucous laughter of the pub sector of Thenis loomed in front. He knew this way too, alley to the left, to the right, straight ahead, step-step-up, and he was running on the tin roof of a narrow set of back-alley businesses, his footsteps so light they didn't even resonate. Running, running, running, until he came to the place his informant had indicated. It was a tenement and not a tent, so the assassin's business must have been good, and it had a back entrance. Even better, it had wooden walls, so Dorjan's specially designed boot bottoms and gauntlets stuck to the wall, allowing him to climb up the side of the building like an arachnid.

He slid in through a second-story window and caught his breath, knowing he'd feared this and not sure what to do about it.

The tenement was a flophouse, three men to a room. Dorjan supposed most of the men or women who slept there would engage in their sexual activity in a brothel or a bathroom or against a wall—but not in a room with two roommates. Not even here in the stews.

No. These rooms had one purpose only: to be slept in. There were still day labor jobs, honest or not, to be held in Thenis, and these were the folk who did them.

Dorjan didn't hesitate before he reached for the last of his weapons, the one Areau *hadn't* given him—the last legacy of his father. He wore it always. It was in the shape of a nisket flower, which was only fitting because that's what dwelled inside.

He held the little pendant in his palm and thought carefully about what he wanted, and felt the thrumming in his blood. It was an exciting feeling, for something his father had told him meant that somewhere in his family tree was a criminal, and nothing more. It was a fact his peers on the Forum had been quick to exploit—the family of Kyon's Gate was on the Forum because they controlled the mines and for no other reason. Sometime back in his history, before the Forum's demands that the asteroids be depleted too quickly caused the gravity rolls to afflict the continent, someone in Dorjan's family tree had been harnessed to the nisket mines. Back then, before the full danger of unregulated resourcing was known, criminals were attached by a tube to the umbilical, sharing the same power source that they were mining, the same metals that the metallurgists enhanced with ambulatory properties and more. At some point, the original miners must have also shared the heartblood of the tiny creatures who were ever so excited to have the big lumbering humans help them in their natural tendency to burrow into the asteroids until there was no asteroid left.

The miners who had come to own the land had guarded that secret so jealously that the niskets were only a child's story in every other keep and province on the planet.

No one knew how long they lived, but their memories—either race or individual—were very, very long. Dorjan's father had treated the niskets exceptionally well, as had his father, and his father before him, and so, Dorjan assumed, had they all, right back to the criminal who had probably figured out without help that life in the mines was far easier with the niskets to help than without.

For one thing, the little metal creatures were extraordinarily good at ferreting out whatever their masters needed, be it copper, tin, or lumium. Whatever the asteroids were being mined for, the niskets could help, and they had a few other benefits. The humans they bonded with—and in the past few generations, it had been the entire adult population of the keep—were easily healed and, in fact, had better immune systems than the non-nisket bound. They also had the uncanny knack of knowing when an asteroid should be cut free or whether it could be mined some more without gravity repercussions. They were the only ones capable of attaching umbilicals to the asteroids and keeping the number balanced so that the gravity stayed as steady as it could—which was a necessary thing. And they had a weakness for the gas byproduct of mining lumium, which meant they were as eager as the humans to find it. Lumium powered the steam for everything—the armor, the crickets, the rabbits, everything.

So the nisket that lived contentedly in Dorjan's pendant had been in Dorjan's blood for time immemorial, and as Dorjan set her free, he could feel the hot exultation singing between the two of them.

She had loved Kyon too, and they were both parched for the taste of a vengeful death.

She disappeared, her glow masked by her understanding that she needed to hide, and Dorjan followed closely. It was a room-to-room search, and he clung to the shadows, moved silently in his clever armor, padded like a wraith in the wake of the nisket. She knew what they were hunting, and she held to their purpose with the surety of her kind. Burrow burrow burrow, a tiny metal flower with insect-like appendages, she burrowed through the sleeping strangers to the heart of their quest in this rank stew that smelled of sweat and piss pots and too much sex in dark corners where no one could see.

When she found their target, Dorjan felt the shock of it thrilling him to the pit of his stomach and up his spine, enough like an orgasm to make him long for one, and he padded through the next two rooms toward his victim. In the second room, before the tiny glow of the nisket, he saw a woman's eyes open, and he clapped his hand over her mouth before she could scream.

"I'm not here for you, little sister," he murmured, although she was probably twice his size. "Live a good life, and I'm sure I never will be."

He faded out of the room, relieved when she didn't give alarm. He risked a look back and saw that she had rolled over and was huddling, the blanket pulled around her chin, probably praying she never knew what happened next.

Erskin Nenk was a small man with almond-shaped eyes and sallow skin. Dorjan had gotten a few glimpses of him as he'd followed the man through the stews and pretended not to notice him in the courtyard of the Forum. He paid the flophouse to sleep there full time but only stayed one out of three or four nights at the most. The flophouse was the final address Dorjan had for the man; the other three were in brothels or gambling hells or behind a fish market. The flophouse, his one place of peace—*this* was the most likely place for a hit.

Dorjan recognized his sleeping face as the nisket hovered over him, humming somnolently, guaranteeing that he would sleep through much. Dorjan didn't want him to sleep through this. He wrapped a length of black linen over his mouth and shoved a wad of it inside before securing it with the rest of the length. Then he looked at the nisket and nodded.

Nenk opened his eyes and started to thrash, then stilled as Dorjan flicked his hand and palmed the knife that slid from his gauntlet straight into his grasp.

Dorjan held the knife to Nenk's throat and murmured in his ear. "All men leave a hole in the world when they're torn out," he said softly. "But sometimes the hole is like a lance through festered flesh. When you are dead, the world will ooze pus, Erskin, and then, perhaps it will heal."

And with that he dragged the knife hard across Nenk's jugular, and stayed there for the count of ten, twenty, fifty, ninety, before his breathing stopped and the man who had murdered his father was no more.

The nisket, not to be deprived of the rewards of a job well done, sipped at the blood as it spilled hot and thick across Nenk's chest and face. When the man was dead, Dorjan took a shuddery, triumph-filled breath and readied himself. Getting out undetected was going to be slightly more work than getting in.

HE SLID into the stable a few hours before dawn, breathless, exultant, and dripping blood, some of it his own. On his way back, he'd run into a press-gang invading an orphanage (it had supposedly been hidden, but if Dorjan had known about it, everybody had) for recruits.

Dorjan hadn't cared why. He had been shaking with unrealized fire after escaping the tenement, his blood thundering so fiercely he hadn't heard the sobs of the children until he was almost upon the press-gang itself.

He was only too happy to engage.

It was visceral—stab, punch, kick, *crack*, *rip*, *maim*, and when he was done, the children huddled in a knot, staring at his masked, shadowy figure in horror. He'd looked around at the bodies—some still moving—panting for breath, and felt… *alive*. Oh, Bimuit! He was *alive*, and he could *hurt*, and he could defend and do all the things he'd wanted to do as an officer in service of his land. He was not even disturbed by the change in his own heart. He used to think violence was a necessary evil. Now it was simply necessary. Deeply, deeply necessary.

He'd noticed the children at that point, huddled in the corner, looking at him in fear. He tried to get himself under control, running a shaking hand over his mouth, which was barely exposed by his cowl.

"Go back into hiding, little ones," he growled. "They will be waking soon."

Some of them. Some of them would never wake up.

"They killed our guardian," one of the bravest said.

Dorjan had to close his eyes and breathe deeply some more before he could stop thinking like an animal.

He knew the stews—knew the brothels, knew women who whored because they needed to feed their families, or whored because they were afraid of their pimps, or whored because…

Because they'd lost their families and had no one to care for and empty, aching hearts.

"Go back inside," he murmured. "I shall find you a new one."

She'd propositioned him many a time as he'd wandered the stews, and he'd always put her off gently and firmly. Finally, at the end, he'd told her that he was sly, but he'd give her money for information.

She'd laughed bitterly. "Of course you're sly," she murmured. "Why do you think I've been hounding you? I wanted company, sly boy, nothing more!"

She'd been helpful since, and he had spent company, stolen minutes in the crowded corner room that was her boudoir. He was sure she was not prepared for him to come bursting into her bedroom in the small hours of the night, covered in blood and violence and about to send her life into upheaval.

She was with somebody, a man who stared up from what he was doing with the slack-jawed look of a drunkard and whose eyes widened theatrically when he saw Dorjan, masked and hooded, covered in blood, standing over her bed.

Dorjan didn't have time for him. "You," he said shortly, "out. Now." He must have looked serious, because the man fled, pulling his pants up around his waist and juggling his shoes as he went. Then Dorjan turned to Jely.

"Don't be afraid," he said softly. "I can give you things you crave, right here and now. I can give you children to care for and a safe place to do it, but you need to dress, and you need to be ready to abandon this place, and you need to follow me."

She had dark hair, dark eyes, and a pale oval of a face that glowed luminously in the light of the two moons that shone through the window.

"Sly boy?" she asked, her voice shaking, and Dorjan held his fingers to his lips.

"Can you do it?" he asked. "If not, I need to make other provisions."

She nodded.

Later, he thought it was as if she'd been waiting for rescue, because she took one gauzy silken scarf and filled it with a heartbreaking clutter of treasures—her dead husband's ring, her dead son's carved wooden cricket, her dead daughter's hand-sewn poppet—and, without shame for her nakedness, threw on a plain handspun dress and bound her hair behind her in a braid.

He must have made a sound of impatience because she looked at him sharply. "I won't care for children as a whore," she said. "Give me this."

And he had no choice.

They made their way through the city streets quickly, and when they arrived back at the orphanage, some of the bodies were gone, leaving bloody trails in their wake. Some of the bodies would need someone else to make them bodies and not people. Dorjan had no moment to linger over his handiwork, to ask himself if the violence was as glorious now as the bodies cooled—the children still needed a guardian, and the guardian still needed a plan.

After that it was easier than he would have thought possible. He had gold—his mines produced far more than his government knew about, mostly because Kyon hadn't trusted them either. Dorjan poured a handful of gold credits into Jely's hand after purchasing the tickets via millipede himself. He sent them to Dre's keep with instructions that if Dre couldn't house them, he was to send them to Kyon's Gate. What was important (and he told Jely this specifically) was that they couldn't be immediately tracked to Dorjan himself. Jely was not stupid—she'd managed to survive on the streets of Thenis, after all.

And at last it was done, and dawn was barely creeping over the horizon, and Dorjan stumbled into the stables of home.

Areau was waiting for him that first morning—in fact, would be waiting for him all of the mornings that followed. His eyes were wicked bright, his face was pale, and the faint sheen of sweat shone in the glare of lumium-powered electric lamps.

"Is it done?" he asked, his voice a bizarre mixture of giggles and harsh question. "Is it done? Did you kill the bastard, spill his blood, rip his skin…." He rubbed his hand over his face and across his mouth repeatedly, chattering and gibbering into it, and for the first time, in the sad aftermath of adrenaline and murder, Dorjan looked at him through clear eyes.

This hadn't made him better.

Dorjan had hoped…. He'd endured the obstacle course, fixed the vengeance firmly in his head, and followed that course like a nisket homing in on blood and metal, hoping without ever framing the thought, that revenge, this one revenge, would make Areau… better. Just better.

It had seemed to. It had given him purpose for the four months leading up to this moment, and he's spoken clearly, made decisions, planned, even looked forward to the coming day with something akin to expectation.

Dorjan hadn't seen him like this since his final bandages had first come off in the month after Kyon's death.

"It's done," he said, swallowing, hoping the move would soothe the boy who had used to laugh so infectiously. "It's done, and more besides. I think," he said—and it was reluctantly, because he knew what he was committing to, even then—"I think this is not going to be the last time I venture out into the stews of Thenis."

Areau's laugh was unspeakably ugly. "Oh, I hope not," he giggled. "Oh, I hope not! You and me… we have some damage to do!"

"I'm not an assassin!" Dorjan snarled. "That's not the purpose here!" He felt a slick knot of nausea in his stomach. He wasn't an assassin? Oh, he'd certainly killed easily enough, oh yes he had!

"You liked it," Areau said, his eyes burning feverishly as he trembled on the balls of his feet. "Tell me you liked it! You loved it! Your knife sinking into flesh, the force of your body cracking bones, ripping skin—"

"Stop it!" Dorjan cried, his entire body shaking. For a moment the nausea warred with the cold pleasure of adrenaline, and he ran his own hand over his mouth. "Stop it—this isn't fun, Areau! What I did out there, it's brutal and it's ugly… you stay here in this safe house and you make these plans for bloodshed—"

"Oh I *do*!" Areau cackled. "I *do*! I make plans for you to cut, to kill, to maim… I get hard in my study, do you know that? I think about you, the person I love most, killing and hurting and—"

"*Stop it*!" Dorjan swung out blindly, aiming for Areau's shoulder, but Areau—oh seven hells and nisket dung, did he duck *into* the swing? He must have, because Dorjan's fist made a sick thud against Areau's scarred and tender jaw, and Areau staggered back, coming up against the wall of the stable, where the tack for the hexahorses was kept. The horses themselves snorted mildly and shifted on their six legs, and Dorjan looked at Areau in horror.

Areau's return grin rang of nothing less than vicious, feral sanity. "That was good," he purred. "That was excellent. Now more… more…."

Dorjan wanted to—his muscles ached with the need to beat his friend, his brother, until he was insensible, until he bled, until the boy Dorjan had fruitlessly loved returned to the battered husk of his body, just as he had left. But they were not children, and Dorjan turned away, fury and grief aching in every sinew of his shoulders.

The riding crop thrown recklessly at his head made him whirl. Areau stood naked, his hands against the wall of the stable, and he was weeping with need.

Dorjan looked at him and gasped. The scars on his face—well, Dorjan saw them, was used to them, had even started to think they gave his friend a certain barbaric beauty, but this?

"Those aren't burn scars," he said, his voice as thin as wire. "What did they do to you?"

Areau's smile burned. "They hurt me, Dorjan, and they...." He shuddered. "And it felt good. But first the pain... would you hurt me? Please... oh, Bimuit, Dorjan! Hurt me!" He undulated that scarred, glorious body, making sure his erection—unscathed and long, glowing like marble in the dim light of the stable—was abraded against the rough wood of the wall.

"Stop that!" Dorjan said sharply, and Areau did. Oh Bimuit help him, his cock was hard under his armor, and Dorjan loosened the stays on the thin synthetic metal plates and let them fall to the floor in an acrylic clatter. He pulled off his triangular mask with its goggles and the cowl under it and looked at all his friend was offering.

Areau looked him in the eyes and spread his legs, aware, so aware of what he was putting on the platter.

Dorjan made a gruff sound in his throat.

"I'll do anything you ask," Areau whispered. "They popped my cherry with a mop handle in the asylum, Dorjan. There was blood, cherry rip, cherry ripe! I could stretch it for you this time, just... just give me the pain...."

Dorjan's cock throbbed viciously, and he closed his eyes, the thrill of the kill, of the city, of revenge, still coursing through his veins.

He came closer to Areau, thinking *I could talk him down, I could gentle him, send him back to his room.* He ran his hand over Areau's shoulder, the ripples of tissue rough under his palm.

Areau recoiled like he was tainted. "Hurt me," he hissed. "You have the crop in *your hand*! Don't tell me you don't have the stones for it! *Hurt me!*"

Dorjan's engorged cock brushed over Areau's backside, and Areau shuddered. Dorjan startled back, and Areau whimpered at him, "Please, Dorjan, *please—*"

"I said no," Dorjan whispered, but Areau stuck his ass out and whimpered, and he thought about a little redness, just a little smack, to punish Areau for just... just *doing* this to him, on this night when Dorjan needed gentleness more than he'd ever needed it in his life.

"You don't have the stones for it!" Areau hissed. "You were always the sweet one, remember? I could go and throw stones at birds but you couldn't—I could tease the niskets until they drew the hexas' blood, but not you! You're weak! You stood there and *watched* those children burn, and you *listened* to me scream, and you didn't fucking care!"

"That's not true!" Dorjan cried, knowing what Areau was doing and not able to stop the lurch of panic in his chest. Bimuit, was it true? Was he weak? Had he caused all of that? Oh *hells*, had it been his fault?

"You *liked* it when your father died, didn't you? You didn't have to live up to any standards, and *that's* why it took so long for you to avenge him—"

"You shut up about my father!" Dorjan pulled his hand back with the crop.

Later, he'd know that even as he stopped, his body thrumming like a plucked string, the moment he raised his arm was the moment Areau won.

"You liked that! You could grieve him and you didn't have to *do* anything, just cry in your room like an infant, pissing away your manhood like a gelded hexahorse or a neutered nisket. You *wanted* him to die—"

"*Shut up about my father!*" Dorjan screamed so loudly spittle flew out of his mouth, and he sliced the crop across Areau's shoulders with a vengeance.

"*Yes!*" Areau gasped. "Do it again! Harder! Harder! Oh God, Dori, I've needed... I've needed so badly! *Harder, you gelded hexacow, fucking harder!*"

Snarling, rabid, rutting beast that he was, Dorjan struck him harder, but when a line of blood followed the welt, he hesitated for a moment, frozen in horror at what Areau had made him do. But he was still grunting, panting, aroused beyond endurance by the thrill of giving pain when it was begged for, and that was when Areau spit on his fingers and reached behind him. With a triumphant crow, he thrust his own fingers up his arse without mercy or hesitation.

"*God, yes, it hurts!*" he howled, and Dorjan, Bimuit help him, Dorjan shoved his cock where those fingers had been, and Areau screamed in pain and ecstasy and came against the stable wall. He screamed again, and again, as Dorjan plowed his untried cock into his friend in an act of brutal agony and craved pain.

His release, when it came, hurt—it flooded his nerves with blazing ice and tore his synapses asunder. He moaned and collapsed against Areau, aware of the stickiness beneath his chest that was blood and sweat, and of the stickiness flooding his groin that was blood and semen.

Blood. Any way he looked at it, there was Areau's blood.

"I'm so sorry," he whispered in Areau's ear. He was suddenly exhausted, drained, barely able to raise a shaking hand to pull his friend's hair back from his sweating face.

Areau slithered out of his embrace. "Don't be," Areau mumbled, throwing his trousers on. Dorjan's seed was tracing the inside of his thigh, and Dorjan watched it, numb as a frozen tree limb. "Don't be sorry. But don't be kind, either. Kindness makes me vomit."

And with that he was gone from the stable, leaving Dorjan to fall to his knees and weep into the clean straw, so empty that sobs were beyond him, so weak with self-loathing he couldn't even reach for the knife in his armor to slide across his wrist.

TEN years. It had been ten years since that first seduction of Areau and his pain, and for ten years Dorjan had played the fool in the Forum and vengeance at night. For ten years he had come home from his bloodier missions to find Areau in the stables, or in Dorjan's room if Dorjan managed to escape him in the stables—hell, in the kitchen, in the privy, Areau would be there, naked, angry, bitter, and needing, and Dorjan would give in.

Every morning Areau would apologize, but he would run, unable to be touched by the man who had fucked him the night before, unable to stop forcing Dorjan to give him the thing he craved but that was destroying Dorjan flog by fuck by folly.

Dorjan watched him disappear now, thinking that the scars from his time in the asylum had faded from Areau's back but that in his heart, on his mind, they were more raw than ever.

They'd been doing this for ten years, and every time Areau came looking for sex and pain, Dorjan died a little more inside, and Areau got no better and no worse. What they did, the blood Dorjan stripped from his back, the degradation of fucking someone who only fed on his own self-loathing, the excruciating remorse of the morning—it was a stopgap measure, good for maintaining Areau at a working level. Areau had to work or Dorjan couldn't go out on the streets at night and visit the only justice working on the streets of Thenis. Very often, Dorjan was the one who kept the street hierarchy and press-gangs from devouring children whole. Dorjan was the one who kept the whores from being beaten to death by corrupt landowners, and Dorjan was the one who kept the asteroid dust trade at a minimum. The Forum was ineffectual, the long-term war waged on, and the lack of able-bodied adults in the city left the criminals and the weak and nobody in between.

Sure, there were strides being made in the Forum—subtly, and without being accused of using too much brain, Dorjan had been maneuvering some Forum members into standing against Septra on key issues. They'd been voted down, but their influence was gaining. Dorjan had long ago abandoned the idea of a strong leader—even himself—emerging and claiming the land for good again. The war was too entangled, the corruption too deep. But, he thought painfully even as he came awake this bleak morning, if he could get enough people on his side, when he finally assassinated Septra, the government would not fall apart.

Even Dorjan knew that *no* government was worse than *bad* government, and considering what bad government had cost him personally, that was saying something.

But he couldn't go on like this. Even with what he had to do that night—*had* to do that night—he could not promise to come back again and debase himself in Areau's bed to keep him functioning.

But he couldn't just stop, either.

He'd tried to stop a few times, had refused to rise to Areau's baiting, had simply done what he should have done in the first place. He'd found Areau the next night in the stews, in a brothel known for its twisted tastes, half-dead from blood loss and begging for more pain. Areau needed it like the asteroid-dust users needed their next touch of powder, and the only person Dorjan trusted to administer his fix was Dorjan himself.

Dorjan rolled over in bed and buried his face in the pillow, closed his eyes tightly, and tried very hard not to remember his beautiful friend daring him to climb just a little higher in the apple tree and hang from an asteroid umbilical. Dorjan had done it, and had nursed the burns on his hands and a broken ankle from letting go, and Areau had visited him every day in remorse. Areau hadn't been able to sit down because his father had tanned his hide, and the two had sworn then, solemnly sworn, not to put the other in danger that he was not willing to face. Dorjan went out on the streets each night, and it put Areau's sanity in further jeopardy. Dorjan came home and tried to make it right.

It was a pretty thing to tell himself, lying in sheets stained with blood and come. It was a pretty thing to believe as he went out on the streets and killed and maimed and hurt. It was a pretty, pretty lie that let him try desperately to keep the pieces of world from flying outward, like asteroids without tethers, to scatter into the blackness of space.

HE FORCED himself to make it to breakfast and to talk to Areau like they were human again, because he had no choice.

"Again?" Areau asked, surprised. "You need to make another run so soon?"

Dorjan looked at his steamed grains, made special by Areau with honey and nuts and butter, and tried not to heave. He had to eat. Food powered his body like lumium powered their steam engines and lights, and at best he was an effective killing machine.

"I've found the man who's been killing the little girls," he said gruffly, not wanting to think about the tiny violated bodies he'd been finding in his other nightly adventures. Nearly twenty in all, starting with the girl who had brought him the information on his father's killer for silver coins. The money Dorjan gave her for informing had eventually not been enough, and she'd gone to working the streets.

In less than a month, she'd been dead.

The loss hurt—Dorjan had felt like her protector, and he'd obviously failed—but back then he'd assumed it was a random killing. The stews of Thenis were dangerous, and he could only do so much.

And then he'd found another tiny body of an underage prostitute. And a few months later, another. The girls were the smallest, the youngest of the streetwalkers, and Dorjan started to warn the madams at the brothels to watch their youngest, and to warn the girls on the street too. His warnings must have held some weight, because a sultry, violent summer passed, and there were no deaths—and that was Dorjan's first clue.

His second was when the next body was not the body of a prostitute, because the younger girls weren't being allowed to work without supervision.

His third was when the girl who died was last seen getting into a rabbit—something that only the landowners could afford these days, when even the public centipedes were offline for lack of funds. Suddenly Dorjan felt as thick as he pretended to be on the Forum floor.

Areau was lifting a piece of fruit to his mouth. Mrs. Wrinkle had prepared his favorite—she was in her fifties now and had garnered more wrinkles than she should have. Dorjan knew that not a few of those were from the washing their sheets, from seeing the fresh marks on Areau's back, from hearing Areau mutter, screech, and chatter to himself as he worked in his laboratory, and from watching Dorjan drag himself in night after night, dripping death from his battered homemade armor.

As of yet, she hadn't issued a word of reprimand or censure, and Dorjan had made sure her children and grandchildren stayed out in the provinces and very, very far from Thenis.

"He's a Forum member, Ari," Dorjan said quietly, and Areau set the fruit down in the bowl.

"A what?"

"It's Ibram. Ibram Manste."

Areau blinked hard. "Wait—isn't he...?"

Areau's distress was gratifying. Unless they were playing the pain/fuck game, it meant he was still listening to Dorjan when Dorjan spoke politics, and that he was still applying his fine mind to strategy and not just his fix.

"He's the biggest supporter of reform, yes," Dorjan said quietly. "And apparently he's also visiting the stews and picking up the youngest girls. And sometimes, when he can't hold his water, he's beating them to death."

Areau groaned. "Are you sure?"

Dorjan looked away. "I grew suspicious when the killings stopped over the summer. The only people who have enough money to leave during the summer are the landowners—the Forum. And the girl talked about a rabbit. I searched them all, Ari. Remember when I had you make me a master key?"

Areau's lips went blue with shock. "But… but a *Forum* member?"

"His rabbit had blood all over the inside. More than one girl, Areau, because some of it was fresh and some was older. He needs to be stopped. We're the people who stop him."

Areau let out a whine. "But you can't kill him, Dori—he's the—"

Dorjan nodded and shook out a sigh. "He's the leader of the rebellion party. He's the one that the other Forum members listen to about policy. Yes. I know."

Areau scrubbed a hand across his eyes. "But… but without him, the rebellion will fall apart. Dori, we'll never go home!"

Dorjan gaped at him. "That's what you're working for?" he asked, and Areau turned a pale, sweating face to him.

"I've just been thinking," he said slowly, darting his eyes to the side. "What are we working toward? What is our reward for this? For my scars? For yours? What do we get? And… I loathe this city, Dorjan. I hate it. The only time I've been happy for the last ten years has been when we've blooded with the niskets. When you've sent me home."

Dorjan started laughing helplessly. Of all the silly things—"Home? Is that all you want? Bimuit, Areau! I'll put you on the millipede myself!"

But Areau shook his head. "Not just me. *Us.* Don't you see? At home, we are friends, and you don't hate yourself, and our bodies only touch in the mines, and I can love you too. I can't go home without you, Dori. You know that."

Dorjan closed his eyes against the plaintive, childish notes in Areau's voice. It happened sometimes. Sometimes the bitter masochist, the manipulative deviant, became the little boy Dorjan had loved, both in Areau's own head and in Dorjan's heart.

"Yeah, Areau, I know," he murmured. "I know. But we can't do it on the blood of children. I have some pull on the floor now. I'll simply have to glad-hand a little more, right?"

Areau looked at him helplessly. "There's not a whole lot of you now," he said, more lucid by the moment. "Bimuit knows I take my share."

Dorjan shook his head. "I'll simply have to give a little more." He'd stopped eating moments before, and Areau's hand suddenly covered his quiet, chilly one.

Dorjan couldn't look at him, couldn't look at this vulnerable, thoughtful academy graduate or the bright-eyed boy who had dared him to climb just a little higher.

"You won't need to come to me tonight," Areau said softly. "I think maybe, this once, I won't need fixing."

Dorjan kept his gaze fixed at the stone ledge around the little window by the breakfast table. "Thank you," he choked out, because Bimuit, it really had come to that, hadn't it? The thought of killing a man was not nearly as repugnant as the thought of coming home and fucking his best friend.

Taern

TAERN had seen the man, or flickers of him, as he'd walked the streets. The stews called him the Nyx because he was like a black nisket, something that was only whispered in legend. He was silent, deadly, and thirsty for blood.

The stews of Thenis lived in hope and fear of Nyx.

The street gang leaders, the dust dealers, the weak and corrupt military who were supposed to be patrolling for crime but who more often took money from the criminals—they lived in fear.

Taern? Taern had learned to love the man, and he'd only ever seen his shadow and heard the whispered stories of his deeds.

Taern had been surviving since his arrival in Thenis when he was ten. He'd been footsore and tired and getting damned good at picking pockets, but he still might have been conscripted to a street gang if Madame Matiya hadn't taken him into the brothel as almost a pet. He'd picked her pocket first—she'd been so impressed that he'd succeeded that she told him she needed someone that smart and that good working for *her.* At that point she'd held a blade under his throat until a thin line of blood appeared, and told him what would happen if he double-crossed her.

By then he'd seen enough of the streets of Thenis to want that knife on his side. Besides, he may have been picking pockets to survive, but he'd been brought up honest. He knew how to keep his word.

When Taern got busted in his room with a john who hadn't been able to perform with a girl (and was enjoying himself enough to be noisy about it!), Matiya asked him if he wanted a contract. He said yes—he'd have been a fool not to. Matiya wasn't a run-of-the-mill street pimp—by Karanos, she did things right. First thing she did was take one of her sly boys, one of the older ones who made good money in tips and was in high enough demand to have his own room, and lock them in that room together for two days with nothing but room service, milled oil, and several sets of sheets. When all the sheets were soiled, she unlocked the door.

Taern had emerged, exhausted, with come dripping down his thighs and from his chin and from the end of his own oily cock. He'd stumbled to his own bed to sleep for two days. He and Yael had fucked each other so often, so hard, and so well that his stomach, chest, flank, and thigh muscles ached from coming, and his jaw ached from blowing and his ass ached from being reamed and his cock burned from reaming. Matiya believed that a good whore was a happy whore, and the first thing she taught her people was how to love their job.

Taern had been a star pupil—and sometimes, on their days off, he and Yael still got together and kept each other company, just because the johns didn't always know what they were doing and Taern and Yael were damned proficient at keeping each other happy. In fact, they got along well enough to move a cot to Taern's room for Yael to sleep in so they could use Yael's old room to fuck johns in. It worked, because when they weren't fucking, they could pretty much leave each other alone, and because the smell of sex got old when you were rolling around in it all the time.

But Yael was working in the house tonight, and Taern was working the street. Although it wasn't true winter yet, it was nippy enough for Taern to miss their sexing room (as Yael called it) and yearn for the winters, when they greeted johns in front of a roaring fire, with mugs of hot cider, and the johns were happy enough for the warmth to leave healthy tips on their pillows, or at least some chocolate or a bauble or two.

The feasting days were coming, and Taern had to comfort himself with that. The sex with strangers was not too bad if there were feasting days with his fellow whores and moments of laughter as they kept Matiya's great house. The moments when he and Yael were fucking were nice, although Yael was taciturn and sarcastic most times, so really, the fucking was the only thing they had in common. Taern yearned for the feasting days and those bittersweet moments during the solstice when only the two moons and Karanos were watching, and he could allow himself to remember his family.

His moment of nostalgia was broken when the rabbit came tooling by on the public rail. Abruptly Taern looked to his left, where Krissa was sitting, looking both demure and decadent on the little stool she brought to rest on during her stroll. Krissa was not yet twenty, but she looked younger, and Matiya had warned him not to let her get into anyone's conveyance. Nobody talked about the killer that stalked the streets or the disappearing young women and girls, but all of the whores Taern knew were frightened and being as careful as they knew to be. Of course, Madame Matiya was an ideal boss if you were whoring—not all of the people on the streets had someone looking out for them, someone who was more interested in their safety than their take. Taern had seen enough girls strolling to know that some of them were more afraid of the beating they would most certainly get than of a phantom maybe.

The rabbit slowed down right in front of Krissa, and Taern was just about to speak and warn her when her brown eyes grew huge and she gasped. Taern turned and looked and caught his breath too.

The Nyx was on top of the rabbit. It could only *be* the Nyx, a figure dressed all in smoky black, crouching deftly, holding on to the shiny bronze hull of the vehicle by some sort of techno-magic and force of will. He was gazing fiercely at Krissa and shaking his head. The message was unmistakable: do *not* enter. The rabbit came to a stop and the door opened, and Taern and Krissa both looked hesitantly inside.

The interior was... odd. It was plush—lots of cushions, a small bar with probably a choice of drinks and dainties—but it was... dirty? Was that the word? There were stains, old stains, that had been washed at and washed at and had faded, but were still there. The gentleman inside was not old and not young, well cared for, and a little portly but still handsome. His smile would ordinarily have been kind and disarming, but the Nyx was perched on top of his carriage, and Taern looked a little closer.

And shuddered.

The man's chin was shiny like he'd been foaming at the mouth, and even as they watched, he pulled his arm across his face. His eyes were vacant, and his lips were not so much smiling as twisted. Taern took an involuntary step backward, and Krissa stood up so fast her stool shot back and clattered to the concrete of the sidewalk behind them.

"No," Krissa said, her voice rough but strong. "Not you."

The man's eyes widened, and he wiped his slavering mouth. "You can't tell me no," he said, his voice cracking a little. "Nobody tells me no, little girl. You need to get in here now!"

He sounded like an irate father—even Taern thought about doing what he asked, the compulsion to obey a father was so strong. Taern looked up and saw the Nyx shaking his head and waving at the two of them to move.

Taern grabbed Krissa's arm and pulled her back. "We can say no." His voice was stronger than he felt. "We have the right to say no, and we do. No." From the corner of his eye, he saw the Nyx nodding and rolling his hand as if to say, *Keep talking!*

"You're *whores!*" the gentlemen sneered. "You have no rights!"

"Have they been taken out of the ruling articles now?" Taern snapped tartly.

"What would you know about the articles?" the man asked.

Taern found himself spouting his schoolboy lessons as if that time in his father's study had been yesterday.

"The Articles of Biemansland are the envy of all the other provinces," he said, aware of the irony dripping from his voice. "The document was the first to give individual rights to citizens and not just landowners, the first to protect all tax-paying occupations, and the first to ensure that things like medical assistance and transportation were equal for all citizenry." Above the rabbit, Nyx startled, looking at Taern through the triangular shape of his armored mask as though he'd never seen someone recite lessons before. Even the gentleman in the rabbit was arrested, looking at Taern as if he were a speaking hexabeast.

Taern paused, uncomfortably aware of this attention, and he looked imploringly at Nyx. Karanos! If the man was going to do something, he should do it now, right?

Nyx shook himself and gestured again for Taern to keep talking, and Taern dug deep for the rest of his father's lesson.

"Uhm, right. Every land in the northern hemisphere modeled their own government after this one... until you pieces of nisket shit began to wage war on Karanos for no reason anybody could logically explain. Now we just want the paper to piss on it!"

The Nyx shot him what could have been a very annoyed glare as he finished up. He bent and put his hands on the edge of the raised door, flipped inside the conveyance, and pulled the door shut with one hand.

Krissa and Taern looked at each other, and the night was, that suddenly, silent. Taern looked around and saw that the other whores on the stroll had all vanished, smoke on the wind, and he nodded to Krissa that she should do the same.

She turned and glanced back fiercely for him. "Come *on!*"

"No!" he hissed back. "I want to see what happens!"

"Dead whores are what happens!" She took two more steps down the walkway and turned back again. "Please, Taern—I don't mind being a whore, but I'd rather be a live one!"

Taern glanced at her before looking back at the rabbit. There was a brief thud from the inside, and the vehicle rocked sideways on the rails before it began to move. Taern and Krissa looked at each other for a tense moment, and then the door opened and the Nyx slid out to run at pace with the conveyance when it started down the rails. They couldn't see what was inside, but as the Nyx ran, catching the door and heaving past the hydraulic resistance in the hinges to slam it shut, a spatter of red caught the light of the two moons, and Krissa's indecision was over. So was Taern's.

"You'd better come back tonight!" she whispered and whirled back toward Madame Matiya's, where, Taern was sure, she'd be given enough money for the story to make up for the night's loss of income.

Taern had more important things than money to worry about. He shrank into an alcove, a space between buildings with a closed end to the alley, and he knew the shadows were blacker than the Nyx's armor. In these same shadows, he hid and looked to where the conveyance continued on the monorail, bound for who-the-sky-cared. The Nyx was bent over slightly with his arm wrapped around his middle, and as Taern watched, he turned back toward where the rabbit had stopped and walked—soundly but slowly, as though he ached—in that direction. He drew near Taern's position and looked around, cocked his head, and listened. His shoulders shook slightly—with a chuckle, maybe?—and he spoke, his voice clear through the hole in the mask that hid his face.

"You've nothing to worry from me, little brother," he said softly. "I would pay you for your night, that is all."

Taern peeked out from the shadows enough to be seen and dodged back into them in blatant invitation. The Nyx took him up on it and slid into the alley as though he belonged there, then leaned heavily against the bricks. Carefully, he pulled the armored mask up. His face was still obscured by the cowl, but his next breath in was deep and even.

"Hard to breathe?" Taern asked, and he nodded.

"Bloody thing blocks my nose. New and improved version my skinny arse!"

Taern bit back a laugh, although the Nyx's voice was irritated and in pain, and he obviously hadn't meant to be funny. But it *was!* This great scary god of vengeance, swearing at his equipment like any whore swearing at a mop bucket! By Karanos, it was good to know this man was human!

The cowled head looked up, and Taern was treated to two very human, very *brown* eyes, although the skin around them was covered in dark smudges—probably to keep the skin from contrasting too badly underneath the cowl. When the Nyx closed his eyes, his face looked blank, devoid of human expression, especially when the cowl obscured that flat, grim mouth, and Taern suddenly appreciated how much work went into just *looking* like the Nyx. The laughter died in his chest, and he grimaced.

"Are you hurt?" he asked, and the Nyx shook his head and propped himself back against the wall again.

"No," he said shortly, and it was a lie.

"Hexashite!" Taern muttered and moved in. There was a tear in the garment over the Nyx's armor, and the Nyx startled back against the wall as Taern widened it. "Karanos! It looks like you were... what? What could make a dent like this?"

"A steam spear," the Nyx told him, and Taern glanced up at him, those eyes so close, the smell of his sweat bitter against the synthetic metal of the armor. Those eyes were narrow now, and Taern looked down again and started investigating the armor itself.

"Karanos! Really? What did he have a steam spear for?"

"I have no idea," the Nyx hissed and then batted at his hands. "The same reason he liked to kill little girls walking the streets—stop that!"

"But you're hurt!"

"I've been worse!" Two gloved hands closed over Taern's wrists firmly but not cruelly. "Please, boy—I'll get healing for it, yes? Is your friend all right? The girl? Will she be all right after tonight?"

His voice was deep and gruff, and Taern wasn't ashamed to admit it left a little chocolate thrill in the pit of his stomach. He lifted a shoulder. "Krissa? Aye. She's probably back at Madame Matiya's, making her living off her story. You could be the best night off she'll ever have. Someone will tend to you?" he asked, because the hands, with their bloodied leather gloves, had loosened on his wrists, and he took that as leave to do whatever the hell he wanted. At his words, though, there was a sudden intake of breath, almost like the Nyx had sustained another blow, and Taern looked way up. The Nyx was tall—much taller than Taern would ever be—and his shoulders were as wide as a rabbit's back end.

"I tend to myself well enough," the Nyx said in a small voice, and Taern squinted up at him.

"That's shite," he decided. "I may be a whore, but I got beat once? The whole house came in to make sure I would be all right. You don't need to tend to yourself, Nyx. Find some girl to tend you."

Those gloved fists again, but this time their touch was almost gentle—and very reluctant—as they moved Taern's hands from the catch he'd felt in the armor. "You're kind, boy," he said gruffly. "But you are a boy. I'd like to pay you for your help, and then I'll find my way home."

Taern waited until the Nyx had dropped his hands back to his sides before fumbling again to work the catch on the armor. An entire section of the plating—which was curious, with the suppleness of thick leather and the shiny smoothness of metal—fell sideways, revealing a light shirt covering a concave stomach. The shirt was ripped, showing a dark trail of fur, and cotton smallclothes tight at the hips. Taern tunneled under the shirt to find a bruise already starting on the bottom of the ribs and the top of the stomach—Taern could see it even in the shadows because the Nyx's skin was so very pale in the slivers of moonlight that crept through.

"See?" the Nyx murmured gently, reaching down for the armor so he could relatch it. "I'm fine. A hot bath, some cold compresses, I'll live to fight another day."

"Wait!" Taern protested, glancing quickly at him. The Nyx's breath had quickened, and his stomach fluttered with the movement, but it was more than that. He'd allowed Taern to touch him and hadn't objected, and there was the gentleness in those hands as they'd gripped Taern's wrists. Taern reached out again and stroked the silken skin of that concave stomach softly.

The Nyx's breath stilled, and Taern looked up into his eyes. "I don't want your payment," he said, his voice low enough to make the Nyx drop his head to hear. Yes, it was a trick picked up from Madame Matiya, and yes, Taern used it shamelessly. "Did that man—was he the one killing the girls?"

The Nyx expelled a quick breath. "Yes," he said, and something in his voice was sad and bitter at once. "Their blood—it was all over the inside of the rabbit. He washed it out, but… he hadn't bothered replacing anything." The Nyx shuddered. "I think he liked it like that."

He sounded so dejected, and Taern realized that it was horrible not just for Taern and the girls at Madame M's to contemplate, but for this man too. This man who had just killed a monster—it had been horrible for him to do and horrible for him to know about.

"I should be paying you," Taern said softly, reaching up touch the Nyx's face.

The Nyx moved to stop him, but he wasn't fast enough. Taern was stroking his cheek before the Nyx could do so much as stop leaning into his touch.

"That's not why I do it," the Nyx said harshly. He stepped sideways, toward the light, and Taern stepped with him.

"I know it's not why you do it," Taern retorted. "You do it because it's right, and nothing's right here. You do it because you can. I understand. But somebody should thank you." He stroked that tight, fluttering stomach again, and it wasn't his imagination. He knew that intake of breath, the way it shuddered on the way out. Oh, nobody had ever claimed to be the Nyx's lover, and now Taern knew why. Bad enough to thwart the ineffectual authorities—the Nyx was apparently sly, and while it wasn't yet a crime, it wasn't a blessing in this place either.

"Boy—"

"I'm nearly twenty," Taern told him, and the Nyx let out a wordless chuckle.

"That doesn't make this better. Don't you have a... a... a keeper? A pimp? A—"

"Madame M would give you any girl in the house," Taern told him. "And any boy too, although there's just three of us right now. You'll want me. Yael's a right prick if you touch his stuff or snore in your sleep or don't pick up your clothes. I'm a much nicer person. You'll want me."

"I don't care about your cl—*othes?*" His voice cracked as Taern thrust his hand down the Nyx's smallclothes and looked with wonder up at the man he could only see through spaces in the armor. Underneath all that getup, the skin of his stomach was soft, and the hair on his abdomen and at his groin was silky, but his cock?

Oh, that was hard on the inside and silken on the out, and dripping with precome too.

"You're ready!" Taern murmured, thrilled. "You've wanted me this whole conversation!"

The Nyx took a step to the other side, deeper into the alley, and Taern followed him. He took another step in the opposite direction, like that last was just a feint, and Taern gripped his prick hard enough to make him moan softly, and brought him to a stop.

"How long?" he asked, sinking down to his haunches and nuzzling that soft, furry belly. "Brother, how long has it been since someone touched you like you needed?"

"I *need* to get out of here!" the Nyx muttered, and Taern grinned up at him, seeing that his eyes were screwed closed and his mouth was pulled back, almost like he was in pain.

"You could, if you really wanted," Taern said softly. "You took a steam spear to the gut—you could go if your life were in danger or if you thought this was bad. I've had to fight my way clear a few times, and I know *you* could get out, if you wanted. You especially. But you *need* this." Taern set the Nyx's cock free and stuck out an experimental tongue. The skin at the head was clean as it peeked from the foreskin, and his precome tasted sweet, like he ate fruit. Taern smiled because this was his best sort of customer, the kind who was clean and healthy and who cared what his whore thought of him. And he'd saved Krissa, and probably a lot of other girls as well. Oh yes, Taern could sink to a squat and blow a hero with a lot of gusto, especially if he bathed like this one did.

He looked up again and saw that the Nyx had stopped breathing. Those gloved hands came up to Taern's head and the Nyx burrowed his fingers through Taern's hair. It was a caress more than an urge, but Taern took it as a signal to proceed. He opened his mouth and clamped his lips over the head of the stranger's cock, then sucked it deep into the back of his throat.

The low, soft moan started at the base of the Nyx's stomach and shuddered its way out of his mouth. Karanos, how long had it been since someone had touched this man?

Taern pulled his head back again, those fingers tightening in his hair gently. Oh, he wanted, oh yes he did, but this man was reluctant to take. It made Taern even more determined to give. He lowered his head again, as far as he could go. Not far enough to tickle his nose on the dark curled hair—no, this cock was too long and fat for that—but far enough that with a little help from Taern's fist, he could make the Nyx groan again.

Oh yes, the man liked it. His stomach fluttered with the force of aroused breath, and Taern put the hand *not* wrapped around his cock up to his chest, past the bruise, and petted him gently. He wished abruptly for a bed because he wanted to touch *all* of this man, wanted to stroke his nipples and see what color they were, but he couldn't. He could just pet him softly up near his sensitive ribs and keep him in place so Taern could give him the best alleyway blowjob in Thenis.

He moved his head and his hand faster, because this wasn't going to take long. The Nyx didn't make a lot of noise, which was probably a habit from his occupation, but the way his body tensed in waves told Taern he wasn't that far from climax, not at all.

Sure enough, when Taern moved his hand down to the man's balls to cup them and massage them just a little, he gasped and shuddered, his cock pumping hard into Taern's mouth. Taern was a pro, though. He'd practiced on Yael for a week, learning not to gag on a man's seed, and to swallow every bit. It wasn't even hard with the Nyx—his seed was a damned sight sweeter than most johns', that was for damned sure.

Eventually the Nyx was done, his breath still sobbing but his cock growing soft, and he offered Taern a hand up. Taern took it and put the man's smallclothes and shirt to rights before he fastened the armor again and pulled his torn tunic over the gap. His own cock was aching and aroused, but he was a whore and he'd offered his service for free—he was certainly not going to ask this man to relieve him when the man was embarrassed about being serviced as it was.

The night had grown colder as it closed in on morning, and Taern shivered, his body acknowledging that it had been too long in the chill. Without warning, the Nyx wrapped an arm around his shoulders and pulled him in to warm him. His armor was heated with his body, and that helped, but Taern was struck by a desire—so strong it clawed at his chest—to see this man naked and vulnerable, sprawled on a bed for Taern's taking.

"You should go home, boy. I can walk you to within sight of your house, if you like."

Taern looked at him and smiled a little, and to his surprise, the stranger dropped his head and pressed a careful kiss against Taern's mouth.

Taern opened immediately, thrilled with the advantage, and invited a heated exploration. He tasted the Nyx's tongue, and the Nyx tasted his own spend on Taern's, and when the Nyx pulled back, his mouth was twisted in a pained line.

"You're sweet, boy," he said gruffly. "You're sweet, and I'm beyond grateful, but it's time for all smart boys to go home."

"I'm a whore," Taern said boldly. "Good whores go back to a whorehouse. Good boys need to find a home."

The Nyx sighed. "Well, maybe we can arrange that," he said thoughtfully. "Now lead the way."

It was not far; Madame Matiya wouldn't have wanted them strolling too far from safety as it was.

"This your house, boy?" the Nyx asked as they approached the neatly painted two-story white structure, with the columns and the porch and the stately gracefulness from another time and another city.

"Yes," Taern murmured. "So you can find it again if you need to."

The Nyx made a grunt. "Does your Madame M—does she have girls who can dish out pain?"

Taern turned toward him, indignant and sickened. "You don't even *like* girls!" he protested in a hoarse whisper. "And I *know* you don't like pain!" No—this man had needed all the gentleness Taern had to offer. Pain wasn't on the table, which was good, because pain was Yael's thing, not his!

"Not for me!" the Nyx replied in an annoyed whisper. "And I'd need to buy her contract. Does your madam have anyone like that?"

Taern shrugged. "There's a few. Krissa might go—but the offer would need to be sweet. She's almost got enough saved to buy her own contract, and she doesn't mind getting smart with a whip if you ask pretty. Is that what your friend wants?"

He was concerned when the Nyx closed his eyes, looking in more pain from the question than from the truly glorious bruise blossoming on his stomach.

"Bimuit, oh gods, yes, I truly hope so."

Taern was not surprised then, but he was charmed as the Nyx, scourge of the gangs and the drug lords of Thenis, bent stiffly and kissed him on the cheek through his cowl and the armored mask he'd put on as they'd walked. "Thank you, boy. It's been… sweetness. Sweetness I'd not expected. I'm grateful."

And with that he turned and disappeared into the alleys of Thenis.

Taern watched him go, still hard and aching but now also wondering, hoping. Karanos! How long before Taern saw him again?

THE next afternoon a stranger walked into Madame Matiya's. A Forum member, judging by the tiny gold star on his lapel. (Some of the Forum members wore their stars large, on thick, ostentatious chains. Taern was fascinated by that tiny pin. He wanted it, wanted to push it through his ear like a stud and claim it for his own.) The stranger was tall, with shoulders as broad as a rabbit's backside, dressed finely in a black suit with tight black breeches, a coat with long tails, and a black cravat, tied simply at his throat.

He bore himself quietly, as quiet as smoke, and bowed slightly to the girl who greeted him at the door as he asked to speak with Madame Matiya by name.

His voice was deep and gruff and left a little chocolate thrill in the pit of Taern's stomach when he was done speaking, and Taern gasped from his place at the top of the stairs.

The eyes that flicked up to him widened in recognition. Set in a fine, handsome face with a wide, long jaw and a bold, once-broken nose, they were a warm, kind, *familiar* shade of brown.

Familiar Beginnings

DORJAN hadn't gotten a good look at him in the dark. He'd seen the pale oval of a face, with the high cheekbones and the pointed chin, and glimpses of eyes that were dark enough that they were probably brown.

They weren't. They were blue. And the hair was black and curly and silky looking, silky enough that Dorjan regretted not feeling it between his fingers. Oh, glory be to the niskets and their kin, he was beautiful. His lips were full, not just with youth but with nature too, and dark pink, and there was a wicked curl to them, even as the jolt of recognition passed through him too.

Dorjan swallowed, suddenly embarrassed by how much that meant. He hadn't just been an exciting cock in a blind alley—the boy knew who he was too.

"Dorjan of Kyon's Gate?"

Dorjan nodded, the flush of heat catching him unaware. Bimuit, he was a murderer, an assassin, a covert agent out to destroy his corrupt government. He'd been emotionally blackmailed into doing things so perverse to his own sexuality that he was surprised his equipment worked at all, and there was no reason a visit to a whorehouse should cause him to—oh nisket shite. The boy was watching him and laughing.

Dorjan scowled at the boy, who laughed right back, and then turned to nod curiously at the woman who could only be the madam of the brothel.

She certainly didn't hide it.

For one thing, she was nearly as tall as Dorjan himself, with hair that had been tinted until it was a blood black with glittering ruby highlights, piled high on her head and spilling down her back. Her face was square-jawed and handsome, with an elegant brow and artfully plumped lips. She wore a skirt that was hiked up to a shapely muscular thigh, clean of all hair, and a bodice that split down to her navel, revealing a cleanly muscled chest and the unapologetically developed Adam's apple of an adult human male. Apparently Madame Matiya's gender was a matter of identification as opposed to the gifts of nature.

Dorjan looked up at the boy again, and the curl to his lip bordered on derision. Ah, and so it should be. The boy's entire good opinion rested on Dorjan's behavior in the next moment.

Dorjan bowed low and sincerely and placed a respectful kiss on the lady's hand. He was the last person to judge the things sexuality demanded of a person, male or female, sly or straight, gifted by nature or by desire. The boy obviously considered his boss a lady, and so would Dorjan.

"Madame Matiya," he said pleasantly.

The woman replied in a throaty contralto. "Forum Master. How is it we're graced with your presence?"

Dorjan looked up at the boy and then regretted it. This visit was on the boy's recommendation, but that didn't mean Dorjan needed his permission. "I have a friend," he said, aware of a tightness in his chest. He saw the beginnings of a smirk and changed the tack of his introduction. "Madame, I myself am sly, a lover of men. This is a request for a woman—it truly is for a friend. A friend with special requirements, my lady." He closed his eyes, aware that they were standing in the vestibule of a great house and that every ear in the house was tuned to the needs of the Forum Master. "May we speak privately?" he asked, feeling pained. "My friend's failings are...." He closed his eyes more tightly, aware now more than ever of the boy's eyes on him. There was something so familiar about the boy in the light. He'd *known* this boy. His manner, his voice—except not so deep. He needed to figure out that voice. It was driving him to distraction.

"I understand," the woman said, and she smiled graciously and bowed, her movements so exact and feminine that Dorjan had no doubt she really was every inch a lady—in spite of what genitalia she might sport between her smooth-skinned thighs.

She led the way to a small study, complete with an oaken desk and a dumbwaiter, ostensibly so Madame could work uninterrupted. If it weren't for the pale-green wallpaper with the darker-green curls of ivy that graced the walls, it could very well be Dorjan's own desk, which was designed much the same, except with dark paneling and blood-red velveteen fabric on the chairs. Areau had designed the place, and Dorjan loathed it. Madame Matiya probably left her study with a much lighter heart.

There were two brocade chairs with stubby wooden legs in front of the desk, and she sat in one and gestured for him to take the other.

"May I offer you any refreshment, Forum Master?"

He shook his head. "No, I'm sorry. Feel free to take some yourself if I've intruded upon your lunch hour."

She inclined her head graciously and rapped twice upon a tube on the wall. Behind the wall, he heard the dumbwaiter in operation and wondered what sort of dainties her kitchen would produce. He was charmed by her, by her operation, by the cheerful working voices not only of the people in the house but of the servants working behind the scenes. His father had always taught him to treat people of all occupations with dignity, and he'd never thought a brothel should be any different. He'd seen enough miserable whorehouses in the city to know that this place was special and safe for people who had not had a lot of safe for the past ten years, and he respected it.

"So," Madame Matiya asked delicately. "Your friend?"

Dorjan swallowed again, choking on the shame. This was so not anybody's business but his own. But he couldn't do it anymore. His day at the Forum had been ghastly, and he was going to have to politically maneuver until he bloody well kissed his own arse in order to get the Forum and Triari back to where they had been in terms of looking at Alum Septra with suspicion and withdrawing from the war. His heart and soul were shredded thin like curls of cheese or frozen meat, and he needed *not* to sell his flesh by the pound whenever Areau needed the screaming pleasure that Dorjan so loathed to inflict. He'd refrained from doing this before out of fear—whom could he trust with the secrets of his house? But that moment, that breathless moment in the alleyway that he wished badly he could forget, had taught him that maybe some people in this city would be willing to ignore the goings-on in his home for the potential good they could bring. It had brought him the hope of trust.

"My friend was kept in the asylum for a month," Dorjan said through a rough throat. "They botched the healing of burns on his body, among other things. He has scars—not as disfiguring as he believes, but not pretty either. They...." Dorjan grimaced. "They made him love pain. I don't know how—I don't." Well, Areau had told him about the dust, but since that should have condemned Areau to a messy, painful death, Dorjan figured he'd keep that to himself. "Every time we try to think of how to undo it, it only makes him worse. We...." He looked her directly in the eye. "Madame Matiya, this friend and I, we have an undertaking, great and hopefully to the benefit of our whole province, and it cannot be done

without him. But I'm the only one he can trust with this craving and I...."
His voice derailed, broke track, and refused to go on. He looked at the
hands clasping his knee and realized they were shaking and that the air
was chill on his face.

He was surprised when he looked down to see her large well-
manicured hand, with scarlet polish tipping each nail, resting on his own
clasped fingers.

"You have been filling this craving?" she asked gently, and Dorjan
pulled his hands back, uncomfortable with the sympathy.

"I loved him once," he said apologetically, feeling weak, and her
sympathy almost undid him. Ten years he'd been carrying this secret, him
and Areau. Perhaps their housekeeper had suspected, but no one had
known for sure. This woman suddenly knew, and Dorjan felt naked. He
lived his entire life ensuring that he was never this exposed.

"You don't anymore?" she asked, carefully keeping her hands folded
in her lap.

"Not that way," he said, sure of himself. "Not... he never wanted my
touch. Ten years he's been craving it because it disgusts him. That...."

"Oh," she said. And that was all. Just "Oh."

Dorjan closed his eyes again and gathered himself. "I need a girl," he
said again. "One who can administer pain but who will stop even if he
doesn't ask it. She needs to be willing to live with us so that he may have
his bloody pain whenever he needs it, and she will be paid well for her
services. She needs to be prepared to watch out for him—the last time I
refused to...." Dorjan was tired of blushing, but that didn't stop the hated
heat from trapping him inside it. "He disappeared. I found him in the
worst brothel in the stews, and he almost died of infection. She needs to be
prepared to be his babysitter and his lover and his pain-giver. I will pay
her, pay her in buckets, if only she consents to stay with us for two years,
to live with us, to keep our secrets."

"What if she wants to leave after that?" Madame Matiya asked, and
Dorjan shrugged.

"What else would I do but let her go and find a girl who would want
the same position? This girl could leave earlier if she needed to—as long
as she knew she wouldn't get the full payment, there's no reason for it to
be a slave indenture. I just...." Ach, Bimuit and Karanos. "I need to
sleep," he murmured. "I need to sleep and know I'm not go be wakened to
wage war on my brother."

"Sh," Madame said, patting his shaking hand. "You've been a good friend, Forum Master. Let's talk about other things while I send for a couple of girls who might meet your requirements." She stood and hit the metal tube with the small hammer hanging from it, and the dumbwaiter opened. She pulled out the food tray that sat upon it and clanged again, then turned and wrote a brief message in handwriting that was both elegant and clear. She put the missive in the dumbwaiter and turned to Dorjan with the tray, which she set up on the small table between them.

"Have some tea, at least," she urged, "and let us talk of other things."

"Such as?" he asked, accepting the tea in a delicate white cup. It was herbal, fragrant, and almost flowery, and he sipped it appreciatively. He didn't drink a lot of tea, but he enjoyed it when it was offered.

"Such as the boy you wanted but did not ask for," Madame said coyly, and Dorjan almost spat out his tea. She threw back her head and laughed. "You're adorable," she said, a sweet smile playing with the corners of what could have been a lean mouth. "Look at you. Did you think Taern wouldn't come straight to me last night and tell me about his adventures?"

Dorjan swallowed and wiped his mouth. "I hope he didn't get in trouble," he said softly, because the thought had preyed on him. He'd seen the lives of whores on these streets, even in the best of the places.

Madame rolled her expressive honey-brown eyes. "Please, my darling. I would have done more than played your instrument in an alleyway to have my girls safe—and I wouldn't have let you get away at the end, either."

"That is...." Oh Bimuit. "For the last ten years two people in the world have known that," he said quietly. "Two. And now four know. It was a mistake on my part, one I can't afford to repeat. I can trust on your discretion on this?"

Madame blew on her tea and eyed him over the rim. "Oh, now you're insulting my professional ethics. And Taern's as well. You get nowhere in this business without discretion. And," she added soberly, "that goes for the girl—whichever girl—you decide to hire at the end."

Bimuit. Dorjan took a breath and let the blush just wash right over him, and tried not to count the minutes until he could leave this place with a solution to his and Areau's dilemma. "My apologies." He inclined his head. "But about that boy—where did he come from?" he asked, that niggle of curiosity, of *familiarity*, unable to leave him alone.

Madame Matiya raised a perfectly sculpted eyebrow. "Of all people, you should know, Forum Master."

Dorjan startled and scowled. "Why me?"

She startled and scowled back at him for a moment, and for just a moment, he saw the very strong man inside (or outside) of the very strong woman. "Does the world really have such a short memory, Forum Master Dorjan of Kyon's Gate?"

Dorjan maintained her gaze steadily, refusing to be unnerved. "I am unaware of what it is supposed to remember," he said politely, and she shook her head and tilted her lips in a disbelieving smile.

"Oh, you're good. You're better than most of my whores at dissembling. Do you get paid to pretend to idiocy, or is that a perk of the job?"

Dorjan swallowed and maintained his polite smile. "Let's call it a perk, shall we?" he said, so grateful for the solid ground of dissembling and maneuvering that it didn't even occur to him to tell the truth.

Madame nodded and took a breath, obviously to quiet a zinging temper. "Yes, yes. I understand. Your need for secrecy is very likely more important than my own. I'll bend to that and say it outright. I am old enough to remember Kiamath Keep, Dorjan. The streets were whispering about you for years—you made a wonderful tale. The young man who dared to question his superiors and almost died of his injuries. We don't get any Forum gossip down here, but the idea of you there, working to restore Thenis to glory—don't think that hasn't put some children to sleep with more security than we've had in years."

Dorjan sat up straight and fought to breathe. Black spots danced in front of his eyes. "Kiamath Keep?" he asked, his throat almost too tight to let the words through. He remembered the flashes of midnight blue, the dark hair—it had been straight and glossy. Sometimes hair did that, he thought randomly. It was a thing that happened at puberty. Mostly he remembered the attitude, the courage, the insistence from a young boy. Uncomfortably, he juxtaposed that memory with having a hell of a time keeping a grown young man from finding the stay to his trousers.

Madame regarded him steadily from under lashes thick with something black and purposefully sooty. Her eyelids were powdered in purple and green, and she really was exquisite. He had a thought that in spite of what genitalia she may have been sporting beneath her dress, she was far too much of a woman for his tastes, and he wondered if she would be flattered by that. He hoped so—it was a compliment.

"Yes, Dorjan," she said simply. "Does this mean something to our young friend?"

Taern. That was his name. Dorjan nodded. "He should know his sisters live," he said gruffly. And then, because he must: "And that his parents do not."

"You should tell him," she said softly.

"If he wishes to go visit his sisters, may he?" He ran a shaking hand over his face. He didn't want to do it. He didn't. This was not within his purview, speaking to the people he had failed. Was it not bad enough that he failed? Was it not horrific enough that he was damned near ineffectual in his work to change his city, his people, his world?

"Would you be interested in buying his contract?" she asked, her voice sharp. Of course. Of course. He was already buying one employee out from under her. She would need compensation.

"If he wishes to go," Dorjan said honestly. "If he wants to leave here—"

"Thank you," Madame said quietly, and he pulled himself out of his own anxiety enough to see that her eyes were lowered and that she meant it.

"For what?"

"For not assuming that anyone would rather be anything than a whore."

"I spend all day in the Forum," he said absently, "pretending to be a moron so that I can lead gullible men. Quite frankly I'd rather fuck men for money. That, at least, is honest. How am I supposed to tell him?"

It was Madame Matiya's turn to spit out her tea. "Bimuit!" she coughed, and Dorjan stood courteously and clapped her on the back a few times. When she was done coughing, she looked up at him with amused exasperation. "You're perfect for each other," she said when she could speak. "Don't worry how to tell him. Buy his contract, and I'm pretty sure one of you will blurt out an uncomfortable truth within seconds of speaking."

There was a banging down the pipe, and she stood. He rose to accommodate her, and she walked to the door and opened it.

"Hello, ladies. Krissa?"

"Yes, Madame."

Dorjan recognized the girl from the night before—tiny, delicate as porcelain, barely of age. But she'd stayed there and stood next to Taern as he'd faced down a man who was obviously dangerous.

"Go fetch Taern and then come back and join us, please."

Krissa curtseyed and grinned up at Dorjan impishly. "Taern will be happy to be summoned," she told him exclusively, and he found himself smiling. Brave. She was exceptionally brave. He turned toward the other women and tried to look at them objectively.

The first was as tall as Madame Matiya, with white-blonde hair and an icy demeanor. He gave his best bumbling smile, the one that seemed to have all of the men in the Forum convinced that he was a nice, well-meaning man, just easily led astray.

He was rewarded by a cold disdainful smile, and he paid that back with a raised eyebrow. No real smile, no contract, he thought grumpily. He had to live with this woman too.

He smiled at the next girl and was graced by a smile in return—a distracted smile, to be sure, from a plump girl with enough curly red hair to choke a hexacow.

He bowed to her, and she bowed low enough for something to fall out of her cleavage.

"Let me retrieve—ow!" Apparently it was a race to see which one of them could get there first, and both of them backed up, glaring, rubbing their heads after knocking them hard.

"I'm sorry," she fluttered, and then she squatted like a peasant to get the damned pen and tiny pad of paper. "I'm a bit of a dangle-weed. I think Madame M just asked me here so you could see the bottom of the scale."

He laughed at her, charmed. "I'm sure that's not true," he said, trying to reassure her. "But while your friend here leaves me with no doubts, I do need to ask—I need pain." Madame Matiya cleared her throat, and he rephrased that. "My friend needs pain—this is, honestly, for another soul, and it is not an option. You seem sweet, but...." He trailed off delicately, and she grimaced.

"Don't get me wrong," she said frankly, pushing that mass of hair back from her face. "I'm a right whipcrack at the pain thing, Forum

Master, but...." She grimaced and looked apologetically at Matiya. "This is to buy a contract, is it not?"

Matiya grimaced. "Paenny—"

"She won't make it without me," Paenny said soberly. "I know I'm a right mess—"

"It's asteroid dust, Paenny. She... she won't make it at all."

Dorjan grimaced. Asteroid dust—it wasn't really from the asteroids at all; it was, in fact, a dried distillation of flowers that only grew in Karanos and the blood of a rodent commonly found in Biemansland. Highly addictive, instantly pernicious, it could reduce a user to a coughing husk of humanity within months.

He looked at the absentminded Paenny with new compassion. Distracted for a sister? A lover? It didn't matter. Yes, a loved one with an addiction—it was not like he didn't know what one of those was like, was it?

"No," he said gently. "You wouldn't be able to visit your friend on the streets if you came with me."

The girl looked beseechingly at Matiya, who grimaced and sighed, and at that moment the other door opened and Krissa came in, her dark hair pulled back from the tumbling fall down her back into something more like what the blonde ice queen wore. She was pushing a hairpin into place, and Taern was behind her, securing everything there, and Dorjan had another moment to smile.

"You don't need that show for me," he said, sharing a look with Madame Matiya. "Krissa, Taern, if you could stay for a moment, I have an offer for you." He dismissed the cool blonde with a nod, and she flounced off without uttering a word. For Paenny, he took her hand and kissed the back gently.

"Don't let your friend's misfortunes be your own," he advised soberly, feeling like a hypocrite, but it must have meant something to her, because she dabbed at her eyes and curtseyed before turning from the room.

Krissa was looking up at him, her dark eyes impish and dancing, and he felt another unlikely urge to laugh.

"Bimuit, you're not lacking for spirit, either of you!" he said, feeling grateful. This had been a day of surprises and of painful revelation, but the thought of this bright-eyed girl in his sullen, cold household, eating at the table with him and Areau, speaking with them on the odd days when he could linger in the sitting room in the evening... it was beguiling, that's what it was, and he was suddenly grateful for the perky resilience of the children of the streets.

"Krissa?" he said gallantly. "I do have an offer for you." He outlined the situation as cleanly as he could, without any of the hesitation that had plagued him with Madame, and he was reassured as she nodded and hesitated thoughtfully at some points. When he got to the part about the time span and the option to leave, she looked almost disappointed.

"What if I want to stay?" she asked almost plaintively. "You're asking me to exchange one home for another... what if he dislikes me, and yet I want to stay?"

Dorjan blinked. He honestly hadn't thought of it. Then his common sense reasserted itself. He ran his keep's affairs from his loathed office in the town house. He knew the rules he and his father had always abided by.

"No one in my keep who wishes to earn a living of any sort is ever forced to leave," he said after a moment of quiet regard. "If you and Areau are not compatible, I swear to you, you may either stay at the town house in some capacity or, if you like, you may go into the country and spend your time working in Kyon's Gate. I doubt you will find the *same* employment, my dear, but my mother will find you *something* to do."

Krissa smiled confidently and then bowed to Madame. "May I go pack my things?" she asked, and when Madame M nodded regally, Krissa launched herself into the woman's arms for a strong, content hug.

"You'll be magnificent," Madame Matiya murmured. The women released each other, and Madame looked directly at Dorjan. "I shall leave the two of you alone."

With that, she and Dorjan's new employee left, and Dorjan was left looking into a pale oval of a face with midnight eyes and an impish grin similar to that of his friend's.

"So," Taern said grandly, "what is it you wanted to discuss?"

Stubbornness and Tea

TAERN scowled at the bloody stubborn man. *Yes*, he understood that his sisters were alive—he even understood that Nyx had saved them, had, in fact, been the same soldier who had listened to him at the beginning of that bloody awful night and gone bounding up to Kiamath Keep on the great metal cricket. Madame Matiya had brought him square with the odd and amazing history of Forum Master Dorjan, son of Kyon, during the long winter nights when they'd sat and sipped their tea and told stories of the appalling state of the world.

It hadn't been that hard to put together. Forum Master Dorjan had tried to save his family, and until this very moment, Taern thought he'd failed miserably, but that was not the case. His memory of his little sisters was dim yet powerful, and yes, oh yes, he'd love to see them again.

But not right now, and that was what he didn't understand.

"You wish to buy my contract," he asked for what must have been the fourth time, "and send me to some keep on the edge of the gravity roll so that I may... what? Go be schooled with my sisters? Don't you think I've learned enough on the streets of Thenis to make that unlikely?"

Forum Master Dorjan had short-cropped hair, a wide-cheekboned face, and a lantern jaw that came to a rather abrupt point. He had a bold nose and large brown eyes that might have been limpid and expressive, but Taern couldn't tell; the flesh around them was puffy and sagging from lack of sleep, and Taern thought that this could be the one man in the world who needed to buy himself a whore as a matter of medical necessity. Taern was up for that job, oh yes he was.

But not for that other thing, oh no he was not!

"Don't you want to see them?" Nyx (as Taern would forever think of him as) asked, sounding weary.

"Of course!" Taern snapped. "Of course I do. I want to see them. I'd love for them to know I'm alive as well! And...." He had to breathe deeply here. He'd *thought* they were all dead. To *know* that his parents had died, that was something different. But he'd learned, these ten years, first on the streets and then in Madame M's place, how to think about the now. Don't think about the customer and his sneering use of your body, think about whether what he's doing feels good. If it feels good, enjoy it. If it doesn't, adjust your position until it does. Life could be boiled down to the simple if you thought of it that way, and Taern was good at boiling life down to the simple.

The simple right now was that he'd finally found a reason this Karanos pissed-on city held any appeal whatsoever.

"I'd like to grieve my parents," he said after a moment in which the silence stretched too long. "It is true. I would. But what you do at night—*that* looks interesting! I'd very much like to be a part of that."

Dorjan's eyes nearly bugged out of his head, and for the first time since he walked into Madame M's, the man looked truly awake. "*That* is out of the question!"

Taern scowled. "So let me get this straight—you'll buy my contract to put me on a millipede like a good little schoolboy and then send me out to gravity's edge so that I can see my little sisters, avoid telling them what I've done for the last few years because *that's* something you want impressionable young girls to think is charming, and then find some sort of activity out there that doesn't involved sucking the cock of handsome strangers in an alleyway, right?"

Dorjan glared at him crossly. "Succinct," he muttered. "Yes. What you tell your sisters is your choice, but yes. I would dearly love to know that the boy I saw ten years ago was finally safe with the family we could save. Is that so bloody awful?"

Well, yes and no, right?

"That time has passed," Taern said brutally, thinking about it. "I'm not saying I plan to be a whore all my life—I didn't plan to be one for this much of it! But I am saying I don't want to be a farmer. I don't want to mine asteroids. I don't want to be a steward or a housekeeper. I'd love to be a soldier, but not for this bloody province, and I'd love to be a peacekeeper, but the same thing goes. What I want to be... *truly* want to be, is *you.*"

"Absolutely *not!*" Dorjan sputtered, and Taern looked at him in surprise.

"Why not? It seems to me like you'd want some help!"

"What I do at night? What *I* do at night?" Dorjan cut a fine figure in that suit, with the long tails and the responsibly tied cravat. It was amusing to see him destroy that impression with the flailing of arms and the mouth that opened and closed independently of words. "It's *awful*! *Nobody* wants to do that!"

Taern took a breath and looked at him. "Then why do you?"

Abruptly that amusing loss of control ceased. Dorjan drew himself up, and the face he presented to Taern was, no doubt, the same face he wore under the mask and the cowl. "Regardless," he said with icy calm. "Regardless of what I do and why, you will go pack your things. I will buy your contract, and you will have the life you could have had, if you had not been a bloody-minded child and run off into the night."

Taern raised his eyebrows. Oh really? "I was frightened," he said rationally, and that grim-faced scowl intensified.

"I was *worried*. Now go pack, and we can make the station before the last millipede leaves."

Taern laughed outright, but he didn't contradict the man. "Right. I'll go pack. You just keep deluding yourself that this is going to turn out the way you think it should."

He left Dorjan gaping and trotted out of the room—and practically into Madame M's waiting chest.

"So?" she asked, looking at him as though she expected him to gossip immediately.

Well, it wasn't as though he'd ever disappointed her, was it?

"He thinks he's shipping me off to my sisters and some sweet little hidey-hole in the country," Taern snapped, charging through the foyer and to the stairs.

M was right behind him, bustling like the lady she was. "There are worse things!" she said, and he turned to see she'd hiked her skirts almost to the danger line (which was a bit lower than for other women, it was true).

"Not for me," Taern muttered, "and definitely not for him!"

They arrived in Taern and Yael's room, and Yael rolled out of bed sleepily, glaring at Taern as though his sleep were the only thing at stake.

"You'll have the room to yourself forever," Taern told him baldly, "but you need to get the hell out for half-span an hour, yes?"

Yael's narrow-set eyes widened, and he looked around for trousers. Taern found them, neatly folded on the chair at the foot of his bed, and threw them at him. Yael caught the trousers, hopped into them, and ran a hand through tousled sand-blond hair, then wordlessly thunked to the door. He turned to Taern with his hand on the knob and said, "It's been nice fuckin' you, flower mouth," and then left, shutting the door firmly behind him.

Taern didn't even pause as he grabbed a duffel from under his bed and started throwing his clothes, his few knickknacks, his shoes, his scarves, his pleasure toys, all of it, into the bag in a muddle. M took a moment to look behind her, though.

"It's a good thing that boy has a mouth like a vacuum tube and a cock the size of a bell jar," she muttered.

Taern barely spared the energy to roll his eyes.

"And an arsehole like a wet rubber ring," he added, because it was true, and for all his lack of personality, it was good to remember that his roommate had saving graces. "But I'm not going to miss him." And that was the end of Yael.

"Now explain about *your* life!" M said irritably. "You're taking him up on his offer—don't tell me you're going to default!"

Taern turned toward her in indignation. "Have I *ever* broken a promise to you, M?" he asked, truly appalled, and she shook her head.

"Of course not! You're the most honest whore on street or in brothel—but *explain!*"

"He wants to tuck me away in the country—keep me safe, I think."

M snorted. "He doesn't know you very well, does he?"

Taern looked away. "It's tempting," he admitted. He remembered the girls, lively, squealing, fighting, hugging, singing nonsense songs to each other when they played. "I'd like to see my sisters—they'll be young ladies now, and a handful."

"Then why not?"

Taern looked back. "Did you see him?" he asked, trying to keep the sentiment out of his voice. "Wasn't he handsome?"

M shook her head and narrowed her eyes. "I taught you smarter than that, boy."

"He *needs* me," Taern argued. "He's... he's *exhausted*—"

"And hurt," M said reluctantly.

Taern nodded. "He tried to hide it, but he was moving stiffly—that armor he had on was something, but a steam spear—he must be trying to breathe through that bruise!"

"That's not what I meant," M murmured, "but that too." She shook her head. "But he's grown—"

"And so am I!"

"Yes, but not so long ago that I'm going to let you run out of here with the first john to drop his guard!"

"He didn't pay me," Taern said, curling his lip up impishly. "Not a penny. And he kissed me when it was done."

M jerked her head back with one of those surprisingly quick gestures that showed she had more muscle than most women. "So that means marriage?"

Taern shook his head and dropped his overflowing duffel. "I saw him that night, as a soldier, when he was young as me. This whole battalion was trooping by in stiff bronze armor, and their feet were all in time, and every footfall felt like thunder, right?"

M nodded, listening avidly. M loved a good story—was known to sleep with a man for the gift of a story. "You were a child."

"I was nine—just that month, actually. I was out that far in the bogland flying my new kite, but I saw the battalion and let it slip into the sky, then hid, but he saw me and broke ranks. He was...." Taern looked down, remembering how angry he'd been, how frightened. "He was appalled. He took me seriously, him and his lokogos, and suddenly he just raced into the night, trying to fix things. At first, when the news caught up with me on the road and I realized they were all probably dead, I hated him for that, but later? When the stories reached me here? Think of it—he risked everything... *lost* everything, on the word of a boy hiding in the brush." Taern pulled himself away from the dark night, the handsome young soldier, the blinding blue flare of the cold magnesium fire sweeping the bogland.

"A good man," M said evenly, "but that doesn't mean—"

"He hadn't been touched in forever," Taern told her baldly.

"You don't know the circumstances...." M sounded reluctant, and Taern looked up and tried to put things together.

"You mean the friend and the pain?"

She shrugged, and he knew he would get no more from her. She loved a good story, but part of the reason she held them in such high esteem was that she kept a confidence tighter than a dead man's fist.

"I don't care," Taern said recklessly. "He needed my touch. He will need me!"

He stilled in the act of fastening his duffel bag and looked away, and behind him he heard Madame M let out a shuddering breath.

"Taern—"

"This isn't what you think," he said, but his voice sounded weak, even to him.

Madame Matiya had been his confidante and friend from that first day when she'd chased him down in the market place, wearing four-inch heels and a corset. She got him—by the scruff of the neck—and said in a nut-shrinking baritone, "Junior, if you ever make me do that again, I'll kill you."

Taern had stopped struggling immediately and glared at her. "Lady, if you can catch me in those shoes, you can do whatever you want!"

She'd laughed then, heartily—and it was one of the few times Taern had heard her deep-down belly laugh. He'd discovered as he'd grown that she didn't let it out often. She'd taken him to her place and, up front and without hesitation, told him the facts of life. When he asked if he had to become a whore, she replied, "Only if you have aptitude and inclination when you are grown."

He'd grown up a few years before she would have chosen for him to, but he'd enjoyed those years, and so had she. She'd taught him everything he knew about the business, and one of the first things she'd taught him was that love and business had absolutely nothing in common, *certainly* not when sex was involved.

Suddenly her strong, blunt fingers with their scarlet-tipped nails were under his chin, and she forced him to look into eyes so brown and liquid that they had beguiled a hundred straight men to ignore the cock and believe in the woman.

"Say it again, Junior, so I can believe it."

He faced her this time. "You've told me to believe in my instincts, M. My instincts tell me that this man needs someone. Whether that's on the streets or in the sheets, I want to find a way to be that one."

She dropped her hand and slumped back dejectedly on his narrow cot. "You rhymed that, you wretched brat," she said, and he pressed his lips together and bent down to hug her.

"I'll take care of myself," he promised, and she glared at him with dignity.

"You'd better. That's how I trained you!"

He kissed her cheek, which probably needed a touch-up with the razor this time in the afternoon, but nobody in her house told her that. "It is indeed," he murmured and then threw his duffel over his shoulder and turned to change his life.

HE WAS not surprised—even a little—when Dorjan ordered the rabbit to the train station. Krissa looked surprised, but Taern wasn't. He smiled pleasantly at Krissa and pleasantly at Dorjan. Dorjan frowned thoughtfully and twitched his shoulders a little, and Taern's smile only grew more pleasant.

Good. The man *should* be uneasy, because in their short acquaintance, Taern had yet to give up with this little fight. It spoke well of him that he could read the signs.

The entire trip, Dorjan sat back on his cushion with a fountain pen and a parchment on a board, and when they arrived, he folded the parchment carefully, put it into an envelope, and then pulled out a small clever torch to melt the wax. He used the pendant at his neck to make the seal, and Taern noticed it glowed an intense blue after it had been forced into the wax.

He didn't say anything, though. He planned to get *much* closer to that pendant before this adventure was through.

The door of the rabbit swung up and open, and Dorjan stepped through, then stood at attention, his hands folded neatly at his back, while Taern said his good-byes to Krissa.

"Put a bright scarf outside an open window," he whispered into her ear. "Preferably his, if you can manage it, you hear?"

She nodded slightly as she pretended to wipe her eyes and then bussed him by his ear.

"You'd better be sure of your welcome," she hissed, and he grinned cheekily at her and winked before swinging out of the rabbit and shaking hands with and taking his letter of introduction from the very stern and forbidding Dorjan of Kyon's Gate.

He swung up into the millipede through one of the doors in the sectioned cars and then hustled to the very front of the train before it could power up. He smiled gaily at the conductor at the front and then hopped out the other side of the neck. He'd circled around and was out of the station, sprinting across the next trestle bridge and toward the Forum Master section of town, before the millipede even started its steam-powered clatter down the tracks.

Sure enough, in one of the newer houses—a big one, with black shutters and gray paint, which must have been fashionable but certainly was not cheerful—a bright fuchsia-and-puce scarf fluttered from a window on the third floor.

It appeared that he was done with whoring, and for a moment Taern was a little put out. He very much wished he had a way to put silver in his pocket, because as he spotted his route over the drainpipes and the cornices of the roof, he thought that he owed Krissa at least a week's worth of wages.

Refuse, Reject, Deny

DORJAN was relieved that the boy left without much of a fight, but he wasn't sure he trusted it. He waited until the millipede pulled completely out of the station before he got back into the rabbit, and tried to deny the sharp poison of disappointment. He reminded himself that he visited his family for a moon cycle and that he usually made it out to Dre's keep to see the orphans his old lokogos had taken in. He'd see the boy again—and possibly hear stories of his recalcitrance then.

The thought cheered him, and he turned his attention to not chasing Krissa away with his dourness—or with Areau's theatrics, when they arrived.

"Your…." He grimaced. "Your companion doesn't know you're coming," he said baldly. "I haven't told him about this. There will be some unpleasantness when we return."

Krissa widened her eyes and arched her eyebrows. "Well, I'll just have to punish the man for unpleasantness, won't I?"

Dorjan was forced to make a sound that resembled a laugh. Bimuit, he was tired. He'd arrived late to the stables the night before and found that Areau—Areau, who had promised that Dorjan wouldn't need to practice their perversion of pain and sex that night—had apparently forgotten.

He was naked, his wrists bound from chains and manacles he'd outfitted above the iron pipe that delivered steam power to the rabbit as it slept in its stall at night. Dorjan hated those chains, hated the nights when Areau bound himself to them and begged. One night Dorjan had refused, and Areau hadn't told him where the key was until Dorjan flogged it out of him. Areau… oh, damn him. It was Dorjan's punishment to flog his friend until his back bled that night. Dorjan had never refused since.

So the night before, Dorjan had left his armor on and taken up the riding crop next to the whip and the flogger. He liked the crop—pain, but not damage. "You promised," he whispered. "You promised we wouldn't do this."

Areau's look over his scarred shoulder had been shamed and eloquent. "No fucking," he offered. "I can spare you that. But… you were out on the streets tonight… look at you! It….” Areau wiggled, his engorged cock scraping roughly on the wooden wall of the stable. “I’ll come from the pain alone, Dori, but I need it. Please. I need it from you tonight.”

Dorjan whistled the crop through the air and tried hard to forget the tender, happy touches of young fingers on his skin. The boy had wanted…. Yes, it was his profession—but Bimuit, Dorjan hadn’t paid him, had he? The boy had simply wanted. He’d been eager and excited and… soft. No pain. No disgust. Given what he and Areau had been engaging in for the past ten years, a whore on the streets of Thenis was practically virginal compared to Dorjan.

Dorjan thought of that touch as he sliced the crop and smacked Areau’s bare, scarred bottom, and wished his balls would shrivel up and fall off in shame. *Switch, switch, switch.* Dorjan had learned long before that he could get Areau off faster if he varied the strokes, surprised him with pain rather than deadened him to it. He’d studied hard, how to be good at this, because the quicker Areau whimpered, moaned, and screamed his way to a climax, the less likely he needed Dorjan to….

Dorjan shuddered.

The thought of his flesh sheathed in Areau’s bowels, plunging away like an animal while Areau begged and screamed for harder, more painful, rougher, made him feel physically ill.

Just as well the boy had gotten on the millipede. He would have wanted a thing from Dorjan that Dorjan could probably not ever give again without the sickness that tainted his every breath in his own home.

He realized that Krissa was looking at him, her fingers knotting in a brilliantly colored purple-and-green scarf, and that he’d been silent for several seconds. “Punish him as you see fit,” he said weakly. “What needs to happen is that I cease to be a part of it. I don’t know if you recommend weaning him from my touch or simply cutting him off from it—he… he finds it loathsome. He was never a lover of men. But I was the only one either of us trusted with him for so very long.”

Krissa’s eyes widened. “You’re not that old, begging your pardon, Forum Master.”

Dorjan smiled thinly. “You’d be surprised,” he said, then took a deep breath and continued. He told her about his odd hours and how she needed not to worry about his appearance when he showed. He attempted to make up a story about a boxing club and other Forum Masters indulging in senseless violence. She tilted her head skeptically and raised her eyebrow, but she didn't gainsay him. Good. Even if she suspected—even if she *knew*—she could pretend otherwise if Dorjan was ever apprehended. She was just an innocent whore, shanghaied to tend to a friend's twisted perversions. It was no less than the truth.

"When we get there," he said as the rabbit left the stews behind, "we shall find a room for you, preferably near his and far from mine, so you will not be disturbed by my hours. The house is very large—Forum Masters used to bring their families in from the country during the seasons, but not as much these days. Mrs. Wrinkle will help you decorate: you'll have a budget, feel free to make your space...." He smiled, remembering his mother's tidy sitting room, his older sister's flouncy pink meringue of a bedroom, the elegant, feminine space of Madame Matiya. "Make it you," he said with an inclination of his head. "The house is musty and haunted at present. Don't hesitate to breathe life into it, if you have such a penchant." He tried for a tired smile. "It certainly couldn't hurt things, could it?"

Krissa nodded and then smiled brightly. "You're paying me generously, Forum Master. You'd be surprised what some silver and a willing body can do for a place!"

Dorjan nodded and felt some of the tarnish fade from his smile. "Excellent, but," he warned, "Areau has certain rooms in the basement for his experiments. Those are his rooms—not even I venture into them."

Krissa's eyes widened a fraction. "Warning taken, sir. Now are you sure you don't want to rest up?"

Dorjan grimaced and reached into another compartment for his parchment, quill, and board. "A lovely suggestion, my dear, but would you believe that Forum Master is actually a job? I have taken the day off from it, but that does not mean the work has disappeared."

He submerged himself in his details for the memorial service of a certain Forum member who had been found dead of a heart attack in his personal conveyance. Of the Forum members attending the funeral, he wondered how many others knew that the heart had been attacked by a knife.

HE HELPED Krissa carry in her belongings, trying not to hold his stomach and cringe. That wretched steam spear had left his ribs tender and the very act of breathing normally an effort in theater.

A very surprised Areau greeted them in the foyer.

"Who is this?" he asked baldly, and Dorjan grimaced at Krissa. She had been nothing but pleasant, brave, and willing. It would be nice to make a better impression.

"She's your new companion," he said, keeping his voice even.

Areau flinched as though struck. "Were you hit on the head last night?" he asked, his blue eyes wide with shock. "Tasting asteroid dust? Sucking niskets through a straw up your nose? Did you bugger the wrong whore and—"

"*Enough!*" Dorjan roared, and Areau closed his mouth with a snap. Dorjan so very rarely yelled, so very rarely fought back from any of Areau's demands. But he had to. He *had* to. His country was falling apart, and sometimes it seemed as though he and Areau were the only ones holding it together. They couldn't do that and sustain their destructive dance. Not anymore. Dorjan was... Bimuit! For a moment, he'd considered letting that spear find its mark.

"She's your companion, Areau—not a slave, not a whore."

"But—" Krissa protested, and Dorjan looked at her sharply.

"You're a paid companion with specialized talents," he said, not backing down.

Areau only visited the streets to seek degradation. Ten years ago the two of them would have tittered and giggled like schoolboys at the thought of visiting a whorehouse. Unless he was looking for a whore on purpose, or to whore himself out for the pain, for the most part, Areau had spent ten years in this house, visiting the courtyard for exercise—plenty of it—but not venturing beyond the gated gardens. Dorjan understood that a whore was a businessperson, nothing less. Areau still thought like a schoolboy.

"Nobody in this house"—Dorjan glared at the boy he'd once loved, at the man he struggled daily not to hate—"is anything less than a lady or a gentleman. You are to treat her no more crudely than your sister or my mother, do we understand?"

Areau did a curious thing—a sad thing. He backed up and bowed from the waist. "Yes, Forum Master," he said formally.

"Ari," Dorjan protested, but Areau had already turned on his heel and started down the hallway. Dorjan caught hold of his temper and called after him in the same voice that had stopped him short in the first place. "Areau, son of Coreau, of Kyon's Gate!" he barked, and Areau turned around, surprised again.

"You left your companion in the foyer without so much as an introduction," Dorjan snapped. "Your father taught you better manners than that, and your mother would be ashamed. Come back here and introduce yourself."

Areau glared at him but turned around reluctantly and made a short bow. "Areau, son of Coreau, my lady," he said shortly. "I apologize for my rudeness."

"Not good enough," Krissa said smartly, and Dorjan looked at her in surprise and approval.

"I beg your pardon?" Again, Areau flinched back.

"This man went to the trouble to procure you a companion to help you satisfy a need he never should have been asked to fulfill, and you're *rude* to him? He claims you honor your parents. I've yet to see it happen!"

Areau opened his mouth and shut it and straightened his spine. "I—"

"You what?" Krissa asked, her voice brooking no argument.

Areau looked at Dorjan and managed some shame, or some reasonable facsimile thereof. "I'm sorry, Dori," he muttered. "You should have told me you didn't want to do it anymore."

Dorjan felt a flare of temper. "Every time I tried, you did something so horrible, I had no choice," he said honestly, and Krissa turned to Areau, her eyes narrowed.

"I was told you were a gentleman, and I find a spoiled child," she said coldly. "Clearly, we have things we need to work on." She turned and bowed to Dorjan courteously. "Forum Master, if Areau may show me to my room, I can get settled in here. There is work to be done."

Dorjan bowed to her. "Agreed. If you could meet me in my study in two hours' span, I would be honored, my lady."

Krissa bit her lip—the first bit of uncertainty he'd seen. "It would be good if we could all meet at mealtime," she said, and he felt bad that he couldn't accommodate her.

"Forgive me, my lady. I often have other things to attend to. Areau and I usually take breakfast in the kitchen together, but very rarely am I here for dinner."

"Tonight?" Areau asked plaintively. "Really, Dori? Again?"

Dorjan grimaced and looked pointedly at Krissa, and Areau flushed and tried again. "It's been two nights running," Ari said, still looking lost.

Dorjan usually only ventured out in his armor a few times a week, but the night before, as he'd slid back slowly and silently through the shadows, he'd overheard something he couldn't overlook.

"It's important, Ari," he said earnestly. "And since Lady Krissa is here to take some of the burden off my shoulders, it's best that I use the time I'm given."

Areau nodded and bowed. When they were children, they had joked about Dorjan's status, had mocked the social hierarchy that would have Areau bowing to his oldest friend in public. Now, at this moment, there was nothing of mockery or of play in his bow, nothing of the snide and acid disposition Areau had shown since his time in the asylum. Simple deference. Simple concern. Dorjan felt like his next breath was his first true one in ten years.

"Be safe," Areau said quietly. Then—"This way, my lady. I shall find Mrs. Wrinkle for you, and you can give her a list of your needs."

"I think you should transcribe it for me," Krissa said, her voice not breaking a bit as she issued the order. "I like to keep my crop hand fresh."

Dorjan noticed that Areau had turned down the hallway and that she had not attempted to move. He got halfway down and looked back. Krissa looked him calmly in the eyes until he looked beside her and saw the battered cardboard case that she'd brought with, Dorjan assumed, all of her earthly possessions. It lay at her feet, which were covered in cheap cloth slippers, but Lady Krissa didn't bat an eyelash as Areau turned around, bowed deeply, and picked up the case.

"It's down the hall and to the left, my lady. I assume you will want the room next to my own?"

"Does it have an adjoining washroom?" she asked tartly, and Areau conceded that yes, yes it did.

Dorjan watched them disappear down the hallway and wondered, truly wondered, what it was like to be young again. Perhaps... perhaps he could almost stand without ache and breathe without that binding across his chest that he'd felt for the last ten years.

It would be nice to see.

A FEW hours later, he was working in his study, nibbling fitfully on the small sandwiches he'd asked Mrs. Wrinkle to bring him for supper. He looked up happily from the tentative knock on the door and stood to usher Lady Krissa inside.

"It's a bit foreboding," he apologized as she came in. "But please, make yourself comfortable. Would you like Mrs. Wrinkle to bring you something?" He reached for the button that would ring the bell in the kitchen, but Krissa shook her head.

"He's worried about you," she said abruptly, and Dorjan smiled his most disarming smile and shrugged.

"And I him. It is what we do," he said. "I will be here for dinner tomorrow."

Krissa looked around and wrinkled her nose. "Did he design this?" she asked, and when Dorjan grimaced, she finished the thought herself. "Of course he did. It was to punish you for an imaginary wrong," she muttered. "Or to punish the rest of the world. Something." She glanced at the heavy metal monstrosity of a desk he was sitting behind and shuddered. "Would you like me to design something less…." She made a fussy gesture with her hands, and Dorjan decided he liked her very, very much.

"Gothic?" he asked, and she laughed faintly.

"Look," she said after a moment, "I'm going to cut to the chase here. I know you're the Nyx—I'm not stupid, and I was listening through the dumbwaiter when Taern was talking to Madame M. Don't worry," she forestalled him when he felt his heart try to burst out of his chest with a delayed fright reaction, "I will tell no one. But I knew what it was I was agreeing to when you bought my contract."

"But why?" he asked, trying to stay calm. "But… *why?*"

She cocked her head and thought. "Thenis is a horrible place," she said seriously. "My whole life—what there's been of it—I've thought of getting out. You *could* get out. You could have a proxy, spend all your time in your keep—hell, a lot of Forum masters already do that. But you don't. You stay here and try to make it better." Krissa shrugged. "Who doesn't want to be a part of that?"

Dorjan shook his head. "Most people," he said bluntly. "But since most people aren't caring for my dearest friend, perhaps your opinion has more weight."

She nodded. "He's going to be… difficult." She looked down at her hands and blushed, and it was the first time he'd seen her discomfited since that tense moment the night before, when he'd been hoping she and the boy by her side would run for it.

"I am aware," he said, hoping that helped.

"I just thought that if we're going to work together on him, you should be able to be honest with me. It would be easier, I suppose, if I started with the honesty, so I did."

He nodded and then saw perhaps what she was getting at. "Our past pattern," he told her carefully, "was for him to greet me in the stables. He started out by... by picking fights and driving me to strike him." He looked down, shamed. "When I realized what he was doing and that he wouldn't stop, even if I said no, we turned it into...." He swallowed on the nausea. "Foreplay, of sorts. I would come back and he would greet me, asking me for... for his choice of pain."

She nodded and then asked, "Do you perhaps have some sort of permanent restraint? I would prefer leather, but—"

"I've got some leather ones in my room, if you like, and he's bolted manacles to the barn door," Dorjan said through a dry throat, and she nodded too.

"Is he capable of moving them to his bedroom on his own?" she asked seriously, and Dorjan shrugged.

"He's a genius with all things mechanical," he told her honestly. "If he tells you no, he's lying."

Her smile was both grateful and impish. "Very helpful information!" Then she sobered again. "Tell me now—and don't be afraid if the answer is yes, because I'm stronger than I look. Will he strike me? Will he try to fight me back?"

Dorjan thought hard and swallowed against a suddenly dry mouth. He stood restlessly, then came to sit on his desk instead of behind it, the better to dangle one foot off the thing and try to touch the floor.

"When we were children," he told her, "I would have said no. He was the gentlest child. He didn't... drown kittens or pull the wings off flies. He used to protect his older sister—and me, for that matter, if the children of the workers tried to bully the keeper's boy. He was gallant and funny and frenetic and charming...."

"But not after the asylum," she supplied when he couldn't go on.

"Or my father's death, which happened the night we freed him."

She closed her eyes and covered her mouth with her hand. "That's awful. I'm so sorry."

"Not as sorry as the two of us." That was enough. He was done briefing her on the most painful moments of his life. It was necessary, and he knew that, but it was old.

"So I don't know," he said seriously. "I like to think that there is still that kernel of boy inside him, who wouldn't hurt a woman, but—"

"But you never foresaw the two of you like this," she supplied, and he inclined his head.

"Does that help you?" he asked, and she nodded.

"Oh, very much."

"Good. Then if you don't mind…." He trailed off delicately, but she refused to take the hint.

"I have one more question, and I'll let you return to your work, sir."

"Indeed."

"So, you attended his 'needs'," she began, her inflection over the word obvious, "but who attended to yours?"

He stood coldly. "That is a very impertinent question," he said in dismissal, and this time she took the hint and stood too.

"And you just answered it," she said, her voice gentle. "Be careful on the streets tonight, Forum Master. They do not get any safer as the time passes us by."

She curtseyed then, deliberately, and he bowed and let her leave. But when he sat down again, it was impossible to work. He hadn't wanted to talk to her about that, hadn't wanted to tell her anything at all. But he couldn't help it. She had asked him who cared for his needs, and all he'd had to answer her had been a single moment in a dark alleyway with a young man squatting at his feet. He had black hair and midnight-blue eyes, and if Dorjan could do anything right at all, the boy was currently bound by millipede to the edge of the province to see sisters he'd long thought dead.

WHEN the bell rang for supper two spans later, he left his study and went upstairs to change.

The boy was lying there in his great ebony four-post bed, naked under the covers, waiting cheekily with his hands behind his head for Dorjan to come in.

Dorjan gaped at him for a moment and then shook his head. "I don't have time for this," he muttered and went to his armoire for the black wool smallclothes and a new overtunic that he wore with his armor.

It was the boy's turn to gape. "You don't have *time* for this?" he asked, and it was *almost* worth the headache he'd just caused Dorjan to hear him flounder for words. "I'm likely the only man to come to your bed happy for years!"

"Try ever!" Dorjan snapped, too out of patience to be tactful, and he hated the way the boy's eyes widened with pity. "But I need to leave on the half hour, or my entire strategy for this evening will be for naught!"

Taern blinked at that and looked twice at the black smallclothes that Dorjan was putting on. "No," he said with authority, sitting up in bed. The sheets and comforter slid down, revealing a smooth chest, pale but defined, and Dorjan had to force himself not to take a moment to look appreciatively.

"You're not even supposed to be here," Dorjan said after allowing himself a sideways glance. "You certainly don't get to tell me what to do!"

"Where else am I supposed to serve out that contract you bought?" Taern replied tartly. "And I'm telling you what to do because you shouldn't do it! Not for your health, not for your household—let Thenis save itself tonight!"

"You're supposed to serve it out getting a stellar education with your sisters at Dre's keep!" Dorjan snapped, going to his armoire without looking, which he felt was some accomplishment.

"I'll send them a letter, I've things to do here!" Taern returned, and Dorjan was forced to glance up from the layers of suits and Forum robes in order to glare.

"I hadn't thought you were cruel," he said darkly, and to his credit, Taern looked away in something like shame.

"I'll meet them," he said stubbornly, "but not now."

"Then why did you get on the train?" Dorjan demanded, whirling around with his clothes in his hands. He usually changed into his sleek black smallclothes here in his room and then padded back to the stables to put on his armor. It needed to live in the stables because Ari was constantly refining it—and fixing dents, rents, and holes. Dorjan thought briefly of changing in the hall or in the washroom, but that would be ridiculous, and he was having a hard enough time maintaining his composure.

"To get you out of the train station, obviously," Taern returned. He looked at the clothes in Dorjan's hand and seemed to consider Dorjan's hesitation, then sat back in bed and smirked. "That way I could come back and enjoy the show."

Oh, niskets take this! "I'm going to change in the stables," Dorjan said with as much dignity as he could muster.

"Why change at all?" Taern asked plainly. Forsaking his own dignity, he swung his feet out of bed and moved across the floor into Dorjan's space.

Dorjan took a step back, and the insufferable boy looked up and matched him. Dorjan couldn't help it—he did it again. In three more steps, his back was against his door and Taern's hands were busy under his coat and starched shirt, fumbling with his smallclothes. His hands were cold, and Dorjan gasped when they got to the bruise on his stomach.

Taern gasped too and yanked on his outer shirt so hard a button popped off and hit the wall and the floor with a tinkle and a thud. The bruise on Dorjan's ribs was spectacular—it exceeded the bandages there to help support his breathing. Suddenly Taern was touching the soft skin above the bandage, his hands delicate as a nisket in flight.

The look he gave Dorjan was eloquent.

"You," he said deliberately, "will get yourself killed if you go out like this. I'm surprised you can walk without stiffness."

Dorjan clenched the two halves of his shirt together. "It's not my first injury," he said tightly, "and certainly not my worst."

Taern parted the shirt again, and Dorjan let him in order to avoid touching his hands. Somehow taking those clever questing hands into his would have been so very personal. "I can see that," the young man said quietly, his fingers brushing upon the scars from other encounters— moments when the armor had failed, or when Dorjan had.

Dorjan grabbed the shirtfront and whirled away from him, deciding that changing in his own washroom was better than this.

"You may eat dinner with Krissa and Areau," he said tightly. "We'll discuss where you're going to—where are you going?" He turned, harried, to find the boy, still naked, right on his heels.

"I'm following you," Taern said, his dark brows drawn tightly over his blue eyes. "You keep trying to get away from me because you're changing. That's not going to happen. If you want to finish this conversation in such an all-fired hurry, you're going to have to take your clothes off in front of me, and that will be a start."

"A start to what?" Dorjan demanded, well and truly flummoxed. "You're a *boy*—"

"I'm a whore," Taern said, his eyes hard, "and you've just bought my contract."

"You're not my *whore*, you're my *ward!*" Dorjan protested. "I'm not having sex with someone I'm responsible for!"

"You would if I were your *wife!*" Taern laughed, and Dorjan thunked the wall next to him solidly with his fist.

"We need to have this conversation at another time," he said, hauling his self-control around him raggedly. "I was not joking when I said my time was limited."

"Well can you at least tell me what's so damned important that you're willing to go out there when you can barely breathe? Don't think I can't hear you struggling for breath, you almost filled the carriage."

Dorjan scowled. "I'm stopping a shipment of meteor dust—"

"There will be another to replace it!" Taern snapped doggedly, and Dorjan took a deep, labored moment and tried to explain.

"Yes, but *this* shipment is going to pay the man who set an army on Kiamath Keep," Dorjan said, fighting for breath. The obnoxious brat was right; breathing had not been easy all day. All he wanted to do was lie down and sleep, maybe take some laudanum for the pain so that breathing was not quite such a chore, but he absolutely could not do that. Fortunately his last statement was enough to get Taern's attention.

"Alum Septra," he said through his next breath. "Alum Septra bought most of the Forum on the night my father was killed—Kyon's death was proof that he had enough power to keep them safe from censure. The few honest Forum members were rallying to put pressure on the Triari—we were a month, maybe, from pulling our forces from your province."

Taern's hands had stopped their relentless quest for Dorjan's skin, but he didn't move back. He stayed, naked and unself-conscious, inches away, resting his hands lightly on the waistband of Dorjan's trousers, and Dorjan had to close his eyes so he didn't just look down at their bodies, so very close but not touching.

"Were?" Taern asked, proving that he was as bright as Dorjan had supposed.

"Well, the biggest supporter of the antiwar movement died under mysterious circumstances in his personal conveyance last night," Dorjan said shortly. "If I can cut off Septra's spare cash, maybe I can make that not the end of the movement."

Taern opened his mouth and closed it and stepped back, cocking his head a little to the right. "But... but... you *had* to kill him!" he protested. "You *had* to!"

Dorjan nodded. "I'm not disputing that," he said. He was running out of time and he still had his smallclothes in his hands. His natural practicality asserted itself, and he began to shed his shirt.

Taern's hands came up to help him. "But... but can't this wait until tomorrow?"

"No." Dorjan looked at those hands—supple, long-fingered, well-manicured. He remembered the night before, when one of them had crept up and stroked his ribs, just to keep him still. His breath came uncomfortably fast. "If I wait until tomorrow, the money will have exchanged hands and Septra's representative will have delivered it. Those votes on the Forum might have been mine. People hate Septra—if he doesn't pay them, they've got no reason to come through."

Taern nodded his head then and slid his hands over Dorjan's shoulders. Dorjan shuddered. Touch. Sweet, gentle touch. The coat and the shirt fell down, and Taern caught them in one hand.

"I'm coming with you," the boy said sensibly, and Dorjan saw red. He was used to pain. He bent down and thrust his shoulder into Taern's midriff, hoisted him over his back, and wrapped his arm around Taern's cleanly muscled thighs. Oh... oh no. Taern's groin... rough pubic hair, smooth-skinned genitals... rubbing against his bare skin. He slowed for a moment but didn't falter. He dumped Taern into the bed and pulled a pair of softened leather manacles from his drawer.

Taern stared at them in shock as one clicked over his wrist and the other over the bedpost. There was a large ball on the end of the bedpost for decoration, and no, not even the soft manacle would stretch to accommodate that.

"What in the name of a nisket's balls are you doing with these things in your bed table, Nyx?" he gasped after they'd stared at each other in shocked silence for a moment.

Unconsciously, Dorjan stroked the shoulder where the boy's cock had touched, closing his eyes to savor the idea, before he opened them again to face what he'd done.

"Areau," he said gruffly. "If I didn't comply with his needs, he liked to wander." Dorjan looked away. "I had to sleep sometime."

It was Taern's turn to close his eyes, and he leaned his head back against the pillows and let out a patient breath. "You need me, Nyx. You need me here in bed, you need me on the street. I don't know how you survived without me this long."

Dorjan's face—and his purpose—hardened to the cold expression he wore under his mask and cowl. "I survived by not worrying who else might be hurt if I failed," he gasped. He turned around then, so he didn't have to see the boy's eyes on him, and made quick enough work of his trousers to don the black smallclothes. They'd been tailored, so they were modest, and they acted as a buffer between the supple armor and his skin. The boy gasped just a little as he was pulling up his trousers, and Dorjan couldn't hide his flinch.

He pulled the long-sleeved shirt over his head and said, "So see? Perhaps you don't want to share a bed with me after all."

"If you think those scars will scare me off, that's the hundredth thing you've been wrong about today!" Taern snapped, and Dorjan looked sideways enough to see him stretched out, pretty and naked, on top of the covers of his bed.

"Or that could simply be your second lie," he rasped, and then he slid out the door and down to the stables. By Bimuit and Karanos, he had better things to do.

Meteors, Asteroids, and Other Things That Crash

TAERN wasn't stupid. He counted to two hundred after he heard the man's padded footsteps on the stairs at the end of the hall. Somewhere in there, he heard the back door of the house—the one he figured was nearest the kitchen—slam, and *that's* when he threw his head back against the pillow and let out a snarl and a scream of frustration.

Then he called Krissa's name at the top of his lungs until the door opened and a small, plump middle-aged woman opened up the door, her eyebrows up to her hairline.

Taern struggled for the blankets to cover up his nakedness and smiled greenly. "I imagine this isn't something you're used to seeing in here," he said, thinking that embarrassment was an unusual emotion and he wasn't thrilled to have it washing over his bare skin.

"Unfortunately not," she said shortly and pulled a key out of her pocket. "The young lady said Master Areau thought you might be needing this."

Taern looked at the key and nodded. "That would be splendid," he said brightly, but she made no move to draw nearer, and he tried a winning smile.

"That would depend," she said measuring him with her eyes. "Are those your clothes?"

He looked down at what he'd been wearing that morning. He liked bright colors—turquoise ruffles at the throat, a brilliant scarlet topcoat, grass-green-and-gold-striped breeches that fit like a girl's tights, and they lay there next to the bed like a circus tent. His smile widened. "Can't miss 'em in the dark," he affirmed, and she humphed.

"They like to think I have no idea," she said shrewdly, "but you and I both know the dark is where he will be living this night. If you're going to follow him, you'll need dark."

Taern's grin settled to its usual cheeky grooves. "It's adorable how he thinks this whole Nyx thing is a secret," he said cockily. "The only person who doesn't know is—"

"Don't say it!" the woman hissed, turning to him fiercely. "If this is all sport to you, I'd just as soon leave you locked to the bed!"

"No, I—"

"Fourteen years I've worked here. When those boys were in school, I made them rolls and sweets for between classes. I watched them, wide-eyed, as they bought their government's lies and killed themselves to be the best soldiers they could be. He spent a month in bandages after Kiamath Keep, and Master Areau...." She shook her head and wiped her eyes with the back of a hand. "I watched them grieve his father, and their boyhood, and their innocence. I watched...." She looked away, her cheeks reddening. "No. I didn't watch that. It wasn't my place. But I could see the rot in his soul festering. For ten years it's been them making a hell for each other and me cleaning up the brimstone and the nisket shite. And today he brings in a girl like warm wind, and there's a boy in his bed. You're hope, boy, but if you don't take this serious, you're a false hope, and you will kill him dead."

Taern stopped and swallowed. "I'm the boy he stopped for," he said gruffly. "The boy who told him the keep was full of people. Don't think he's the only one who takes this seriously." His lips twisted up, and he was aware that *this* smile was not bright or quirky or cocky. It was the smile he used when a john tried to get rough with him or before someone thought he would put out for free. It was flat-eyed and dangerous, and no one *ever* tried to cheat him twice. "I'm just so damned happy I'm alive."

The woman nodded and grunted. "I'll be right back," she said decisively and then turned and left without another word.

Taern stared after her, naked and exasperated. In a moment the door opened again, but it wasn't the older housekeeper, it was Krissa, and she was dressed to work.

Her soft chestnut-colored hair was pulled back into a tight bun, and her clothing consisted of strategically placed straps of leather crisscrossing her slim body and pushing her breasts up and together so they'd look fuller. She'd tucked a riding crop into the strap crossing her hip, and Taern remembered hearing screams coming from Madame Matiya's dungeon on more than one occasion when she'd worn this outfit. When she turned a brown-eyed glare at him, he winced.

"Well done," she snapped.

"Are you going to let me out?"

"Mrs. Wrinkle will, when she gets back with some clothes. I've got about thirty seconds to ask you what the bloody hell you're playing with before I decide to order Areau to throw you out of the damned house."

"You knew I was coming back!"

"I didn't know you were going to… to *play* with him!"

"Karanos!" he swore. "For the love of baby niskets, Krissa, have you ever known me to be cruel?"

Her scowl in no way comforted him. "I've never known you to be serious, either," she muttered. "I just don't want him to be hurt."

Taern snorted. "You know, for a man who boldly professes to be sly, he's got all the women in this house panting after him in a hot second, but the naked man in his bed? No, he's getting no love whatsoever."

Her lips pulled up at the sides, and she shook her head. "If it's love you want, Taern, perhaps you should have taken that millipede. If he's anywhere as damaged as his friend, love is not something that will live easy in his heart." And with that she was gone, leaving him to wait for the nice woman with the key.

"Great. Just great. The whole world knows he's the Nyx, the whole world is trying to help him, but the one man who's got a snowball's chance in a nisket's kitchen? He's handcuffed to the bed naked and hard… oh shite."

Because he really was hard. It wasn't the handcuff, either, because that had never turned his key. No, this hardness was all leftover from Dorjan throwing him over a bare shoulder in order to toss him into the bed. Dorjan's skin was scarred—old scars, new scars, old bruises, new bruises. There were scars on his arms where his bones had popped through his skin and scars on his chest where knives or other pointed things had penetrated. His back was a nightmare of jagged little ones and the occasional long slash, and Taern? Taern wanted time with that naked body to worship every one.

Every. Damned. One.

He'd known—hell, he'd known from the night before, when the Nyx had come apart under his hands—that this man needed in ways Taern had never fathomed. But now? Taern felt it, the clicking of lock and key—

A real key disturbed his thoughts, landing on his lap from the doorway. He looked up in time to catch a set of what looked to be smallclothes, but soft, wool and black, as they came sailing for his face.

"Oh, you darling, you!" he crowed, grabbing the key with his free hand and unlocking the manacles. He paused for a moment to flex his hand and let the blood flow back through his wrist. "I don't suppose you know which way he went, do you?"

Mrs. Wrinkle might have had ginger hair once, and her tanned, freckled face might have been girlish and sweet. She was a "Mrs.," so she might have had children who loved her, and she might have picked them up and tickled them and cuddled and laughed with them, as Taern remembered his own mother doing. Maybe she had laughed like that, maybe.

But she didn't crack a smile, not once, as she told him where she thought he'd gone before he started his night's work.

By the time she was done talking, he was dressed, including a pair of old boots of Nyx's that were only a little big, much like the suit that had apparently fit the Nyx quite well when he was younger, before he'd sprouted three inches after he'd passed his twentieth year (according to Mrs. Wrinkle). Yes, every piece of clothing had a story, and it meant Taern had to roll up the sleeves and ankles of the suit as it was, and it was still too big across the chest and the shoulders, but even then he couldn't spare a smile for the absurdity of slipping around in a larger man's underwear.

Of course, by then he was dressed and she'd given him directions and he didn't feel like smiling at all.

THERE was a graveyard nearby, a place for Forum members and their families. Some Forum members preferred to be buried on their estates far away from the central city, but they still had a marker, a memorial, a "thank you for your service to our province" sort of thing.

It was a forbidding place, the lawns impeccable, the memorial stones in perfect symmetry and alignment, and any statues or busts set strictly within size and display limits. Flowers were cleaned up every morning before sunup, and nothing else was permitted graveside, or the family who had left the picture or keepsake would be charged with the grave's upkeep.

The place was a marker for the path of the Nyx, and Taern slipped through the lengthening twilight shadows of the pretty, perfect houses to find it. He looked four rows up and two columns over and saw the perfectly blown flower—they were sometimes called niskets because they looked so much like the legendary creatures who were described to whirl, full of light—but they were also called meteor roses, and Taern liked that name better. There were two sitting on Kyon's gravestone, one blood red and one sapphire blue, and Taern marked their presence and then moved on. So Nyx was sad about his father—that was not Taern's grief, not now. The marker simply meant he'd gone to his next place in his little ritual, and maybe, with luck, he had lingered just long enough for Taern to find him.

There, two blocks over from the graveyard, Taern saw the house. Mrs. Wrinkle had apparently once told Master Dorjan about it, talking happily about how one of Dorjan's old schoolmates had married and had children, and how the house was pleasant, with gardens and children's swings and a young mother who liked to take her late afternoons outside if she could. It was a reminder, Mrs. Wrinkle said, of the times when many families in Thenis could be found outside, playing with their children. When the poorer quarters had been working class and not poverty class, and before the cardboard cities of the stews had sprung up like mushrooms in the dank loam of Alum Septra's decay.

"He stops there," she said, "and watches. I saw him once, not long after I told him about his friend, and he didn't see me. I began to return that way near twilight from the market—every night he leaves the house wearing black, he stops by the graveyard with two flowers, and then he stops there."

Taern could see it playing out then in Nyx's orderly mind. (Taern thought of him as Nyx, now, especially when he was dressed for battle, or when Taern wanted to engage in one with him. He liked the nickname. It made the man less of a walking heartbreak.) One stop to pay penance to the past, one stop to remind him what he was doing in the present. Lovely. Just fucking lovely. Taking the grief for himself and leaving the peace for strangers. Taern was glad he was apparently good at taking blows as well as grief, because this made him want to hit the man himself.

And there—in the tops of a tree, Taern saw him. Oh, he really was good. The tree was back in a corner of the yard, a place where darkness had already fallen, and Nyx was looking in through a window. Taern couldn't see the window itself, but he could imagine. He'd been part of a happy family once. A mother, young children, a father. Would the father be reading? Would the mother be chasing them after the bath? Would they be eating fruit or cobblers after dinner?

Taern hugged his own shadow next to someone's converted stable and behind their (ugh!) compost pile, and watched as Nyx observed the life he had decided not to have.

The masked, armored figure stayed crouched, head alert, nothing in his movements to show what he was thinking, and Taern wished he could imagine the man happy. But how could he be? Taern had been inside his great echoing, dusty mansion for all of an hour, and two women—one he'd known for years—had come in and warned him not to hurt the man.

How could Nyx be happy?

Taern had known him through but a handful of encounters in two days, and Taern knew Dorjan of Kyon's Gate was probably a step away from leaping off the bridge in the center of town into Thenis's dank river, and seeing if the Nyx's armor bore him down.

But he didn't. No, he spent a scatter of moments here, looking at a happy family, and then he flickered into the night like a moth's shadow.

It was a good thing Taern had needed to practice moving the same way, and an even better thing that his feet could find their way into and through the stews from nearly every part of the city. For his first few years at Madame M's, he'd been her most trusted messenger, mostly because he was fast but also because he was reliable—not just to deliver the message and keep it a secret but to keep himself safe along the way. He was fleet on foot, if (he panted with the thought) a little out of practice. Karanos! The man was fast!

But Taern knew which way he was going, and as soon as he turned left after the river instead of right, he knew which gang's territory they were in and the most likely place for a meet.

Yes—there it was, down past the solarium, to where the school had been before it was burned out. The superstitious held that it was a church and that Bieman and Karanos would come down from the heavens and smite the wicked. Taern had listened at his lessons, though—Bieman and Karanos had been men, two of many, who had gone forth through the northern hemisphere and established cities, governments, and whole provinces. Gods, they were another thing, but when people swore by Bieman or Karanos, they were swearing by the deeds of determined men and not by the superstitious wrath of phantom deities.

Taern didn't tell people that, though. He figured in Thenis, believing that someone could visit the festering bowels of this shithole and give it a good purge, that was as close to hope as you got. Wait… oh shite, had Taern *lost* him?

No. No, and *oh no!* Taern thought he'd been heading for the burned-out school, which was a logical place for a meet and also the home of Flame and Vengeance, one of Thenis's biggest street gangs—but that's not where Nyx was heading.

No, Nyx was heading for what had used to be a bathhouse, back in the day when the people of Thenis could meet without fear. The pool was still there, but instead of being filled with steamy replenished water, it was filled with people—fixing people, dying people, drugged people, high on refined asteroid dust in its latest incarnation, something called comet.

Oh hells! Could Nyx's information be bad? But as Taern ran recklessly across a deserted street, he saw three people striding with purpose into the building from the other side. No. No, Nyx's information was probably spot on. This meeting was being held where the product would be most quickly distributed—which was one of the dumbest things a street dealer could do.

By the time a person got to the Thenis bathhouse, they weren't able to afford their poison anymore, were they? Once a week, the dealers and street gang paid their low man on the totem pole to go in and haul out the bodies, who were then taken to the one thriving business in Thenis—Pauper's Point, the city's funeral plot for the poor. Lately so many poor had been dying that they'd been burning the bodies and burying the vase, with a tiny stone denoting gender and approximate age, if they didn't have a name. Compared to Pauper's Point, Nyx's first stop on his night tour was a sign of hope.

But you didn't want to have a meeting in a drug house with all that product—the folks who could still move craved beyond reason, and they would show no mercy. Someone was being set up—the man with the drugs, the man with the money—*someone* was planning on walking out of here with both.

And Nyx was planning on being caught in the middle, trying to fuck them all!

Taern took a deep breath against the stench of unwashed bodies and ran faster toward the bathhouse. This could go bad so many ways!

He entered the building quietly, but it wouldn't have mattered. Even the human shambles on the outer edges of the pool house had heard the whisper of product there, of drugs, unclaimed and pure. They were stumbling, shaking, making their way back toward the changing rooms, and Taern could hear voices raised in fear and excitement.

"This was a hell of a place to ask for a meet, Uln! Does Septra want his money so badly he's willing to get it coated in junkie blood?"

"No," came the composed voice. "But he doesn't mind it coated in *yours!*" There was a sound there—a hiss and a thud and what sounded like somebody choking on a glass of milk. Taern knew differently, though. Someone in front of him stumbled and someone shoved that person against the wall—against *Taern*—and Taern barely sidestepped him. Hells, there had been a needle in that man's hand! Taern shuddered and concentrated on moving quickly and silently—and not getting noticed by any more users and not getting anywhere near their needles. Suddenly he was praying very much to gods he wasn't sure existed. One prick—that's what they said. One scratch and you were addicted, and it would take the movement of heaven and earth to cleanse that filth from your veins before you died from the need alone.

Two more steps and he'd be near the entrance to the changing room—oh hells. A backup of people and frantic whispers of "He killed him!" "Dust? Did he have dust?" "Who's got dust?" instilled the desperate quiet with mumbling confusion.

Taern took one look at the group of people gathering there and dodged into a crevice where one of the pipes carrying water to the pool was anchored. The junkies, a writhing mass amalgam of something that used to be humanity, all converged into the room, and there was a shout of disgust.

"Oh hell! Who let them in?"

"Don't look at me—you killed their dealer!"

"Bimuit! I knew this was a bad idea! But Septra, he wanted the drugs *and* the silver... hells...." There was another hissing thud, and another, and another, and a weak inhuman scream. "Let's get out of here!"

Taern heard a low roar from the mumbling, driven junkies and realized that the two men who had double-crossed the dealer must have escaped out the back door. Then he heard a shout from one of them and swore at himself. Yes. Oh definitely—would have made *so* much more sense to wait for them from the outside entrance! Karanos, no wonder Nyx had chained him to the bed!

"What in hells—"

"He just grabbed the money—"

"*And* the drugs! He scaled that wall—how are we supposed to follow him?"

And the drugs? What was he going to do with the drugs?

Taern didn't have time to worry about that because there were more shouts and screams, and the drug-addled mob seemed to have pushed its way out the door and... there were more screams. Oh. Oh hells. So much for the fate of Septra's men.

Taern pulled himself out of the recess for the pipe and looked around. There were a few bodies left—some breathing, some not—but no sign of anyone who might be after *his* hide next, and he had a sudden moment of acute vulnerability.

He had to get the hell out of here!

He turned quietly and slid out of the building, thinking he'd had a close call when he was grabbed from behind.

Later, he would wonder why the stench didn't warn him first, and he'd figure that he'd gotten used to it from his first few moments in the bathhouse.

"Hello, pretty shadow." The voice in his ear was slurred and oddly dreamy, and the hand that pressed his chest back was grimy, the fingernails so dirty the filth flaked off the front of them and clung to the skin like scabs. "What do you have for us?"

"Get *off* me!" He swung his elbow back and connected with a prominent rib cage, then broke away before he could hear the *oolf* or the exhalation of fetid breath. Something snagged on his soft shirt, but he was too busy sprinting away to care. He dashed for the end of the street, the better to find the shadows to bring him back to Nyx's great house, when he practically plowed into a man running in the opposite direction.

This man was not a junkie. Instead he looked like a gentleman's assistant in his short-tailed coat in a dark color and an overelegant cravat.

"Who in the hells are you?" he snarled, and Taern didn't bother to answer him, instead turning to resume his sprint back to safety.

Suddenly there was something sharp and broad jabbing into his side. He glanced down and cringed. Wonderful. A steam spear, and here he was without his armor.

"I *said*, boy, who the hells are you?"

"In the wrong place at the wrong time!" Taern gasped. For a moment he'd been terrified that the point jabbing into his shirt had been a syringe, and his relief almost let his water down. Of course, that steam spear in the side wouldn't be any less deadly.

"Shite!" the man spat, and Taern had a moment to rethink his earlier assessment of gentleman's assistant. He might have been somebody's errand boy, but nothing about him screamed gentleman. "You're wearing the same as that other one, the shadow who stole our payload. You with him?"

"No," Taern lied. "I'm a working boy, a hustler… just taking a shortcut, that's all."

"You're lying," the man said unpleasantly, and that was the last thing he said.

Taern didn't even see where he came from. It *seemed* like he came from behind them, leaping in the air and twisting at the last moment to catch the man in the face with a soft-booted foot. The man went flailing backward, releasing Taern, who took four steps to his left and turned in time to see Nyx hold his hand up and release a weapon at the man—and Taern gaped.

It was a simple thing—it looked to be a rubber ball, but a gun of some sort set into the Nyx's armor hurled it at great force. It caught the "gentleman's assistant" square on the nose. There was a crunch and a splatter and the man went down, twitching, as his nose cartilage exploded into his brain tissue and he died.

Taern gasped and looked at him and then back at Nyx, and suddenly Nyx's arms were around his shoulders and he was being pulled against the unyielding armor in a *crushing* hug.

Taern was speechless. The hug was intense, all encompassing, and soundless, and for a moment, he closed his eyes and melted into it, overwhelmed by gratitude—not just that Nyx saved his life but that he… he was offering his body as safety. Oh, blessed Karanos, Taern could get used to this.

Then Nyx's hands started exploring his body, but not in a sensual way. He was, Taern realized, patting Taern down.

"I'm fine," he said crossly, missing that hug.

"I need to see," Nyx muttered, turning him around. "You were in the bathhouse?"

"Yes, but I'm—hey, a little personal?"

"Hells!" Nyx's voice was gruff and unapologetic, and Taern felt something being detached from his sweater. He struggled to turn around, and his eyes grew so wide they dried out.

"I didn't know that was there," he muttered, looking at the half-filled syringe like it was a death sentence.

It *was* a death sentence, and it had missed Taern's bare skin by the thickness of soft black underwear.

Taern had enough time to cast a green smile at Nyx and whistle lowly, and then he was thrown unceremoniously over Nyx's shoulder as Nyx, aided by his armor, went sprinting through the city with a very specific goal in mind.

"Ouch! You're jouncing!" Taern cried out after the first block.

In response, Nyx shuffled his body a little more firmly (to prevent the jouncing) and evened out his original half-mad gait. It was a little better, and nice to know the man cared about Taern's comfort, but Taern was getting woozy.

"I'll puke on your back if you don't put me down," he warned after another block, and Nyx grunted.

"Not—" Gasp. "—too long—" Gasp. "—to go!"

And Taern felt a little bit awful.

"Oh, hells, Nyx, put me down. I'll run where you're running. You're *hurting* yourself, dammit!"

But they were there, apparently. Taern recognized the open wooden pavilion of the deserted train station, and Nyx bent double at the waist and dumped him on his feet. Then he held on to one of the pillars and knelt, trying to get his breath.

Taern bent at his waist and looked up into that triangular mask and tried to peer into Nyx's eyes. Could he see Taern in the dark? Could he see the contrition, the worry on his face?

"You can't put me on a train until tomorrow," he said gently. "Perhaps you want to take me home and we can talk about this?"

He was unprepared for Nyx to straighten, plant one augmented hand on his shoulder, and shove Taern so hard and fast that he stumbled backward and fell on his ass.

"I don't want to talk!" he gasped. Taern imagined he would have shouted if he'd had the breath. "I need you gone. I need you *safe.* Do you have any idea what almost happened to you tonight? *Any?*"

"Yeah," Taern said, shuddering. "I think I need armor too!"

Nyx screamed, the sound echoing off the ceiling. "Armor? You want *armor?* You need to be *gone!* This city is *not* a safe place!"

Taern snorted. "Look, you're telling *me!* That man would have *killed* me!"

The Nyx's mask left his mouth bare, but it was compressed into such a stoic expression that Taern once again couldn't be sure what the man was thinking, but, well, he *did* have the feeling he'd shocked Nyx to some extent.

What Nyx said next shocked Taern perhaps even more.

"I would have written," he said oddly.

Taern blinked, and his jaw dropped open, and he felt like a right fool. "I'm sorry?"

"I wouldn't have just sent you off to a stranger. I would have written, you know, to find out how you were doing. I wouldn't have just deserted you."

Taern stared at him blankly and shook his head. "What does this have to do with—"

"Go somewhere safe! Just because you leave this place, that doesn't mean your life will disappear! You can get out, don't you see? This train station, it can take you away! I worried about you for *years*—and when I found you, it was like... like a *sign* that I could do it right this time and get you to safety. You're not stuck here, just before the cricket landed, like I was before the crash! Get *away!*"

Taern planted his feet as firmly as he could, because it felt like the sands of the earth were shifting under him. "You can get away too!" he said, and for a moment, he thought about what it must have been like here in this city. How many years had he been fighting in the day with people who couldn't even see there was a war, fighting in the night with people who didn't care what he suffered? How many years had Nyx been, from what Taern could see, fighting in his home with someone who was supposed to offer peace? As he thought about it, it felt like the ceiling had fallen on his head and was pressing him, suffocating him, crushing him against the floor.

"Get away!" Taern said now, half pleading. "Go yourself! You have a keep—you can stay there! Why don't you go?"

It wasn't his imagination. For a moment that black figure with the smoky-gray armor and the triangular mask swayed, but Taern couldn't tell if the suggestion weakened him or tempted him. "I have things to do," Nyx said after a moment, with simple dignity. Taern noticed that he had a satchel under his arm, and he wondered at the fate of the drugs and money from that amazing heist he'd just pulled off.

"Then let me help."

Nyx bent his head and sighed. "I just wanted… you were kind to me." Behind the mask, the voice sounded apologetic. "You were kind to me. I just wanted… I wanted to give you that kindness back. Being free, that was the best kindness I could think of. Can't you take that, Taern? Can't you take that kindness and let me think of you free?"

Taern approached him, realizing that for a few moments, he too had fallen under the spell of the anonymity and the darkness.

"I'm angry," he said, surprised when the honesty escaped. "For the longest time, I was angry at *you*." Nyx flinched, and so did Taern, but he went on. "You said you were going to stop it, but nobody stopped it—or so it seemed. And then the rumors started to filter down, about the two boys who wouldn't let the people burn inside and about how they were being punished by their government, and then, you know, I had a much bigger hatred. I didn't know what to do with it, I didn't know where to go to make it stop, but I hated. I let it burn. And now?" Taern smiled brightly because the thought, the *idea* of doing what Nyx was doing, was just so delicious. He was fucking them from both ends, Taern thought savagely. He was fucking the real villain in the day on the political arena, and at night, in the covert arena of the streets.

It made Taern's cock hard just thinking about it.

"You're doing what I dreamed of doing. I'm not going to be free until I get some payback," Taern said, feeling like there should be blood dripping from his smile. "I want some flesh in my teeth for all my family suffered. And you know—of anybody, you know—how I can shed ever so much blood and not much of it my own."

Nyx seemed to shrink before his eyes. His shoulders drooped, one foot came up as though that leg were injured, and his arm went to his side, cradling his ribs as though they were in pain.

They *were* in pain.

"Do you," Nyx said randomly, "have any idea how long it's been since I've gotten any sleep?"

Taern sighed and moved up under his arm to take some of his weight, but Nyx shook him off. "I'll be fine," he said irritably.

Taern tried to insinuate himself anyway. "Sure you will be," he said. "Once we get you back to the house to take off the armor and get you to bed."

"Please," Nyx begged him. "Please? All day, I had this vision, that when I finally got to bed, I could dream of you at Dre's keep, happy with your sisters. It was almost like you were a boy again, and I was young and didn't know what a shithole the world was." Something like a sigh escaped him then, and this time he didn't acknowledge it when Taern situated his body under Nyx's shoulder. "That was the best night's sleep I could possibly imagine," he said, his voice almost dreamy.

Taern wanted to hold him closer, but he wanted to wrap those ribs first. "Brother, if *that's* the best night's sleep you can imagine, you have *not* been finishing your nights off right!"

Nyx straightened and swore, falling back on Taern's shoulder for help. "We're *not* sleeping together," he said crossly, and Taern laughed.

"You go on and think that," he said, as happy as he'd ever been. "Whatever gets you home."

HE DIDN'T accept help for long. After they cleared the train station, he seemed to straighten, gather in on himself, and in a few steps he was the Nyx again, instead of a tired man. He whispered from shadow to shadow, and Taern had difficulty keeping up with him. When they got to the house, Nyx went in through the stables and stopped. There were no horses here anymore, and just as Taern was wondering if there ever had been, that smoky-colored triangular mask turned toward him.

"Go into the kitchen and have a snack, boy," Nyx said quietly. "I'll be there in a moment."

Taern took two steps toward the kitchen before he realized what this was.

"No," he said, moving in to the armor again. He remembered where the catches were from the night before, and he had no qualms about helping Nyx off with it now. Nyx made random, frantic movements over his shoulders and tried to jerk away several times, but Taern estimated his resources were about spent—probably in that spectacular acrobatic twist and landing when Taern had been held captive. But still, it wasn't an easy task when the catches in the armor kept moving, and he finally just turned to Nyx in impatience.

"Dammit! Don't tell me you've never had help doing this! If nothing else, your friend in there with Krissa must have worked as sort of a valet. Stop being a spoiled child and let me unlatch your armor, for sweet hell's sake!"

There was a sound like a growl, and suddenly the jerking and fidgeting stopped and Taern was free to finish his task. It wasn't too difficult—there was a perfect symmetry to the latches, and the armor itself slid off almost like living water.

Taern looked around the stable and saw a closet—a big one, with what looked to be a mannequin in it that was obviously supposed to hold the armor. He picked up the biggest pieces and took them toward the mannequin, and looked up to see that Nyx had picked up the rest.

"I'm supposed to be waiting on you," Taern said lightly.

"You're not my valet," Nyx said shortly. "I... my friend usually helps me, the one who designed the armor. That way he can see if the new features worked." He helped Taern attach the armor around the mannequin, and Taern noticed that now that the gauntlets were gone, he was very, very careful not to let their fingers touch. When they were finished, Taern looked at him expectantly, and Nyx reluctantly placed his hands under the edges of the cowl and mask combined and lifted them both off.

He darted his eyes almost nervously in Taern's direction and looked away, putting the mask and goggle apparatus over the head of the mannequin before turning toward the door that connected the stable to the house.

"Nyx!" Taern called, and he kept walking. "Nyx, wait up!"

"If we're quiet, we can get supper," he said, stopping at the threshold. "Mrs. Wrinkle is kind enough to save some. If she knew you'd be out, she probably saved yours too."

"But wait—Nyx!" He wouldn't turn around. He wouldn't look at Taern. He just kept walking. In the black smallclothes, his shoulders were broad and his waist was narrow (too narrow—he needed to eat), and Taern could see every muscle defined. He could also see an almost conscious effort to... to minimize himself. He didn't slouch, but his height was not imposing, although he was tall. His form was not formidable, although his shoulders were broad. He took off the armor and the mask and he simply became…

"Dorjan!" Taern said, his voice pitched much more softly.

Dorjan froze in the doorframe. "It's late," he said just as softly. "We need to go in."

Taern followed him on padded feet, trying to fight the compulsion to make himself just as small as Dorjan.

In the kitchen it was the same. He took their supper out of the icebox—cold chicken, salad, and some pistachio pudding for dessert—and served it up for both of them, Taern first, like he was hosting a dinner party. Except he didn't make conversation and he didn't make eye contact. When the plates were dished, he sat and ate without ceremony. Taern was damned hungry himself, but when he got to his third piece of chicken, he slowed down a little and looked at the satchel on the table. Dorjan had brought it in from his adventure, and Taern's natural curiosity finally overcame the heavy restraint in the kitchen.

"Drugs and silver?" he asked, and Dorjan looked at the bag, startled, like he'd forgotten what was there.

"Yes," he said. "The silver gets split between orphanages—I drop it off when I run to the Forum in the morning."

"The drugs?" Taern asked, impressed in spite of himself.

Dorjan let out a heavy sigh. "Areau wants them. He's trying hard to find a way to break the addiction—keeps analyzing the chemical, trying to see if there's something close but less deadly, less addictive, that he can substitute instead."

Taern blinked and looked at the satchel again, then at Dorjan. "That's brilliant!" he said, breathless. "That's… that's *amazing*. It's like a *cure!*"

Dorjan shook his head. "No. It's exchanging a larger addiction for a smaller addiction. Right now one use is like a death sentence—the people who have the will to break the habit cold die nearly 100 percent of the time. The heart can't take what the body does. We want… we want a way out for those willing to take it." Dorjan sighed. "No," he said, his voice dropping as though he was ashamed of his earlier passion. "A cure for it is a nice dream. Right now, we'll settle for a way out for the willing."

Taern searched his face, but Dorjan was looking at his plate with determination.

"Did someone you know use dust?" Taern asked, trying not to let his voice sink into that quiet, funereal tone that people used.

Dorjan was surprised enough to actually look at him. He shook his head and said, "No one and everyone." A bitter smile twisted his face. "I run through the stews every day, often two, three times a day. I see children who don't grow up and grown-ups that don't grow old. You get used to a person on a street corner, selling trinkets or shipments of stolen fruit, and then, one day, they're gone, and their twelve-year-old child just… just looks at the nearest flop for the dying, and you know. One day it got to be too much, and they… drifted away."

Taern nodded and took a tasteless bite of the once savory chicken. "Paenny's sister—she'd be someone to test on. She's almost quit… more than once. But…." Taern looked away. He'd been there when the shakes got to be so bad Paenny had needed to give her a small dose, just one, to keep her heart from giving out. But you didn't wean off of dust. The small dose had sucked her under just that quick.

"If Areau comes up with a solution in time, I'll tell Madame Matiya," Dorjan said. "Are you done? I'll clean up and show you to your room."

Taern scowled. "All my stuff is in *your* room," he pointed out, feeling stubborn.

Dorjan was still not looking at him as he took both plates and scraped the leftover salad and bones into a compost bucket. "That's not why I bought your contract." It was clear that he had his own stubbornness to rely on.

Taern stood up and wrapped the cloth around the chicken plate, then returned it to the icebox. When he looked up, Dorjan was leaning over the sink, rinsing the heavy glazed dishware, and Taern had the sudden urge to close the distance between them.

He walked up behind Dorjan and put his hands on his hips, pushing up close against his back.

And Dorjan dropped his dish into the washbasin, where it broke with a clatter.

Taern jerked at the initial noise, which sounded like steam cannon shot in the quiet house, but he was a professional, after all. He stayed pressed up against Dorjan's backside and clasped his hands around Dorjan's middle.

"I don't want to be close to you because you bought my contract," he whispered. Dorjan made helpless gestures with shaking hands to pick up the plates, and Taern moved to stop him, twining his fingers with Dorjan's and pulling both their hands to clasp at Dorjan's waist.

Dorjan's breathing quickened, and Taern was close enough to smell the sudden heat—and sweat—through the wool of his smallclothes.

"I sleep with a knife under my pillow," Dorjan said, his voice far away and remote from his shaking shoulders and the way he tightened Taern's fingers in his grip. "I wake up suddenly. You need to sleep somewhere else." He didn't move for a long moment, and Taern wrapped his arms even tighter around him and squeezed.

Taern had been hustling at Madame M's for a little over two years. He'd touched ugly men, men who sweat, men who were too fastidious to put their cocks in his mouth. He'd had handsome men who knew they were good in bed and wanted to showboat, and ashamed men who didn't want to admit who they were but needed human touch so very, very badly they had no choice. He'd made love to virgins, some of them twice his age, and he'd fucked bullies who wanted it in the ass and wanted it raw so that just once, they didn't feel like they ruled the world. He'd even touched the occasional vulnerable soul who had been beaten by family when they had discovered he was sly, and who chose a brothel over the shame of his family.

Taern had thought he knew all the ways of touching a potential lover—he'd been sure of it. But Dorjan… Dorjan was a mystery.

A mystery who slept with a knife under his pillow and woke suddenly.

"Perhaps," Taern murmured, "if you kiss me before you go into your room, you'll be more used to me in it."

Dorjan laughed a little, but it was not a sound of comfort. "I need to bathe, boy. I have blood on my hands." And those words apparently gave him the strength to break free. He picked up the broken crockery and threw it away before combing the sink to make sure there were no slivers left for any unwary soul. Taern leaned against the sink and heroically refrained from saying that any blood on his hands had been washed off with the food on the plates.

When he was done, Taern followed him silently up the stairs. Dorjan's bedroom, with the bath suite, was all the way at the end of the hallway, so Taern shouldn't have been surprised when he stopped immediately on top of the stairs and opened the first door to his right.

"Krissa and Areau are in the middle two rooms on the left," Dorjan said, his voice still maintaining that unearthly quiet. "This room is the farthest away from any of us—no noises should bother you."

"I doubt they would anyway," Taern said, grinning past Dorjan's sober demeanor. "Krissa's a right hand with a ball gag."

Dorjan swallowed hard and his eyes grew wide, but he kept talking like Taern hadn't ventured into someone else's bedroom without so much as a by-your-leave.

"Feel free to draw yourself a bath," he said. "Your guest bathroom is through the adjoining door." He opened up the armoire at the far end of the room. "There are robes and smallclothes of various sizes in here. I'll have Mrs. Wrinkle put your things in here tomorrow morning."

"Not going to happen," Taern said cheerfully. "I'm sleeping in your bed if I have to cuff you to it to let me!"

This time Dorjan *did* flinch, and then he laughed self-consciously. "Bimuit, boy, the things you say." He put his hand on the doorknob then and turned as though he was going to say one more thing, but Taern knew an advantage when he saw one. He took two steps forward before Dorjan could startle back, and this time, when the Forum Master representing Kyon's Gate and the Nyx, scourge of the Thenis stews, looked up, Taern met his eyes.

Taern was mesmerized. The expression therein was burning, soulful, and, if Taern was not mistaken, frightened.

"Good night," Dorjan said, and he went to turn his head again, but Taern put a hand on each cheek and stopped him.

"Thank you, Nyx, for saving my arse. Thank you, Dorjan, for feeding me and giving me a place to sleep."

Dorjan grimaced as though very aware of the dichotomy in himself that was so painfully apparent. "You're welcome, Taern," he said softly. "Sleep well." He moved closer, and Taern let him, relieved that finally, finally, he would let himself have this freely offered kiss.

At the last moment, Dorjan jerked his head and kissed Taern on the forehead and then pulled away and shut the door in his face.

"Coward!" Taern called, but not too loud. For one thing, it was untrue for most of what he'd seen. For another, this thing between them, it was the definition of private. Not even Taern would sell that moment with Dorjan's full regard on his face, and certainly not to assuage his hurt pride.

TAERN drew a bath and luxuriated in having the hot water there on tap. Madame M had two shower stalls, and she made them all bathe thrice in a seven-day, more if they could manage. Being clean was a luxury, and the bath? It sure did soak away the hurts and bruises from Taern's brief sojourn on the streets.

But it also made him acutely aware of Dorjan settling his bruised body, ribs in particular, into the hot water, to emerge and wrap them all on his own.

Taern wasn't sure he could think of a lonelier image—or a lonelier man.

And a misguided one, if it came to that. The man owned Taern's contract. Taern owed him. Taern drained his tub and rinsed the sides, then dried off and used an available comb to tame his curly black hair for the moment. Men liked his hair, or so they told him. The crude ones said it gave them a good grip, and he thought that was sexy all on its own. Dorjan had seemed entranced by it earlier that day, and Taern would keep it tidy for that alone.

When he was done, he took one of the dressing gowns from the armoire and forsook the smallclothes. After wrapping himself in the gown and then burrowing under the covers (since it was getting cooler and cooler in the big house), he lay still, calming his breathing, and listened with all his might.

Once he got past the beating of his own heart, he could hear Dorjan. First there was the draining of the bath, which was loud enough through the pipe system. When that was done, if Taern held his breath, he could hear him moving around in his bedroom. After a sufficient period of silence, Taern rolled over once and listened again. There was a creak in the mattress, so Taern waited another ten minutes. Then he rolled over and listened again.

And heard nothing.

He rolled over two more times, the usual squeaking and rustling of his bedsprings and the bedclothes sounding abnormally loud each time. Each time he stopped and listened, and when nothing happened again, he threw back the covers and tiptoed in bare feet toward his door.

Still nothing. The house was shrouded in silence, even after he opened his door and padded down the hall, the tiny blade he'd kept up his sleeve cupped in his hand. It was a leftover from his pre-Madame M days, when he'd made his living as a thief, and he hoped he wasn't too bad at it. He hadn't gotten pinched, and that was a relief, since thieves got sent to the military on the worst of the battle lines.

So he was fairly confident when he set his mind to Dorjan's door at the end of the hall. It was an inside lock of a gentleman's home. Taern was pretty sure he could open that with no more noise than a hungry mouse.

Once he was *in* Dorjan's room, *that* was the hard part. Dorjan said he slept with a knife under his pillow, and Taern was inclined to believe him.

With the tiniest of clicks, the door lock gave, and the door swung open soundlessly on well-oiled hinges. Dorjan must not have wanted to make any more noise returning home than Taern wanted to make sneaking into his room.

Taern waited a moment, making sure his eyes adjusted, and saw Dorjan, clenched in a little ball on his side, clutching his pillow to his chest as tightly as a woman would clutch a child.

Taern took a deep, silent breath and hoped, because this could be the toughest prize he'd ever swiped—and the most deadly if he missed.

Slashing Blind

DORJAN sat up in bed, heart pounding, eyes blind in the darkness, and struck out with his clenched fist. The side of his hand hit something, so he leapt to a squat and, still blind, directed a barrage of blows at his opponent, until he realized that the mass of bone and muscle he'd been hitting was out of his reach.

Cautiously, he squinted in the dark and crab-walked back to his pillow to root around underneath it in concern.

"I locked your knife in the armoire," said an almost-familiar voice calmly. "Smartest thing I ever did. Are you awake yet? Can I come back to bed?"

Dorjan crunched his eyes shut and then opened them wide in an attempt to orient himself. "Taern?" he asked carefully. Oh yes, he knew someone named Taern, someone who.... Why would he be.... "What are you doing in my bed?"

"Sleeping with you," Taern said, and he must have taken Dorjan's recognition as permission or safety, because in a moment he'd crawled back under the covers. "Now come on, get under. It's cold out there."

Dorjan squinted at him. "You're naked," he said, and part of him was excited about this, but most of him was puzzled. "Didn't I give you a nightshirt?"

Taern grunted. "Like that thing you've got on? Women wear less clothing to funerals."

Dorjan looked at his gown, which hung about midthigh and had drawstrings at the cuffs and buttons at the throat. "Keeps the chill off," he grumbled and flipped over his corner of the bedding and crawled in. "I could have killed you!" he said, and he knew that through the layers of sleep, he was appalled and ashamed.

"You gave it your best. I'll have a bruise on my shoulder from where you got me with your fist. Does that make you feel better? Can we go to sleep now?"

"No," Dorjan muttered, as confused as he'd ever been in his life. "Why are you sleeping with—" The boy, the *naked* boy—the naked *man*—had taken advantage of his recumbent position and snuck into his body, nestling in against his chest like a baby bird. Dorjan instinctively arched his shoulders protectively over him, bringing him in. His entire body shuddered at the rightness of having him there.

"Me," he finished weakly. "What are you doing with me?"

"Mm?" Taern said sleepily. "What am I doing? I'm going to sleep. It's still the wee hours of the morning, Dorjan."

"I've got conditioning in an hour or so," Dorjan yawned. "Mrs. Wrinkle will rouse me."

"Not if I have anything to say about it," Taern grumbled, and oh! He just felt so good there, in Dorjan's arms, so sweet in a way Dorjan had never felt sweetness. Dorjan's night terror had faded, and he'd get his knife back out of the armoire tomorrow, and in the meantime, he had learned to capture sleep as it came.

HE WOKE up several hours later because Taern was shaking him gently.

"Sorry, Dorjan. Mrs. Wrinkle says you need to get ready for Forum duties. I got you out of conditioning—whatever that is—but even I know you need to be on the floor when it's time."

Dorjan sat up so abruptly he nearly smashed into Taern's chin. Taern jerked back in time and looked at him in amusement. "It's *when*?" Dorjan demanded, his heart beating in triple time.

"Don't worry!" Taern soothed. "You've got time to bathe, dress, and eat—that's what Mrs. Wrinkle said—"

"Oh hells… you're in my bed. With me. What are you doing here?"

"Well, sleeping when you weren't trying to kill me. And then ducking, and then some talking, and then mostly sleeping." Taern's leer looked particularly dirty when his little apple cheeks popped.

Dorjan felt heat wash his face, and he looked down as he struggled to get out of bed.

He was arrested by Taern's hand on his wrist. "Mrs. Wrinkle is bringing breakfast. Don't break her heart and get dressed before she gets back."

Dorjan looked at Taern's hand. It was well manicured and moisturized, like any one of the Forum members. He knew—he paid attention to such things. His own hands were rough and hard and muscular. He'd taken to wearing gloves lined with lotion whenever he could get away with it so his callused hands didn't attract undue attention.

He looked at that pale hand and swallowed. "She'd understand," he said softly, but he didn't move.

"Then don't break *my* heart," Taern said, the laughter in his voice gentle. "I mean, it's the least you can do after you whacked me in my sleep."

Dorjan looked up quickly and searched his face for a mark. "I didn't bruise you, did I?"

Taern winked. "If I said yes, would you search my body and make it better?

Dorjan pulled back and glared at him. "I warned you of the risk. Is Mrs. Wrinkle really coming back?"

"Yes," Taern said unrepentantly. "Now scoot back here and talk to me for a while so we can give the old girl a thrill and let her think the worst."

Dorjan's glare grew sterner. "Is there any *possible* way you can try not to shock me with every other word?"

"Hey, you're the libertine bastard who bought two whores from Madame Matiya. The least you could do is reap some of the benefits of all that notoriety!"

Dorjan felt as though his eyes were the size of dinner plates. "People will know about that?" he asked, horrified, and Taern shrugged.

"It's possible. Madame M won't gossip, but the whole house knew. We both had regulars. They'll ask."

Dorjan dropped his face to his knees and groaned. "Oh well," he muttered. "It can't hurt my reputation as it is."

Taern pulled up his knees under the covers, and Dorjan allowed his body to go off of high alert. "What is your reputation?" he asked, and Dorjan half laughed.

"Just that I'm Kyon's half-witted son." Taern's amused snort was a balm to his soul. "It's nice that *someone* doesn't find it easy to believe. It's convenient," he explained before Taern could say anything else. His world got tangled every time that boy opened his mouth. "Septra spread the word when I was recovery," he said meditatively. "It was almost funny. Men who had known me all my life, who had praised my studies in front of my father, suddenly started talking slower and ribbing me about how to read orders correctly." He shrugged and studied his armoire, wondering if he could find a way to pick the lock or if he would have to search Taern's naked body for it.

"But... why didn't you... you're obviously not... why didn't you set them straight!" Taern was sputtering, his arms pinwheeling even as he sat, and for the first time in forever, Dorjan felt like smiling. He didn't, but he felt like it.

"Because they're easier to manipulate," he said frankly. "And because the odds of me catching an assassin's blade to my throat lessen considerably with every Forum member who thinks I'm dimwitted." He shrugged. "They let things slip too—you become part of the wallpaper if they think the best you can do is open your mouth and breathe in and out. It's like you're a spy in plain sight."

Taern gaped at him. "But... when did your father die, Dorjan? How long have you been... spying in plain sight?"

Dorjan had relaxed for a moment—it had been lovely. Now he remembered how he had survived so long, and he dropped his gaze to his knees again, and then to the door as someone shot it open in a way wholly uncharacteristic of Mrs. Wrinkle.

It was Areau.

"You slept *in!*" Areau accused, stalking into Dorjan's bedroom like he belonged there. Well, he had woken up here his share of times, but never willingly.

"Mrs. Wrinkle was—" Dorjan looked at Taern, who was glaring at Areau with a hatred like poison. Oh no. This did not bode well, not if the boy was as stubborn about leaving as he had been about everything else. Dorjan took a deep breath and started again. "There was a miscommunication," he said shortly. "But a useful one. I needed the sleep." He smiled and tried to appeal to Areau's humanity. He'd had it once, but now nothing softened his glare. "Three nights in a row, Ari. Even the niskets take rests!"

Areau's glower continued to burn. Apparently his humanity was not making an appearance today. "The niskets don't need to plot strategy in the morning, Dori. They're niskets. Their job is in their blood! Vengeance is something you need to study!"

"Have you even asked how he is?" Taern said suddenly from Dorjan's side, and Dorjan shook his head to warn the boy off.

"I'm fine, boy—"

"What are you even doing here?" Areau asked, glaring at the boy through his long ringlets of once gold hair. "Don't tell me he bought a whore for himself! What, Dori, was it a two-for-one—"

Dorjan knew his vision must not have been as red as it seemed, because he saw well enough for his punch to land, and Areau went staggering back into the dresser behind him.

"*Dorjan!*" three people shouted—because Mrs. Wrinkle had ventured into the room too, and apparently seeing him in his nightshirt was just as shocking as him throwing a right cross at Areau. Later, he might think to be grateful about this, but right now—

He'd just taken a deep breath to yell for everybody to clear his room when Lady Krissa joined the party and did it for him.

"Areau?" she said, her voice very exact, and Areau stood up from the dresser.

"Yes, my lady Krissa," he responded almost automatically.

"Are you in another lover's room?"

A twisted expression crossed Areau's face, and he glared venom at Dorjan. "No, my lady."

"Be honest, Areau," she said, brooking no argument, and Areau cringed and looked straight ahead.

"Yes, my lady."

"Does he want your attentions?"

Dorjan closed his eyes, and suddenly everyone in the room disappeared, and it was just him and Areau, and he was finally, finally getting a choice.

"No, my lady," Dorjan answered truthfully, and Areau's scorn vanished to be replaced by a terrible, terrible hurt.

"Dori!" he protested, and Dorjan took a deep breath and kept his eyes closed.

"I'll come talk strategy after breakfast if there's time," he said, not responding to the plea on Areau's face. "But in the meantime, I need everyone to clear the room."

"Except me," Taern said from behind him, and Dorjan turned with every intention of telling him that of *course* Dorjan meant him, he was the one Dorjan needed to leave the most. The movement twisted his core, though, and he let out a gasp at his sore limbs, and Taern met his gaze mockingly. "He's not all right, Areau, and he needs me to wrap his ribs after breakfast. Thank you, Mrs. Wrinkle!" he called cheerfully, and Mrs.

Wrinkle did for that impudent pain in the arse what she'd long ceased doing for Dorjan, and bowed. Then she left the tray of food on the dresser behind her, and in a moment, the room was clear.

"Was any of that necess—augh!" Damn, there went his ribs again. "Necessary," he said, trying to keep his breath even, and it was Taern's turn to glower.

"Get in the bed, Dorjan, and let me serve you."

"I didn't buy your contract to make you my servant," Dorjan snapped, taking a step away from the bed.

"I know you didn't. You bought it to set me free. Well, I'm free, and what I choose to do with my freedom is serve you breakfast, you stubborn, irritating man, and when I'm done feeding you breakfast, I'm going to tape your ribs. But first, *get in bed and eat!*"

Dorjan grunted and shook out his hand, which was aching from contact with Areau's jaw. "I suppose I've had enough conflict this morning," he muttered and followed orders.

Taern hopped out of bed stark naked, and Dorjan was just bemused enough to allow himself the pleasure of watching that taut backside as Taern sauntered toward the tray. He quickly averted his eyes when Taern returned, and he saw the boy smirk.

"I saw that," he said softly, setting the tray over Dorjan's legs and pouring the tea.

"So did I," Dorjan returned, refusing to be cowed. If he hadn't wanted Dorjan to ogle, he would have put on clothes.

"Good." Taern grinned. "I was starting to think that whole moment in the alley was my imagination!"

Dorjan started scooting backward, and Taern put a hand on his shoulder.

"Please, Dorjan. You can't run away every time I bring that up or question you about your sex life or get personal. If you'd wanted me to stay uninvolved, you shouldn't have bought my contract. You could have left it a blowjob in an alleyway, but you made it personal, and now you've got me, being personal. Take it like a man."

"Shut up," Dorjan grunted, but he stayed put.

There were two plates on the tray, both of them with scrambled eggs, toast, and two sausage links, and Taern took one in his hand, then sat at Dorjan's feet, held the plate up to his chest, and started eating. Dorjan took a forkful of eggs, and for a moment, they were silent. Another bite later,

Taern spoke into the silence, his voice low and probably designed not to spook Dorjan, but that was too bad because Dorjan dropped the food off his fork.

"Was he?" Taern asked and then picked up the toast and used it as a scoop for the eggs.

"Was who what?" Dorjan asked, but he was pretty sure he knew.

"Were you and Areau lovers?"

Dorjan forced himself to swallow a bite of eggs. "In the loosest sense of the term," he said, hating to confess to even that much.

Taern looked at him, a toast scoop of eggs halfway to his mouth. "I thought your friend liked girls."

Dorjan dropped his fork and shoved the plate across the tray. "He does," he admitted. "Begging me to fuck him was part of his pain."

Taern swallowed and shuddered, then turned to him. "Eat that," he said shortly. "If I can eat mine hearing that, you can eat yours living with it."

Dorjan let out a breath of what might have been laughter. "Yes, but you've heard it for five minutes. I've lived it for ten years."

Taern suddenly pinned him under those midnight-blue eyes. "But no more," he said seriously, and Dorjan shrugged.

"I hope not," he agreed. "It's why I bought Krissa's contract, and she seems happy about the job." He snorted. "She's certainly good at it!"

Taern shook his head. "No. I'm telling you—"

"Telling me?"

"Yes. Telling. You. I, street whore, Taern of Kiamath Keep, am telling you, Forum Master Dorjan, also known as Nyx, that I will not allow you to sleep with that man again. Find another whore if you must, although that would be a damned waste of this one, but not him."

Dorjan squirmed and looked mournfully at his breakfast. He'd been looking forward to actually finishing it this morning. "I have no intentions of doing so," he said honestly, and then he stopped squirming. "But it's not that simple, and as you just saw—" He sighed and flexed his hand with the three knuckles that had popped up purple as he ate. "—Areau does know how to work my cricket console."

Taern put his plate down deliberately and then hopped off the bed and cornered Dorjan as he sat. "I'm not telling you to stop for me," he growled. "If it made you happy, I'd say fuck him all the time, twice a day. I'd come watch and beat off. But I'm telling you, we're going on three days of acquaintanceship here, and that man is *bad for you.* Anyone could see it. If you hadn't gone to get Krissa, one of you would have snapped and another one would have ended up dead, and don't think it might not have been you. So I will say this one more time, Nyx. Not again. Not with him. You're a smart man. You keep dodging the oath because you take them seriously. Well, I'm not letting you out of this bed until you swear it. Then you'll have to, you hear me?"

Dorjan reached out an uncertain hand and smoothed the soft skin along Taern's collarbone. "I could overpower you," he said rationally, and Taern agreed.

"I know you could."

"I could leave this room without making this vow."

"I have no doubt."

Dorjan felt the oath forming in his chest before he spoke it, and what felt like iron plates falling from his shoulders as he gave it breath. "I, Dorjan, Kyon's son, swear I shall not engage in sexual relations with Areau, my oldest friend, anymore."

"Even if he begs?" Taern asked, and Dorjan looked at him levelly.

"I swear it."

Taern nodded and then leaned forward and very, very softly met Dorjan's lips with a kiss. He backed away after Dorjan had a scant taste, and smiled sweetly when Dorjan brought his fingers up to brush his tingling lips.

"If you're done, I'll tape up those ribs now," Taern said practically, and Dorjan made a sound in agreement. Then Taern's natural impish smile asserted itself. "Of course, I'm going to have to see you naked."

Dorjan put on his breeches first and ignored the fact that Taern was looking at him avidly when he turned his back. Finally he sat patiently on the bed while Taern dug the bandages and tape out of his drawer. He taped a solid support wall over Dorjan's bruises and then wrapped the bandage tight around his middle.

"It's a good thing you don't have a lot of hair," Taern said appreciatively as he wrapped. "It'll make tearing the tape off not as painful as it could be."

Dorjan grimaced. "None of it is enjoyable," he stated grimly, and Taern grinned up at him, his head almost in Dorjan's lap.

"Oh my. Almost humor. I'm impressed. I would have said that part of you withered and died."

"It did." Dorjan grunted as Taern pulled the bandage particularly tight. "All I have left is understatement and an acid tongue. Fear my irony, it may draw blood."

Taern's shoulders jerked against his as he passed the bandage around his back, and when he spoke again, his face was right... next... to Dorjan's.

"Your irony, I'll fear," Taern said soberly, and Dorjan got to look deeply into those midnight-blue eyes. He swallowed and noticed that Taern had fading freckles on his apple cheeks and the beginnings of crinkles at the corners of his eyes from smiling so often. Taern let out a breath from an open mouth, and it puffed up against Dorjan's cheeks.

Dorjan licked his suddenly dry lips and tried to force some sanity into the closeness between them. "I am not a good person," he confessed painfully. "I'm not gentle, I have no kindness. Fear all of me, Taern. Don't ever let your guard down. I wouldn't forgive myself if I hurt you."

Taern didn't move. He stayed right there, barely a kiss away. "Wouldn't it be a shame, Dorjan, if this was as close as we ever got?"

Dorjan opened his mouth and barely felt the cool air as Taern moved, his lips not quite touching Dorjan's, and then the boy was doctoring him again.

Dorjan closed his eyes, counting to one thousand by prime numbers while praying to a higher authority than Bimuit to help his erection go down easy.

About the time he hit 997, Taern was done, and Dorjan stood up quickly, grateful that he could. "Nice job," he said, inclining his head. He pulled a fresh undershirt from his dresser and slid it over his head, then moved to the armoire for the rest of his clothes. Taern got there first and picked the lock with what appeared to be a metal tooth from the comb that had been on the bureau in his room.

He opened it and grinned and said, "Turn around."

"I'm running late—"

"Then don't fight me on this. Turn around."

Dorjan complied hastily. He would have to sprint this morning to make up his usual time as it was. After a few moments, his Forum robes were thrust at him, as well as one of his newer topcoats and a cravat. He took all three items and folded them up neatly on the bed, still keeping his back turned. Taern was rooting around, grunting and muttering to himself, and Dorjan hoped seriously that he'd be able to undo whatever he was doing back there.

"My long satchel?" he asked.

Taern said, "Hmmm? Oh." And then it was being handed over Dorjan's back.

He was sliding his clothes in neatly, with the ease of long practice, when Taern suddenly realized what he was doing.

"Why on earth would you do that? I thought you were getting dressed."

Dorjan couldn't help a little smirk of gratification. It's not like he hadn't felt exactly like that since he'd found the boy naked and in his bed. "I have enough time to run to the Forum through the stews. How do you think I keep up my knowledge of them? My time is limited, yes? Now can I get my boots? I can't venture out without them!"

The boots appeared at his side, and Taern went back to his dissatisfied sounds and increasingly frustrated movements. Dorjan sat the other side of the bed to pull on the specialized boots Areau had designed and that he had made twice a year. Soft rubber and cloth that gave, they were soaked in oil and buffed to look like leather. Dorjan could run in them with ease, but they *looked* like the damnably uncomfortable things every other Forum member wore.

And still Taern was rummaging around in his armoire like a shopkeeper after a rare item, and Dorjan stood and sighed.

"You're incredibly resourceful, Taern, and I have no doubt you'll find whatever it is you're looking for, but I do live here, you know. I may be of service."

Taern grunted. "And?"

"It would help if I knew what you are trying to do?"

"Fine. Turn around."

Dorjan did and saw nothing remarkable except that the clothes in the armoire were in disarray. And that Taern was *still* naked, and that he looked *amazing*, with defined muscles on his arms and chest and shoulders, but hardly any bulk at all. Dorjan kept his eyes resolutely away from the boy's manhood, though he did get an impression of curly black pubic hair.

"And?" he said, feeling a muscle in his cheek twitch.

"I need a place I can hide your knife!" Taern gestured with it in exasperation. "I don't want you to be able to reach for it in your sleep, but I *do* see why you might want to have it handy in your line of work!"

Dorjan took a deep breath, fighting against the tape on his ribs, and tried to put his world in order. "You could solve the whole problem by sleeping in your own bed," he said, making his voice as reasonable as possible.

He wasn't even finished with the sentence before Taern rolled his eyes. "I've seen your body, Dorjan. I've actually had my hands on your skin. If you think I'm leaving this house without tasting your cock again? Having you inside me? You're mad."

"According to some," he said evenly, hoping the boy couldn't see how tight his breeches had suddenly become, and Taern rolled his eyes at that too.

"Bollix. Now do you have anything useful to say or not?"

Dorjan wasn't sure what made him do it, but he put his satchel down and moved to his writing desk. "I have no idea," he said shortly. "Between the mattress and the box springs, perhaps? Maybe between the mattress and the frame. You're a clever boy—maybe fashion some place with spare pieces of wood and glue. I'm going to leave it up to you." He paused for a moment and pulled out a piece of parchment and his fountain pen, and the only thing that could be heard in the room was the scritch scritch scritch of pen on paper. Before he was done, Taern was right at his shoulder, crowding his space. Dorjan turned his head and glared at him.

Taern looked up and grinned. "Really?"

Dorjan folded the parchment carefully and held the end of the wax taper up to the electric bulb in the sconce until it melted enough to stick to the page. Before it had cooled, he'd reached around his neck and taken his necklace off to seal the letter before putting the silver chain and pendant back on and tucking them under his shirt.

"You know what the catch is," he said as he handed the folded missive over to Taern's greedy hands.

"He's going to be angrier than a horny hexabull?" Taern said, eyes wide and apparently undeterred by that fact at all.

"Angrier," Dorjan said, looking at the clock above his desk. "Because I'm about to run out of here without a strategy meeting."

"I don't care!" Taern said happily, clutching the letter to his bare chest.

"Make sure he gets the satchel in the bottom of the armoire!" Dorjan cautioned as he got to the door. "It might put him in a sweeter frame of mind."

"He can rut with a rusty saw and come on it too!" Taern said, consigning Areau's comfort to the four winds. "I'm going to get fitted for *armor!*"

Dorjan couldn't fight the smile this time, and he even let Taern get a glimpse of it before he trotted out the door and down the stairs.

HE BARELY made it to the gentlemen's room of the Forum and changed before the bell rang to convene, and he had to hustle back to the floor to hear whatever hexashite bill being debated with breaths to spare. (The last bill had been to make it illegal to buy more at a market than could fit in a standard-sized market bag. Dorjan had voted against it because it was an asinine endeavor whose only purpose was to distract the Forum members from the food riot that had occurred the week before. It had passed. As if the average citizen of Thenis could afford that much food.)

He was halfway down the corridor, a number of Forum members lingering in his wake, when he suddenly found himself matching strides with Alum Septra himself. Dorjan put on his best "pleasantly surprised" expression.

"Triari," he said respectfully. "To what do I owe the honor?"

Septra had aged well in the past ten years. Unlike Dorjan, who'd had Areau razor the back and sides of his hair close to his head and high off his collar when it proved too bothersome for his nighttime activities, Septra had a queue hanging long and silver from his widow's peak to midway down his back, braided neatly and still quite thick. His long face with the lean lips and hollowed, austere-looking cheeks and cheekbones was still handsome and had, in fact, become sharper and more distinguished with age.

"I was hoping that I could speak with you again about your keep's effort toward the war."

Oh, I just bet you do! "I've told you before, Triari Septra, my family's keep is donating its full tithe to the government. I've shown you the records detailing what we mine—"

"You still haven't answered my concerns about mining more to my satisfaction," Septra snapped, and Dorjan fought to keep his even-keeled idiot's smile on his face.

"Mining the asteroids too fast causes the gravity ripples, Triari. My father told you that for years, and the one time he mined beyond his conscience, the series of earthquakes almost destroyed Karanos. I grew up in those mines, Triari—my blood runs in them, so to speak. Destroying our society now will not help us win a war. It won't help us feed the hungry. It will not help us rebuild our ailing city. It will only hasten our bitter end."

He kept his voice reasonable, made it sound as though he was parroting his father, but he couldn't help it. The shortsightedness... the *gall.* Septra looked at him sharply, and Dorjan smiled blandly back.

"I'm sorry, Triari—I am running decidedly late if I'm to sit the floor before you speak. Silly me—my clock ran down this morning. We men of leisure do enjoy our sleep!"

With that, Dorjan tried to make a quick left into the center of the dome that housed the Forum, only to find Septra's hand tightening around his arm. For fun, Dorjan tightened his bicep and pretended not to see Septra's eyes widen at the wiry power of a body that did a lot more than gad about the Forum floor and complain about the smell from the stews.

"I would like to see your family's records again," Septra hissed, and Dorjan nodded pleasantly.

"Of course, Triari. Should I run get them from home, or would you like to see them tomorrow?"

Septra looked startled. "You have them *here*? In the city?" he asked, and Dorjan found he was enjoying this conversation more than he should. Yes, he had the *fixed* books in the city, and no, Septra would *never* get his hands on the real figures, which he and his foreman had hidden in a safe *underneath* his desk at Kyon's Gate.

"Why, yes! I keep in constant contact with my foreman, Coreau. You do remember his son, Areau, do you not?"

He watched a muscle twitch in Septra's cheek as Septra had to admit that yes, he had known the boy he'd confined to the asylum and ordered tortured into madness. Dorjan was not sure if he acknowledged that the boy still *lived*, but he did know that name. "I was aware. I'm sorry that ended so badly."

"Endings are only new beginnings," Dorjan said vapidly, and Septra's smile was all patronization.

"Well, I'm sure you will be able to find a woman who will fill that void," Septra said, and Dorjan hoped Krissa didn't mind being used as a blind.

"Oh, I already have. She's lovely—she certainly brightens up my bachelor pad, and that is the truth!"

And another hit. Septra was, as far as anyone knew, single. Dorjan would have suspected he was just as sly as Dorjan himself, except Dorjan knew the signs. Septra had been surprised by Dorjan's strength but not attracted to his body. Apparently power was for Septra what sex and family was for the other Forum members, and Dorjan had a vicious moment to imagine the man next to him reeling from a financial blow to the bollocks. He hoped they were swollen and blue by now, and the hope made his smile even wider and more vacuous.

"Wonderful," Septra said thinly. "Wonderful. I look forward to seeing you a bit less in the Forum, since you will be distracted by family."

Oh, you wish! "My older sister is doing quite well by the family way, sir, and my lady fair has plenty to keep her occupied. I'm free to serve my province with all my heart."

"Such a shame, really," Septra said, condescension dripping from his every syllable. "The task would have been so much easier were you gifted with your father's same sense of business."

Calling me stupid. Yes, because I haven't heard that *before.* "I'm lucky to have people back home who can make up for my lack. My father was good at teaching us to work as a whole. You'd be surprised how much an average man can accomplish if he's willing to appreciate men of greater gifts."

Septra literally jerked his head back. "Such men usually covet power of their own," he said, his voice saturated with disgust.

"Not if you treat them well." Dorjan was in a fine mood this morning—he could have sparred happily with Septra for another hour, but even *he* recognized the danger. He pretended Septra's bony fingers weren't trying to bury themselves in his still-flexed muscle and simply continued walking toward the center of the Forum, his expression of openmouthed idiot joy for once only partially a work of clever fiction. He managed to maintain that look right up until the primary speaker spoke, and then his entire day was spent wiping the expression of burning and sickened fury off his face.

Conditioning

IT WAS true that Dorjan had warned him, but no amount of warning could have forged the cast-iron plating Taern wanted for his balls earlier that morning when he'd gone downstairs to where Areau sat at the breakfast table next to Krissa, and presented the letter Dorjan had written. He also presented the satchel, which was, Taern noticed, light on the silver but still heavy on the drugs.

Areau checked the contents of the satchel and nodded, then stared at the letter and then at Taern. Taern stood in his brightest topcoat and most outrageous pair of breeches and wished he'd simply come down in the black smallclothes he'd worn the night before.

"He wants me to what?" Areau repeated, and Krissa grimaced at Taern quickly, before Areau could see her slip into her Madame Dominatrix character.

"Are you *dim*, Areau?" she snapped, and Areau's neck drooped subserviently.

"No, my lady."

"Do you *know* how to read?"

"Yes, my lady."

"And what does it say that's so difficult to comprehend?"

"That I'm supposed to set him a training regimen and fit him for armor!" Areau snarled. "Does he think it's that easy? Does he have *any* idea how long it took me to get his armor to where it is now? Is he not *aware* of how important my chemistry experiments are—"

"Why yes, Areau," Krissa said mildly, "I believe this part here makes it quite clear that he doesn't expect it to happen overnight. He's asking for a few hours a week spared from your other endeavors, that is all." Krissa refolded the letter and put it back under Areau's plate so he could lay claim to it as it was addressed. "So you see, Areau," she said, her voice gentle and firm, "he completely respects your time. He's just asking to add another member to your team. If you think about it, that's really much safer for him on the streets. You didn't see him as Taern and I did. He was *very* vulnerable the night we met. I'm surprised he made it out alive."

"He caught a steam spear in the side," Taern said bluntly. "He wouldn't have made it out alive if not for your armor, and he wouldn't have made it out one more time after last night without rest. He needs somebody to have his back—"

"What do you think I'm doing with the armor!" Areau snapped back, his voice rough with anger. "I wouldn't send him out there if I thought he wouldn't come back!"

"But you wouldn't mind if he was injured, would you?" Taern asked nastily. He knew some of the story, but given this man's corrosive attitude… oh, heavens, he could guess at the rest.

"Fine lot you know!" Areau spat. "I *needed* him to come back in sterling condition. Besides being my friend, no one else could give me my…." He trailed off as Krissa brought out the riding crop at her side to tap under his chin.

"And is that the only reason you want him back?" she asked sweetly. "Because he's a friend of mine too. Now that you two have an altogether different arrangement, I would be very interested to learn whether or not you intend for your friend to return home."

Areau gaped for a moment, and his mouth opened and closed in surprise. "You mean… sabotage?" he asked, and he seemed so genuinely hurt that a part of Taern relaxed. He hadn't realized until just that moment how worried he'd been that Dorjan placed so much faith in this individual with the tangled hair, the dirty cravat, and the blistering, necrotic hostility.

But he had to make sure. "Yes, I mean sabotage!" Taern retorted. "As far as I can tell, you were just using him for your own dirty little deeds. I don't even know if you really cared for him at all!"

Areau yanked his hair out of his eyes, and Taern saw them then, bitter, festering scars, bubbled skin from botched healing, and a flat pink spot where his hair should have been growing but only scraggle grew now.

"I cared enough to jump in and get these, didn't I?" He yanked at the throat of his shirt beneath his frayed and stained waistcoat, revealing more bubbled scarring. "And these, and these—and yes, our little street waif, they go all the way down my body, and yes, barely miss my manhood! Have I given enough for him? There we both were, heading for a commission and brilliant bloody careers, and he's got to spoil it all by listening to some brat in the rushes—"

"That was me in the rushes, you self-pitying git, and all those pretty scars didn't save my parents, did it!"

Areau gaped, and Taern scowled right back. Dorjan... Dorjan didn't speak about his commission or the things he'd given up. Dorjan just worried about giving enough.

"Dorjan has his own scars," Taern added, his voice bitter. "And a lot of them are recent. You may think you've done your part by making the armor, but I don't know if you've *ever* had his back!"

"Well it's a wonder you want my services at all, then," Areau sulked. "If I'm that incompetent—"

"I have no doubt you're bloody brilliant!" Taern didn't either. He'd seen Dorjan's armor, felt it, seen how cunningly engineered it was and how much freedom it gave Nyx as he was darting among the Thenis shadows. That armor was more than a defense and more than a weapon— was, in fact, a work of living, sculpted art. But it was the man beneath it who made the supple plating feel like warm skin. "I'm saying that it's been more about turning him into a weapon than caring about him as a man—"

"I'm not sly." Areau's voice dripped with disdain. "I'd say that's probably more your purview than mine."

"You're not sly, but he's an old lover," Taern said thoughtfully. "How did that work?"

"He forced himself upon me," Areau said, his eyes open wide with a sort of manic glee. "It was terrible. I loathed every minute of—*ouch!*" The exclamation was followed by an ecstatic shudder as Krissa's crop came down on the back of his hand hard enough to leave a bright-pink mark over the scarring.

"Be. Truthful," she said, her voice as icy as Taern had ever heard it. Taern's gaze flew to her face, and he realized that at this point, her grimness wasn't a façade. She was truly this angry and, it appeared, on Dorjan's behalf.

"He did!" Areau snarled back. "What does he think of his hero now that he knows he's no better than a common rapist, rutting with orphans in the—*augh!*"

Krissa locked eyes with him and watched him shudder, then wipe the bloody back of his hand across his mouth. He lapped a little at the blood that welled up from the finely sliced welt left by the sharp edges of the leather crop.

"Do you want me to fill your craving, Areau?" she asked gently, tracing the crop along the top of his hand.

Areau watched it move, mesmerized, and laughed a little like a boy about to get a favorite sweet.

Krissa withdrew the crop and ran it lovingly along his cheek. "I will. I will fill every need your twisted heart desires, Areau, son of Coreau. But you need to do everything I ask, as I ask it. Wasn't that our agreement yesterday?"

Areau nodded eagerly. "Yes, Mistress," he said, giggling a little to himself.

"Well, then tell Taern the truth."

Areau slunk a glance toward Taern, and Taern answered with his own rage. The things he was saying about Dorjan... the terrible, terrible things, about the terrified, gentle man Taern had been trying to seduce....

"I made him," Areau whispered, obviously proud of himself. "He's got such a code of honor, that one, and I broke him. See? I made him. I hit him and I hit him and then he hit me back... and I bared my ass to him, and he wanted it... and it was rage, always it was rage. He took me in rage, and it was *sweet*, because I hated it, and hated him, and he fucked me and then...." Areau smiled a child's smile and hunched his shoulders around his ears. "And then I ran away like I was afraid." He narrowed one eye and looked at Taern with cunning intent. "That was the best part. Watching him wake up in the morning and loathe himself. Now he knows how I feel, looking down at this body."

That quickly, Areau's frightening glee turned to self-pity. "Ruined," he said softly, looking at his hand, raising it up to finger the differences in his face. "I'm ruined, ruined, ruined...."

Taern turned away, sickened. Oh... oh hells. His Nyx. His innocent, innocent Nyx. And he'd been betrayed in the worst ways by his friend, by his body.

Taern would be lucky of Dorjan ever let himself be touched again. He was an honorable man, Taern was sure of it. The... the dishonor of the sort of relationship Areau was describing... oh, it must have fermented, rising to a chemical boil in his breast.

"You enjoy yourself," he muttered. "I'll expect that armor by the third of never."

Krissa stopped him. "Wait, Taern." She turned to Areau and whispered something that was probably filthy into his ear, because he brightened and nodded his head, as besotted as any puppy being offered a scratch on the arse.

"Lunch," Areau gasped, and Taern didn't even need to look to know Krissa was massaging his cock through his breeches. Excellent. The fucker could still get off with a woman. Dorjan would be lucky if he ever got off again. "After lunch I'll measure you, give you a list for a regimen. I'll need to see you move. After we eat, have Mrs. Wrinkle get you some smallclothes, and we'll meet downstairs in the gym." His breath came faster and faster, and Taern turned around and walked away. Whether she meant to bring him off at the breakfast table or do something painful and perverse that would get him to their quarters, for once, he really didn't give a good damn about what kind of sex another person was going to have.

He was too busy worried about what kind of sex he and Dorjan might never get to experience.

HE SPENT the morning hanging his clothes up next to Dorjan's in the wardrobe and doing quick calculations. He had silver—he'd been saving his money when he was tricking, because as much as he'd loved coming into his sexual maturity in a gourmand environment, he'd known, even at sixteen, that he would eventually develop a taste for a specialized meat.

He figured that Nyx was as specialized as meat got, but looking at his child's paint box palette of clothes next to Dorjan's somber gentleman's dress, he had to concede that maybe he should spend some of his silver refining his image.

Dorjan kept calling him "boy." Taern thought that as he was younger, that appellation might stick for a while, but he wouldn't mind having a slightly more mature look as well.

But that would have to wait. After unpacking in Dorjan's armoire and making room for his shaving kit in the bathroom (there was plenty of space on the counter. Why not?), he resumed his initial task of the morning—finding a place for Dorjan's knife.

He didn't trust the suggestion to put it between the box spring and the mattress or between the bedframe. For one thing, those places weren't easy to get to should they actually be accosted in the night. For another, they weren't... *alien* enough. Dorjan moved better half-conscious than most men did while fully alert, and that was the problem. Taern wanted

Dorjan to have to *wake up* before he had the capacity to do real violence, particularly upon Taern's person.

That meant that the hiding place had to be secure, within reach of the bed, easy to get to, yet difficult to access by accident. He'd seen Dorjan asleep, clutching his pillow. The man practically slept with a knife in his *hand.* He needed to sleep with a knife in....

Hm. In a cunning little box, assembled on the bed frame, that required a simple catch.

That was it. A long spring along the length of the box. That would do.

Taern hadn't worked with wood since that day playing in the rushes as a child, but he *had* worked with wood. He could close his eyes and remember his father in the workshop with a treadle-powered lathe, band saw, and jigsaw. There was not a light fixture in Kiamath Keep that Olem Kiamath hadn't had a hand in crafting. It had been his passion—he'd gone to that shop when thinking, when Taern's mother, Valie, had been angry, when the girls had been too rowdy, or just to do something peaceful and skilled. Taern had followed him in one day, and Olem had given him a whittling knife and a block of wood. The results had been, well, less than artistic, but Taern had learned the basics.

But first he needed to... oh hells. He was reasonably sure that the only person in the house who could help him was Areau.

He walked out of the room and down the hall, paused by the two rooms he was pretty sure belonged to Krissa and Areau, and listened. Through the door, he heard the whistle and snap of a whip—probably one of the softened ones Krissa had shown him were often used for this purpose, but still, the snap had been cruel, and Areau's gasp of pain sounded genuine.

Krissa's voice purred, and although Taern couldn't make out the actual words, he was very clear on the fact that Areau would very much not be available until after lunch.

He ventured downstairs to find Mrs. Wrinkle, and *she*, at least, was helpful.

"What is it you need?" She was at the clothesline in the courtyard, and Taern couldn't help but finger the fine lawn of a simple white shirt. She must have been one of those servants with laundry secrets, because it was soft. He'd felt Dorjan's clothes, and although they were nicely ironed, with creases, they had none of the stiffness of starch, and he was glad.

Dorjan probably didn't pay much attention to his clothing as long as it was comfortable, and apparently Mrs. Wrinkle made sure it was comfortable.

"I need a box for him to keep his knife," Taern said boldly, "so that he doesn't kill me in his sleep."

Mrs. Wrinkle actually dropped the basket of wet laundry at her hip, and Taern spent the next several moments helping her pick the scattered wet clothes up and take them back to rinse before shaking them out to dry. By the time they got back to where she'd started, she had apparently overcome her shock.

"He sleeps with a knife under his pillow," she ventured, and Taern nodded and then explained his plan for a box.

"He needs to be able to get it easily, but he needs to be able to get it *consciously*," Taern said with emphasis, and Mrs. Wrinkle nodded vigorously.

"I understand, young master, and I even have a friend who will do that." She paused in the act of pinning up yet another shirt and looked at him kindly. "Are you sure you wouldn't just rather"—her cheeks stained a blotchy orange—"return to your own quarters for sleep?"

Taern resisted the urge to tell her that as a whore, sleeping with a man had not been part of his duties, and that it was the sleeping that would make his relationship with Nyx so very special. Instead, he simply shook his head. "If I'd wanted to sleep in my own quarters, dear, I wouldn't have snuck into his bed, now would I?" He winked at her then and was gratified when her blush intensified.

"Yes," she muttered. "Yes, I see. Well, if you give me the knife, I'll see if Mr. Innes can't fix it."

"Mr. Innes?"

"He's our handyman. He keeps the place shipshape, but he's sort of a free contractor, seeing as we don't have enough work to hire him full-time. He's a right hand with wood and metal. Tell me what you want, and I'll have him make it."

Taern wasn't comfortable with that. "Uhm, Mrs. Wrinkle, you understand that the sooner we get this thing back, the better, right? I can hide it from him tonight, but he'll be… uhm, extremely uncomfortable without it by his side for longer than that."

Mrs. Wrinkle's eyes got extremely large. "He should be next door in the next five minutes, young man. If you can hang up the rest of this laundry, we can have it tonight!"

Taern didn't mind hanging up the laundry after that, and when Mrs. Wrinkle returned, she said the box should be ready after dinner.

"Will he be home for dinner?" Taern asked, and she let loose with a pleased smile, although her eyes were strictly focused on the dry laundry she (with Taern's help) was taking off the next clothesline.

"I think, with you here, he might."

Taern suddenly liked her very much, and he felt a compulsion to be honest with her. "You know… you know what Krissa and I were before he bought our contracts, right?"

Mrs. Wrinkle shrugged her shoulders. "Same thing about half the city has done at one time or another to make ends meet. Not all of us get the good fortune to work for Mr. Kyon, now do we?"

Taern smiled at her and ducked under the clothesline to kiss her impulsively on the cheek. "You're a good dame, Mrs. Wrinkle. I think we're going to be great friends."

She let out a schoolgirl's giggle, and he finished helping her with the laundry.

WHEN he was done, he took a good look around the courtyard and allowed himself to be seriously impressed. There was a giant barrel set up to spin in place, rings to run through, two climbing structures united by suspended and free-falling ropes, and a number of cannons that confused him at first until he hit a spring button on the end of one and launched a small yet heavy sandbag about twenty feet in the air. At first he laughed, because the thing was not traveling fast enough to seriously injure anybody, and then he stopped laughing because the fact of the matter hit him: that was the point. The sandbag cannons had the same purpose as the rings and the rope structure and the cave of barbed wire and all of the other hard, practical items parked on the acre of land behind Dorjan's town home. They were part of an obstacle course—this was how the Nyx trained for what he did on the city streets, and a confused battle of anger and gratitude occurred in Taern's chest.

He settled on anger.

Oh, how Areau must love it when one of those sandbags found its mark.

Taern left the courtyard quietly fuming, and unfortunately, his next stop was lunch.

Areau had bathed and dressed to eat, and his hair had been combed and pulled back in a queue. For a moment Taern had hope. This could be civilized, this thing with him and Areau. Areau was Dorjan's oldest friend—that's what Dorjan seemed to think.

Then Areau turned those beautiful blue eyes on Taern and sneered. "I see we're still here."

"I can say the same about you," Taern muttered, and Krissa cleared her throat. Taern took a deep breath and looked at her resentfully. She shrugged, and the message was clear. They'd both enjoyed Dorjan's house so far. Obviously neither of them was looking to leave this new position. Taern needed to make nice with Areau or all of that was at risk. "You're looking fit, my lord," he said brightly, meaning it, and Areau flicked a spoonful of soup at him.

Taern gaped. "What in the names of—"

Krissa was faster with her riding crop than Taern was with his soup, and Areau received a blow to the cheek. Taern had soup dripping down his face, but that didn't stop him from gaping at Krissa, whose fierce gaze didn't waver from Areau's cowed demeanor.

"I warned you," she hissed. "I've given you what you said you craved, and you promised to behave. That will be the *last* blow you receive until you live up to your part of the bargain."

"I can't help it," Areau rasped. "He's here… he's here to steal from me!"

Taern grabbed Areau's napkin, which was resting by his plate on the small homey kitchen table where they'd been eating, and wiped his face before throwing the napkin back at his opponent. "You can't steal something somebody's thrown away," he said icily and then picked up his bowl of soup and drank it efficiently before something untoward could happen to it. Like Areau's spit.

Mrs. Wrinkle came by with plates of warm sandwiches then, and Taern and Areau contented themselves with exchanging mutual glares until she left.

"You still need to come get fitted with armor," Areau muttered. "I'll still see you in the gymnasium."

"Looking forward to it," Taern muttered, and then he looked at Krissa, who blew an imaginary piece of hair from her forehead. Apparently that lie was for the both of them, then.

She was there, of course, and Taern could truly appreciate why Dorjan would keep cuffs in his drawer and why there had been the manacles that had disappeared from the stable. Areau needed constant supervision, and the thing the man wanted the most was to prove Dorjan wrong.

He spent half an hour measuring Taern, and he misaligned the tape on purpose often enough that Krissa finally took it from him, took the measurements, then made Areau write them down and looked over his shoulder to make sure he did it correctly. When they had a satisfactory set of figures, she gave him the tape and told him to return it to his laboratory, which is where he'd brought it from, and while he was gone, she sidled up close to Taern.

"Are you and Dorjan…." She trailed off delicately and blushed, which ordinarily would have struck Taern as funny, but it wasn't—not in their new set of circumstances it wasn't.

"Are you joking?" Taern asked irritably. "After what that one's put him through? It'll take me months to fix all that damage."

Krissa stopped and cocked her head. "But you intend to? After only a couple of days, you intend to?"

Taern shrugged. "Try ten years, Krissa. Ten years ago he was a god. The god fell that night. Knowing what the man has been through has only made him more interesting."

Krissa raised her eyebrows. "Good. As long as you're in it for the long haul, you should know that tonight is going to be horrible. Areau's going to want to be whipped and gagged and restrained, and all I'm going to do is restrain him so I can get some bloody sleep. His shouting is going to keep the entire house up, but I would like him to be obedient, at least, before he starts firing those sandbag things at *you*, do you understand?"

Taern nodded vigorously, and she grimaced.

"All I'm saying, Taern, is that tonight might not be the most romantic of times. Nor tomorrow. It sounds like you were planning to take things slow. I'm telling you it might be slower than you think."

Taern grinned at her, suddenly tickled. "Slow is good," he said, excitement tingeing his voice. "Haven't done slow before. It's new!"

She rolled her eyes, and he wrapped his arm around her waist and kissed her cheek, just as he had Mrs. Wrinkle. God, he loved women. Had no interest in fucking them, it was true, but from his mother to his sisters to Madame M, he'd had no problem earning their adoration, and the feeling was mutual.

That was good, he thought as Areau clattered back and he stepped smoothly away without being told. It was good to have allies in a place where a man's oldest and dearest friend had to fight himself daily not to have you killed.

Taern took his time to wander around the gym as Areau sat at a small desk in the corner and nattered to himself about circumference and joins. Like the courtyard it looked out upon, the gym was a utilitarian place—there were weights and bands in one corner, with a chin-up bar and a mirror, presumably so Dorjan could make sure he was lifting correctly. There was a small punching bag and a heavy leather sandbag and a sparring ring (which apparently doubled as a tumbling ring, given the number of extra mats at its side) and jump ropes, and Taern found he was eyeing the place with a combination of interest and dislike. There hadn't been a place like this at Madame M's; all of Taern's conditioning had come from walking the streets, although not always on the job. He was starting to feel a little stir-crazy and thought the gym or the courtyard might take care of that, and that was good.

But he thought about Dorjan, that fabulously muscled body, those amazing moves on the street, and the high price he'd paid for all of it, and the place suddenly took on the colors of a prison. How long had Areau been imprisoned and tortured? Areau had his scars to show for it, it was true, but then, so did Dorjan.

Taern had seen them himself.

Still, he did ask Krissa's permission to strip to his smallclothes so he could avail himself of the jump ropes and the tumbling mats, and she asked Areau courteously if that was all right. Areau barely glanced at him, then went back to his diagrams and his muttering, so Taern did so before leaving his clothes in a muddle in the corner and setting up the tumbling mats with as much speed as he could.

When he was a kid, he used to be good at this.

He took a few tumbling runs—easy things, front rolls, cartwheels, walkovers, flip-flops—and stood excitedly. He was *better* at this than he'd been as a child. He took a few steps back and made a run, then vaulted up into the air and spun twice before he landed and tucked into a front roll. He came up with his arms over his head, doing a little dance of triumph.

"I'm a *nisket*!" he crowed, and Krissa shook her head.

"No, moron, you grew up in Karanos during the gravity rolls," she said tartly, although she did not sound unimpressed. "It makes doing that kind of thing when you get *here* crazy easy!"

Taern made a face at her. "Well, it wasn't *that* easy," he grumbled, because he was starting to sweat, but that didn't stop him from making more passes until he was sopping with it, and sore to boot. But he was excited, happy, and triumphant, and that's when Dorjan stalked in.

Dorjan was wearing one of his outfits of black smallclothes that he'd apparently had made for working up a sweat. He didn't seem to pay attention to anyone else in the room; instead, he spotted the giant leather sandbag and went charging for it, then let out his frustration in a long, wordless howl, beating on it savagely with his bare fist.

An hour later, Taern was at an end. It had been an hour of watching Dorjan, sweat pouring from his hair and sopping his clothes, pummeling the bag with no less ferocity than he'd started. Every now and then he would roar, "*Eight bloody thousand fucking men!*" and throw a punch that, with any other man, would have broken his wrist.

Oh, hells and aether, his voice shook, but his assault on the helpless leather bag never relented. Areau finally met Taern's gaze, his expression miserable, and Taern wanted to smack him. Yes, oh Karanos yes, he was despondent over the losses Biemansland had suffered in the constant war she was waging, but Areau, his oldest friend, could only stand there and watch? Taern needed to do something. The fact that even Areau was concerned meant it was time—finally—for someone to step in and save Dorjan from himself.

Taern looked at Areau again and saw that his initial concern had been replaced. His eyes were glazing over now as he watched Dorjan throwing himself again and again at the bag, his knuckles splitting and scraping and bleeding. Areau's mouth was open, and his breath was coming fast, and oh hells! His hand was rubbing at his crotch. Taern's fury practically stopped up his throat, but he did manage to keep his head.

"Krissa!" he snarled, and she snapped her gaze away from the vision of Dorjan lost in violence.

"Wha—oh. Fuck."

Were it any other time, Taern would have looked at her twice when she swore. Krissa rarely polluted her language—she tried, in fact, to carry herself like a lady born and bred. Most days, she succeeded.

"Oh hells, Taern," she muttered, picking up her riding crop and walking toward Areau with purpose in her eye. "Could you have Mrs. Wrinkle set a tray outside my room near dinnertime? I'm starving."

"For both of you?" Taern asked, mostly just willing her to get Dorjan's curse the hell out of there.

"Fine. If you insist." It did his heart good to know she'd just as soon Areau starve at this juncture, but it would do his heart better if the pain in the arse was just gone. "Areau!" she snapped, smacking him smartly in the swollen groin with the riding crop.

Areau groaned and fell to his knees, looking at her with a combination of recrimination and awe as he shuddered and came from the blow alone. "Mistress!" he whined, and she looked down at him.

"Did I give you permission to be aroused?"

"No, Mistress."

"Did I give you permission to touch yourself?"

"No, Mistress."

"Did I give you permission to climax?"

"No, Mistress."

"Follow me, then, and we'll discuss terms of punishment."

Areau made feeble attempts to stand, and Krissa looked down her nose at him. "Don't. Bother." She turned on her heel then, and Areau followed, wretchedly, on his hands and knees. The idea that he had to crawl up three flights of stairs might have made Taern's day.

But first he had to fix the man in front of him.

"Nyx!" he snapped, and Dorjan launched a right hook that would have shattered someone's jaw if they'd been in front of him, followed by a left cross that would have had an opponent biting off his tongue. "Nyx!" Taern screamed, and he realized that Dorjan was in the same sort of trance Areau had been, except—and Taern checked to make sure—he was not aroused.

"*Dorjan!*" Taern shrieked, and he coupled the name with a low tackle to the man's knees. He rolled away as soon as the two of them hit the ground, because he wasn't sure what was coming next, and rose to a crouch, panting.

Dorjan crouched, facing Taern, hands balanced in front of him. He was clearly ready to rush Taern and take him out. Taern leapt as Dorjan pitched forward, and literally vaulted over Dorjan's shoulders, but Dorjan was quick. He pivoted on the very next step and swept his leg out—if Taern hadn't been ready for it, he would have gone sprawling.

As it was, he executed a dive roll and a quick turn and came up facing Dorjan, who had resumed his crouch. They circled for a few moments, and Taern grinned fiercely. This was *fun!*

Suddenly Dorjan leapt on top of him, pinning his hands above his head and straddling his torso. Taern struggled beneath him for a moment and felt—

He smiled up at Dorjan lasciviously, and Dorjan wiggled his hardening cock against Taern before letting go of Taern's hands in surprise. Taern rolled, throwing him, and they both rose to their fighting crouch again in no time. Taern shifted for a moment, adjusting himself, and realized that his cock was half-hard from the thrill. He was watching Dorjan the entire time and knew exactly when Dorjan saw that too.

Dorjan sat down suddenly, wearily, all of the fight out of him, his breath coming in hard pants. "Go bathe," he said gruffly. "Go bathe and dress and go down for dinner. Tell Mrs. Wrinkle I won't—"

"The hell I will!" Taern said, standing up fully. "That woman is cooking something special for you, I just know it!"

Dorjan smiled faintly. "As kind as that is—"

"What got you? Was it noticing my cock? It's all right, Dorjan. We're sly. I don't mind if you notice. Was it that you were hard? We were wrestling together—I know you like my body. I took it as a compliment."

Dorjan cringed and looked at him with hurt eyes. "I would *never* force myself on you!"

Taern closed his eyes and swallowed. "I know you wouldn't," he said softly, and then his hands went to the drawstring waistband of his soft pants. He unknotted the drawstring and pushed down his pants, knowing his cock would be hard just from being bared in front of Dorjan.

"Does it look like I'm afraid?" Taern asked, making sure Dorjan held his gaze. "Does it look like you were forcing me?" He took a step closer. "Look at it, Dorjan. It's my manhood." Taern grabbed it from the base and stroked, then tilted his head back and closed his eyes because it was hard, and it was good, and because Dorjan was watching him. He felt the little bit of wetness at the end, and he rubbed it with his thumb. Catching Dorjan's gaze again, he popped his thumb in his mouth and suckled.

Dorjan's lips parted, and he licked them without seeming to notice.

"Do you like my cock, Dorjan?" Taern asked slyly. He nodded, knowing that Dorjan would do the same.

"It's beautiful," Dorjan whispered. "But I am not the man who—"

"If not you, who?" Taern took another step forward. "I've had hundreds, you know. If I'd stayed on the streets, it would have been thousands. I know men, have held them and fucked them and been fucked by them." He wrapped his fist around the base again and heard Dorjan suck in a tortured breath. Taern stroked himself enough for more fluid to spurt out, then stepped close so he could feel Dorjan's breath shiver across the end.

"I am aware," Dorjan said, but he was now as mesmerized by Taern's cock as he had been by his own violence moments before, and Taern considered that an improvement.

"Blow on it," Taern urged. "You're the only man I want to see it at present, the only man I want to touch it. The least you could do is... ah, yes...." Because Dorjan obediently pursed his lean mouth and was blowing gently across the wet head. Taern closed his eyes and stroked again, drizzling precome at the pressure. He felt the whisper of something soft and wet, and his eyes flew open so he could *see* Dorjan sticking out his tongue to catch it as it dripped.

"Lick it," he begged. "Please, Dorjan. It feels so good, and I'm longing to feel your tongue."

Dorjan looked perplexed for a moment, as though he'd never done this before. Taern thought perhaps that was true. He wasn't a virgin, technically, but he'd never done *this*—tender, exploratory, gentle experimentation—before.

"C'mon, Dorjan," Taern whispered. "Pleeee—oh, *Karanos, yes!*" The flat of Dorjan's tongue swirled around the head of his cock, which was peeking from his foreskin hood. Taern pulled his fist back, exposing the head entirely. "All of it," he said. "That's right, around the... oh, yes, the crown. The slit at the top... oh, yes. That's special, right there. Mmm...."

For a few moments, it was enough to let Dorjan explore with his tongue. Dorjan pulled back and Taern almost wept; then he realized Dorjan was pushing up so to sit back on his knees to make his angle better. When he opened his mouth again, Taern said, "Now suck it in... there you go. Careful of the teeth...." Although the edge of a tooth could sometimes make him hotter, that wasn't the point of this exercise, not if he wanted Dorjan to feel good about it. "Ahh... that's right. Deeper," he murmured, and very lightly, so lightly he wasn't sure if Dorjan would feel it, he rested his hand on the back of Dorjan's head. Dorjan pulled him deeper, and Taern thought he would die from the exquisite slowness of the whole act.

"Now pull back," he ordered, massaging Dorjan's scalp very gently through his shorn hair. "Good, now swirl your tongue...." He shuddered, because Dorjan was good at that. "Nice," he gasped. "Now suck me deep. That's right. So good. You're making me feel *so good*, Dorjan," he said deliberately. He pulled his hips back and thrust forward, pleasured when Dorjan swished his tongue like Taern had begged.

Dorjan looked at him, those brown eyes expressive and hopeful and eager to please.

"Yes," Taern murmured. "I'm gonna...." He pulled back and thrust forward because he *had* to, and tried to finish the teaching thought. "I'm going to just fuck your mouth, if that's all right. Keep swirling your tongue if it's good." Dorjan did it again when Taern pulled back, and Taern let out a sigh of satisfaction. "Feel free to... ahhhh... yes. Improvise. Wrap your hand around my shaft or cup my bollocks... *yes!*" Because Dorjan did both. First he wrapped his hand around Taern's shaft and stroked up when Taern thrust forward, and then he used his other hand to gently, gently.... Oh, Taern yearned for it harder. He liked a stiff, rough, violent fuck as much as any whore in Thenis, but not today. Today it was enough that Dorjan was fondling his balls and sucking his cock and—*Karanos!*—doing that magic thing with his tongue, and Taern's hips jerked hard and his fingers tightened in Dorjan's hair.

"It's good, Dorjan. So good. I love your mouth on my cock. Just... just keep doing that. I'm going to come in your mouth, yes? You may swallow or spit it out or wait for me to kiss you and get it back—*ahhhhhh!*" That last thought must have aroused Dorjan beyond measure, because he sucked on Taern *hard,* and oh, that edge of pain did it. Taern closed his eyes and hurtled toward the black-exploding-white of oblivion, pulling Dorjan's head to his groin and spurting, urgent and thick, into his mouth.

Dorjan's throat worked once or twice, and then Taern felt him holding the spend hotly around his cock head. Dorjan pulled back slowly, suckling as he went, and Taern spurted twice more, responding to the extra pressure. When he was done, Dorjan looked up at Taern, his eyes wide and limpid and hopeful, and Taern sank to his knees and kissed him, taking his own spend and swallowing, and then kissing more, and more, and more. He licked the inside of Dorjan's mouth, cleaning his come from every corner, and Dorjan let him in, allowed him access, allowed Taern to clean him and suckle on his tongue and take care.

When Taern pulled back from the kiss, he reached into Dorjan's lap to finish him off, and he was met by a spreading wetness across the front of Dorjan's pants. He looked at Dorjan in wonder, and Dorjan broke away, stood up quickly, and grabbed a swath of linen hanging from the side of sparring ring to wipe his mouth and then to dab at his soft-knit long underwear.

He was looking anywhere but Taern, and Taern, after spending those precious moments having Dorjan's thoughts mirrored in his eyes, was not going to let him turn his back again.

He didn't say anything, he just walked into Dorjan's heat until their chests touched, and cupped Dorjan's cheeks between his palms.

Dorjan looked up, surprised, and Taern pulled him down for another kiss. "I really enjoyed that," he said against Dorjan's lips. "It would destroy me if you were ashamed of it."

Dorjan didn't say anything, but he nodded in understanding and kissed Taern again, roughly and quickly. Then he grabbed the towel and looped his arms around Taern's shoulders.

"We need to shower for dinner," he said, his voice almost apologetic, and Taern nodded. "Should we tell Krissa and Areau?"

Taern shook his head, unwilling to explain. "I think we should have Mrs. Wrinkle bring them a tray," he murmured. Did that little interlude count as slow? He hoped so—it was apparently as slow as he could go without jumping his personal cricket over the bloody bridge. Besides, if Krissa was right, it could be the sweetest moment Dorjan had for a couple of days. Perhaps slow was not as important as teaching lessons when the opportunity arose.

DORJAN was quiet as they took their turns at the shower and then dressed for dinner. (Taern insisted on them using the same bathroom, enjoying Dorjan's discomfiture immensely.) Dorjan was polite and courteous and didn't argue at all with Taern's decision to move his belongings into Dorjan's room. Of course he was also extremely distracted, but Taern figured he was allowed to be. The thing that had set him to beat the sand out of the poor defenseless leather bag had not gone away. But when

Taern got out of the shower, he found Dorjan trying to tape his own knuckles, and he decided to put a stop to that right quick.

"Here," he said shortly. "Sit down before you hurt yourself. Move." He pulled on his third-best suit (since the second-best suit was still in a puddle in the gymnasium) in an all-fired hurry, leaving the smallclothes since he didn't see what the big deal was to be dressing so close to when you were supposed to be going to bed anyway. Especially when he slept naked, which wasn't the point. The point was, he didn't want Dorjan confusing what he was about to do with sex—not this time.

"Here, I'll button the shirt in a moment," he muttered in exasperation.

Dorjan sat patiently, his mind most assuredly elsewhere. Taern caught his attention, though, when he picked up his one hand and daubed antiseptic on it from a brown bottle. Dorjan hissed and Taern shrugged. "You could have avoided these," he admonished. "I have no pity for these. The next time something heinous happens, come home and talk to me— don't beat up helpless gymnasium equipment."

"I'll do whatever I bloody well please," Dorjan said, but he said it without heat.

"Oh yes, because that's what you always do—what you bloody well please." Impatiently, Taern started wrapping gauze on the clean scrapes. "It's why you risk your neck on the streets and why you risk your family's holdings living a double life. It's why you keep Areau here, although it must have crossed your mind more than once to send him back to your father's keep—"

"I need him," Dorjan muttered. "His armor, his training—"

"You could live without," Taern said smartly, finishing the gauze up on one hand and moving to the other. "You could live without being the Nyx—but you bloody well please to try to make it up to Areau and you bloody well please to try to fix your festering province when it should probably just be allowed to self-destruct, and you bloody-well please to live like a monk—

"I do *not*—"

"*Except* for that abomination with Areau, of which we won't speak for a moment. Yes, Dorjan, you bloody well please to throw away your life. You bloody well please to continuously flog yourself for things which are not your fault. And you will bloody well please to do that mentally and I can't stop you, you will *bloody well please* to not beat yourself against helpless gym equipment to the point where you hurt yourself!"

Dorjan glared. "I'm not going to stop doing it just because you yell at me," he said patiently. "I'm not a child."

Taern knew it. But *Karanos*, it hurt him too. "Well, could you at least tell me what it was all about so I can think that maybe it was worth it?" Taern finished the gauze, and Dorjan sighed and scrubbed his face with his hands.

"During dessert," he said after a moment. "I'm hungry, and I need to gather my words."

DINNER really was good. Served in the dining room, at one end of the long table, it was the most formal thing Taern had seen about Dorjan's mansion. He smiled at Mrs. Wrinkle as she brought out their covered plates, and although she winked at him, she didn't smile back, apparently taking her role as servant/matchmaker very seriously this evening. The meal itself was *wonderful*—stuffed pheasant and rice, with a cucumber salad and warm soup beforehand. Mrs. Wrinkle had baked fresh bread, and it was crusty on the outside and soft on the inside, and there was fresh butter to go with it. Taern loved the old girl all over again, just eating her food—especially because he knew the food had been made for Dorjan.

Taern dug in and ate with enthusiasm, and he saw Dorjan watching him from the corner of his eye and then joining him. Good. During his time on the streets, Taern had not always been well fed. Even at Madame M's times had been hard and they'd had to pool their resources sometimes simply to afford thin potato soup. But Dorjan's family keep was one of the best managed in the province—even Taern had heard that. Very often, if there was a shopkeeper who had food in a time of want, he was supplied from Dorjan's keep, and the prices were kept low too. Taern knew that more than one of those vendors had slipped him an apple when he'd first arrived in this city, and those apples had been the difference between an alive Taern and a dead one.

He appreciated the food, and it was nice to know he could spread that sort of joy.

Mrs. Wrinkle brought them apple pie and ice cream for dessert, and it seemed like some sort of a sign. Taern refused to speak during the apple pie, because it was sublime and required his full attention. Dorjan didn't speak either, but after they'd cleaned off their plates and Taern had licked his finger of the last sticky bit of syrup, Dorjan pushed his chair back and sat for a moment.

"Do you know the names of the six provinces, Taern?"

Taern blinked. Schoolroom stuff.

"Karanos, Biemansland, Conrad, Gretzky, Davanos, and Corian. Biemansland has the asteroids as its main asset but also a lot of pastoral farmland and the river to help with transport before the millipedes were adapted to be powered from the lumium. Karanos has…." Taern rolled his eyes. "Swamp gas, mostly—marshland. Lots of hieters—those big, scaly prehistoric land-roaming ichthyosaurs that like to eat people. My father once told me that he made the entire keep's food money exporting those skins to Thenis so ladies could have fashionable boots."

Dorjan nodded. "Good. Your father ran a tight schoolroom in his keep."

Taern smiled, lost in memory. "He used to remind us all the time," he said, thinking. "He would remind us that the provinces were founded by the men who found the world. Each one of them took their portion of colonists and set up a government and a trade, and their one goal was to trade equably and fairly. They were not"—Taern's eyes found Dorjan's face, and he felt as though this one thing was of great importance—"*not* to be confused with gods."

Dorjan nodded. "Your father was a wise man. That's what my father said too. He told us to swear by them all we wanted—but to believe that there was a force in the universe stronger than men and stronger than commerce, and that good and evil were defined by that and no other."

"They would have spoken well together, our fathers," Taern said softly, and Dorjan nodded and leaned forward.

"Alum Septra—one of our Triari—was the stratego who ordered the assault on Kiamath Keep. He told us—told the Triari, told the Forum—that we were assaulting a cache of weapons. When he was asked why Karanos would be stockpiling weapons, he reminded us all that Karanos didn't have the resources that Biemansland did and that instead of trading, your government was thinking about taking it by force."

Taern wrinkled his forehead. "I don't remember politics that way," he said politely. "But then, I was only nine."

Dorjan closed his eyes, and when he opened them, there was the faint memory of their moment in the gymnasium in his expression. "Yes, Taern, you were only nine," he repeated and grimaced. "And now you are only nineteen. And I am—"

"Not going to start doing math," Taern announced grandly. "It makes me fall asleep. That would be bad form."

Dorjan shot him a droll look. "I must correct myself. Your father kept an *outstanding* schoolroom and probably had the patience of a saint to deal with you. But let me continue."

Taern stuck out his tongue, vastly relieved that Dorjan could still speak lightly.

"Anyway, Septra lied." Dorjan inclined his head. "A fact you very kindly tipped us off to. But when the news of the battle got back to the Forum and the Triari, Septra had a month to start bribing men who had formerly not been bribable. I was, at the time—"

"Recovering from your wounds," Taern said quietly. "The whole city knows the story, Dorjan. I'm no different."

Dorjan inclined his head. "Yes, well, by the time we sprang Areau from the asylum, Septra had enough people in his pocket to have my father assassinated and have the Forum turn a blind eye. And in the meantime, he continued the fiction that the other provinces were a danger to us. It's a hideous cycle, you see. We squander all of our resources on the war, and so Septra says we need to wage more war. In the meantime, we have barely enough resources to feed our population, so Septra reduces the population by squandering them in the war too. It's an elegant solution, really, and it means that no one dares gainsay a madman, because everyone is terrified that if they're wrong and Septra is right, their argument has just condemned our province to death."

Taern shuddered, suddenly cold. "Squandered the population," he quoted. "Just say it like it really is. You're talking people and soldiers and—"

"And lives," Dorjan said, his voice shaking. "Yes. Exactly. Your father raised a smart son."

"But why?" Taern asked, shaking his head. "What does he stand to gain from all of it?"

Dorjan looked thoughtful. "I think," he said after a moment, "that in recent years, the power has become its own end. But that's not how it started."

"No?"

"No. Originally he simply wanted more lumium. More of everything, really, but the lumium that powers our steam conveyances— that was his special desire."

Taern's gaze darted to Dorjan's face, but Dorjan wasn't meeting his eyes again.

"Isn't the lumium taken from Biemansland?" he asked, not following the logic.

Dorjan nodded. "More specifically, it's mined from the asteroids in my father's keep. See, that was the one resource that the other provinces couldn't manufacture or mine on their own, and do you know why?"

Taern shook his head. "No—that wasn't covered in our schoolroom."

Dorjan nodded again, his eyes still off in space. "See, the asteroids were initially harvested by criminals, and it was dangerous, dirty work with few survivors. Harnessing something that big to the earth? Feeding it oxygen through an umbilical tube? It's insanity. Or it would be without the niskets."

Taern sort of grimaced. "Yes," he said, feeling embarrassed. "We're taught that those are old wives' tales. We talk about them a lot, but no one's ever seen them."

Dorjan did meet his eyes and smile then, and at the same time, he brought his hand up to the pendant around his neck. He stroked it gently and closed his eyes and then cupped it in his palm.

The thing opened right before Taern's eyes and started glowing, rain gray and sky blue, whirling in Dorjan's cupped palm.

"Hullo, my pet," Dorjan murmured. "Meet Taern. Taern, meet...." Dorjan looked at the tiny glowing creature and grimaced. "Have we changed our name again? Really?" An extremely self-satisfied humming emitted from the thing. "Flox," Dorjan said, rolling his eyes just a bit. "Today she's Flox. Anyway, feel free to meet."

With that, the tiny flower-shaped metal-textured thing took off in a spinning, dizzying flight across the room, bumping into the chandelier and making it jiggle and then bumping into Taern's glass of wine. Taern barely saved the wine, and then he held his cupped hand imperiously over it.

"Here," he said sternly. "You'll only hurt yourself if you keep dancing around like that."

It settled then, primly on the palm of his hand, and Taern studied it, trying to find some sort of human equivalent for eyes, ears, mouth, nose, and wings. In the end he realized that two of the petals with highly distinctive markings were really eyes and the little thorn at the bottom that kept poking him was really a proboscis, and it was....

"Eww." Taern grimaced at Dorjan. "It's drinking my...."

Dorjan nodded. "Your blood. Be honored. It means she thinks you're worthy."

"Worthy of what?"

Dorjan shrugged. "Worthy of whatever. The niskets are great believers in shared endeavors. And they *adore* mining the asteroids or digging tunnels or a thousand other things that the original colonists set their lawbreakers to do. But since the asteroids were only harvested in one province—"

"The niskets only stayed in one province," Taern deduced. "Which explains why the rest of us only think of them as fairy tales."

Dorjan nodded. "You see, the niskets and the asteroids are the key to supply. Septra doesn't know about the niskets, but he did want the supply. He kept asking my father to mine faster."

Taern pursed his lips. "Well, the man is a git—I can see why your father wouldn't want to—"

"Start another earthquake like the one that leveled Karanos and reduced your entire province to rubble, marshland, and those horrible lizard creatures?"

Taern gasped, and Flox the nisket flew off his hand and pressed herself flat against Dorjan's. Dorjan opened the necklace at his throat and Flox fit right in, looking like a hammered piece of metal and making the entire man's locket a novelty item and nothing more. "That was caused by—"

Dorjan nodded. "It was the one time my father acceded to the Triari's request for more, and within two days...." Dorjan shook his head. "I was... no older than you were, when my province destroyed your life. I remember my father hearing of the earthquake, then facing down with Septra. We were here in the city, and that day, my father packed my mother, my sister, Areau, and his family—all in one go, we were sent back home. I'll never forget that. *Bimuit!* The fights we got into—Areau more than I, because he liked to protect me back then. But word of the battle on the Forum floor trickled down, and Areau and I were called traitors and...." He shook his head. "Child's play—but it had an impact. When I found that the young nobility was being pressed into service for fear of aggression from another province, I was the first to sign up, and Areau— he was right on my heels."

"And your father?" Taern asked, and Dorjan shrugged.

"Septra was clever about that, you know. His sources were always from other keeps. He always presented their information without any semblance of collusion. My father bought the line. He thought that perhaps we had brought the action on ourselves, but never did he doubt that there was an action until...."

"Until you were almost killed." Taern's stomach clenched as he said the words, and for a moment, he regretted eating all of everything, even his dessert. Oh, Karanos, he'd come so very, very close to never eating dinner with this man, never seeing him move, never tasting his skin. It would have been a crime, he thought now in sudden fright, a true tragedy, if Dorjan had not survived that dreadful night. There were so many terrible losses from that time as it was!

Dorjan nodded. "I was lucky," he said, his voice ringing with sincerity. "My father believed me and believed that Areau needed to be rescued." Dorjan looked down. "My father was not so lucky. He believed and knew just enough to be killed."

They were both quiet for a long moment, and then Taern spoke up and tried to bring the conversation to the present. "So today...." He inclined his head, waiting for Dorjan to proceed.

"So, today," Dorjan sighed heavily. "Today there was a military contingent that was still around from that day ten years ago. They have been bringing back reports of confused populace and betrayed citizenry and a general puzzled demeanor from the other provinces for why our province would simply go mad. Military men are taught to follow orders, but they're also, heavens willing, taught to have honor, and the courage to make honor a true thing. This particular branch of the army had stopped raiding keeps unless their own intel backed up that the keep was empty—and very often, it didn't. This particular branch of the army had a very brave, very smart stratego, a friend of mine, actually, who ran the keep closest to my father's keep. The keep where your sisters are housed, actually."

"My sisters?" Taern sat up suddenly, and Dorjan reassured him with an open palm.

"Are fine. I sent word to the keep this afternoon." Dorjan grimaced, his look growing bleaker. "Anyway, this contingent was not... obedient. And three days ago, as a cost for their lack of obedience, they sank into a swamp filled with napalm and were eliminated to the last man."

Taern groaned. "Eight thousand," he murmured, because *that* had been what Dorjan had been screaming as he'd worked out. *That* had been the loss he'd been mourning. "It is no small thing."

Dorjan raised his eyebrows and nodded. "My old battalion went down," he said quietly. "My first and only command. And you know what the best part is?"

Taern had no idea what could possibly be more awful.

"None of the other provinces manufacture napalm. It was a trap sprung by Septra's allies to get rid of the last moral fiber in the military. It worked."

Taern had no words. He simply looked at Dorjan, sorrow in his heart for what neither of them could fix. After a moment he reached across the table and clasped Dorjan's shoulder, and then slid his hand down Dorjan's arm to clasp the back of his hand over the bandages on the knuckles. To his immense relief, Dorjan turned his hand palm up and accepted the comfort. It was all Taern had to give.

They sat like that, without speaking, until Areau's piteous screams penetrated the walls of the great mansion and echoed down into the dining room.

Dorjan startled and almost jerked out of his chair, but Taern kept their handclasp and shook his head. "Sometimes," he said, feeling like a horrible person, "sometimes, things have to get much worse before they get better."

Dorjan's whole body was on high alert, and his gaze darted frantically overhead to where Areau's cries were coming from. "But Areau—"

"This is the worse, Dorjan. Have some faith in Krissa. She just wants to make it better."

Dorjan nodded—but he also jerked his hand from Taern's and stalked away. Since he wasn't heading for the stairs, Taern didn't follow for the moment. He needed to gather his own inner resources before he could comfort Dorjan with any competency whatsoever.

TAERN found him outside in the courtyard in the fading twilight. For a moment he almost missed his silhouette because it was crouched on top of one of the rope-climbing structures. Taern noticed that all the ropes connecting the two structures had been taken down and that the only way to get up to where Nyx—and he was very much Nyx at the moment—was standing was to climb the pole, splinters and all.

Taern narrowed his eyes. The pole across from Nyx was metal, he thought, considering. The only way to get to him without an armload of splinters was to climb the metal pole and use the ropes—the ones Nyx was in control of. Well, Nyx had better give up some of that control. Taern was damned if he would let Nyx isolate himself now, not after so much effort getting him to open up.

"I will be down soon enough." Dorjan's voice floated down to him, and Taern looked up, realizing he couldn't even make out the lantern jaw or the faintly almond shape of his brown eyes because the twilight was so thick.

"I worry," Taern said shortly.

"I'm tired of talking," Dorjan said mildly. "Can you respect that?"

Taern nodded, but that didn't stop him from shimmying up the metal pole in his last set of decent clothes and standing atop the T-bar at the apex of the pole. Once there, he hauled up one of the ropes and swung it forward, back, forward, back, and then forward, releasing it at the height of the throw and allowing it to sail to where Dorjan crouched on the crossbar between the two wooden posts that made up his structure.

Dorjan watched him impassively, and for a moment, Taern feared he'd be making a foolish gesture without Dorjan's help. But when the rope came Dorjan's way, he reached out and grabbed it and secured one end around a hook on the crossbar, apparently made just for that purpose.

"There are gloves hanging from the end of the T-bar," Dorjan called, and his voice was reluctant. "The rope is harsh on your hands."

Taern grinned even though Dorjan couldn't see it in the near darkness, and tested the rope with his foot. When he had the slack figured out, he ran lightly over it, not looking down, grateful for what Krissa had pointed out to be the natural advantage of growing up with fractured gravity.

In a moment he was crouching next to Dorjan, who cast him a slanted look and murmured, "Show-off," but there was affection in his voice, Taern was almost sure.

They squatted there for long moments until the sky was completely black and the stars were diamond peaks in the velvet. Taern looked up and searched out the Nisket Flower, thinking that now he knew for certain there was such a thing, the constellation felt close enough to touch.

The city was quiet from here, and Areau's calls for pain and pleasure couldn't be heard. Taern could see, down by the laundry room, Mrs. Wrinkle sitting in the rapidly cooling night and shivering, and he bumped Dorjan's elbow. Dorjan looked and sighed, then ran across the rope and shimmied down the metal pole.

Taern listened and heard Dorjan offer to escort her to a nearby house for the evening. He heard her say no, thank you, she would be fine. Her bedroom was in the farthest corner from their part of the house anyway, but thank you. Dorjan was returning to the structure when Taern decided they had hidden enough and ran across the rope on his own, then slid down the pole, almost into Dorjan's arms.

He recovered his balance and grinned, and Dorjan smiled like an automaton in response.

"I need to ask something," Dorjan said, and he didn't back away, didn't try to widen the distance between them, as awkward as it was.

Taern turned and leaned against the pole, spreading his thighs a little suggestively and pulling Dorjan's hips toward him so they could stand together, groins touching, as intimate as two men could be when fully clothed.

"I'm right here," Taern said, half a cocky grin on his face.

"Why?"

"Why what?"

"Why? Why... why the alley? Why not go see your sisters? Why... if you were going to come here and... and do what I do, why do you have to slee...." He swallowed, and Taern knew he was having trouble finishing the sentence.

"Why do I have to sleep with you? Touch you? *Be* with you?"

Dorjan nodded, and with no conscious thought of what he was doing, Taern cupped his cheek. "See, Dorjan, if you'd ever had a real relationship—even one that lasted but a night—you wouldn't have to ask that. Our relationship has lasted three days. It's the longest one I've had and the only one where what we're going to do tonight when we climb into bed is not a foregone conclusion. But that doesn't make it any less real. It doesn't make me want you any less."

"I'm... I will find a reason for you to want to leave."

It sounded enough like a vow for Taern to pat his cheek with a little bit of force. "If you can't simply tell me to go away because you don't want me, any reason you find will be a lie. You're not a liar, Dorjan."

"No. I'm just a rap—"

Taern kissed him so he wouldn't say the word. Dorjan kept his mouth sullenly closed, but he didn't finish what he was about to say. "I said you weren't a liar, Nyx. Don't make a liar out of me."

Dorjan closed his eyes and nodded. Then he stepped away and adjusted himself in his tight breeches and turned to walk back to the house.

"Oi!" Taern called, drawing abreast and deciding they'd had enough of the deep quiet. "I've got a question."

"I'm deeply shocked," Dorjan replied dryly, and Taern grinned at him.

"Yes, I can tell. Anyway, I've got silver. I'm running out of clothes, and next to you I look like I'm ready for the circus anyway. What can I do to order more clothes from the git who makes your kit?"

He saw a smile flirt with the corners of Dorjan's mouth. "You ask Mrs. Wrinkle. She'll have Gustal come and fit you for as many suits as you like."

Taern glared at him. "Are you deaf, Dorjan? I said I had silver—I'm not to take your clothes like your kept man!"

Dorjan emitted an actual muted chuckle. "You allow me to buy your contract on false pretenses, sneak into my bed naked not once but twice, *steal my knife*, and force yourself into my personal life and space with the tenacity of a bog leech burrowing through a man's foot, and *you* don't want to take my generosity?" Dorjan snorted. "Too. Damned. Bad."

Taern opened his mouth to protest—he did. But they were at the back door by then, and as Dorjan opened it, they could hear Areau's piteous sobs quite clearly.

"*Please, Mistress! I only want one blow! Just one! Grab my cock, spank me... just touch me with some fucking pain!*"

Dorjan turned to him seriously. "My conveyance has furs and a fold-out bed seat," he said quietly. "If I were to fetch some pillows and some blankets, how would you like to spend the night in the stables?"

Taern couldn't even summon a cocky smile. "I think that's the most romantic offer I've ever had," he said, and he meant it, heartily, with every fiber of his soul.

Wind Changes

THE rabbit was actually a very snug place to sleep. Once the cushions were pulled out and arranged, the bed was more than big enough to sleep the two of them, and although the autumn night was chill, the furs and the blankets more than made up for the lack of a furnace. Dorjan brought paperwork from his satchel out to work on and brought Taern a book— one of the ones he'd read as a young man, full of action and adventure, a story of spacefarers in faraway stars—in case Taern wanted to read. He also brought robes and smallclothes for both of them so they would have something to wear into the house when Mrs. Wrinkle came to fetch them in the morning.

"So," Taern said as he was stripping off his "circus" clothes, shivering in the chill of the stables, "what sort of strategy meeting will you hold with Areau if he's able?"

Dorjan stripped off his suit coat and his cravat, then laid them carefully over the controller's seat. He kept his eyes aimed out the front of the vehicle and resolutely did not think of Taern naked, not even when the boy (man, wasn't he?) left his clothes in a puddle and scrambled under the blankets and furs.

"I gave you smallclothes," Dorjan said, risking a glance over his shoulder.

The horrible man grinned at him. "I'm aware."

"I *know* you must have worn smallclothes to sleep sometimes, when the weather turned bitter."

"Oh, I did," Taern agreed, still grinning.

"Then why do you refuse—"

"Because. Because the more often I sleep without smallclothes in your bed, the more likely you will roll over one night and forget all the things you shouldn't do to me and remember all the things you want to do to me."

Dorjan looked away, remembering his earlier behavior and feeling a little ill. "Has it occurred to you that this thing you are talking about is irrevocable?"

Taern looked a little surprised. "It's just sex," he said and then grimaced, as though it had occurred to him that maybe Dorjan couldn't look at it that way.

"You'd think it was," Dorjan said quietly. "I'd like to believe it was. That it can't scar a person for life because both parties profess to want it. But…." He shook his head. "What has happened to Areau—"

"Is not your fault!" Taern snapped.

"I made it worse!" Dorjan told him firmly. "I never should have given in the first time. After that…." He looked away. "It was… I didn't know what to do. We had started something by then. That first time was right after I killed my father's assassin. Both of us knew—right then, we knew—that we were not done, not by a scant mile. So we weren't done, and he knew I needed him. And if I needed him, he needed…."

Ten years. Ten years they'd been doing it, and he couldn't bring himself to say it.

"I know what he needed," Taern said, his voice hostile and brittle. "He needed you to feel like hell. You have—you paid your debt. It's time to pay in different currency, that's all."

Dorjan grimaced. Taern was young. It all seemed so cut and dried, so black and white, when you were young. He turned back to the window and kept undressing, then went to pull on his gown.

"No," Taern said, and Dorjan arched an eyebrow and pulled it on anyway.

"*Karanos!*" Taern threw himself back against the pillows in a huff. "At least take off the briefs. I've never seen anybody wear so much underwear!"

Dorjan shook his head and left the briefs on, and Taern covered his eyes with his hands and let out an exaggerated growl of frustration.

"I brought you a book," Dorjan said, walking to the side of the bed and handing Taern the little volume. "Since I'm going to be doing paperwork, I thought you'd enjoy something as well."

Taern took the book from his hand and leafed through it, looking reluctantly impressed. "What every growing boy needs," he said. "Are you going to bring me a sweet before bed and then make me brush my teeth?"

Dorjan looked at him sideways as he set up a lap desk and the forms he needed to sign. "Do you need to be coddled?"

"You didn't answer my question," Taern said. "If we actually *get* a strategy meeting, what will you tell Areau?"

Dorjan shrugged and dashed off his signature on the top paper as a matter of rote. He'd checked the "reject" box on the bill, even knowing that his signature would have no impact on the already decided vote, and simply cement his reputation as an imbecile more firmly with the Forum. In the past ten years he'd decided he'd rather be imbecilic and moral than corrupt and brilliant any given day.

"I'll tell him what I told him today. When his duties permit, please manufacture a suit of armor to meet your particular needs and give you a training regimen that will help make you ready to aid me in my endeavors."

Taern was moving his lips contemptuously, and when Dorjan looked closer, he realized the obnoxious brat was mimicking "aid me in my endeavors" with a curling lip and rolled eyes.

Dorjan picked up the sheaf of papers and smacked him on top of the head and then went back to his paperwork, wishing the lights in the conveyance were a little bit brighter or that he'd get over his silly pride and have another pair of spectacles made for reading. He was not yet thirty, but already the job of Forum Master was starting to make itself felt.

"You have a problem with that?" Dorjan asked mildly, skimming his next document, and Taern grunted.

"Only that you make running around the streets in costume like lunatics and saving the populace from evil greedy men sound about as exciting as… whatever it is you're doing, that's all."

Dorjan allowed one of his half smiles and looked warmly at Taern. "It's much more exciting than this," he said, and then the half smile turned into a grin, which he probably ruined by biting his lower lip almost shyly. He looked away. "Trust me. I'll hasten Areau along with that armor."

Taern groaned and threw his arm over his eyes. "Killing. Me. Dorjan. You're *killing* me!" Suddenly he sat up, and Dorjan made a messy blotch on his next form when Taern grabbed his thigh through his gown, rucked the gown up and put the soft skin of his hand on the almost hairless, tender part of Dorjan's upper thigh, and then curled his fingers in.

"Is it more exciting than *this*?" Taern asked, putting his lips next to Dorjan's ear and whispering.

Dorjan's whole body broke into a cold sweat, and he almost threw Taern's hand off his thigh. "I used to come home from a job and find

Areau manacled to the stable wall, naked," he said harshly, and he knew that if Taern's manhood had been feeling adventuresome, it had certainly shriveled now. "If I ever take you in the stables, Taern, I'll take my life shortly thereafter."

The words were precision clean, and Taern's next touch at the small of his back was not sexual at all.

"Please don't say things like that," he said, subdued. "I'll behave out here if you just don't think like that, yes? There's not much I wouldn't forgive you for already, Dorjan. Please, be prepared to forgive yourself for the same things?"

Dorjan didn't even look at him. "I forgive myself nothing," he said coldly. "I forgive myself less if it should result in you getting hurt."

Taern didn't move his hand from the small of Dorjan's back. In fact, he leaned his cheek against Dorjan's shoulder and moved his other hand— holding the book—in front of him, and after a moment, Dorjan could move on to his other duties.

Eventually he packed up his paperwork and made it ready in its case for the next day. He looked to his side and saw that Taern had fallen asleep with the book over his face, and he laughed a little as he took the book and a spare scrap of parchment to mark it, then placed it on top of Dorjan's soft leather satchel. He reached up and turned off the electric lamp in its sconce and lay down on his side. When he was in this position, he could watch the rise and fall of Taern's chest. That was enough to send him to a peaceful sleep.

THREE mornings later they were still sleeping in the rabbit because Areau's cries could still be heard ringing through the house. And that morning on the third day, Dorjan was not awakened by Mrs. Wrinkle's tentative tap on the outside of the rabbit or by the spring-and-gear timepiece on the dashboard of the conveyance. No, he awakened to Taern clutched tight to his chest and struggling against his embrace.

"Oh hells, Dorjan, I need to go use the necessary!"

Dorjan blinked. "You have to piss?"

"Yes!"

"Well, do it!" he muttered fuzzily. "What's stopping you?"

"You, you big lummox! You're practically choking me you're holding on so tight!"

Dorjan grunted and rolled to his side, squinting at the clock on the dashboard of the conveyance. He'd had no idea sleeping in a rabbit could grow so comfortable so quickly.

It was their third morning in the damned thing, and Bimuit take it all, he hoped it would be the last. The past three days had been an exercise in careful control.

In the morning he and Taern would awaken, dash inside to bathe and dress, grab something to eat, and then Dorjan would take Taern out to the courtyard and run through a few of the drills Areau had started him out with. Taern would accompany him on his dash to the Forum, see his routes, wave to the folks Dorjan waved to, and then promise to run back to either Madame M's or the mansion.

Dorjan had never asked, but Taern had always been there, at the small entrance between the great buildings, like the rot behind an apple's beautiful skin, as Dorjan emerged. As they dashed through the city— taking another route from any of the others—Taern would tell him about his day.

Dorjan had to give him credit. Taern did his best to make the world easier on the people around him. He talked about spelling Krissa, allowing her to go take a soak in the tub, encouraging her to go out to the courtyard and take a few turns. Apparently he had convinced Mrs. Wrinkle that it was not yet too chilly to eat outside, and they had picnicked out in the courtyard as well, watching the leaves above them turn from fuchsia to scarlet to brown, or violet to plum to black.

Dorjan had offered to spell Krissa too, but apparently he wasn't allowed in Areau's quarters. When he told Krissa he'd never been allowed in Areau's quarters, her jaw tightened and her eyes narrowed.

"He's no longer allowed in yours, either," she said, and Dorjan shrugged, blushing under her stern gaze. In the past seven-day, he had accustomed himself to the idea that there was nothing childish about her, in spite of her diminutive size and apparent fragility.

"Honestly, Lady Krissa, most of the activity you're trying to forestall occurred in the stables. You've handily removed the manacles. It certainly won't move into my bedroom without them."

Krissa sighed. They'd been having this conversation in the hallway, and she took the last step out of Areau's room and closed the door. "Forum Master, may I ask about Taern?"

Dorjan wished heartily for the days when his personal life had been just that. "Taern and I are forced to share quarters. That is all we are doing."

"At present," she said, snorting as though the climactic end to the terrible tension of having that bothersome, pesky, irksome, persistent pain in the arse was both foregone and desirable.

"I am trying to remain honorable, my lady!" Dorjan objected, his voice rising a little hysterically. It had been difficult, walking up the stairs and offering his services so that she might leave the room where Areau still sat—naked, from what Dorjan had seen—and tried to learn how to obey simple human rules of behavior.

"Honorable, Forum Master? Taern's nature functions on sort of an opposite pole, if I say so myself—"

"He's been nothing but—"

"Sneaky, irritating, and compassionate as he has always been," she interrupted. "But not honorable. He has no use for something that hurts as you have been hurt. He'll have his way with you, of that I have no doubt."

"My lady—" Dorjan protested as she was about to go back into Areau's room. "Is there nothing I can do?"

Krissa thought for a moment. "Is it true you're having Taern fit for new clothes?"

Dorjan blinked. "Yes, my lady."

"Does the tailor make women's as well?"

Dorjan laughed a little then and felt better. "No, my lady, but the city's finest dressmaker will be here before lunch tomorrow. I will give the woman your spending limit, but don't worry about it unless she does."

At that moment Areau began calling, "My lady!" through the door, and Krissa brightened.

"I'm thinking that tomorrow night, you may be able to sleep in your own room," she said happily and then turned back to the room Dorjan had begun to think of as the slough of despond, and continued to clean up his mess.

That was two days ago, and Dorjan had taken care to stop at the tailor's to secure the commission yesterday morning. Both Gustal and his recommended female counterpart should be arriving sometime the next morning. Dorjan knew that in the past two days, the young man currently struggling out of the awkward portable bed in the rabbit had escorted Mrs. Wrinkle to the marketplace twice and had run those preliminary regimens faithfully and as often as possible, if his snores by Dorjan's side at night were any indication.

And not once had he trespassed against Dorjan's request not to exceed the bounds of intimacy—as long as they were in the stables.

Taern made his laughing exit from the rabbit now, and Dorjan passed his hand over his eyes and thought he should take this opportunity to put on his robe before Taern could come back and harass him for the extent of his propriety. And he tried not to think about...

Stolen kisses. The night before, they'd been walking from the courtyard in the frigid twilight, panting slightly after exerting themselves on the equipment. Dorjan hadn't yet fired the sandbags at Taern—unlike Areau, Dorjan wanted to wait until the boy had some protection before putting him through that. But not now. Now, Dorjan felt...

Relaxed. He and Taern had set up two parallel courses and raced companionably to see who could complete the course first. Dorjan won, but it had been close, and he'd had to exert himself in the extreme. He had the feeling at the end that Taern had pulled back a little, humoring Dorjan's older body, and that made Dorjan determined to practice more. They'd rounded the alcove to the back entrance of the mansion in the middle of banter, Taern calling him old, him calling Taern inexperienced, and suddenly Taern stopped, his back against the door, and looked at Dorjan devilishly.

"So I'm inexperienced?" he asked, and Dorjan was suddenly tripping on his own tongue.

"I, you know that's not what I—"

"Because I've been very patient, my virgin prince, but I think you need a reminder of which one of us here knows which end is up!" And with that, Taern seized Dorjan by the front of his knit sweater and pulled him close for a hungry, laughing kiss.

The laughter faded and the hunger remained, and when Dorjan pulled away, shaking, Taern didn't let him get any farther than the bump of a nose or a stroke of lips along his jaw.

"Dorjan?" he whispered in Dorjan's ear, and Dorjan should have been ashamed of the whimper he made. In frustration, he seized Taern's hips and pulled him forward until they were flush and tight together, both of them engorged through their knit exercise trousers.

Taern laughed and ground back roughly. "This is what I'm talking about," he said softly.

Dorjan jerked back, away from his body, out into the silver-lit night, and stood there, panting, until he mastered the urge to touch the boy. "Taern," he said softly, trying hard to find a tone of warning, but Taern shook his head.

"Dorjan," Taern said, his grin unbreakable, "you're going to have to face that fact that Areau is getting better. In another day, he might be human enough to come out of his room. And then it will be you and me in the same bed, because that hasn't changed. And it won't," he added to forestall the useless protest Dorjan had been about to make. "And you're going to have to either articulate to yourself why you deserve us or articulate to me why you don't. Make your choice—but remember, I'm almost as quick with my tongue out of bed as I am in it."

Dorjan startled as the image. Oh, heavens… that image. After their interlude in the gymnasium, he now knew what *his* tongue could do on bare skin. He could barely tolerate the idea of what Taern's tongue could do to *him.*

"It's so unfair," he blurted suddenly into the quiet. "You… you know everything about this. All I know is when it's wrong." He sounded childish, and he hated that. Nearly thirty, wasn't he? Nearly thirty, and he could predict the delicate shifts and balances that could redeem or ruin his country just by seeing which politician had visited his mistress or his favorite brothel in the morning, and he couldn't answer a single question about what it was like to have a relationship that didn't end with abomination.

"Scratch that," he said irritably, taking another step back into the darkness. "Tomorrow night I need to venture out. The gang that was going to profit off of that sale we broke up slid back into the sewer, and there's a power vacuum. There's going to be violence tomorrow, mark my words." Excellent, a political crisis to help him put off impending adulthood—he was thrilled.

"Which gangs?" Taern asked. In spite of having lived in the stews, Dorjan had realized that Taern knew little about the gangs. Although some of them ran brothels near Madame M's, there was almost a mutual accord not to pursue violence in the brothel district. Too much bloodshed was bad for business—even fools could figure that out.

"Death Mask and The Hieters," Dorjan said, thinking that naming one's social group after something as unpleasant as a real hieter should have given those people the idea that this was a destructive life choice.

Taern blew out a breath. "What do you think is going to happen?"

Dorjan shrugged. "It's... it's a visceral thing," he said thoughtfully. "It's... it's watching the shopkeepers let their stock in front be sold to almost nothing so it's easier to pack it all up. It's watching the number of children roaming the streets diminish in number. The girls in the gangs start wearing trousers and wrapping their hair tightly in cloth to make fighting easier. The young men start sporting new tattoos or rips to prove they're able." He shuddered. The tattoos—those could have value. Some of them could be damned beautiful, if there was an artist at the needle. But the ripping? Taking a knife to an exposed strip of skin up near the shoulder and then ripping the skin down until it broke, exposing a long, shallow wound? Dorjan wanted to scream when he saw the young men doing it. Pain! Oh, Bimuit and the powers above, why would somebody choose a life of pain?

So when he started to see bloody shirtsleeves and pale men with death-rictus smiles, it was time for the armor to come out of hiding. There would be blood on the streets, and more often than not, without some intervention, most of it would be innocent.

"There is something brewing," he said to Taern, aware that he'd been quiet too long. "It won't be tonight—for one thing, the cold snap will keep them inside—but if it gets warmer tomorrow, it will be then, and if not, it will be the night after."

Taern nodded unhappily. "I shall just have to train harder," he said after gnawing on his lower lip. "I hate to think of you alone."

Dorjan shook his head, thinking that what was really unfair was how young Taern could be when he *wasn't* seducing Dorjan one determined moment at a time. "And I hate to think of you out there at all," he said grimly. "Gods... I should have tied you up and stowed you aboard one of the empty trains that night in the station."

Taern's expression grew unaccountably sober in the light from the alcove sconce. "You were in no shape to do it—that's the only reason. That alone should tell you that you need me."

Dorjan opened his mouth and closed it, then opened it and closed it again. Damn him. Damn him for being right—about all of it. Dorjan wanted to tell him he needed Taern alive more than he needed him as a brother-in-arms. He wanted to tell Taern that he needed him desperately, but he needed Taern to respect Dorjan more than he needed a lover. Dorjan wanted to tell him his weakness that night had been mental more than physical—it had just been so long since a conversation with a partner, an equal, hadn't been filled with scorpions and hieters, and he'd loved Taern's smart mouth as much when the little snipe was talking as he did when....

Dorjan didn't finish that thought. Didn't finish any of them. He simply brushed by Taern and opened the door without preliminary, and the two of them listened for Areau's weakened and hoarse groans. Some of them sounded satisfied, and Dorjan wondered listlessly if Krissa and Taern had been right and Areau really was getting better.

Most of him wondered if the course of his relationship with Taern was going to be dictated, in one way or the other, because he could not say what needed to be said. Or, at least, he couldn't say it with enough venom to get the boy to see why Dorjan was the last person he should squander his energy on.

That had been the night before. What he recognized this morning, as he quickly donned his robe and slippers, was that the first night, he'd woken up huddled in a tight little ball on the side of the rabbit, his hand clutching convulsively for something that wasn't there.

The second night, it *had* been there, in a cunning little box that wouldn't open if Dorjan just grabbed blindly at it but would open *instantly* with the slightest pressure from his fingers in an obscure place under the lid. It was easily felt but *very* difficult to open by accident, and Dorjan had been moved and relieved when Taern had presented it to him as they ate their dinner at the small table in the stables their second night hiding from Areau's recovery. The second morning Dorjan had awakened still tight in the corner and clutching the knife box to his chest.

But this third morning... this third morning he'd been clutching neither the pillow nor the knife. This third morning he'd been clutching Taern, and clutching him so tightly he could barely breathe.

"What are you brooding about now?" Taern asked as he hopped back into the rabbit through the smaller door by the head. "You look downright thunderous!"

Dorjan shook his head. "If I agreed to pursue a relationship," he blurted before he knew which way his mouth was heading, "would you agree to not venture into the street with me?"

Taern crossed his eyes and stuck out his tongue. "Dorjan, when we get home this evening, it might be quiet in that house. We might have dinner with one perfectly nice person and one almost human being. After that, you will go up to your own armoire to change, and I'll follow you up, and if I'm good, I'll get your trousers around your ankles as you're changing, pull out your instrument, and blow on it until it fountains joy. If I do all that, is that going to keep you from donning your armor and venturing out into harm's way?"

Dorjan swallowed and shifted his hips miserably. "Oh, fuck a rabid hieter, Taern," he snapped. "Must you?"

Taern was never going to apologize—his fierce look straight at Dorjan's swollen groin proved that. "Yes," Taern said, then grabbed his own crotch and thrust straight into his hand. "Yes, I must. Because you're talking about fucking rabid swamp lizards, and I'm telling you I just might if you make me wait much longer. And I'm telling you that the *only* thing keeping me on my best behavior is that promise of armor you've made Areau make. Krissa said he'll work on that and the cure for dust and nothing else in the next week. Besides that, I think I smell desperation rolling off of you, and you may very well cave to my prurient desires before my cock shrivels up and falls off in frustration."

Dorjan looked away, knowing he was sweating a little with the implications. "Well, let's see if I survive tonight," he said, thinking of some way of avoiding this conversation *right now*. He had to go back into the Forum and once again feign idiocy, and considering the fact that no amount of asking guilelessly, "If our enemy got this napalm from us, why didn't we report it stolen?" was making anybody more eager to face the truth, the Forum charade was less and less attractive. He'd tried to raise a widows-and-orphans fund for the families of the fallen and had been told that they didn't have resources to feed their *live* soldiers, and his proposal hadn't even made it to the floor. It was just as well—he'd had Coreau set aside some of the many resources he failed to report every season and send them to Dre's hold. Dre's widow had assured him in correspondence that she would see the food, silver, and lumium was given to the people whose husbands, sons, wives, and daughters had been lost when Stratego Dre led his unit into a trap set by his own corrupt government.

Given that, death on the streets was beginning to sound damned attractive.

But not to Taern. "Don't even say things like that," he snapped, and Dorjan shrugged.

"I'll say things like that until going out into the streets with me or sleeping with me seem like less attractive ideas," he said stubbornly. "And if or when I get home tonight, maybe I can... I can penetrate that thick head of yours!"

Taern was clutching a robe to him against the bitter cold of outside, and suddenly he opened it. Dorjan gasped because his cock—which was not quite as long as Dorjan's but almost as thick—was fully erect, and the head was shiny with slick fluid.

"Nnngghh." Dorjan couldn't keep his eyes off of it.

"Why do you think it took me so long to pee," Taern asked, out of temper. He wrapped his hand around it at the base and squeezed, shuddering, and Dorjan watched when his thigh muscles shook as he attempted to remain standing.

Dorjan whimpered and looked at that fine, toned body, open for him, with a mixture of starvation and revulsion. "Not in here," he managed to whisper, not wanting Taern's body or his soul or any of him tainted by the things he and Areau had done not ten paces away, outside the conveyance, in the corner by the door, where the manacles used to hang.

Taern shuddered hard and pulled the sides of his robe together. "How long are you going to make me do this dance, Nyx?" he asked, and Dorjan knew his expression was bitter and couldn't help it.

"A seven-day? That's all you've known me?" Dorjan sneered. "Areau's carried his scars for ten years, and I've carried our sins for most of that same span. Tell me when a man can wash that out of his soul, Taern, and I'll tell you how long we shall dance."

It was a pathetic attempt to build a void around himself, to keep Taern and the dazzling promise of intimacy he offered at a distance, but for a moment, it felt like it worked. He gathered his leather satchel for work and set his feet in his slippers and tightened up his robe with unnecessary force.

"I'll go inside first," he said, his voice kinder now that he felt girded. "If he's not quiet, I'll go fetch your running kit and bring it down after I change."

Taern sighed. "Right, Nyx, fine. If running by your side is as close as I'm allowed to get, then so be it."

"Imagine the fine young man who would fill the void when all your attention is no longer squandered on me," Dorjan said and knew it for an awful attempt at levity even as he uttered the words.

"No time with you is squandered," Taern told him firmly, but his face was turned away. "Even when you pay for it with blood and pieces of your heart." He dashed the back of his hand under his eyes and Dorjan realized that... oh no.

"See!" he cried, panicked, with his hand on the door. "This—this is why you shouldn't waste—"

"Just go!" Taern snarled, his voice thick. "It's a wound, Dorjan, and not a mortal one. Let me tend to it, since you refuse to, and I'll be up for the battle again."

"I'm sorry," Dorjan muttered, but he meant it. "I'm sorry I can wound you with words." And then he couldn't stand the rabbit or himself anymore. "I'll send Mrs. Wrinkle if it's not horrible inside."

He didn't wait for a reply, but then, he didn't expect one either.

BESIDES being liberating, there was something almost... mystical about that run together through the back alleys of the city. They both wore stocking caps on their heads, and although the caps didn't hide their faces, the black clothes, caps, and silent boots made them feel almost invisible.

People dodged them and walked around them, certainly, but nobody ever called out to them and nobody threatened them. There were plenty of thugs walking around with blood dripping down their arms from their latest tattoos or their latest rips, but none of them snarled at Taern, for instance, when he went rebounding off the side of a building to avoid a vendor's cart and then leapt over a Hieter's bald head. Nobody called out to Dorjan when he brought Taern up and over the tin-roofed shotgun apartments that made up the spaces of the alleyway, and nobody tried to stop them from scaling the smaller buildings and running along roofs to save time. Dorjan took a different route through the stews every day. He should have been as strange to the people on the streets of Thenis as they were to him, but in the same way he recognized which shopkeepers were still in business and saw the ebb and flow of families moving in, moving out, being pressed to service, disappearing, resurfacing in worse circumstances still, somehow the people of Thenis came to recognize that the young master and now his friend, were simply part of the ebb and flow of the streets.

It comforted him as he and Taern leapt, ran, and dodged the crowded thoroughfares that were now too crammed with people and detritus to let the monorails run. As far as he knew, nobody had put together the idea of the Forum Master who was too stupid to abuse his job and the darkly dressed young man who pattered through the city streets nearly every day. He liked it that way. The fewer people who put that together, the less likely anyone would ever look at him and see the Nyx.

And that run through the city was... exhilarating. Leap, dodge, spin, flip—every step, every turn was an adventure in finding the quickest, most efficient way through a landscape that refused to sit still. Although Dorjan hadn't thought of it before Taern accompanied him, this time in the morning or afternoon, when he wasn't wearing his armor but was allowed to run—that was the time he felt most free.

That didn't change with Taern at his side. It was, instead, intensified: every moment Taern spent leaping into the air or running up the side of a building was a moment Dorjan was unfettered by gravity as well. Watching the boy was a pleasure, and running with him, knowing that when Dorjan vaulted the gaping hole in the sidewalk, Taern was behind him, finding his own way over or around—it was better than having wings.

It occurred to Dorjan that having the boy there while they were both masked, both of them moving without fear, both of them ready to execute violence if it were so needed—

He dropped to his knees and tumbled backward as a cart suddenly crossed his path and he had no room to slow his momentum and not enough momentum to leap the cart. As he was somersaulting backward, Taern executed a dive roll both over his tumbling body *and* over the cart, landed on the other side, and looked at him with triumph on his face.

Dorjan couldn't help but laugh back.

He picked himself up and trotted around the cart, then joined Taern again, thinking that having company on the streets at night might not be the worst thing ever to happen to him.

They came to a stop in an alley about two blocks from that dismal entrance, and Dorjan turned to him, grinning. "Great move," he praised, still excited from watching Taern's grace and fluid body. "I love how you—mmm...."

Taern seized his shirt in both hands and hauled him down for a hard, breathless kiss. Dorjan melted, thrusting his hand up into Taern's thick, curly hair and tugging so Taern's head would tip back and Dorjan could have better access. Ah... oh yes... warmth and excitement and laughter and...

Oh... Bimuit. Arousal. Dorjan wanted so badly. He bent and cupped Taern's tight bottom in his hands and hauled up. Taern took the hint and hopped, then wrapped his legs around Dorjan's hips and ground them together hard enough to make Dorjan break off and gasp.

"Ah...." Taern moaned. "This is a really bad time for this!" Then he pulled Dorjan's head down for another kiss.

Dorjan kept tasting, kept plundering, until Taern bucked up against him and howled into his mouth, shuddering and trembling and shaking, and Dorjan was shocked, appalled, and so aroused he almost couldn't breathe when he realized there was a spreading wetness and warmth against his crotch from Taern's climax.

Dorjan groaned and whimpered, and Taern stayed up in his arms, wrapped around him, for a moment, resting his head on Dorjan's shoulder.

"Oh Nyx," he said softly, almost tearfully. "What are you doing to me?"

Dorjan groaned again, and Taern slid down and thrust his hand down Dorjan's trousers to pull the front just low enough for his cock to stick out into the open air. Dorjan felt that clever hand wrap around him and squeeze and jerk, once, twice, three times, and then he buried his face in Taern's neck while Taern stepped aside to let his spend arch whitely through the air and spatter on the brick wall behind him.

Dorjan couldn't take his face from the hollow of Taern's neck and shoulder. Taern smelled like sweat and the coffee they'd had at breakfast and like... like sex, which Dorjan could smell even above the fetid morning stench of the alleyway. Taern's hand was gentle on the tender skin of his cock, even though his newly formed blisters caught a little when he tucked Dorjan back into his trousers.

"Bimuit!" Dorjan wanted a stronger word. He wanted a universal power to apply to, because the founder of his province did not seem big enough to give his blessing or curse to the painful drug thundering through Dorjan's veins right now.

The summoning bells permeated his thoughts, and he straightened reluctantly, pausing for a brief kiss on Taern's cheek. Taern closed his eyes as Dorjan touched his lips, though, and Dorjan needed to make that right. He shifted, captured Taern's lips briefly, and Taern answered him. Dorjan pulled back before it became too heated, and leaned his forehead against Taern's while they caught their breath.

"You're late," Taern whispered, and Dorjan nodded.

"I am aware."

"You were going to let me go."

"It's what I said, yes."

"Can you really do that?"

"Hells, Taern, I can barely stop kissing you."

Taern nodded, their tiny alleyway closing in on them, becoming womb-like, dark and close in the heart of the bustling city morning. "I won't push you," Taern whispered. "I won't. But you gave me hope today. Don't take it back, Nyx. You're afraid of being a cruel man—the cruelest thing would be to take that back."

Dorjan made a sound then, something sad and hurt he couldn't believe he let escape. He pressed a brief kiss on Taern's full mouth and backed away.

"You'll be here at the end of the day?" he asked, hating that he sounded needy, hating that he sounded uncertain, but unable to change it or fix it or even address it with those damning bells still ringing from the courtyard but a sprint and a leap away.

"Have I let you down yet?" Taern asked, that surprising dignity surrounding his body like a brightening aura.

"Not once," Dorjan told him truly and then turned and sprinted for the entrance to the courtyard, vaulted to the tin roof of the corridor in one smooth leap, and ran with steps that felt impossibly long.

SEPTRA was apparently feeling the pressure for resources, and Dorjan didn't blame him. There had been food riots in the rural areas, as the military had come and confiscated harvests from farmers who were working their land with their children and their pensioners, since their hale and hearty workers had been pressed into service. The Triari needed to start farming his land instead of ravaging it, but that was not where Septra was looking to solve his problems.

"Really, Dorjan," Septra cajoled, "what is one or two more shipments of lumium, or even gold—"

"When weighed against the lives of citizens who have never lifted a finger to hurt us? Nothing, Triari. Nothing at all. I'm glad you agree, completely unnecessary to increase the mining. Now if you'll excuse me, I've got a meeting about the widows-and-orphans fund—"

"Did we not decide—"

"Well, yes, Triari. But what is a Forum Master's new conveyance or summer home when meted against the families who have sacrificed for their province?"

Septra smiled indulgently and patted his cheek. "Such a good-hearted boy," he said. "Your father would be proud."

Dorjan smiled back with as many teeth as he could show at one time. "You have no idea," he said and then turned around, wishing he could look behind him and see if Septra was afraid yet.

He should be.

THAT night, Taern was there to meet him in their pickup spot, but he didn't greet Dorjan with a kiss, and Dorjan didn't blame him. The pressure on the streets was palpable, and the two of them didn't showboat as they pelted, as fast as their soft-booted feet would allow, back through the streets. It seemed like no time before they arrived at Dorjan's sweet neighborhood with the great houses and the manicured lawns and shrubs and the hectare-sized courtyards in the back. They were truly invisible in their black, unadorned with blood or open weapons, and Dorjan headed straight for the stables, where he started stripping without a word in front of the armor cabinet.

"No dinner?" Taern said, sounding strained, and Dorjan shook his head, reaching for the armor practically before the satchel with his robes and paperwork hit the ground.

"Did you feel the temperature?" he asked, struggling to take his left boot off so he could put the armor on. Taern trotted over in front of him and yanked at the boot without saying anything. "The rain isn't going to break until later. That's wonderful. It can wash away the blood."

Taern pulled the boot off with a pop and went to work on the other one. "Hold just a moment when you get it on," he said quietly. "I know you'll bring your satchel—you can put a sandwich in it."

Dorjan looked at him, condescension in his eyes, and Taern snapped at him.

"No, a sandwich isn't going to save the fucking city, Dorjan, but it could give you energy when you need it. I'm looking after you, don't laugh at me."

Dorjan relented then. "It takes me a minute anyway," he said, nodding. "Go. I can wait."

He was, in fact, still struggling with the catch on the side of his healing ribs when he heard Taern come back.

"How is the household?" Dorjan asked without glancing up. "I forgot to ask."

"Much improved," said Areau dryly, and Dorjan looked up. He knew his expression was half-hesitant, half-hopeful, but he didn't seem to be able to school it to his usual expression of complete neutrality.

"Master Areau," Dorjan said, inclining his head. "I trust you're feeling better."

Areau's hair was clean and queued back from his eyes, and his suit was new, pressed, and buttoned impeccably. When they'd been children, Areau had always been so beautiful. He'd known he was beautiful, and Dorjan had paid for him to have the best suits, the trendiest clothes—straight from Gretzky province, which specialized in those things—so his friend could be the prettiest one.

It was that young man, the beautiful, charming companion he had loved, both platonically and, for a while, romantically, who stood before him at this moment, and Dorjan was uncertain whether or not to trust that vision at all.

Areau inclined his head. "I am, thank you," he said, and then his face darkened. "It's like dust, though, Dori. That craving—I shall always have it, and sometimes I shall need it indulged." Areau flushed and looked around the stables and then at Dorjan in his armor. "But not by you," he said formally.

Dorjan shook his head rapidly, nervously. "Good," he said, meaning it. He took a step or two forward and offered Areau an awkward embrace. "It's good to see you looking happier, Ari," he said into Areau's ear, and then he stepped back, his flesh still shrinking from the taste of Areau's like a slug would shrink from the sea.

Areau gave a partial bow. "Lady Krissa said I was not to stay too long," he said by way of apology, and he turned around and brushed past Taern, who stood near the stable door with a paper-wrapped sandwich in his hand.

"I shall be working on your armor tomorrow, Taern," Areau said with something approaching civility. "I do hope you can forgive me the delay."

"If he comes back in one piece tonight, I'll think about it," Taern muttered, and Dorjan grimaced.

Areau turned and looked at Dorjan, seeming to see him from his distracted air of inner serenity for the first time. "It will be dangerous in the streets tonight?" he asked, and Dorjan shrugged.

"As it ever is."

"Take care, Dori," he said, his low voice graced with concern since the first time in... Dorjan didn't want to think about it.

He gave another incline to his head. "As I ever am, Ari"—and on that note, Areau nodded thoughtfully and left.

Taern huffed and walked up with the sandwich, shaking his head.

"I'm not buying," he muttered, finding Dorjan's smaller satchel and putting the sandwich in it, as well as a small flask of what Dorjan hoped was water.

"He seems much improved," Dorjan said cautiously, and Taern shook his head.

"I don't give a hexashite," he said bluntly. "He could be as sane as Bimuit and Karanos on their best days, and I'd still hate his guts until his entrails boiled."

Dorjan grimaced and struggled with the catch, wishing twisting were not quite so difficult.

Taern walked over to his side and clicked the armor together in two deft moments of his fingers and then picked up the gauntlet. "Here, give me your hand."

"Can you *not* complain about Areau as you're helping me?" Dorjan asked, mostly seriously.

Taern grunted. "I still think it's a load of shite. Yes, I think Krissa groomed his pubes until he likes the way they lay, but... he still hates you.

He still wants his revenge for the shite-dump his life has become, and he wants it from your skin. I won't trust him until he stops looking at you like he'd like to dissect you like a hieter on a student's table."

Dorjan grunted. "I take it that's a no, you can't not complain about Areau," he muttered and went to pick up the other gauntlet.

Taern took it from him and held it out so Dorjan could put it on. "I'm fighting your entire childhood whenever I look at him," Taern muttered. "Not to mention the last ten years of suffering he's put you—"

"I think we did it to each other," Dorjan sighed, flexing his fingers to make sure the gauntlet was tight enough. "There's no denying that."

Taern grunted. "Give me some time out of this wretched stable, and I will tell you, in detail, why deny it you should. But in the meantime, here—your greaves aren't hooked yet, and they're attached to the groin plate, and I think we need to make sure that whole area is put together right so you get a chance to use it as it's intended to be used."

Dorjan laughed a little and took his help gratefully. He was just about to slip on his black knitted mask when Taern stopped him.

"Not before a kiss for luck, Nyx," he said soberly, and Taern's lips on his were an unhurried, sweet miracle in a night that crackled with tension and violence.

Dorjan smiled as he pulled back. "You have nothing to fear from my memories of Areau," he said quietly, thinking he should give Taern something before he ventured out into the night without him. "Were it not for the... the perversion that followed our grief, he would have been a crush, nothing more."

A wholly adult look crossed Taern's face as Dorjan pulled the knitted mask over his head. "You are so very young," he said gruffly, patting Dorjan's cheek.

Dorjan was stung. He pulled on the metal mask, with the great bug eyes and the shape like a diamond with the bottom point cut off. "I am over ten years your—"

"Not that way," Taern snapped. "I've taken the virginity of men who had done more than you." He took a deep breath. "It would be a real shame if you died on the streets before we had a chance to fix that. Do me a favor, Nyx, and come back to me tonight, do you hear?"

Dorjan nodded soberly. "I'll do that, Taern. You do me a favor and think of what you want me to call you once you have your armor. If I'm

Nyx, you must find a name that suits you. I won't be calling your real name when we're on the streets together."

Taern shook him off, which was too bad. Dorjan hoped that subject, at least, would have distracted him. "You can call me Prick Face, Nyx, as long as you come back. Now go. Stop trying to cheer me up and get out there and do your job."

"Yes, sir," Dorjan said, grinning past his mask. He wanted to touch Taern's face or pull him in for a kiss or let slip some of the tenderness he had welling up in his breast. But he couldn't, and he'd been there entirely too long. "I'll see you at breakfast," he said, heading for the door.

"You'll see me in here," Taern snapped. "As Karanos is my witness, you will not bandage your own wounds, Dorjan. Now go."

Dorjan had no choice.

Flight

TAERN stalked back and forth in front of the doorway of Areau's basement workshop. He was not allowed in—Krissa was the one who laid down that edict, or he would be right in there, right over the bastard's shoulder, urging him on with every fucking breath.

"I can hear you out there!" Areau shouted. "Hear you! Hear you muttering! Hear you cursing! Go the fuck away! Give me a fucking hour to do my job! I've got asteroid dust in here, you ass-fucking rabbit—let's see how you like a lungful!"

Krissa sat patiently in a new gown, doing some sort of complicated needlepoint thing right there in the hallway, and she looked up, some of the strain of the past days showing in the shadows under her eyes. "Come along, Taern. Let's take a turn around the courtyard, shall we?"

"I've taken turns in the courtyard," he snarled. "Several."

Krissa jerked back, and he felt like hexashite. The past three days hadn't been easier on her.

"Forgive me," he said, swallowing. "Please, forgive me. Let's go steal an apple from Mrs. Wrinkle, shall we?"

Krissa nodded and smiled, obviously relieved, and stood up. She set her needlework down on the cushion and grasped Taern's hand as they walked up the stairs in the back of the house to the kitchen.

Mrs. Wrinkle was in there, cutting up autumn apples and crying. She didn't make any sound, but her shoulders shook, and the paring knife wobbled as she cut an unbroken strip from the skin of the fruit. Taern let go of Krissa's hand and took the apple from her before she cut herself.

"I think Krissa and I need to pull our weight," he said stoutly. "How many bushels do you need skinned?"

Mrs. Wrinkle wiped her eyes on her shoulder and shook her head. "Just the few there," she said. For a moment she looked indecisive, and then her jaw firmed with resolution. "I know Master Areau's down there making you some armor," she said lowly after a moment. "When? When can you go help him come home?"

The stews had turned into battle zone, and the Nyx was everybody's enemy. Dorjan hadn't come home that first morning. Dorjan hadn't been home in three days.

The first morning Taern had fallen asleep in the rabbit, covered in furs. He'd awakened with a start, aware that it was past Dorjan's usual sleeping time, and rushed out to see if he'd arrived and Taern had slept through it.

No armor in the closet, no Dorjan in the bed. Just a faint roaring from far away, like a thunderous ocean pounding on the crumbling concrete streets of Thenis.

Taern had torn inside to get dressed to go out to find him. He'd been upstairs, putting on his running kit, when Mrs. Wrinkle had opened the door and two girls barely in their teen years had entered, shaking and tearful. Krissa greeted them, and Taern recognized them too. They were daughters of two of the serving women who worked at Madame M's. They both had satchels over their shoulders, and as soon as they saw Taern running down the stairs, they handed him a small envelope with Madame M's simple flower sigil stamped in scarlet wax on the back.

Taern broke the seal and pulled out the missive, painfully aware that his lungs were blazing with held breath and his hand was shaking almost too hard to hold the page. Krissa's hand closed gently over the back of his, and he focused. This sort of hysteria did nobody any good.

Taern,

I trust you and Krissa are doing well—would it kill you to visit, you horrid brat? I do miss you. A mutual friend of ours spent an hour or two sleeping on the couch in our basement room. I worried over the girls in the city during the riot, and he worried about his household. He agreed to escort the girls to safety if they would deliver a message for him. He promised they could spend the remainder of the riot safe with you, and the house is much grateful to him. He said to tell you not to worry, and to wish the others in the household well. When I asked him if he had something in particular he wished for you to know, he said, "Yes, but as with so many things, I have no words. Tell him I have every intention of returning. Tell him"—He paused quite some time here, my boy; what have you been doing to tie this boy up in knots?—"Tell him he's a reason to return."

Now I'd say that's *high praise. Tell Krissa I miss her, and it wouldn't kill her to write back—but not right now. The streets are dangerous. Stay safe, my lovelies.*

Madame M.

Taern read the letter twice and then sat down abruptly on the stairs. He looked up at the girls—Evvy and Alla—and tried to gather his thoughts.

"These riots," he said after a moment of trying desperately to think like Dorjan. "Tell me about them."

Dorjan's feeling of trouble on the streets had been dead on—the two gangs had started a showdown on the fringe of the stews, near the river, and according to what the girls knew, it had seemed like the usual. Nyx had been there, keeping civilians inside, keeping the violence away from the doors of the innocent, kicking the people who wanted to kill each other back into the central playing field when they strayed.

Taern was aware that this happened three or four times in the course of a year, and that he was lucky. As Dorjan said, the violence very rarely escalated to the brothel district—just like a barn animal didn't like to shit where it ate, even the lowest man on the street didn't want to bleed where he fucked.

But in the past, the vestigial military that served as law enforcement had left the gang justice alone.

"What would compel them to interfere *now*?" Krissa asked when the girls had finished their story.

Taern shook his head, having his suspicions based on what Dorjan had told him, and looked at Evvy and Alla. "Would you two like to go eat? I'm sure Mrs. Wrinkle hasn't tended to little girls in quite some time."

The girls smiled tentatively. Evvy was a big blonde girl with wide blue eyes. She was smart enough to survive on the streets, but there was something… untouched about her, in spite of where her mother worked. Madame M made sure the servants' children stayed far away from the true business of the brothel, but she was also willing to let them help their parents. It was difficult to find a safe place for children on the streets— Madame M tried to make one, as much as it was possible in a whorehouse in the slums.

Evvy's companion, Alla, was tiny and quick, with caramel skin and dark hair, and if Taern wasn't very much mistaken, she was a year or two older than Evvy.

"Alla," he said quietly as they turned to follow Krissa. He knew the girl would remember the times he'd snuck down to the kitchens to play jacks with them. "How far did the Nyx escort the two of you?"

Alla thought a bit. "There were patrols on the edge of the stews—even some of the safer neighborhoods were locked into the pit of it. He took us to where we could see the great cemetery, the one with all of the Forum Masters, before he turned away."

Taern grunted as though struck in the stomach. "Why... did he say why he didn't come farther?" he asked, and Evvy made a hurt sound.

Alla grabbed her hand. "There was... there was a gang of men raiding a house—looked like just a regular house, but there were screams from inside. Nyx picked both of us up and ran until we were safe," she said, and then her voice dropped. "But I think he went back to help those people. They... you could hear their screams really loud."

Taern nodded his head then and watched as Krissa disappeared down the hallway toward the kitchens with them before he pounded up the stairs and hammered on Areau's door.

"What in the fucking he—"

Taern grabbed him by the front of the tunic and bore him back against the wall. "Not another word. We sat patient while you mewled like a fucking kitten and hauled the whole lot of us down into the cesspool in your head. Well, you're out of it now, and *he's* outside, trying to save the city from a fucking riot while the goddamned soldiers have a hazard zone marked to make the place like a pressure cooker, you understand?"

Areau blinked hard, but suddenly the petulant expression on his face sharpened, and Taern could see the young military student he'd once been. "What do you mean, pressure cooker?"

"*Nobody* can get out. Not the innocent, not the frightened. They're locked in there by curfew, and the military"—Taern shuddered hard—"the girls say they're the worst of the lot. The criminals, the ones pressed to service and full of hate. They're equipped with steam spears, you hear me? They're killing anyone who tries to get away."

Areau shuddered. "He's still there?"

Taern closed his eyes and released him, taking a step back. "He brought two friends of mine within eight blocks of home."

"He *what*?" Areau roared. "That selfish, self-righteous, presumptive *git*! What did he do after that? Go save some child's kitten? Go redistribute the wealth of the whole quarter? Bring all the junkies soup? What was so *bloody important* that he had to go running back into that bloody hieterfuck of violence!"

Taern opened his eyes and looked squarely at Areau. "The same thing he's been doing for ten years. And I'd be happy to help him, but I'm not a martyr. I need some *fucking armor*, and that means you need to be functional for more than five minutes at a stretch. Do you think you can master it, Areau, or do I need to go knock some soldier over the head?"

"Their armor is hexashite!" Areau snapped. "I came up with the design ten years ago, and it's a child's toy compared to what he's wearing right now!"

"Then *you* need to come up with something better so I can save his arse, now don't you?" Taern snarled, and Areau bared his teeth.

"Someday, you snotty little prat, this isn't going to be about him. It's going to be about you and me, and then there'll be a reckoning," Areau hissed. "Now get out of my way so I can make your bloody armor!"

That was three days ago. From what Taern could see, the people in the gentry section were pretending it wasn't happening. The dressmaker and the tailor had shown up not too long after Evvy and Alla, and although the joy had gone out of it for both of them, Krissa and Taern had both ordered clothing. Krissa had ordered a dress for each of the girls, much to their excitement, and Taern was pretty sure Dorjan wouldn't mind. Besides, hearing them excited, picking out ribbons and pretty cotton prints and eyelet trim? That was something that kept spirits up, and Taern and Krissa desperately needed that.

The market had stayed open, though Taern escorted Mrs. Wrinkle in the morning and they wrapped up their business as quickly as possible. Taern could make out shouts and screams and weeping, individual sounds that made up the general roar, but nobody in the better quarters said anything. They didn't make eye contact with each other, but they didn't say anything either.

Taern seethed and decided that very few people in general deserved saving, until he felt Mrs. Wrinkle clutching at his sleeve and remembered himself. People were afraid. That was no reason to condemn them to die in their own violence like a goldfish died in shit.

And Areau had worked obsessively, night and day, in his cluttered, oddly beautiful workshop, so Taern couldn't even be angry with *him*, as much as he'd like to.

He'd spent the past two nights sleeping naked in Dorjan's bed, clutching the knife box obsessively like a stuffed toy and feeling oddly out of sync. If he wasn't working at Madame M's, if he wasn't challenging Dorjan, if he wasn't joining the Nyx on the streets, who was he?

Apparently he was the man who cheered up the children, supervised Areau when Krissa was losing her mind, and kept Mrs. Wrinkle company when she claimed she'd been a solitary worker most of the time before and there was no reason for her not to work alone now.

In a very short time, he'd managed to make himself at home here in Dorjan's home, and it galled him that he was doing such a smashing job of it when *Dorjan wasn't there.*

Bimuit, Karanos, Gretzky, and sons—he wanted his Nyx home!

But until this moment, late in the afternoon of the third day, he had managed to keep his anxiety contained (if not exactly to himself) and not let it spill crazy into Areau's overflowing vault of it.

Areau had worked—Taern had to give him that. His workshop was an odd place. There was the eclectic mix of beakers, bubbling experiments, distillation glasswork, and general miasma on one table; and gears, springs, tiny weapons, and diagrams on the other. Taern had pretty much expected to see those things—they were mad-scientist staples, and Areau was nothing if not as crazy as a hieterbird. What Taern had not been prepared for was the fey and lovely hanging sculptures Areau had crafted out of extruded nylon wire and spare parts. He must have spent hours on them, standing on a ladder, pinning each wire to the vaulted ceiling, following it down, deciding which gear to put at the end of it, at what length. The results were ever-shifting mobiles that actually hung in distinct shapes—a jointed man much like the Nyx, a double helix, and a curling, crashing wave. The sculptures were large—as long as a man, with a width almost as great—but they were kept shallow, perhaps two layers of tiny gears and metal parts. They hung about chest high for someone like Areau, so that, were you tall enough to pass through them, they parted like a curtain.

The sound they made when a breeze hit them, a sort of tinkling, delicate shatter, was what Taern had imagined a nisket's laughter sounded like, when he had been very young. Now that he was older and knew they were real, the impression was much the same.

It was harder to fume and rage at Areau when he worked in a place with such beautiful craftings to his credit, but that didn't mean Taern didn't feel like he was coming apart at the joins.

He looked at Mrs. Wrinkle, crying softly, trying to hold the little household together with pie, and realized he didn't have the luxury of coming apart.

"Yes," he said, meaning every word of it. "I'm going to go bring him home."

STRONG words, when he was waiting on someone else's labor to make them happen.

He was in the middle of his final pass along the courtyard obstacle course in the lengthening shadows of the autumn afternoon when Krissa came hurrying out after him.

"It's done, Taern. It's done. It looks sound—I tried it on myself. Come see."

Taern was in the middle of running backward on top of the spinning barrel, and he stopped running and let the barrel throw him off. He used the momentum to take a diving leap onto the padding beneath the barrel, did a roll, and came up to his feet quickly. He didn't waste breath or words asking Krissa questions but followed her back inside.

Areau was in the workshop, tinkering with some part of it, but he stepped back when Taern entered the room.

"You're wearing the knit smallclothes?" he asked quickly, but it didn't warrant asking. Taern had worn nothing else unless he was escorting Mrs. Wrinkle to the market, because he spent most of his time running the obstacle course in order to keep himself sane.

Without bothering to answer, Taern started sliding on the armor, testing the joins at his knees, elbows, shoulders, thighs, and core very carefully. The armor was wonderful stuff—supple, soundless, fluid in movement, damned near impenetrable—but it was not bare skin. Areau held out a gauntlet and Taern slid his hand in, listening as Areau explained the bells and whistles.

"If you fling your hands out like so"—he demonstrated, throwing his hands out to the side—"your main knives will slide forward off your forearms. Dorjan has a spare blade coming out of his gauntlet, but yours are smaller. No room for the curved blade, so I added the tiny throwing stars instead. You have a grappling hook at your belt and a pocket full of smoke tablets. Watch out—the white ones make smoke, the red make flame, and the green ones make a sleeping gas that will work on you as well. There's a long knife at your waist and a shorter one at each ankle. If you throw your hands out like this, tiny spikes will come up from your gauntlets. They're not for battle but to help you scale walls. I have a satchel for you—it has first aid supplies and a sort of astringent. If you get dust or anything questionable on your skin, wash it off immediately, and it should reduce risk of contamination. If you get injured, or if he is injured and bleeding, dump it in the wound and it will prevent infection. You move faster than Dorjan—I made your helmet smaller and sleeker, and your armor is not quite as thick—"

"What's this roll at the neck?" Taern asked impatiently, tugging at it because it was extra bulk.

"I was getting to that. If you need it, it's a cloak—use it to hide, use it as a weapon, they're surprisingly helpful. Feel free to exploit it."

Taern nodded and looked down, surprised to find himself outfitted and ready to hit the streets just that quickly.

He looked at Areau and bowed shortly. "Thank you for this," he said, meaning it. "This… this puts paid to many things."

He did not care for the look he got in return, but he couldn't deny the armor was a gift. He looked at Krissa, who gave him a quick hug, armor or no. "Be careful," she muttered. "Bring him home."

"Tell Mrs. Wrinkle I shall do my best," Taern said. And then he grinned as he pulled his black cap and facemask over his head, followed by the sleek helmet, with the goggles that went over to protect the eyes. "And tell her I'm taking some of those apple tarts. I'll bet he hasn't eaten in three days."

And with that he ran out, hitting the kitchen first and then going through the side door to the stables. From the stables he slipped into the shadows and began sprinting with all his speed to the source of the ocean roar, of the smoke, of terrible noises of screaming, destruction, and death.

SLIDING past the guard was sickeningly easy. They all stood with their backs to the good quarter, intent on keeping people locked inside the violence instead. The guards in their bulky urban armor didn't see him, which was good, but after that he was almost at a loss.

They had gone running for three days—only enough time for Taern to see six routes through a city with a thousand of them. He ran one of the ways familiar to him, but he was running for a specific place. He figured he'd go to the place Nyx had last been seen.

The streets were labyrinthine and eerie. Through some blocks, there was nothing, not a sound, not a peep, just trash—broken furniture, strewn clothes, the sad and rare child's toy. Taern ran full-out through those places, not even wanting to imagine the tension of being a family in one of the silent houses, tucked into the basement, shivering with fear, praying it was over. Taern rounded the corner from one such block and almost ran straight into an epic rumble—mostly men, fighting so hard they didn't bother to shout. There were grunts, the thuds of flesh on flesh, the occasional roar of exertion as someone launched a kill-or-die effort. Taern stumbled back as he watched a fist hit a mouth and explode in a cloud of teeth and blood from a distance of not two arm's lengths away.

He found the shadows then and scrambled—the tops of trash cans, fire escapes, window ledges. He cleared the rumble and realized he was three blocks from Madame M's. Good—a fair place to start. If anyone knew where Nyx was, she would.

He slipped in through the basement window, which was harder in his armor than it had been when he simply hadn't wanted to face anybody coming through the foyer, but he made it. As soon as he landed, he took off his mask, because most of the people here knew how to use a knife too. He took a brief, hopeful look around the basement room and saw the scattering of furniture on top of Madame M's oldest rug, the racks keeping the liquor, the cabinets that held the extra clean linens, and the hampers with the dirty ones.

One of the hampers caught his eye, because most of the linens were white, but there was a sodden heap of brown-red, and Taern had to swallow hard. Lots of people were getting hurt out there—there was no reason to assume that was *his* blood just because he'd slept down here.

He had just shored himself up to go upstairs and ask Madame M when he heard a rustle. When he looked up to the top of the stairs, he realized that she had come to him.

"Taern?" She looked him up and down with hard eyes, her throat bobbing as she took in his armor. "What are you doing?"

"Where is he?" Taern asked, trying to keep his voice steady. "Is the blood his? Is he here?"

She shook her head. "Where is he? Fucking everywhere, sweetheart. He's saved more lives in the last three days than the entire fucking military in its entire wretched existence. But as for where he is now?" She looked at the linens and nodded, and his stomach clenched. "Yes. That's his. The wounds aren't mortal, but they're not child's play either. I don't know if they were enough to send him home."

Taern growled and thought about kicking the couch. "No, of course not. Rather die a martyr on the fucking streets than come home to me."

"I don't think that's what he was thinking," M said kindly, and Taern glanced at her.

"Did he say anything?" he asked, feeling pitiful, and she smiled gently.

"He said you were a colossal pain in his arse and that you were—his words—'the most recalcitrant brat I've ever yearned to spank'."

Taern grimaced. "Is that all?"

"No. Every other word he utters is about you. I think that is the point."

Taern rubbed his hand over his mouth. "I've got to find him, M. We've got things to finish."

She nodded. "The fringe houses—the nice neighborhoods that were going a bit shabby. Those are the places he's been helping the most, because they've got the most silver on hand. The fucking soldiers—" She spat. "—they've killed almost as many people as the thugs. That last wound was a steam spear, and not the first one, or the armor would have held."

Taern snarled. "He's fucking *done*! I don't care if he's rescuing a kitten from a tree, he needs to come *home*!"

M sighed. "He's done his part. Tell him I said he could quit now."

Taern heard the regret in her voice. "Did you tell him something different before?"

"What do you want me to say, Taern? This is *not* about you getting laid or meeting your meal ticket or even about true love. He's saving *lives*. And right now, this quarter of the city has damned few people who give a hexashite about that. We need him, and if you're on his side, we could use your help as well!"

Taern growled and kicked the couch, the enhancement of his armor knocking it back against the wall, where it collapsed, all four legs breaking off at the same time. "Do you not understand?" he asked, looking at the couch through a haze of red. "If he'd been in the Forum the last three days, he might have been able to do something to keep the soldiers out of it. He's one man!"

"Yes, well right now he's one man who's single-handedly taken down two street gangs, and he needs to go home. We can discuss politics later, Taern. Go find him. It's why you came."

Taern nodded and lowered his mask before he moved toward the window to hoist himself out through it again. He turned before he pulled himself up. "Thank you for taking care of him. He's… he's a good man."

"Honey, he's a great man. That's going to make your life harder, you know that, right?"

Taern had a breath of humor, much needed. "Parts of me!" he said cheekily as he chin-upped to the opening. "Parts of me are spending time very hard indeed."

He held himself up for a moment, looking to make sure no one else was out there, and then wiggled his shoulders through. His feet scrabbled on the wall and then he felt two strong, wide hands on his backside through the armor, and he was shoved through the window with spirit. When he'd picked himself up from the ground, he turned and looked back down and waved at Madame M, and she waved back jauntily.

Later he would be glad he did that, the wave, the joke. Some things are meaningful when the world is on fire.

HE HAD to stop more than once. The first time was to scale the wall of a building next to a burning tenement and pull out three children who were hanging out a window. He got them down to the ground, and one of them started to wail for a parent just as the tenement collapsed. All the children started to scream hysterically after that, and Taern gave them to the nearest adult, a middle-aged woman who looked shell-shocked and tired but who took the children automatically, as though it had been preordained.

He continued on through the back alleys then, thinking he would move faster that way, when he almost ran into a thug who had the flat of his hand on a screaming woman's back as he was rucking her skirt up and fumbling with his breeches.

Taern pulled his foot back and swung, forgetting about the armor until he heard the man's spine crack. Very possibly Taern had punctured something inside of him as well.

The man screamed and pitched forward, and the woman started to scramble out from under him. Taern took four steps back, shouted, "Duck!" and ran forward with enough momentum to use the side of the building to vault the moaning rapist. The woman was whimpering, pulling her skirts down, but when she turned to see who her rescuer was, she started to sob harder, probably frightened by a man in armor and a mask. Taern didn't bother to stop—there was nothing he could say to her that would mean anything, nothing he could do for her that would make the last five minutes of her life any better, and any attempt to communicate with her would just frighten the piss out of her some more.

He continued to run.

There was smoke on the streets, and he actually thanked Areau for the filter built into the facemask, not that Areau could hear. Some of the violence seemed to be dying down as he ran, and he was almost sorry for it. He was furious, angry, downright wrathful, not just at Dorjan but at *everybody*. Looters, rapists, soldiers, politicians—all of them. It was *all* of their doing, and now he was plowing through a human trash heap trying to find one just man.

His blood was up, and his heart hammering with violence when he kicked through a pile of trash cans and burst out into his second-worst nightmare: Nyx, bleeding, weakened, standing in the middle of the street, in the center of what seemed to be ranks upon ranks of the Forum's soldiers, armor shiny, clubs raised.

"This isn't going to end well for you!" Nyx called out, and although he sounded winded, he also sounded confident. Nyx gestured with his chin. "It didn't end well for them!"

Oh Karanos! Between the advancing soldiers, the street was littered with bodies. Death Masks, Hieters—whatever they were calling themselves, they lay crumpled and inert. Some of them moaned and shifted, and some of them would never move again.

"Yeah, but we've got armor, Nyx!" one of the soldiers called out. He had the rank and insignia of lokogos, and as Taern took in the situation, he realized that he was, in fact, looking at one small battalion—and one badly trained lokogos—and that he had arrived just in time.

"My armor's better!" Nyx said. He made a show of bouncing on his toes, and Taern wondered if he was the only one who noticed Nyx's movements were frantic, the last adrenaline spurt before the total collapse.

"Yeah, but you're still alone!" the lokogos called out.

In the tense pause that followed, Taern took five steps back and called out, "Yeah, but not for long!" before running forward again and using the side of the building to boost himself up and jump into the middle of the fray.

Chaos. All battles were chaos. The boosters in the armor enabled him to leap over the heads of the first couple of men and land exactly where Nyx was: in the eye of the storm. For a moment there were shouts as the soldiers turned and looked at this new development, and some of them flinched from the armor, but the lokogos was not *that* green.

"Kill them both!"

Taern pulled his first punch back a little, remembering the man in the alleyway with his spine kicked through his spleen. But these men had armor too, and after the first pulled punch almost bounced off the soldier running at him full tilt, Taern ducked his swing with a short sword and planted a solid metal-denting slug in the man's gut. He groaned and went down, and Taern swung backward with his foot, caving in the armor above the next soldier's kneecap, and he fell screaming. Taern flicked his hands down to his side and pulled them up, armed with short, sharp knives. He sliced through the shoulder join in the armor of the man in front of him and then threw both arms back, knives pointed backward, and sliced through the metal and flesh of the two soldiers on either side. He whirled and kicked, knowing there would be a soldier behind him, and that man went flying, knocking the two men behind *him* into the street.

He laughed then, loud, exultant, and bloody, because there were more soldiers, many more, and he was ready to take them all on.

"Bimuit!"

The oath caught his attention, and he had enough breathing room to look over as Nyx, in a seemingly impossible move, squatted down and leaped, scattering soldiers in his wake. He came down on the head of another soldier. Before that soldier could crumple, Nyx pushed off of him to the shoulder of another, and another, running lightly across armored people like Taern had seen him run across rooftops. The smart ones dropped to the ground before he landed on them, but many of them waved their swords in the air and had their wrists broken when he grasped them in passing. His final leap was off the head of the lokogos, and he added a backward kick as he went, sending the man sprawling to the ground before he launched into a handspring and bounced up again, landing on his feet in time to take out the soldier advancing behind Taern.

"Nyx!" Taern gasped, sending a kick to the kneecap of the man in front of him.

"Prick Face!" Nyx panted, landing his own blow. "What in hell's name are you doing here?"

"Came to fetch you!" Oh hells! These bastards didn't know when to quit! Kick, punch, slice, duck, whirl, kick, punch, breathe. At his back, Nyx was doing the same, again and again and again. Taern was already tired.

"I would have made it home eventually!" Nyx was getting winded, and Taern didn't blame him.

"Dinner got cold!" he snapped. "Karanos! Have you been doing this for three days?" His fury spiked and he used his blades this time, making sure the two men flanking him would not get up again. Some part of him might object to killing so easily, but that would be later, when he and Nyx were safe and this moment was far behind him.

"The soldiers are new," Nyx replied evenly. His solid body faltered for a moment and then stabilized. "For niskets' sake, boy, try bashing them on the head! The blood makes it slippery, dammit!"

Taern grimaced. Oh, yes. Everything had a price, even ending the lives of the mindless soldiers who had been pressed into service and were doing whatever duty came easiest.

"Bash 'em on the head! Got it, Nyx!" The next two he bashed on the head, but the one after that had a steam spear aimed directly at his gut. "Spear!" he yelled and leapt sideways. Nyx looked behind him and leaned backward, falling into Taern's arms just as the spear was shot. The spear punched through the armor of the soldier who had been facing him, and the momentum shot the man backward to take out some more of his compatriots.

Taern shoved at Nyx's shoulders, throwing him back into the fray, and both of them stood back to back again, ready to take on the rest of the fucking Thenis legion.

They may have done just that, but the lokogos, who had gone down from a kick to the back of the head, made his groggy way to his feet. He stood up and looked around and realized that more than half his battalion was down and many of them would not be getting up.

Apparently even morons have sudden shafts of clarity.

"Retreat!" the man screamed. "Retreat! Retreat! To the Forum! Run on the fringes, stay out of the gentry, ignore the civilians! Retreat!"

Taern and Nyx stood back to back, hands at the ready, as half a battalion ran screaming away from two men.

As the last one disappeared around the corner, Taern felt Nyx waver, just once, at his back.

"Ready to go home, Nyx?" he asked, throat tight.

"I'm feeling a bit peckish," Nyx replied. "It's been a long time since that sandwich."

They took a moment; Taern slid his knives back up into the forearm sheaths of his gauntlets, and he was pretty sure Nyx was repositioning his weapons as well. As one, the two of them turned together ran for the shadows of the nearest yard. As they emerged from the space between two older houses, Taern realized the light was turning the faintest bit gray.

"You haven't slept in my bed in four nights, Nyx," he whispered as they slid to the next shadow. "You owe me."

"Can I have dinner and a bath first?" Nyx asked a little plaintively, and while Taern's breathing was starting to recover, he still sounded desperately winded. "We can discuss it then!"

There was a rabbit along the next street, a sure indication that they were in a better area, since the monorails were no longer maintained in the shabbier parts of town. They waited in the shadows for it to pass by and then made a run for it before the next one.

"No discussion," Taern said as they cut through someone's side yard and then scrambled over a fence to make it to the next block. Nyx made a sound as they were scaling the fence, and Taern looked down, realizing he'd left a smear of blood on the wood as he pushed up. He was, in fact, leaving a track of it through the increasing green of the better-manicured lawns. They landed in the backyard of a house Taern recognized, one not too far from the graveyard.

Taern edged out to the front of the house and looked both ways. "Come on, Nyx. If we run between the space of the houses, we don't have to leap any fences. And this way leads directly to the stable."

He led and Nyx followed, and it wasn't his imagination—Nyx left blood with every footstep across the street. When they got to the next set of shadows, he stopped.

"Where are you bleeding?" he said, keeping his voice even. "We've got to stop it now, or anyone will be able to follow you back."

Nyx took a labored breath. "Ah, hells. I think the question is, where am I *not* bleeding, Prick Face. Did the girls make it?"

It was such a non sequitur that it took Taern a moment to figure out he was talking about Evvy and Alla. "Yes."

Nyx was putting more and more of his weight against the wall. His armor was torn in places, the supple metal peeling back like a violated flower, and the flesh under it didn't bear thinking about, not now when they couldn't do a thing about it.

"Good. Have them sneak down here with a bucket of water and rinse away our tracks. None of the gardeners start work until full sunrise, not this late in the fall."

Taern nodded. "All right, then. Let's move. Two miles to go, Nyx. It can't be more than that."

They turned around and started a slow trot. By the time they'd finished one block, Nyx was down to a labored walk. By the time they passed the graveyard, he was starting to sway. Taern muttered, "Fuck it," and wrapped his arm around his higher, broader shoulder, and Nyx put his arm around Taern's waist.

By the time they struggled to the back of the stables, Taern was bearing most of his weight, and they barely made it into the barn before Nyx collapsed on the straw.

"Fuck," he muttered succinctly and started to struggle with the catches at his core.

Taern ripped off his gauntlets, careful of the repositioned knives at his forearms, and started to quick release all of the catches in the armor, throwing the pieces in a pile as he went. When he was done, the Nyx was gone and what was left of Dorjan laid in his place. His sweat-soaked hair was plastered to his head, and his mouth was swollen from what looked to be repeated blows to the face. Taern thought detachedly that he was lucky he still had his teeth, but that wasn't the worst of it. His blood-soaked smallclothes were rent in several places, the flesh underneath the holes torn or bruised as well.

Taern sat on his knees, looking at him for a moment, trying to keep from screaming. A gentle hand at his chin stopped him, and he grasped Dorjan's fingers and lowered his arm.

"Don't waste your effort comforting me," he said gruffly, concentrating on Dorjan's eyes. "As soon as you can stand, I'm going to beat the hell out of you. I don't need your pity."

"I don't need you looking me like I'm dead," Dorjan panted. He smiled a little, the expression so incongruous that Taern almost didn't recognize it. "Go. Go get some warm water, some disinfectant, some linen. Get me some water, oh, Bimuit, please, some water, and some fruit juice or bread. Get me a change of clothes. I don't want to frighten anyone, Taern. Let me wash, we can bandage my wounds. I'll get to my room under my own power."

"Karanos, you arse! Would you stop giving orders for one bloody minute!" Taern felt his voice break. "That was really close, you know that?"

Dorjan laughed a little. "Have I thanked you yet? For hauling my bollocks out of the forge?"

"Not yet, you fucking prat." Taern closed his eyes tightly. This was why Dorjan issued the orders—because someone had to keep his head. "I'll be back, you hear me?"

Dorjan nodded and closed his eyes. "I trust you," he said, still smiling, and Taern had to run out of there before he lost his composure completely and bawled.

KRISSA and Mrs. Wrinkle were up, literally pacing the kitchen floor in their dressing gowns, waiting for him. He ran in, saw them, and took a page from Dorjan's book, issuing orders before he had a chance to get bogged down with questions. As Mrs. Wrinkle started heating the water and Krissa went off to fetch the linens and the extra clothes, he took Krissa aside and told her to ask the girls to rinse off the blood before the sun got much higher.

She looked at him, eyes wide and bruised from lack of sleep. "That's ghastly," she said quietly, and Taern grimaced.

"Well, wait until you see him." They had both been young and had spent time living on the streets. "He looks worse than the last dead body I saw," he said seriously, and she shook her head.

"Mine died of an overdose. As long as he looks better than that, I think we can manage."

He rounded up some juice and some soft bread with honey, and by the time Krissa met him with the clothes, he was already outside with Dorjan again.

"You ready to get off your arse?" he asked as he knelt by Dorjan's side and shook him gently.

Dorjan groaned and opened his eyes. "Right. Sure. We'll run more races in the courtyard."

Taern shoved an arm behind his shoulders and helped him sit up. Dorjan let out a whimper and Taern held up the juice, which he started drinking in strong, steady sips. He'd finished the cup and Taern was wondering if he could work the pitcher one handed when Krissa came bustling in with the bucket, gauze, linens, and smallclothes all balanced in her arms. She set the bucket on the ground next to Taern first and then set the rest down on the table that usually held the armor.

"Oh no, Taern," she said briskly. "He looks *much* better than the last dead man I saw."

Dorjan's chest rose and fell. "Excellent. Glad to hear it. My lady Krissa, I do hope you won't be offended, but I believe we're going to have to cut my knit suit off."

Krissa exchanged rolled eyes with Taern. "You do remember where you found us, right, Forum Master? It's hardly been a fortnight!"

"I have no recollection," Dorjan said with a straight face. "As far as I recall, you're the children sent to me from one of the families in a nearby keep. Need to keep you safe, then. Precious to me."

His voice faded with the bit of fanciful lying, and Taern used his fingers to push his forearm knife slightly out of its sheath. "C'mere, Kriss, and hold him up for me. We'd better start tending while he still has blood to keep in his body."

Very, very carefully, he began to slice off Dorjan's clothes.

It was both better and worse than he'd imagined. It was better, because the armor had done its job and holes in his flesh had missed anything major, but it was worse because the major parts of his body to which injury would have resulted in his death were nearly the *only* parts that weren't rent, punctured, cut, abraded, or ripped.

"Karanos, Dorjan," Taern breathed. "Would you like me to get some sandpaper and take off what skin you have left? You could start all over again; it would be like being reborn."

"I'll pass," Dorjan said, grimacing. "You're just going to have to stitch up the skin I've got!"

It took them more than two hours after Mrs. Wrinkle brought them the disinfected needle and thread. Krissa sewed with delicate, neat stitches, and Taern dumped disinfectant all over the cuts and cleaned out the gravel with water so hot, he kept his gauntlets on to stick his hands in the pot. Dorjan closed his eyes in the middle of all their tending—Taern wasn't sure if he passed out or simply fell asleep, but when they were done with the stitching, they had to rouse him to sluice clean water over his head and wash him top to bottom. Then they dried him off and wrapped gauze over the cuts to keep them clean and absorb the seeping blood.

When the cleaning up was finished, he leaned on Taern and slipped into the clean smallclothes. Krissa got on his other side, and they helped him in the house. They were at the foot of the stairs when Areau came out of his room, complaining loudly.

"Krissa! Krissa, is nobody eating break—" He stopped. "—fast?" He came down the stairs, looking at Dorjan in confusion. "You're home," he said, and he smiled.

It was a normal, plain, *sane* smile, and for a moment, Taern saw a concerned friend and a boyhood companion. In that moment, he saw someone worth all of Dorjan's pain.

"Sorry I'm late," Dorjan said, going limp in Taern's arms, probably under the weight of that smile.

"Yes, well, we didn't hold dinner." He looked at Taern and Krissa. "Are you two really necessary?"

"Without them, I'm not sure if I could make the stairs," Dorjan said softly, and Areau did something unexpected.

"Well, they're both doll-sized. You need a man's help, Dori. Here, let me."

"I've got him!" Taern hissed, tightening his arm around Dorjan's waist until Dorjan's breath caught.

Areau rolled his eyes. "You look like hell. What have you been doing, wallowing around in—"

"Buckets of Dorjan's blood, Areau," Krissa muttered. "And some of his own, if he's honest. Are you going to help us or not?"

Taern had never minded being small and wiry. It had served him well in his former profession, and he knew without conceit that when he'd trained some more, he would be as fast or faster than Dorjan, because his body was built to be quick and light. But Areau was a big man, a few finger-widths taller than Dorjan, with wider shoulders, and when he stepped forward and thrust his arms under Dorjan's knees and took his shoulders from Krissa and Taern, he carried that weight easily, making it up the stairs far faster than they could have if Dorjan had walked on his own.

Taern growled under his breath, and Krissa said, "He's being nice, Taern, don't be an arse. You can hardly stand up as it is."

"I was out there for one night. Dorjan was out there for three."

"Yes, well, he's had more practice. When we get up to his room, how about you draw a bath for yourself. I'll bring you up some food before you fall asleep, how's that sound."

Taern looked at her. She was tired, cross, and giving orders just like Dorjan. "I saw M," he said out of nowhere, thinking that the bath and the food sounded heavenly.

"What'd she say?"

"She said he's not just mine. He's bigger than that. The city needs him."

Krissa sighed. "M's very wise." They reached the landing then, and Taern hurried to pass Areau so he could go draw back the covers. It was something, he thought, feeling pathetic. Anything so Dorjan would know that he might belong to the city, but Taern belonged to him.

Almost Everything

DORJAN startled awake, reaching for his knife. "Taern?"

"Sh," Krissa murmured. "He's asleep next to you, do you see?"

Dorjan turned and there he was, curled up under the blankets, his black mop of hair visible but nothing more. His form under the sheets was rising and falling, and Dorjan put his hand out on top of it so he could feel the boy's breath.

The moment he felt it, he fell back against the pillows with a groan. "Bimuit—how long was I unconscious?"

"A couple of hours, no more. Areau insisted we take turns to watch over you for the first day. Said he'd never seen your wounds this bad. Is he right?"

Dorjan groaned, and tried to remember. "They've been worse," he confessed, thinking of the increased security immediately after his first exploit with the assassin. "But I was younger, and Areau was apparently more self-involved." He'd found a chirurgeon who had doctored his hurts for enough silver to leave the city.

"Well, I'm sorry, then, if you've been hurt worse than this," Krissa said softly. "Here, drink some more juice. We've laced it with some painkiller, and it will help replace the blood volume you lost." She shuddered. "I've helped women give birth, you know. I've doctored hurts after street fights. I've seen dead men in the gutter. I've never seen that much blood. I don't know how you're still awake, much less talking to me."

Dorjan allowed a dry laugh. "Practice," he said, knowing he was falling asleep in spite of the pain. "Is he really here? Really all right?"

She reached out for his hand and rested it on Taern's softly moving chest on top of the covers again. That gentle rhythm calmed his heart, calmed his pain, and he slept.

WHEN he woke up again, it was dark, Taern was gone, and he had to use the loo. He pulled back the covers and grimaced, because the sheets were sticking to his seeping wounds. Bimuit, he didn't want to think yet about what a near thing it had been. Easy not to think of death now. Everything hurt, including his bladder. He groaned and pushed up on the end table and was disgusted when his arm buckled and he fell back down on the pillows. He kept the sound in and just lay there, seeing stars and feeling stupid tears starting. Hells, he'd left half his flesh on the bloody city street, and it was a child's dilemma that almost broke him!

One more time. He braced his arm at his side and swung around, gasping as the stitches on the slice over his stomach pulled, as did almost every damned thing on his body, but he was sitting up, and that was good.

Now, standing.

It took three tries to stand, and he was tottering there, seeing through the darkness in his eyes and trying to calculate how many steps it would take to get to the wall, when his door opened and Taern started swearing at him.

"Karanos take it, you bloody fucking git! Sit the hell down! Where do you think you're going now!" Taern was standing at the doorway with a tray, but he put it down and moved to Dorjan's side.

Dorjan felt absurdly near tears again. "To piss," he muttered. "I have to piss. Is that so bad? It's five bloody paces, maybe ten!"

"Yes," Taern snapped. "Yes. We have a mason jar for just that reason. But no. You and your dignity, you think you're going to walk. Get the hell back in bed and be grateful that breathing is still an option."

Dorjan took one stubborn step forward and, to his horror, felt his leg give way. Taern was pushing up under his shoulder, bearing his weight, before he could fall. One step back, then sitting down, then lying down, and he was back in bed, nauseous, dizzy, and in more pain than before. And....

"Mason jar?" he begged, feeling pitiful. The indignity was excruciating, but Taern didn't seem to care. He watched as Dorjan relieved himself, then took the full jar and actually examined it, grunting when it was merely pinkish from some bruised kidneys before taking it to the privy to dump it and wash his hands. He came out dabbing at his eyes, and Dorjan grimaced.

"I'm fine," he said kindly.

"You can't even get out of bed to piss," Taern snapped. "Not. Fine."

"I could too get out of bed," he snapped back and then deflated a little. "It was the walking that got in my way."

Taern sat down next to him on the bed and sighed, then reached out and cupped Dorjan's face, stroking his cheek with a bony thumb.

"Dorjan?"

"Yes?"

"Have you ever taken your pleasure with a man?"

Taern's eyes were a lovely, mesmerizing midnight blue, and Dorjan found he was too weak to look away. "With you, more than once," he said. He was trying to be light, but his voice came out husky and sincere.

"No. That's not what I meant. Have you *ever* had a man in your bed, spent the night exploring and making love and laughing? Touched someone just to touch them? Kissed just to kiss, with no end in sight? Have you ever moved inside someone who craved your touch? Had them move inside of you? Ever?"

Dorjan's jaw tightened and his eyes narrowed, and he jerked away from Taern's hand. "You know the answer to that," he snapped, and Taern grunted.

"I suspected. But see, last night, we were fighting back to back, and it kept flashing through my mind. *He's got to live through this night. He must, because he's never done that.* Look at me, Dorjan!" Taern commanded, and Dorjan was too weak to evade him. "I want you to do that. I thought fighting by your side, that would be enough, but it's not. I want to *be* by your side. I want you to know what it's like to be loved, Dorjan son of Kyon. I need you let me do that."

Dorjan felt helpless, and he hated that. "You'll leave me?" he asked, everything, *everything* hurting at once. He hadn't acknowledged pain like this since he'd awakened in the hospital outside of Karanos.

"No," Taern whispered, looking down. "Don't you see? There's no 'or' here. There's no ultimatum. I will not blackmail you into loving me. But you've needed for so long, and you've never voiced it. And I need. I need you like breath. I may not get what I need, but I'm not strong like you. I need to give it voice when you're too weak to tell me I'm mistaken."

Dorjan tried hard to look past his own pain. "I'm sorry I scared you," he said after a moment. "I'm sorry I'm… damaged—"

"Don't apologize for that," Taern said fiercely. He moved his hand to his lap, and Dorjan missed it. "I don't want any apologies, Dorjan. I just… just needed you to know."

Dorjan closed his eyes, because Taern's face was so open, so naked with emotion, that for a moment Dorjan felt violated by Taern's intimacy.

"I thought of you," he said, surprised when he said it. "Your snotty little smirk, your eyes—they're really extraordinary, you know that, right? How excited I was to think I'd actually wake up next to you, and how I trusted it would happen." He opened his eyes. "It's not such a bad thing, that you need me." He was growing tired again. "Please. I don't want it to be a bad thing that you need me."

Taern smiled a little and dashed his hand under his eyes. "It's actually really wonderful," he confessed. "When I'm not afraid that you're dead." His voice cracked on the last word, and Dorjan lifted up his hand and pulled the boy gently onto his chest.

"I'm relieved," he murmured. Taern had bathed, and he smelled clean and warm, with an animal male component that comforted Dorjan in a thousand ways. "I'll try not to be dead that often."

"Don't be dead at all, you prat!"

"I'll see what I can do."

They were quite for a moment, and Dorjan found himself absently stroking Taern's hair.

Taern moved gently and turned so he was looking up into Dorjan's eyes again. "Dorjan, have you thought about when this thing—this Nyx thing—when is it going to end?"

Dorjan was almost asleep, and he spoke through a yawn. "In death," he said.

He had a bigger plan than that, something that would change the political climate, pull them out of the war. He had a plan for altering the balance of power, for filling in the power vacuum so that no more lives were spent, no more unnecessary violence occurred when trying to heal the wounds of Biemansland.

Taern jerked upright and glared. "Take that back!"

"Not mine," Dorjan murmured, too groggy to elaborate. "Not mine. Found something to live for."

Taern put his head down then after that, and Dorjan fell asleep with his fingers stroking the boy's hair.

There was a haze then—hot skin, sweat, body aches, wounds on fire, and bowels of ice. Taern was there a lot, and Krissa, as well as Mrs. Wrinkle and, surprisingly, Areau. Those moments with Taern felt real, felt sweet. Dorjan remembered trying to make him talk because the boy was always talking and it didn't feel right when he wasn't. He was embarrassed with Krissa and Mrs. Wrinkle, because sometime in there he lost his smallclothes, although neither of them seemed to care they were changing a naked man's bandages. Areau was neither awkward nor necessary. He was happy to see his boyhood friend, and although Dorjan remembered he should shy away from Areau's touch, in his delirium, he couldn't remember why.

When he came to, he was naked, he seemed to have fewer bandages, and Taern was asleep on the coverlet next to him, this time nearly fully clothed. Dorjan thought about struggling upright but knew, objectively, he was too weak to do that.

"Awake?" Krissa said by his side, and he blinked at her.

"How long?" he asked hoarsely, and she brought water up for him to drink. When he'd sipped that, she brought fruit juice, and he drank that gratefully.

"Well, you woke up the afternoon and evening after you arrived, and we thought everything was blue skies. And then that night, infection set in—that was three days ago, my friend, and I must tell you, you've had me, at least, wondering who was going to pay my milliner bills when you couldn't anymore!"

Dorjan managed a tired smile at her, because his last actual conversation with Taern had been a little emotional, and he was too tired to do emotional right now. "Will Taern forgive me?" he asked, and his voice was gruff with disuse.

Krissa wrinkled her lovely nose and shrugged. "I don't know what you said to him before your fever set in, but it made him absolutely adamant that you were going to live. The rest of us weren't so confident, let me tell you!" Her asperity eased, and the lines in her face settled into something less young and animated, something much more exhausted. "I've grown rather fond of you and Areau in the past weeks, Dorjan. Could you not scare us all again?"

"Areau was worried?" That seemed a wonder. "Thank you," he said, because he had no doubt it was all her doing.

"He's not an evil man," she said quietly. "I know… the relationship you two had, it must have felt that way. Evil. Corrupted. But I think you were right to keep him from self-destructing. There is something very"—Krissa blushed—"appealing about him, when he's not being a right cunt."

Dorjan choked on a laugh, and she brought up another sip of water. When he was done with that, he had to remember that he wasn't allowed too many sweet, personal conversations, whether with Taern or about Areau. He was more than the sum of the people he loved or who loved him. "The Forum," he said softly. "I know they didn't ring bells for the three days of the riot, but after that?"

"Not the two days after that, either," Krissa confirmed. "But they rang them this morning."

Dorjan closed his eyes and tried to do the math. "Rest days?" he said, groggy. "Forgive me if I'm wrong, but wouldn't that make tomorrow—"

"Yes, it's part of the two day. But Dorjan, you'll barely be able to walk in two days!"

Dorjan tilted his head a little on the pillow and realized his neck was stiff. "Well, Krissa, I do have a personal conveyance," he said, trying to be jaunty. "And that's what those are for. But I need to be there. It's not even necessary that I do anything—if I sleep through the meetings, people will assume I'm just that dim. It won't be the first time." The fact was, sleeping through pointless meetings where the conclusion had already been determined by graft and greed was one of the benefits of being considered an idiot by most of his peers. Go ahead and let the poor boy sleep—it's not like he'd have anything to contribute to the conversation, right?

"Why?" Krissa asked, her voice thready with what must have been exhaustion. "Why does it matter if you're not doing anything there?"

"Because I don't want them to think I'm not capable, for one," he said honestly. "Triari Septra is just waiting for me to die—*hoping* for it, actually. If I die or am found guilty of treason, he'll find a way to get my family's keep. I'm the only one stopping him now, and it's a daily battle. Once that happens he can mine the asteroids until our planet shakes itself to dust. He's shortsighted and egomaniacal and...." It was getting hard to breathe, just talking about it. He closed his eyes and calmed down. "I can't appear weak," he said finally. "Do you understand?"

He opened his eyes and saw that she was nodding. Her face looked pinched and sad, but she understood. "I'll tell Taern," she murmured. "It's going to be hard to make him understand."

Dorjan smiled tiredly. "I'll have to make it up to him," he said quietly, and although he'd stopped fantasizing about sex long, long since, when he closed his eyes, he held a single image in his mind: Taern, naked, straddling his body, head thrown back, eyes closed, with the sun coming through the shades and illuminating his face as he gave himself over to Dorjan with every quivering atom.

He wanted that, he realized as he fell asleep. All these years of thinking he had given the best of himself away, and that was the part of him that wanted that moment, needed that moment, in the same way Taern had said he needed Dorjan too.

HE WOULD have to wait far longer than either of them wanted for that moment to arrive.

The next morning, he was awakened by a terrible pounding at the door. He was struggling to sit up when Taern sprang out of bed—bare naked, which was nice because it meant he'd stopped worrying—and glared at him. "Sit down. I'll go see who that is!"

"Dressing gown!" Dorjan snapped. "They're trying to make it a death sentence to be sly in the Forum—are you looking forward to that?"

Taern stopped and gaped at him. "I hate your bloody province," he muttered, stomping for the armoire. "There I was, trying to fly a bloody kite, mind you, and your entire fucking army comes along and destroys my home, and then tries to kill you off, and then does *that* until it gets old, and now they want to take away the one bloody thing that makes my life worth living? If it wouldn't cause global destruction, I'd tell you to let them all suck hieter eggs and we'd better off for it!"

Dorjan closed his eyes against laughter. "One for me," he said past the tightness of bruised ribs and healing stitches. "And one of those nightshirts you despise so much."

"You think *you're* going out there?" Taern stopped right in front of Dorjan as he was sitting up, and Dorjan couldn't help his eyebrows arcing to his hairline.

"Don't you look pretty," he murmured and then tried to clear his head. "That depends," he murmured, "on who it—"

"Master Dorjan!" chirped Mrs. Wrinkle from outside his door. "Master Dorjan? There's soldiers down here to see you. They say that they tracked some sort of prowler to this neighborhood—I tried to tell them we haven't seen anything, but they wanted to talk to the Forum Master himself."

Dorjan took a deep breath and replied, "Very well. Tell them I'll be down in just a moment, if they don't mind cornering a man in a dressing gown!"

Taern gaped at him. "You'll *what?*"

"Taern, if you could put on some fucking clothes and go ask the lady Krissa to let you into her room and then emerge in her own dressing gown as I pass, I would be much obliged."

Taern glared at him, and then the logic started to permeate his outrage. "You can't see more than my room from the bottom of the stairs," he said, holding out Dorjan's nightshirt. Dorjan took it, and Taern helped him throw it over his head.

"Yes," Dorjan told him. "And it shall simply look as though I sent my mistress to her room to dress. I do hope she doesn't mind—"

"She won't. She can help you stand—it will look as though you're simply an established couple. I understand."

He most clearly didn't like it, either, but he did put on a dressing gown and came over to shove his shoulder under Dorjan's arm.

"C'mon, Nyx," he muttered under his breath, and Dorjan pushed with all his strength. There wasn't much. But together, they made it to the door. Dorjan leaned heavily on it while Taern slipped through, and Dorjan had to smile—he was running on his toes, and his footsteps did sound decidedly feminine. He didn't knock, and Dorjan hoped that Krissa was ready for this, but he knew she was a quick girl, and rather thought she might be.

The door closed, and Dorjan leaned heavily on the wall and took a few steps, and then a few more, and finally, finally, made it to where Krissa stepped out of her room, looking resplendent in an obviously new dressing gown in a glorious wine-colored velvet with champagne-hued trim. It looked both decadent and innocent, and he smiled at her even as she offered him her arm.

"You look lovely," he murmured. "A gift from me?"

"Yes," she said back quietly. "One of my favorite kinds of wrapping!"

"Almost makes me wish I was the one opening the present," he murmured sincerely, and she laughed—loudly, for the benefit of their guests—but also sincerely.

As they neared the top of the stairway, she leaned over and said, "Let's see if we can stay up here. I'm not sure the two of us are going to make it down. I'm not that strong."

"There's always the railing," he said tightly, "but yes. Let us see." He looked down toward the foyer and was almost glad for the pain, because it kept him from reacting when he recognized the lokogos whose head he'd stepped on five nights previous.

"Lokogos," he said, inclining his head and speaking genially. "Forgive me for not dressing to answer, but…." He smiled winningly and inclined his head toward Krissa, who simpered and blushed. He made a vow to buy her another dressing gown for that alone.

The lokogos was obviously not sly, given the way he almost swallowed his tongue when Krissa appeared, and Dorjan gave thanks for that. She moved innocently and exposed her ankle and calf; Dorjan thought there might not be enough dressing gowns in the world.

"I can see that, Forum Master, but this is important. Yer remember the ruckus, few days back, do ye?"

Dorjan blinked from the sheer understatement alone. "Well, I assumed there was a reason they didn't ring the summoning bells, Lokogos, but that was, as you said, some days ago."

"I know it. But we tracked some of what's responsible to this quarter o' the city, and we're goin' door to door to see if anyone saw or heard nothing… queer, that might not be our fugertives."

Dorjan blinked again and dared not risk a look at Krissa. He could tell by the way she held her shoulders she was laughing so loudly inside it was a shame she couldn't rock the chandeliers.

"Well, as luck would have it, we did see and hear nothing 'queer' from that night. Do you have any evidence that says your fuger, uhm, tives passed this way?"

The lokogos looked disgusted. "Naw. They was bleeding somethin' fierce. Left a trail almost to the bloody great graveyard, they did. But the blood track disappeared, and we ain't been able ter find where it picked up again. We'll get them, though. We'll get them what started the riot."

Dorjan fought the urge to roll his eyes. "Two men started that great riot?" he asked innocently. "May I ask what the military was doing to stop it?"

"We was doin' our part, Forum Master! We was under Triari Septra's direct orders to shoot anyone out of doors."

Dorjan heard Krissa gasp next to him, and he found his own temper spiking. "Even the innocent civilians trying to get away from the people robbing their houses? I'm sure the Forum Master didn't mean that too!"

And to his disgust, the lokogos shook his head eagerly. "Oh aye, Forum Master. Triari Septra didn't want nothing stirring in those quarters when we was through with 'em." He shook his head proudly. "We did a right good job too!"

Dorjan was suddenly besieged with darkness. "I'm sure you'll do a right good job apprehending the two villains you are searching for, as well," he said gravely, "but I'm afraid you will not find them here."

"Oh, aye, sir." The lokogos's shoulders drooped. "Let us know." He turned away and spoke to his companion, a lowly sergeant judging by his uniform, before they even cleared the doorway. "Ye know, I think the Triari's mistaken about this one. He said the boy'd be a right idiot, but he was all right!" And the two of them walked out the door and closed it behind them without bowing either to Krissa or Mrs. Wrinkle or even begging their leave.

As soon as the door snapped shut, Dorjan's knees gave, and he sat down hard right there in the hallway, disengaging from Krissa before he could carry her with him.

"Lock the door, please, Mrs. Wrinkle," he said calmly, and she did so, guaranteeing them at least some warning should the two soldiers return. "Is it my imagination," he said idly, leaning his head against the staircase railing, "or have the requirements for the Biemansland military gotten less strict than they were when last I served?"

Areau spoke up from his side, shoving one hand under his back and the other under his knees. "Oh, no. You were really as stupid as that prat, I just didn't have the heart to tell you."

Dorjan chuckled weakly. "You think you would have mentioned it when I told you we were going to frag our careers."

"No—I wanted to see the blast pattern when they imploded. Spent the last ten years studying it from the inside of my eyeballs. It's glorious."

With that, he stood up and carried Dorjan, and Dorjan allowed him to do so. It was Areau. He trusted Areau.

"Hey, Areau!"

"Yeah?"

"When I pass out again, do me a favor and buy Krissa a whole new wardrobe."

Areau shouldered his way through Dorjan's door without hesitation, and Dorjan had no problem with him in the bedroom. That wasn't them anymore. It was no longer a fear. "I thought you'd already done that."

"Well, find something better to get her, you git! She's totally fucking earned it."

Areau set him down gently on sheets it looked as though Taern had changed while Dorjan had been clinging to the stair rail and a girl's arm. "That she has. I'll try to find her a trinket that will do."

"Good man. Taern?"

"Karanos, you arse!"

"Wake me up in two days, right? I've got something I need to do."

Dorjan's eyes closed again, and Taern was right next to him, kissing his temple and smoothing back his hair.

"That's something to wake up to," Dorjan murmured and fell asleep once again.

HE DIDN'T get out of bed for the next two days. Taern would wait on him and keep him company until Dorjan harried him outside for exercise and fresh air. It was getting cold outside, and Taern would come in hours later, his fingers cold and pink under the light gloves and his face chilled, and then come and bury his face in the hollow of Dorjan's throat, just to make him giggle.

When first day came around, Dorjan got up early and Taern helped him dress carefully, padding all of his hurts with extra gauze and making sure his coat and loose breeches hid all of the lumps that indicated healing flesh. Areau carried him to the stable for the rabbit, and Taern piloted it while Dorjan dozed fitfully on the cushions. As Taern followed the directions to the front of the Forum, he gasped.

When Dorjan looked out the window, he saw it as Taern would. The Forum of Biemansland was supposed to be the model government for all of the provinces: it stood four stories tall, with straight beveled columns supporting half of the great height of it. It was built on granite foundations, out of marble, with marble steps leading up to the main floor. Speeches were given on the steps of the Forum, and great things had been heralded from the Triari platform that sat square in the middle. The making of the monorail system, which utilized their power resources the most efficiently and had once kept the streets from being too crowded or polluted, had issued from this building, and Dorjan still thought it was a wonderful testament to what a government could do.

"This?" Taern breathed, looking up even as he followed the monorail to the multilevel stable used to house the conveyances of the Forum Masters.

"Yes, this." Nobody rode the hexahorses anymore, but the design had stayed the same. Dorjan had a slot specially made for his rabbit, just like the others, but it was dusty with disuse when Taern swung it in. Once Taern had parked the vehicle, he dimmed the windows and turned to Dorjan, who hadn't moved yet, because he was trying to gather his strength.

"You said you could do this!" Taern muttered with supreme unhappiness. "You promised. 'It will be no problem. I'll make it to my seat and sleep!'"

"I will," Dorjan affirmed, knowing he could do it, just needing that last mental push to get him up.

"But Karanos, Dorjan—"

"See, I'm up! Glory under the aether, Taern, I've heard fishwives nag a body less than you!"

"Fishwives aren't as handy with a knife as I am!" Taern shot back, and Dorjan was relieved. If Taern was bickering with him, Dorjan must not be in too much trouble.

"It's not your knife I'm worried about, it's my sword. Now do you remember the directions?"

Taern nodded seriously. "Yes. Should anyone ask me, I'm a page. I run down to the courtyard and slip through the alleyway, and it leads straight to the stews—I still can't believe that, by the way, I can't wait to see it for myself. I go down to Madame M's and find a way to slip silver to her or aid to as many people as I can." Taern had his armor on underneath his page's robe, and his mask as well as silver in his heavy satchel.

"And if anyone stops you?"

"I'm your page, and I have an important message for you and you alone!"

Dorjan nodded. "Excellent. And if they try to send me home?"

"You'll sleep in the rabbit and wait for me," Taern sighed. "Dorjan—"

"We've gone over this," Dorjan said patiently. "Any sign, Taern. He'll use any sign to strip those mines from me, and this is not going to be it. I *can* do this, I have in the past. Not with quite so much fanfare, but I'll take it in the spirit with which you meant it. Now are we ready?"

Taern grunted. "Aye, sir. Just a lowly page reporting for duty, sir. Do you have your walking stick with you?"

Dorjan nodded and grasped it, glad that he had enough of a reputation as a dandy to make it look as though he didn't need it. "I'll leave first, right?"

Taern nodded, and then, before Dorjan could open the side door, he ran up to Dorjan and gave him a gracious, gentle kiss. "Just imagine," he whispered. "Someday you will go up in front of these wankers and you'll be able to tell yourself that you've been inside my body, felt me move around you, and you know the noises I make while you're fucking me until the world turns white. How're you going to do your job then?"

Dorjan groaned and pulled back. "It's a good thing we have to wear robes," he said, meaning it. "I've had to disguise wounds before, but I've never had to hide my erection."

Taern snickered. "Good. It'll help you remember why you're fighting. Now go!" And with one step down the side of the rabbit, Dorjan reentered the fray.

Not the greatest day, no. The blessing was he could only remember some of it, because he did sleep through quite a bit of the most onerous meetings. He woke up at one point in the middle of a debate about the sly and the straight because a fellow Forum member poked him in the side.

"Look here, Dorjan—you're young and hale! Why should we let these sly ones corrupt the city from the inside out?"

Dorjan squinted and tried to orient himself against the seething pain that permeated about everywhere. He'd missed a step coming down into this conference room, and he was pretty sure he'd torn his stitches.

"The sly corrupting the city?" he asked groggily. "Honestly, Colny, what will you think of next? Why should what two people do in the privacy of their own bedroom have any more impact on the state of the city than what they serve for dinner! Our own military was ordered to fire on civilians and damned proud of it too, and you're debating whether you have the right to care whether two men want to touch each other or not? What's wrong with you?"

There was a startled silence, and Colny, who was probably old enough to be Dorjan's grandfather, laughed for a moment. "Well, if you're not going to contribute anything *useful*, you might as well go back to sleep!"

Dorjan grunted and would have done just that, but someone—not one of Dorjan's compeers—spoke up. "But what you say about them not affecting the city isn't true! The military reports that the two masked cowards who fought in the riots were sly!"

Dorjan lost to his gut reflex and blurted, "How in six hells would they know that?" When he realized he was on the receiving end of several startled stares, he went with logic. "They were busy fighting off half the bloody militia, from what I hear." (He hoped. He *hoped* that's what people were saying.) "They weren't bloody likely to start having sex in the middle of the street while they were fighting off steam spears, were they?" That garnered laughter, and for a moment he felt equilibrium. He was back to being a clown—he knew that role. "Besides," he muttered, an ache settling into every pore of his skin, "I was *in* the military, remember? They called a man sly if he even adjusted his equipment to the wrong side. And in the days when Thenis thrived and Biemansland remembered it was an egalitarian society, nobody gave a festering shite. There are children starving in our streets, gentlemen. I may be a fool, but even *I* know how to set a priority like that!"

There was some muttering, and they agreed to table the issue to a later date. Dorjan suggested they put their energy toward a soup kitchen or a donations center, since winter was nearly upon them and many were going hungry. He was laughed at. One of the Forum Masters said that's what wives were for, and Dorjan made a mental note to rob that man's house. (He was almost incoherent with pain by then. He would awake later wondering where the notion came from but positive the victim would deserve it if Dorjan ever followed through.)

He finally dragged himself off to his cubicle, where he lay down on his couch for the rest of the day. Taern woke him up there, long past the hour he was supposed to have met in the rabbit, and Dorjan glared at him in concern.

"Ta—"

"Alder," Taern said, his jaw clenched. "Remember, sir, it's Alder, your page?"

Dorjan nodded, feeling slightly less stupid. He looked up and realized that Taern was not alone. The plump little Forum Master who had made his afternoon a misery was there as well.

"Master Colny!" he said, slightly surprised. "I'm sorry—I must have fallen asleep." Stupid thing to say, of course he'd fallen asleep. He peered about him with bleared eyes. "It's fortunate my young page here woke me up. My household will be quite in disarray."

Taern rolled his eyes and watched painfully as Dorjan pushed himself up. He managed a sheepish grin in Colny's direction. "It was quite a couple of rest days," he murmured, wishing that, like Krissa, he could blush on command.

"So I heard from the lokogos," Colny said coldly. "Dorjan, where did this young man come from?"

Dorjan blinked at Taern good-naturedly and wondered what Taern was trying to tell him with his stolid glare. "A keep near my own," he said blithely. "My old lokogos"—and he didn't have to feign the sadness here—"Dre. He became a stratego and died with the rest of his unit. Before the debacle, he had a young man at his place who wanted to see the world, so he asked if young Alder could come visit." He smiled indulgently at Taern. "As you can see, he's well worth his ticket!"

Colny's manner thawed a little. "Yes, Forum Master. He has been quite devoted to his duty."

Dorjan winked. "Well, sir, there's a young lady he's been talking to who will be sorely disappointed if we don't get moving. Thanks so much for helping him find his way!"

Colny nodded, and as Dorjan took fluid steps to his desk to start rounding up his paperwork, the man bowed and excused himself. Dorjan put his paperwork into his satchel, looking at the tiny dark-wooded desk in the middle of the bright marble room and wondering when it had gotten so close and stuffy in there, when the door closed.

Taern was there to take his weight as soon as it did, and to help him gently into his office chair.

"Karanos!" Taern gasped. "That was close. Your wounds are seeping through your gauze, Dorjan. I don't know how you think you're going to do this again tomorrow!"

"What was all that?" Dorjan asked, not wanting to answer his question. "He was after something, but I don't know what!"

Taern grunted. "Oh, that."

Dorjan widened his eyes. "That?"

"Yes, well, how was I to know two in ten of you Forum Masters are sly. That one was a regular—Yael's, mostly, but I've had him a time or two. Bottoms like a rutting rhinoceros and likes us to call him 'baby boy'."

Dorjan worked so hard not to laugh that he actually felt a stitch pop over his stomach. "Bimuit!" he gasped. "*That* one? Arse. Keeps trying to make being sly illegal. Would be lovely to hold that over his head!"

"You can't," Taern muttered. "You hold it over his head, you'll have to tell them where you *really* got me, and then they'll start asking questions from everyone's favorite piece of pretty. Now are you ready to go home? Krissa really *will* kill us if we're much later."

"Right," Dorjan muttered as Taern got under his arm and lifted with his knees. "So, does that mean you're going to throw me over now?"

They paused at the great hallway, with its marble floors and white stucco walls, and looked both ways to see. There was darkness coming in through the high windows and the skylight. The contrast of the dark and the light was formidable, but Dorjan had always loved this time of day. None of the Forum Masters remained, Colny being perhaps the only other person who would work late anyway. It had just always seemed to Dorjan that there was a chance with that overeasing darkness that maybe the sins of the day could be washed away with it by the great oceans near his home, and the real use of the Forum would be all that remained.

"You never answered me," Dorjan panted, mainly to distract himself from the fatigue as they made their way down the halls. "Are you going to throw me over, now that you know you've had other Forum Masters?"

Taern snorted. "What, do you think the novelty will be gone?" He was bearing a great deal of Dorjan's weight, and his voice sounded strained as well.

"It's a possibility. I'm pretty sure it was only the robes that caught your attention in the first place."

The walls may have been marble, but there were enough corners and couches and padded niches to absorb much of their talk, so when they heard something down the hallway, they separated and walked very quietly and waited for the night custodian to pass.

As he rounded the last corner, Taern took Dorjan's weight again and allowed himself to snort. "No, I'm pretty sure it wasn't the robes, you prat! The armor, maybe, but you already wear too bloody much underwear as it is."

The laughter was good. It helped Dorjan make it to the rabbit, and he didn't remember much after that.

THE encounter frightened him, though. Taern admitted he'd recognized several other Forum members as he'd walked through the hallways, and at least four of them had visited either him, Yael, or the other boy at Madame M's.

"That doesn't, uhm...."

Dorjan had been lying back in the cushions of the rabbit on their way home that first night, and he pulled himself back from oblivion to figure out what was making the boy so uncomfortable.

"What doesn't what?" he asked, forcing his eyes open.

"I was a whore," Taern told him frankly, and Dorjan blinked.

"I am aware. I was fairly certain I didn't buy your contract from a landowner or a schoolmaster."

Taern programmed home into the conveyance and came to settle back with Dorjan. He leaned close and started running his fingers lightly through Dorjan's sweat-soaked hair. "I'm being serious."

"A fact that does not cease to surprise me."

"Dammit, Dorjan—"

"Every time I fucked Areau, it felt new," Dorjan said brutally. "For ten years, I let him bait me, let him enrage me, until I was ready to do anything he asked, anything he begged for. I knew it was wrong—"

"It wasn't!" Taern cried, obviously upset, and Dorjan managed to raise a hand to his mouth to silence him.

"It wasn't right," he said quietly. "It hurt both of us, every time. But every time, it still felt... new. Like there was a chance this time, he wanted it for real. This time, he would be my friend again when it was done. This time, we could go back and start again and make it...." He couldn't meet Taern's eyes.

"Sweet," Taern murmured, and Dorjan nodded, fighting the tightness in his chest.

"If that could feel new, if it could feel hopeful, *that*, Taern, which... which churns my stomach to even think that it was me...." He trailed off, not sure how to put the rest into words.

"You think that you could feel shiny new to me," Taern finished for him, and Dorjan felt a small smile flutter at his mouth.

"Is it too far away to reach?"

Taern shook his head. "It's right on target, Nyx. From my first taste of you, everything about you is new."

Dorjan slept after that, but he held the words and their promise to his heart. They sustained him, really, for the next four days. He was careful—exceptionally careful—after that to make sure to meet Taern at the conveyance, no matter what their plans had been during the day proper.

Taern fretted on the last day of the working days, because he hadn't been able to connect with Madame M. He'd left her notes and cash to distribute, but in spite of their final peace at the end.... "Our last words were hard, and we were both upset."

"Why?" Dorjan asked, thinking he felt just well enough to stay awake for dinner this night. "What was happening?"

"I was looking for you," Taern said sourly. "But you're taking so long to get better, I'm starting to wonder if it was worth the effort."

Dorjan chuckled softly. "I always thought you were a smart boy, Taern. If you were to answer that truthfully, you'd know the answer was no, it never was."

Taern had already set the controls, and he came to spend the rest of the journey much like he'd spent all of their time in the rabbit or in bed before they slept—leaning over Dorjan and studying his face, his hair, the texture of his skin, his expressions. Sometimes it made Dorjan acutely uncomfortable, and he'd contemplated pushing him to the other side of the rabbit, until a touch, a smile, the way his eyes were starting to crinkle in the corners with maturity—those things would catch Dorjan's attention.

He found he could stare at them constantly, and with the way Taern could look at him, the contact, the proximity, didn't seem so hard to bear.

"Dorjan," Taern said, and then stopped, and then started again. "Dorjan, you do mean for this to end sometime, don't you?"

Dorjan nodded. It was the second time Taern had asked him that. "Yes." He'd always meant for it to end. "As soon as Septra is out of power and our province is stable, the Nyx will not be needed. I can have a proxy work in the government or do what the others have done and leave the city. And I will tend to my father's keep and... I don't know, play with the niskets, mine asteroids, that sort of thing."

Taern searched his face. "That sounds really wonderful. Is your keep... is it illegal? To be sly there?"

Dorjan snorted. "Not even before I told my father that I was. No—Kyon would have said he was too lazy to enforce something that useless. The truth was, he was too much of a good man. Too good, I guess." Dorjan had a hard time saying this, although it had lain quiet in his mind for a long time. "He—he didn't expect it. He didn't expect his government to lie about needing to go to war, didn't expect them to betray him to end his life. Just too good. I wish I could have been like him. I wish I could have been that good."

Taern jerked back. "Why on Karanos's black soil would you say an arse-stupid thing like that?"

Dorjan blinked, closed himself off, realized he'd shared maybe too much. "It was a silly thought," he said, closing his eyes against Taern's horrified face. "I'm sorry I gave it voice."

"No!"

Dorjan's eyes flew open in shock.

"No, no, no, no—answer me, dammit! Your father is *dead*! Why would you want to be just like him?"

Dorjan raised his eyebrows, thinking Taern was very naïve. "Do you think he'd want to live, seeing what I'd become? What I'd let our province become? Do you think he'd be *proud*?"

"Do you think my father would be proud I spent the last three years whoring myself on the streets?" Taern retorted, visibly upset, and Dorjan closed his eyes again because it had been a long day and he'd been on his feet for much of it, though he hadn't told Taern that.

"Yes," Dorjan said softly. "Because you're an honorable man, and you've never caused anyone harm who didn't deserve it, and you've followed your conscience in as many ways as you could."

Taern gathered him carefully close, and Dorjan felt tears in the hollow of his ear. He wanted to smile because Taern was so sweet, so soft—ripe fruit, a kitten's prickly claws and trusting heart. So sweet. Could Dorjan pull him in through his skin, like some creatures gathered in air? That would be lovely.

Dorjan fell asleep dreaming of having Taern sprawled over his body, skin to skin, and lying in a field of butterflies and niskets, the two of them breathing the smells of home.

He awoke in his own bed with the early winter's light streaming in from the window over him, feeling a warm washcloth moving along his body carefully. It started in his hair and scrubbed away, leaving the faint smell of lavender and ambergris, before moving gently to his face.

He closed his eyes and let the massage take its course. From his forehead down his nose to the whorls of his ears and behind, he was bathed and rinsed and bathed and dried, made clean and new in the slanting sunlight. The washcloth was careful around his stitches, and in its wake, there was the mild discomfort of some of the stitches being pulled, snipped, and removed.

"The big one across his stomach, you think?" That was Taern's voice, and he was bathing and (Dorjan came to believe) sanitizing the area before someone else took care of the stitches.

"Still looks a little raw," said Krissa's voice, and Dorjan made a sound, a weak attempt to cover up. He was naked, he thought painfully. Taern he could bear to have look at him, but Krissa? Again? That was like going naked in front of his older sister!

"Stop it," Krissa said crisply, batting at his hands. "Go back to sleep. Dream of whatever you were dreaming about a moment ago. I'm trying to make a decision here!"

"How did you know I was dreaming?" Dorjan slurred, and her snort was reassuring.

However, her reply of "Do you think I don't know what's causing that thing to get bigger?" was not reassuring in the least.

The luxuriousness of the sponge bath gave way to embarrassment, and he struggled for speech. "Do we have to do this with an audience?" he begged plaintively.

Krissa's short laughter disabused him of *that* notion. "Don't worry, Forum Master. I was going to leave before things got too intense."

Dorjan didn't want intense. He wanted pleasant. Intimate. He wanted Taern to look at him with desire, not pity or irritation. Was it really too much to ask? It was a rest day, after all.

"Well, whatever it is he was thinking about," Taern said happily, "it seems to have returned. Yes, Krissa, I say snip as many of those stitches on the belly as you think—but don't leave them all. He's too active for them, see? Some of them are already ripping, and that's worse than taking them early."

"Right. Some of them, then."

The bath resumed, and the stitch removal, and then the second set of hands moved and there was a whooshing of skirts at Dorjan's side. "Don't let him tax you too hard, Forum Master," Krissa said into his hair, "but don't worry too much either. I don't think hurting you is what's on his mind."

She moved near Taern too and told him to be careful, to which Taern replied, "You do realize I did this professionally for a bit, don't you?"

"Yes," she retorted. "But now that money isn't going to change hands, I want to hold you to your standards."

Taern made a rude noise and Krissa swooped out of the room like a queen.

Dorjan would have laughed then, but he was too comfortable. The washcloth continued to move down his abdomen, around his upper thighs, in the crease in his leg. Ooh, yes, that would be... but no. Taern swooped the washcloth down over his thighs and then propped both Dorjan's legs up, knees bent and lewdly splayed. Dorjan grunted and tried to press his legs together, and Taern flicked his knee with a bony finger.

"I'm cleaning your private places. Calm down and spread your knees, Forum Master—don't make me wrestle you, that will wreck the mood."

Dorjan sighed and let his knees fall open. The stretch along his inner thighs was painful but in a good way, and for a moment he was too preoccupied with making the most of that to realize what the washcloth was doing.

Calves, shin, ankles—Taern kept it warm and moist but not dripping wet, and it felt just *gorgeous* to be clean again. There had been no baths because of the stitches, and Dorjan had missed them. But all of the attention to his legs, his upper thighs again, his—

"Roll over, Nyx," Taern said cautiously. "On your stomach. Keep your legs spread, though."

Dorjan was relaxed enough, open enough, to emit a little whimper, and the laughter in Taern's voice was unmistakable.

"So, you seem to think I'm neglecting something." He chuckled. "Here. I'll take care of it for you."

The words were promising, but Taern cleaned off his genitals with brief, thorough touches, and Dorjan groaned when he was done.

"Feeling a bit aroused, there, Nyx?" Taern murmured smugly. "I know it's a hardship. Too bad we're all tired and hurt and everything. It would be wonderful to be able to take care of that condition, you know it?"

"You're a hideous, obnoxious brat, and if touching my privates is such an imposition, I can retire to the bathtub and continue to do it myself," Dorjan snarled, and his hips arched up a little and thrust, because he *needed*. Oh hells... it had been *so* long since he needed that it was frightening to be aroused, to be gentled, to be seduced.

Taern laughed dryly and bent down close enough for Dorjan to see the dark ring around his midnight-blue iris. "Patience, Nyx." He bent closer, brushed Dorjan's lips with his own, and backed away. "Remember, I'm good at this. There's some things I'd like to teach you, yes?"

Dorjan grunted, and Taern laughed again. "Now turn over—I need to wash your back."

Dorjan's back was scrubbed thoroughly, and so were his neck, the back of his head, his shoulders, ribs, and under his arms. He had a couple of gashes that extended around his side, and Taern snipped some of those stitches too, but mostly he cleaned. When he'd gotten as many stitches as he could, he went directly to work on Dorjan's backside, and Dorjan found himself panting into his own pillow.

First Taern traced the crease of Dorjan's bottom with the cloth, then down between the crease of his thighs. He nudged Dorjan's thighs until Dorjan's knees were under his stomach, spread wide. His backside was open in vulnerable invitation, and his cock and balls dangled, fat and thick, between his feet. Taern spent some time there with the washcloth, over, under, around. Dorjan moaned into his pillow, and Taern used his finger through the textured fabric, pushing into Dorjan's entrance. He dipped the cloth into the water again and again, then pushed gently, and gently, until Dorjan started to feel a tingle where before he'd felt only a burn, and his bottom felt loose, spread, and bare to the world.

The thought made him harder, engorged him, and he let out a shuddering breath that had his cock bouncing painfully between the bedspread and his stomach.

"You like this," Taern murmured. "You like being handled, fondled. I knew you would. Weeks ago I saw you with a mask on and knew you hungered for touch."

Dorjan was going to reply, tell Taern he could live quite well without it, when Taern spread his clean backside and started licking at Dorjan's entrance with his tongue.

Dorjan let out a long, breathless moan, and Taern came up laughing. "That was a yes, wasn't it?" he laughed.

Dorjan groaned into the pillow.

"I would have settled for a kiss!" he moaned, and then Taern, the brat, bent his head and did it again. Ah... it was such a gentle sensation, a caress, a promise of something more violent—that was never followed through. Taern kept licking, invasively, aggressively, and then, with his hands, he reached down and started a maddening, slow caress of Dorjan's manhood.

Dorjan moaned some more. "Oh!" And that's all he could voice. It was an amazing feeling, a stroking from the base, hard at the bottom, still firm at the top, Taern's thumb and forefinger seizing Dorjan's slippery foreskin and dragging it over the sensitive head. Dorjan started to pant, to squirm, to wriggle. Taern used his other hand to smack him smartly across the bottom, and Dorjan grew very still.

"But... but *Taern!*" Dorjan complained, because his entire groin was throbbing, and his cock was sore it was so swollen, and because he thought he knew what he was supposed to do with it, but that wasn't the position he was in.

"No, wait," Taern murmured, and he fumbled on the end table for something Dorjan couldn't really see. In a moment there was another feeling at his backside, a slickness, a pressure, a stretching, a finger, then two, pushing past his softened rim and stretching him full.

He screamed into the pillow, but not because it didn't feel wonderful. It did—oh Bimuit, it did! Taern kept penetrating him slowly, gently, with one hand while stroking him with the other, until Dorjan started gibbering, offering, begging, pleading, *exulting*, because it felt good, felt so good, and he wanted more, more, oh hells *yes!* "Yes! Oh Bimuit, *please… please… oh hells* yes!"

He shuddered, and his stomach clenched and released, and Taern dug his fingers in deeply and pushed hard against something inside Dorjan's body. Dorjan screamed again until his throat was raw with it, and he clenched and shook and came.

He collapsed then, facedown, and his bottom would have just stayed there, up in the air, stretched and dilated, but Taern gave him a gentle pull, and his legs straightened out behind him, and there he was, still shaking and exhausted and sinking into the spatter of his own spend.

Taern was at his shoulder as he sank. "Did that feel good?" he asked softly, and Dorjan looked at him and nodded wordlessly. "Good. That's what it should feel like. What you and Areau were doing, it didn't have to be an abomination, do you hear me? It could have been just this good, but he didn't let it be. Don't ever say you want to leave this world, Dorjan. You hear me?"

Dorjan groaned and buried face against the coverlet again. His entire body tingled, and his cock was trying to tell him that they weren't near done.

"Promise me you'll stay by my side, Taern," he mumbled before he fell back asleep. "Promise me you'll stay, and I'll take it back."

"I've been promising that same bloody thing for weeks, Nyx. Karanos, you're dim! Now go back to sleep. If you think we're done with this, you're going to be sorely disillusioned."

The Betrayal of Touch

Taern watched him sleep for a few moments and then stripped off his smallclothes and crawled in bed next to him.

He'd been up already and had run the regimen Areau had set, which was one of the things he'd done regularly when Dorjan was in with the Forum. It had been good for him in several ways—made him stronger, faster, more resilient.

And it had stilled that omnipresent, ever-painful ache of worry.

It had been so close.

He'd *thought* it had been close when he'd arrived in time to help Dorjan fight, but every step closer to the house had driven the point home. It was something he should have learned when he was nine years old and that he thought he *had* learned by living his life exactly as he saw fit, right down to fucking men for money because he *liked* it. It was the thing that allowed every touch of Dorjan to be new and shiny again.

You couldn't be too careful with time. You couldn't use it well enough or take those things you wanted quickly enough. He'd wanted time with Dorjan, time to gentle him, to seduce him, to make him pursue Taern (who had gotten rather used to being pursued) instead of the other way around. But for nearly a fortnight, Taern had been worried about Dorjan, and the one thing the worry had brought home was that there was not enough time for pride.

Krissa must have thought so too, or she wouldn't have agreed to take out some of his stitches, even if she suspected what Taern had in mind.

"Why can't we leave them until the end of the rest day?" she'd asked as Dorjan slept when they ventured into the room with a basin of warm antiseptic water and the sterilized sewing scissors.

"Because he will have popped them by then," Taern responded equably, and she looked at him with wide eyes. "A hazard of the profession," he said blandly. "We're all chair-rutting perverts, you know that."

"It's no longer our profession, Taern. Not even mine, and that's probably what's on my contract. Why? Why can't you wait until *next* rest day? Or the one after that?"

"I don't know," he snapped, feeling miserable and vulnerable at once. "How many times must I almost lose him before I have him?"

Krissa blew a breath out. "I understand, Taern—I do. But… I worry. So much—more than this household, even—hinges on his well-being."

Taern grinned cheekily, then sat down to bathe him. "Well, that's what I'm talking about! Making sure his being is as well as it can be!"

And now, when it was just him and Nyx alone and Nyx was naked and replete, Taern was willing to make himself naked and climb into the bed and stroke the patches of Dorjan's bare skin that held no lasting marks from one near miss of many. He was even willing to admit to himself that it was more than need and more than want, and more than curiosity and more than concern, and definitely more than gratitude. Yes, Taern had been with plenty of men in his past, but they had all ceased to exist the moment he'd squatted in a dark alley and touched his mouth to a masked man's most vulnerable parts. It was a good thing Dorjan had bought his contract the next day, because the thought of being with even one more man after that made Taern sick and sweaty and weepy, and generally it didn't bear thinking about.

So now he slid into bed and simply touched him, savored his skin, kissed him randomly, licked the bare parts of his shoulder, his neck, his ears, until he was squirming on the bed, groaning in arousal, but unwilling to bring himself release because that would mean he'd have to break contact with Dorjan's naked skin.

He groaned in Dorjan's ear and thrust up against his thigh, and Dorjan groaned in return, rolling over to his side and fluttering his eyes open. Taern lay face-to-face with him, touched his chest, and tweaked his nipples between his thumb and his forefinger until Dorjan awakened a little more and started to thrust up against Taern randomly, without rhythm, sleepy enough to be aroused without shame.

Taern kissed him, gratified by his response, and pressed his bare body gently against Dorjan's while Dorjan wrapped his arm around Taern's shoulders and ground against him, his still damp cock growing harder with every meeting of their wet, open mouths. Taern reached down between them and grasped both their cocks in one hand, thrusting against Dorjan and feeling the silk of his skin as his member engorged even further. Dorjan groaned into his mouth and bucked more, and Taern murmured, "Patience!" and then sank down below the covers, needing to taste him before he was sheathed securely in Taern's arse.

It took a touch of his tongue to the pink end to have Dorjan dripping wet, and Taern bobbed his head twice and twice only, tightening his lips as he pulled back and looking forward to another time when Dorjan would dump come down his throat in quantity. But that's not what Taern desired now. He'd told Dorjan what he'd needed before, when Dorjan had just awakened, and Taern had resolved to keep doing that. Dorjan *needed* to know what Taern *needed,* and right now, Taern *needed* to be filled, thrust into, fucked. Taern scrambled up to the top of the covers and reached over Dorjan to the end table, dipped his fingers into the little plate there, and pulled back his hand.

"What's that?" Dorjan mumbled, and Taern rolled away from him and then pushed down the covers and reached behind his bottom.

"Vegetable oil," he said, thrusting two well-slicked fingers into his backside, and the gasp/moan Dorjan let out made Taern's cock even harder. "You see what I'm doing?"

"Nungh...." (Also a good sound. Taern planned to hear that one as often as possible in the future.)

"Yes," Taern gasped. His fingers fit just fine, but he knew Dorjan's cock was much thicker than they were. "See? I'm spreading th—eeem, so you can see I'll be... oh Karanos and Bimuit! I'm stretched, ready, made for your cock, right?"

"Oh," Dorjan breathed, and Taern scooted closer to him, close enough to reach behind him and seize Dorjan's thick, fat cock in his hand and rub his slick fist all up and down its length. "Taern!" Dorjan gasped, and Taern squeezed tighter.

"I need this," Taern whispered. He swung his leg up, spreading his thighs and holding them, and scrunched his bottom down until he felt Dorjan at his stretched, waiting entrance.

"If you need it," Dorjan whispered, "climb on and ask me face to face." And with that, Dorjan's presence at his back was gone.

Taern rolled over in surprise and saw Dorjan was on his back, his cock in his fist and his legs spread wide. "Dorjan?"

"Do you think I don't need?" Dorjan asked, his voice gentle and exasperated. "Do you think I don't dream? Every dream of this for me has been when I can see your face and you tell me that it's good."

Taern scrambled up and got closer, close enough for their skin to touch again, then sat up on his knees and swung one knee up over

Dorjan's thin, scarred midsection. He positioned Dorjan's erection right back where he belonged, and sat very carefully down.

Dorjan let out a long sigh as Taern's body gripped him tightly, in spite of the easing of the oil. Taern threw his head back and allowed a shiver of desire to pass along his spine, and another, and another, as his bottom stretched and stretched and he took Dorjan farther and farther inside. "Ahh...," he breathed and lowered himself down completely, Dorjan so far inside him that when he cocked his hips forward, he pressed against his stomach and—

"Oh!" Dorjan breathed when Taern took his hand and stroked it over the slight bump in Taern's lower abdomen. "That's me!"

"Only because I'm starving!" Taern confirmed, laughing, and then he clenched his bottom and rose and lowered, sheathing Dorjan's cock with his body again, and Dorjan groaned. Oh yes! Again, again, again.... Taern's head tilted back, his eyes closed, and he became lost in the rhythm, the glory of having Dorjan inside him, giving pleasure, receiving it, lost in this act as a joy and not a defilement. Through his haze, Taern felt a hand stroking along his cock, and his eyes flew open. He smiled at Dorjan, who smiled shyly back.

"Good?" Dorjan asked hesitantly, and Taern closed his eyes again and kept moving.

"So good you can't stop!" Taern told him back and kept that gentle, quickening rhythm while Dorjan's hand kept stroking, stroking, easing— "Oh hells, Dorjan! Tighter! Harder! Oh fuck, *faster!*" And with that, Taern's rhythm increased, grew maddened, frenzied, and Dorjan made his caress harder and more aggressive. Taern wiggled, maneuvered, and oh... oh... oh *yes!* He groaned as Dorjan scraped that place, right *there*, and again and again and faster and faster!

Taern moved his legs underneath him so he could bounce up and down while putting less weight on Dorjan's middle. When he was situated, he reached back to fondle Dorjan's bollocks in a rough caress. That lasted a moment, though; Dorjan groaned and Taern felt bad about having to stop, but he *had to* move faster. It was *imperative*.

Oh yes! Yes! He knew this! This was sex at its best! Its hardest! Its most perfect! And suddenly Dorjan groaned and spurted, his hips pumping quickly all on their own, and Taern shuddered with the knowledge that Dorjan's spend swam hot and liquid inside of Taern's body. The thought alone made him tingle, and then Dorjan's hand tightened convulsively on his cock and—

"*Dorjan!*" he gasped, and Dorjan's head was still thrown back in that tight, beautiful grimace of a man pleasured beyond endurance.

That was it, all Taern needed, and Dorjan's next stroke sent him over the edge. He came, sticky, warm, white, all over Dorjan's hand and Dorjan's stomach and his chest, and Taern let him keep milking, keep squeezing, until the goodness of it hurt and Taern threw himself forward so he could just shiver on Dorjan's chest.

Dorjan's grin was blinding and had nothing to do with darkness in the least. "We're shiny and new," he panted, and Taern grinned back, his eyes still stinging but his heart as whole and bursting as it ever had been.

"Like silver or the sky after rain," he said softly. He leaned forward some more, and Dorjan slid out of his body, but that was fine. Taern leaned over and kissed him, and Dorjan's arms slid up around his shoulders and cradled him like he was precious. Taern w*as* precious, important, special, shiny and new.

Taern had always silently laughed at men who'd cried after sex—it had seemed so incredibly emotional for an act that had been, for him, a purely physical release.

Not this time. Not after seeing Dorjan suffer and bleed, no. This act, with this man, was suddenly of paramount importance, more to Taern's heart than Taern had reckoned his heart could hold.

Of course he cried. And because Dorjan was worthy, he didn't question a single tear.

HE GOT up eventually, cleaned them both off, and helped Dorjan scoot up and lean against the pillows. He put on some smallclothes and a dressing gown and went to open the door to the hallway when Dorjan snickered.

"What?"

"You put clothes on. We'll civilize you yet!"

"Hush and let me go fetch food. I'm starving!"

Dorjan nodded and went to swing his feet around to the side of the bed.

"And where do you think you're going?" Taern asked, indignant, as he let the door close and came back into the room.

Dorjan smiled at him with a little indulgence, and Taern thought about slugging him. "I'm going to get dressed. I could use a good work— *ouch!*" Because Taern *did* slug him, right in the shoulder, the one without any gauze, stitching, or blood. "*Taern!*"

"Rest. Days," Taern said implacably, pointing a finger at the bed. "You will sleep and recover for the two rest days. You may, if you are able, start easing back into your regimen, but you need to stand up without bleeding first, and that's already not happening!"

Dorjan looked down, and Taern walked to the end table to grab a clean square of linen and dab at the stitches and lacerations that had opened while they'd been making love.

"I thought you were getting us food," Dorjan said mildly, and Taern narrowed his eyes. Without further ado, he dropped the square of linen, walked over to Dorjan's drawers, and started filling his arms with Dorjan's smallclothes—particularly the pants, but he got as many shirts as he could find as well.

"Taern—ack!"

"Hurt?" Taern asked, his face buried in the smallclothes. He had to look around the pile to make it to the door.

"It all hurts, damn you—"

"Yeah, it hurts. It hurts because you're not supposed to get out of bed!"

"But it's all well if I exert myself in it?" Dorjan asked, the irony searing, but Taern wasn't going to hear it.

"Yes. Sex is good. Getting up is bad. Excuse me, I'm going to go dump these in my room."

"But Taern!"

Taern peered around the mound of clothes in his arms and saw Dorjan struggling to pull the blanket up over his groin, the bruises on his hips, stomach, and thighs standing out in stark relief to his pale, sweating skin.

"If you don't get in bed right now, I'll take out those women's funeral dresses you're so fond of and then the silk dressing gowns." Taern leveled a look at him that brooked no argument.

"But *Taern!*" Dorjan protested, half laughing and half shocked. "How am I supposed to get out of bed if—"

"You may either wear your fancy clothes without your smallclothes, which I suspect would chafe you like rope or worse, or you aren't supposed to. Naked. In bed. Sleeping. Eating. Reading if you like." Taern's voice dropped, because he couldn't say this with insouciance, not anymore. "Making love. Healing. And," he added as Dorjan opened his mouth, "if you bring up my contract into this, I'll take scissors to the shite I hate the most!"

Dorjan fell back against the pillows, a furrow of hurt wrinkling his brows. "I would never," he said deliberately, "bring your contract into this."

Taern scowled, the shame killing his appetite. "Good," he whispered. "Because I have better things to do than destroy your underwear."

He stomped out the door and down the hall, being good to his word and dropping Dorjan's smallclothes on the unused bed in the room Dorjan had brought him to that first night. Then he went down the stairs into the kitchen, surprised when he got there and found the two girls hard at work. Evvy was in the process of cutting up fruit and putting it into bowls, and Alla was putting butter on thick slices of fresh bread and stacking it next to sizzling cuts of ham.

Taern looked at the tray in bewilderment. For the past week, he'd come down and Mrs. Wrinkle had made him breakfast as he'd sat down, but the girls, apparently, had made their own niche since they'd arrived nearly ten days before.

"Where's Mrs. Wrinkle?" he asked curiously, and the girls looked up at him and added some more linen napkins to the tray.

"She's at market with Lady Krissa and Master Areau," Alla said confidently, and Taern blinked.

"Areau? Went *outside*?" Well, Areau *did* run his own exercise regimen, but besides the courtyard, he was usually to be found in the gymnasium or his bedroom doing whatever (and Taern truly didn't want to know whatever) or, usually, in his laboratory, doing unwholesome, unhealthy things with dead animals and poisons.

"He did it to please Lady Krissa," Alla said knowledgably. "I hope she gets offered more on her contract. She seems to be getting attached."

Taern grunted. "Yes, well, it's going around. Thank you for the breakfast tray, sweetlings. I trust Madame M knows where you are?"

"Yes, sir," Evvy said, looking up at him and smiling. "Master Dorjan already sent to her, asking to allow us to change residences. Our mothers are thrilled, and our clothes and such are due from Madame M's at any time, so we can make our rooms our own."

"Really? I had no id—when did he do this?"

"When Mrs. Wrinkle took up his tray earlier in the week," Evvy said, smiling a little. "You were outside, running your regimen at the time."

Taern shrugged. "I can't believe he was feeling well enough to—"

"What's wrong with him?" Alla asked. "Everybody's so concerned, but he keeps going to Forum, same as other days."

Well, maybe all of Dorjan's hard work wasn't for naught, if the girls living in his own house didn't see his weaknesses.

"He was hurt during the riot," Taern said simply. "He's recovering."

"Well, good," Evvy said, adding one more thickly buttered slice of bread to the top of the pile. "The bread is fresh, and it tastes wonderful. That should help."

Taern grinned and ruffled her pretty blonde hair. He remembered her mother, who had often snuck him extra food, even when there wasn't extra to be had.

"There's not much that can be bad in the world when the bread is fresh," he said soberly and then took the loaded tray very carefully upstairs.

When he got there, he found Dorjan rooting through his work satchel, and Taern wanted to smack himself, because trust Dorjan to find the one thing Taern hadn't thought to hide. But Dorjan didn't seem inclined to settle down with it. Instead, he pulled out one flat piece of cheap parchment and grunted, shoving the rest of the satchel between the end table and the bed.

"Please tell me that's not what I think it is," Taern began and then was almost shocked into dropping the tray when Dorjan ripped the damned thing in half, and then in half again, and then in half again and again, until it was only a pile of tiny pieces of paper stacked on his lap.

Taern set the tray down on the end table and picked up the pieces, looking at Dorjan with stunned eyes. "My contract?" he asked, not certain what this meant.

"Yes, Taern, your contract. If you stay, it's out of your own free will, and that includes putting on the armor again and tending to my wounds and… and….” His hands flailed about, sending little pieces of paper scattering over the counterpane and drifting down unheeded onto the floor.

“Making love?” Taern said through a dry throat, and Dorjan nodded, the hurt still there in his eyes.

“Or that,” he said shortly, and Taern sat down next to him and moved the tray into position, thinking that food was the more neutral activity right now.

“Here,” Taern said quietly, putting a piece of soft bread in his hands. “I'd be less inclined to hover if you didn't look so thin.”

“Eat your own,” Dorjan said before taking a bite. “You could shine a light through your hands right now.”

Taern took a piece of bread for himself. “You could shine a light through your entire chest,” he muttered. “Now eat.” He took a bite. “Was that really my contract?” he asked through a full mouth, and Dorjan nodded.

“Worst investment I ever made,” he said after he swallowed.

Taern slugged him once, gently, on the arm, and then they continued to eat. The contract was not mentioned again by either of them, at least for the two rest days. When they were done with the meal, Taern put the tray back outside the door, shut the door, climbed back into bed naked, and watched until Dorjan fell asleep.

THE tactic worked. Dorjan didn't do much out of bed for the two days, and the things they did *in* bed were stunning and poignant.

Taern's mission was to teach Dorjan the things that sex *should* be instead of the misery that it had been, and it seemed Dorjan's mission was to teach Taern that sex wasn't anything without the tenderness behind it.

Dorjan awoke from that first nap and cajoled Taern to let him out of bed long enough to brush his teeth and relieve himself. When he was done, he came obediently back to bed and pulled out some documents to read. Taern pulled the documents out of his hand and replaced them with a book—the same book he'd given Taern, actually. Taern had long since finished it and enjoyed it, and read another much like it.

“I hear it's very good,” he said soberly, and Dorjan shook his head.

“It was one of my favorites,” he said, “but I have things I need to—”

"Ignore," Taern said shortly. "Lay down and read your book, Dorjan. Don't worry. You won't be reading long."

Dorjan did, settling down on his good side, and Taern spooned him from behind. Dorjan let out a sigh as Taern's naked frontside made contact with his naked backside, and Taern used that, undulating gently, massaging Dorjan's body with his own. Dorjan sighed and wriggled backward, and Taern reached around and (very gingerly) started playing with his tiny brown nipples.

Dorjan gasped and pressed back harder.

Taern pinched just a little, and Dorjan made as though to roll over. "I thought I was reading," he breathed, and Taern pushed on his shoulder.

"I didn't say you could stop!" he complained. "Keep reading."

Dorjan groaned but did as he was asked, and Taern continued to drive him mad on purpose. He kissed the space between Dorjan's shoulder blades and flattened his palm over Dorjan's abdomen, all the while grinding himself gently against Dorjan's backside.

Dorjan tried to put the book down more than once, and each time, Taern stopped moving, stopped caressing, stopped playing, and whispered, "Read. You were the one so hells-bent on doing something, now *read*!"

When Taern reached around Dorjan's hips and seized his now erect manhood in his grasp, however, *that* was when he allowed Dorjan to put the book down.

"What am I supposed to do with my hands?" Dorjan complained, grasping Taern's forearm as Taern stroked him slow and hard.

"That's good right there," Taern murmured. Then he pulled his arm away, seized Dorjan's hand, and placed it on his own member. "You can do that for a moment too," he said while reaching for the oil.

Dorjan grunted as Taern stretched over his back, and Taern looked down and saw his eyes, wide and sober, taking in Taern's drenched fingers as he brought them back over Dorjan's body, dripping one thick drop over Dorjan's ribcage. When Taern fumbled between Dorjan's thighs and started probing his crease, Dorjan gasped and crooked his leg up, giving Taern better access—and a great deal of relief.

"You want this, do you?" he asked, rubbing softly around Dorjan's rim.

Dorjan didn't have to answer him, because when his finger slid in, his low groan said everything.

"I told you," Taern gloated. "I told you it was good." He slid the finger in and out, in and out, and Dorjan bucked backward to meet him. "Stop that," Taern whispered. "Just wait, be patient. The good things will keep coming, and then you will too."

With that, he added a second finger, and Dorjan's hand started to quicken on his own cock. "No," Taern hissed. He pulled his fingers away and knocked Dorjan's hand off his cock. Dorjan moaned, and Taern positioned himself at Dorjan's stretched entrance. "Are you ready for this, Dorjan? It will burn some, and stretch…."

"Yes. Please, Taern," Dorjan begged, his body undulating, begging, but not forcing Taern in any way. "Please. I'm at your mercy. Please do anything to me, please!"

Taern hmmed then and very slowly, very carefully, thrust forward. Dorjan keened in his throat, but he didn't drop his leg, and he didn't try to get away.

"How's that?" Taern asked, keeping up a sinuous rhythm, forward, back, forward, back, forward, until he was all the way in, wedged completely in Dorjan's backside. Dorjan was rocking in a gentle rhythm to keep that glide, in and out, continuing the pleasure, but not controlling it, not even a little.

"Ahhh…." Dorjan sighed and then shuddered around Taern's cock, and Taern wanted to chuckle with the flood of power through his body, but he was too euphoric. It wasn't *about* the power, it was about the pleasure, and Dorjan was immersed in it, and that was all Taern's doing.

Taern reached round then and grasped Dorjan's cock, feeling it grow iron hard again in his grasp as he stroked. "How's that feel?" he murmured again, and Dorjan threw his head back and groaned.

"That's amazing, thank you!"

Taern chuckled, the sound raw and strained, because it *was* amazing, and it *was* glorious, and he wanted nothing more—not even his own orgasm—than to feel Dorjan spill, helplessly and gratefully, over Taern's fist on his cock.

He wasn't sure what made him look up in that moment, as his hips were pulsing back and forth and his hand was stroking in counter rhythm. Dorjan had placed himself at Taern's mercy sweetly and without fuss or ego or fear, and Taern was being all merciful in an effort to please him. He didn't hear a noise or a gasp or even get a feeling, but he did look up then, over Dorjan's shoulder, and then had to *force* himself to keep moving smoothly and gently, without stop. Dorjan's head was back against the pillow, and his eyes were closed, and Taern didn't want to do anything that would change that or kill what was happening between them in this magical, weighted moment.

Especially because Areau was watching. Taern locked eyes with him as he peered in the crack of the open door, and bent to kiss Dorjan's vulnerable nape. Dorjan dropped his head and kept meeting Taern thrust for thrust, but that was his only power, his only action here, because Taern literally had him by the cock.

Taern never, ever abused his power. Dorjan whimpered and Taern started to thrust harder, more insistently, and it became harder to keep his stroking in rhythm.

"Take it in your fist again," Taern whispered. "C'mon, Nyx, let me see you come."

Dorjan did, and Taern used his freed hand to brace himself on Dorjan's hip and start thrusting harder, harder, faster. Dorjan let loose a groan, low in his stomach and seemingly ripped from his soul. Taern reached down and squeezed his bollocks while Dorjan shuddered hard and spurted hot, making helpless little sex whimpers as he did.

And Areau watched with large, haunted eyes.

Taern groaned too and deliberately closed his own eyes, allowing his orgasm to wash over him, through him, flooding his body with lightning and Dorjan's with his spend. He groaned and buried his face against Dorjan's sweating back and clenched Dorjan as close to his heart as he could, all the while still joined, still hard and spasming inside Dorjan's willing flesh.

When they finally stopped coming, when their breathing finally evened out, Taern licked happily at the salt on Dorjan's shoulder, and Dorjan kept shivering in his arms. Taern looked up then and to his relief saw that Areau had gone, leaving Dorjan happy and replete, and finally, *finally*, taking his rest days to do exactly what rest days were for.

Areau

DORJAN had been the gentlest child. He'd had big, limpid brown eyes, and his dark-brown hair had always needed combing. He'd had a shy smile, the kind that invited grown-ups to just shelter him and spoil and pet him, and a fluid, noncompetitive intelligence that meant that even if Areau got his way about something, he would realize later that Dorjan had been right all along. Areau had always thought growing up that if Dorjan hadn't been such a kind soul, so determined to rescue niskets, kittens, and butterflies, that Areau himself would have been a spiteful git.

Areau's father and mother were good people—they'd raised him well, with a desire to succeed. He'd also been the eldest, a boy, and told again and again and again that he was beautiful. He had three younger sisters, and their prettiness had been made much of as well. He had been nineteen, in the height of vanity, when that one virtue had been stolen from him.

Growing up next to Dorjan, he had felt like the prettiness and the science were the only things he had.

And it wasn't as though Dorjan was one of those obnoxious children who always had to do the right thing, either. Dorjan was as adept as Areau at getting into trouble. As a very young child, he'd had a fondness for sweets—had, in fact, been plump, pudgy, and freckled. He'd stolen an apple pie once as it was cooling on the kitchen table. The entire keep went searching for him, Areau included, and Areau had been *so* mad, because he'd wanted some pie too. And then, as Areau was passing their hideout in the front yard by the jasmine bushes, Dorjan had called his name. Areau had wriggled in with him, and the two of them had spent a giddy afternoon indulging in pie and watching quietly as people's feet passed back and forth in search of two small boys and one large pie.

They'd been hideously sick afterward, but that moment—the two of them, breathless, stuffing pie down their maws, giggling in the close dark—*that* was one of the best moments of his childhood. Dorjan had included him, had given him a treat, and finally, when they'd been caught, had taken all of the blame.

Areau let him, and felt vaguely ashamed afterward. But after Dorjan was allowed out of the house again, he hadn't held a grudge. He'd been the one to steal the pie; he'd been the one to rope Areau into his (admittedly brilliant) prank. Dorjan was the one who got the spankings and wasn't allowed to go out and play for two days. According to Dorjan it was only fair, and Areau? Had been enchanted. Dorjan was the best friend *ever*.

That hadn't changed after they'd gone to stay in the city and then come home when Karanos had been nearly destroyed by an earthquake. Areau had loved the city residence far more than the country and the keep, and he'd been bitterly disappointed to have their time cut short. But Dorjan had understood.

"Don't you see?" he asked quietly when they'd been in the darkened compartment of the millipede, sharing quarters because they were boys of an age as well as friends. "Father allowed something bad to happen. He feels responsible. He's going to be spending his time fixing it."

Of course, Areau had spent a lot of time fixing it too. When they'd returned to the keep, the other children had been angry—they'd been proud of Kyon's status and success, and suddenly he was out of favor, and their parents had grumbled and Areau and Dorjan had ended up fighting quite a lot. Dorjan hadn't been good at the fight then; this was before military school and training, and he spent far too much time trying to talk the other children out of fighting and not enough time planning to hit the big one in the nose. But Areau had been good about hitting the big one in the nose, and he'd kept Dorjan from getting pounded. Of course, once Dorjan started throwing punches, he could land them like a cannon shot, and that had been good too. The two of them had spent some time back to back, fighting for love, honor, and the thrill of it.

And again, Areau had been taken. His father was a good man and believed very strongly in duty, but his mind was like Areau's: an endless puzzle of numbers and forms, duties and facts, mechanics and details and creative plans for things nobody else could understand. Coreau channeled this into running the keep and calculating how much could be mined and when to set an asteroid free and when to harness another one to keep the complex mechanics of gravity in check. Areau had channeled *his* gift into developing new machines. When he'd been twelve, he'd shown Dorjan a diagram for a functioning vehicle with long-range travel capacity, short-range launch, and a weapons function, all run off of lumium, the same power source he later used for the steam armor. Dorjan had shown the drawings for the cricket to his father, and his father had been the one to submit them to the leading scientists of the province.

The military had picked it up and paid his family a fortune for the plans, actually. Even if Areau hadn't wanted to join when he and Dorjan turned sixteen, he still would have had a place with his province's military research department for the cricket alone. Dorjan had told him it was brilliant, and until Dorjan had told him that, Areau had never believed it. Through his best friend's eyes, Areau saw that he was as brilliant as his own father, that he could do amazing things, had a mind that worked like nobody else's. His father loved Kyon's Keep, and his family had no reason to leave, but Areau—he'd hitched his star to being the man who could make that, could fix things, could create what nobody else could.

It was his defining quality, the thing that made him. That, and his friendship with Dorjan.

He'd enjoyed talking to Dorjan about girls. Areau had thought they were the world's most amazing discovery, better than the cricket, better than the steam armor he'd been asked to set his mind to, just better. He'd been disappointed when Dorjan's reaction to them was not nearly as enthusiastic—he'd wanted his gentle friend's perspective. Dorjan's knack for talking his way out of trouble impressed Areau. Areau hadn't been that good with people, and he'd tried. But enthusiastic or not, Dorjan was still good at coaching Areau on what to say. The first girl Areau ever made love to had fallen for the lines Dorjan had given him before they'd joined the military and the academy outside of Thenis had become their lives.

Dorjan had been so nervous—so very nervous—about telling Areau he preferred boys.

Areau had been upset at first. All those late-night confidences, all of those back-to-back fistfights, all of that shared brotherhood—that had been a *ruse*? That had been an *angle* so Dorjan could kiss him?

"Don't flatter yourself, you git!" Dorjan had snapped. "You're pretty, and I can't say I'd mind, but you're certainly not the only pretty boy out there, and some wouldn't even mind a kiss or two!"

And that had irritated Areau too. "Who! Who out there would you rather kiss than me?" he'd challenged, and Dorjan had assumed a superior smile of his own.

"Your cousin Ciaran, for one," he'd said smugly.

"The weaver's child?"

"That's the one," Dorjan gloated.

"He's my second cousin," Areau replied automatically. "You kissed that simpering prat? Bimuit, Dorjan, I thought you had better taste than that!"

"I did," Dorjan said shortly, "but that git likes girls."

Areau had laughed then, and so had Dorjan. "I'll always love you, Ari," Dorjan had said with that sweet smile, the one that seemed to broker peace in any strait. "However you want me to love you, I'll love you. But I'm not going to whither and pine because you love women instead of me."

Areau had shaken his head. "Well, you could be a little more broken up about it," he groused, but he'd been happy then, honestly relieved. Dorjan was sly, but he was still Dorjan, and Areau wouldn't have to lose his brother or sacrifice his best friend to a desire he didn't understand.

That night, that terrible night at Kiamath Keep, Areau had been honestly surprised that his country was in the wrong. He'd sincerely wanted to help fix it. And, of course, he would have followed Dorjan to hell and back.

But he'd had an arrogance, a blind arrogance, that *Dorjan* was the one who was at risk, that *Dorjan* was the one who needed protection. He hadn't seen, then, the way Dorjan had grown those three years in military school. It hadn't impinged on him that Dorjan had his own battalion now. Dorjan—the Dorjan Areau had grown up with—wouldn't have taken that much responsibility if he hadn't been sure he could lead those men better than anyone else.

So when Dorjan had landed on that cricket, telling Areau to jump aboard, they had to save people, Areau hadn't thought twice. This was *Dorjan*, and Dorjan wouldn't do anything he didn't think was rock-solid right.

That wasn't what the people in the asylum had said.

They'd been terrible people, cruel in the worst ways—objectively, Areau had known that as he'd lain there at their mercy, waiting for them to sprinkle a severely weakened form of dust into his festering wounds. But pain and addiction are not objective. Pain and addiction are a deeply personal whirlpool, and from the moment they'd first rubbed the dust into his skin, addicting him to the pain when the withdrawal from the drug faded, everything in Areau's life had been about Areau.

He hadn't mourned Dorjan's father when he'd lain gasping at their feet. He'd cursed him, because Kyon hadn't gotten him out of that hellhole fast enough. He hadn't rejoiced to see the man he'd loved like a brother alive and whole after his own injuries. He'd envied him with bitter, bilious intensity because Dorjan—in spite of his own wounds, scars, and disgraces—seemed to have gotten off easily, unscathed, the spoiled little keeper's son, hauling the entire world into hell and then skipping away with nothing but a dead father and wounds that might never heal to show for it.

Areau could show him pain! *Areau* could show him craving! *Areau* was the one who awakened every hour, jerking, shivering, *craving* that thing they had given him in the asylum, and, barring that, the thing that had accompanied the ease of the longing: pain.

He had planned Dorjan's first assault on him. He'd built that armor to help Dorjan on the streets, but with every cut of metal, every tempering of the plating, every twist of every tiny screw, he'd giggled, chortled, danced with glee at causing so much pain Dorjan *had* to inflict some upon him. And oh, how delicious! Dorjan would hate it! *Loathe* becoming a bully, a villain, no better than a common rapist on the street, but Dorjan would do it, would *have* to do it, because Dorjan, the fool, the single-minded, dedicated *fool,* loved Areau, *loved* Areau. He'd said it before, he would love Areau no matter what form the love, and Areau needed—wept for—the pain, the humiliation, the self-disgust. Without those things to keep him grounded, he could hear the mockery and the derision of those voices, the many voices, in the asylum, calling him dirt, calling him guinea pig, calling him nothing, and telling him that his hopes for rescue were fruitless because a great man like Kyon wouldn't bother with some shite-crusted steward's son.

Areau, to his shame, had finally believed them. When Dorjan and his father had come to fetch their beloved friend, Areau had been more like a time bomb. They thought they were rescuing an ally, but truth? *Hard* truth? Areau was ticking, ticking, ticking, ready to become a seething ball of emotional shrapnel that would take out all in his path.

Of course, Areau was smarter than that. He didn't need to take Dorjan out quickly and mercifully. He'd leveled Dorjan at the knees, and then built him up, and then leveled him again. *His fault, his fault, all Dorjan's fault. Dorjan did this to him, Dorjan didn't care. Dorjan addicted him. It was Dorjan's job to fill the craving, to fill the emptiness to make Areau better by his own suffering, but it wasn't enough, wasn't enough was* never *enough and Areau shook with pain when pain was in absentia, and craved more and more and more and—*

Watching Dorjan's look of utter self-disgust and abandonment in the morning was almost worth having sex with a man to see.

Or that's what Areau had told himself for nearly ten years.

Krissa had disabused him of that notion right quick.

Areau had learned to be carefully cruel with Dorjan. He'd waited, behaved, been quietly courteous on occasion, and anticipated that flicker of a child's smile on his old friend's face. As soon as Dorjan smiled, laughed at a joke, trusted—even a little—once more, Areau went searching for the pain again. Areau *had* to do that. Dorjan couldn't be driven to hurt Areau unless he had hope. If he didn't think the pain was making Areau better, making him sane, making him Dorjan's friend again, he would refuse, would think that kindness was the better option not just because he'd been on the streets and had the sense of an addict's behavior now, but because Dorjan, for all his so-called "love" of Areau, was not stupid. So Areau would wait and then inflict that final wound of shrinking from their bed like what they had done disgusted him, and then string Dorjan along for a seven-day, a fortnight—once, even a month.

What they had done in bed did not, in fact, disgust him. He was not attracted to men, no, but he was aware that he had the same nerve endings in his sphincter and inside his bowel that any other man did, including the sly. When he baited Dorjan, offered the rough and bloody sex, begged for it hard, he knew the abuse of those tender nerve endings would be exquisitely painful, and that pain would satisfy his increasing yearning for more and more and more.

But it was not enough, particularly in the wait between. Areau had heard of "ripping" from Dorjan. Before Krissa had come to live with them, he had been doing it for years, one strip at a time.

Krissa had seen that the first time she'd had him strip. Areau had expected a gasp, sympathy, horror. What he'd gotten was hard-eyed contempt, and that had stung too.

"Stupid git," Dorjan's purchased whore had spat and had exchanged her gentle leather flogger for a short whip, one that would draw blood. He'd grown erect just looking at it because he knew... *crack!* Ah, yes, he knew that the blood it would draw would be his.

And for two days, she had. She'd moved the manacles to his room— and that had impressed him, as she did that on her own with the handyman's tools—and then, two blissful days of pain. Long enough for him to know she was ruthless, that she no qualms about seeing him suffer, and that she did, in fact, enjoy his suffering as much as he did. She'd masturbated once as he'd stood bent over a chair, his hands chained, a ball gag in his mouth, the smooth wood of a flogger jammed up his arse, and he'd been so aroused by her cruelty that he had come when she had—and earned another beloved stripe down his back for his insolence.

Oh, she was good, Lady Krissa. Areau would never think of her as a whore or bought and sold again.

She had him ready to misbehave, ready to be punished, and then she inflicted the biggest pain of all: the absence of it.

And just like Dorjan had followed him through hell for nearly ten years on the hope, the hope alone, that his boyhood friend could be found under the snarls of bitterness and hatred that had contaminated Areau's soul, Areau had followed Krissa through nearly a seven-day of bilious, hostile, terrifying, screaming, spitting, vomiting, shitting withdrawal on the hope that when it was over, he could have just one more hit of pain.

When it was over, she bathed him, brushed his teeth, and shaved him while he was in the bathtub. She helped him out when his shaky legs wouldn't hold him, fed him some gruel because it would be easier on his abused stomach, dressed the wounds on his wrists from the manacles, and let him sleep for nearly an entire day. She woke him with a gentle kiss on the mouth, and she tasted so sweet, like woman, like gentleness, and he hadn't had that, hadn't allowed that to touch him in oh so long....

They had made love, she riding him proudly, taking her pleasure with laughter and joy, fondling her own breasts as she clenched herself around his cock, and he'd come inside her gloriously, his entire body cleansed from the orgasm that ripped him from the inside out.

When it was over, she fell forward, her dark hair curtaining her tiny heart-shaped face, and kissed him again, smiling. He didn't remember when the tears started, but they ended in her arms.

She'd given him tiny nips of pain since then, playful little smacks, a few sessions with a paddle that was like a chicken feather compared to the sweet agony of ripping a strip of your skin down your own arm. He'd wrapped those wounds tightly and dressed them well, so Dorjan wouldn't know of his little trust-and-betray game. When she fingered the faint scars during their time together, he'd confessed to that, and she'd raised her eyebrows.

"That's diabolical," she'd said, and he'd flushed. Then he'd swallowed and looked away as the true hideousness of his actions settled into his bones.

"I'm a monster," he'd realized and had turned on his side, away from her, knowing that his face and his body might have been scarred, but realizing for the first time that the blackness of his heart was far, far uglier.

And Krissa didn't lie about it, either.

"You were," she murmured. "You *were* a monster. It's like a children's story—a changeling monster reverts back to its first form when it dies. Your monster has died, Areau. What is your first form?"

He'd gasped thinking about it. His first form, the first time he'd seen himself truly, had been through his best friend's eyes.

"Oh, Dori," he'd whispered. "I'm so very sorry."

She'd rubbed his back then, told him that he could make amends with Dorjan in the morning.

That had been the night the riot began.

When Taern had come hammering on his door demanding armor, Areau had snarled at the little snot for form, but he hadn't wasted any time pounding down to his workshop to make the armor either.

Nobody had slept—not even after the message that said he'd survived that first night. In his self-centeredness, Areau was not aware of how the message arrived or even that the messengers still lived in his home. What he had known then, still knew, was that the idea of Dorjan not coming home to this dusty, vaulting mansion was intolerable.

Areau needed to make amends. He was a monster. As far as Dorjan knew, he was a monster, the real Areau had never come back, and all of Dorjan's pain, all of his betrayed hope, was all for nothing.

Areau had *slaved* over that armor, had gone for two days without sleep, had put up with... with... well, with whatever Taern was to Dorjan. He'd put up with Taern stalking, snarling, begging, cajoling, weeping—

Yes, he'd been weeping, hadn't he?

It wasn't until Taern had taken the armor without so much as a thank-you and gone bounding off into what was apparently a very dangerous night that it occurred to Areau that Taern had been weeping.

Areau had always assumed—through the worst of his addiction, through the darkest moments of his craving for pain and degradation—that Dorjan would love him best because Areau loved/hated Dorjan best.

But Taern had been weeping, and he vaulted off to fight at Dorjan's side. Krissa, tough Lady Krissa, who had stood by impassively while Areau vomited out ten years of bitter addiction, wiped her eyes and offered Areau Mrs. Wrinkle's pie in comfort, and it suddenly occurred to

Areau in the strangest, most dreamlike of ways, that his pain was not the only pain on the planet.

And that Dorjan might die, and if Dorjan died, it wouldn't matter whom he loved best. He would never know that Areau still loved him and that Dorjan's love had not been in vain.

Areau had cleaned up his workshop methodically, then gone up into his room to bathe. He'd come downstairs and obediently eaten the dinner Mrs. Wrinkle had prepared, and had insisted Krissa eat some as well. He had heard without hearing the young voices of the girls who had brought the message, and he had summarily ignored them: he was better, yes, but ten years of believing you were the blistering, fractured, volcanic center of the universe did not go away overnight.

And then he and Krissa sat in the kitchen playing whist as though it were the most natural thing in the world, until Taern burst in through the door that led from the stables.

Areau had not been allowed to treat him or to see his wounds. Krissa had smiled tiredly when he'd asked and patted his cheek.

"It's a fine sentiment, Ari, but as you haven't doctored any of his hurts to date, we're not sure he will trust you now."

And Areau had grieved at what he had lost. Carrying Dorjan up the stairs to his room had felt like a benediction and the first steps to forgiveness. It wasn't until he watched Dorjan fight past his healing body to continue his work at the Forum that Areau realized how very much forgiveness he had to earn.

So when he opened up the door to Dorjan's room, it was not to taunt him, not to urge him to continue his regimen, not to do anything beyond check on him and make sure he was resting properly, and maybe have a few words without pain.

He'd been unprepared to see his friend, head back, mouth slack, so lost in passion that the lines and shadows that had layered his face for so long had fallen away. And the boy behind him, the nuisance, the festering little turd Areau had wanted to sweep out of his life, had been kissing Dorjan's nape with such tenderness, such absurd, weighted tenderness, that Areau—who had been congratulating himself on being a better person—found his world remade yet again.

THIS time he knocked and was chagrined when Taern's voice whispered, "Come in."

Areau ventured in quietly, a tray in his hands, and when Taern moved to get out of bed—naked and impudent, of course—Areau shook his head.

"Stay," he said quietly, looking over at Dorjan's sleeping body. Bimuit, but his friend was thin. He grimaced at Taern, unable to resist the jibe. "I'm sure you need your rest as well."

Taern scowled. "Enjoyed looking, did you?" he asked angrily, and Areau found himself flushing.

"Yes," he admitted, remembering all of the times he'd lied to Dorjan. He had felt faint stirrings of desire for his friend—nothing like what he felt with Lady Krissa, but he knew them for what they were. He couldn't lie about that anymore. It was a betrayal of himself, and of Dorjan, and he had betrayed them all enough.

Taern's scowl deepened. "That's not what Dorjan said."

Areau sighed. "Do you like milk or sugar in your tea?" he asked shortly, and Taern snapped, "Both, but I can make my own damned tea."

"Yes, you obnoxious little shite, but I'm trying to be nice."

That seemed to bring Taern up short. He sat up in bed and accepted the cup of tea and the tray of cold dinner with some grace. Areau had to admit—reluctantly, it was true—that the young man possessed his share of grace. He had been running regimens and they had practiced fencing and fighting together, and Areau had been hard-pressed to best him. Give Taern another week of practice and he would be besting Areau. The thought occurred to Areau as he sat that it was just as well he make his peace with Taern now, before Taern grew too sharp in their hand-to-hand training, or Areau might *finally* learn what it was like to have too much pain.

"Why?" Taern asked suspiciously, and Areau shrugged.

"Because I feel like it. Isn't that enough?"

"No," Taern said frankly. "Do you have any idea what you've done to him these past years?"

Areau sighed. "I'm an addict, Taern. Do you think I gave a cricket's shite?" Well, it would have been nice to pretend to be civilized.

Taern took a delicate bite of chicken pot pie. "No," he said after chewing thoughtfully and swallowing with a gulp of milk. "I don't. I think you got off on his misery, which is why I'm not inclined to trust you."

"Well, you're definitely clever," Areau said with reluctance. "I thought you were after his money, which is why I think it's a mistake to trust *you*. Do you feel better now?"

Taern jerked as though he'd been hit. "After his *money*? Are you *dusted*? Do you have *any* idea how much money I sold my arse for every night? *Money* I have!"

"Dusted? No. Not so much. But I wasn't well, no."

"Yes," Taern said with disgust before taking another bite of pie, "we heard."

Oh, lovely. Yes, of course, Areau, you're not the only person in the house. They heard. They all heard you debasing yourself for pain. "Well, you know, mansions aren't as private as a whore's bedroom, now, are they?" He winced when he said it, knowing it made him a first-class arse but unable to stop himself. He was *stung*, dammit, and *humiliated*! But of all the nasty things he could have said, Taern didn't seem to be bothered about this one.

"Yes," he said, drinking some more hexacow milk. Well, he was probably still growing. "I was a whore. I'd still be one now, contract or no contract, if I had any desire to be. Most of the streetwalkers out there, they have to be. I liked it. Does that soften your cock, Areau, to know someone *liked* it?"

"Balls!" Areau snapped, feeling uncomfortable about sex and uncomfortable about the things he'd done and uncomfortable about being in this room with this young man and his friend, sleeping in exhaustion and repletion and probably relief on the other side of the bed. "Do we have to do this? Are you going to make me say it? Or can you simply accept a lousy peace offering and my bloody thanks!"

Taern blinked and narrowed his eyes. "Thanks?"

"For…." And oh, it sounded so trite. After everything, it sounded so very weak, but it was the truth, dammit! "You make him happy. You take care of him. If I didn't give a hexashite, I wouldn't have bothered to drag him down to hell with me!"

Taern grunted, obviously surprised. "I'll be sure to tell him," he said, meditating on the empty glass of milk. "I'm sure he'll be very relieved."

Areau stood abruptly, absurdly disappointed. He'd been *trying*, dammit! "Well, if you're going to be that way, you bloody git—"

"No!" Taern protested. "Sit down, you wank! I'm being serious! He…." Taern looked at Dorjan and, like Areau, softened—his posture, his demeanor, his voice. "He loves you. I may never know why. He... he was at the end of his rope the night he met me, and all of it was over you. It's good to see you somewhat human again. I'll be honest—if you hadn't learned the knack of it, I may have killed you with a knife in the night, just to save him the pain."

Areau gasped. "Pain makes us self-centered," he said automatically, "insular, alone—"

"Unless you're him," Taern interrupted, no pity in his voice at all. "But I don't think you've gotten that far in your human lessons. Let me know when you pick up that chapter, I'll give you pointers."

Areau let out a bitter, muted bark of laughter. "I'm sure you'd be thrilled. I'm glad that he still loves me, never stopped. It may not be the thing I *accidentally* saw a few hours ago, but it—the thing we had between us—was precious to me. I'm glad it's not dead altogether."

Taern grunted and stacked his plates on the tray. "Me too," he admitted reluctantly. "Not that you *accidentally* saw us"—his tone conveyed his utter disbelief, but Areau couldn't change that—"but that he still loves you. Not for you, you understand. You've got Krissa on your side, you don't need me and I don't want you. But for him. I'm glad his faith wasn't for naught. And thanks for being human enough to come tell him."

Areau grunted, about ready to exact a promise from him, but Taern held up his hand.

"And for trusting street trash to relay the message. I understand you, scientist. You'd hoped to catch him awake. Your bad luck, but I'm here. Well, I'm easier."

Areau stood and took the tray. "There is another pie under the napkin," he said, setting the tray down on the dresser and lifting the dirty dishes to take downstairs. "If he wakes, it's for him. If you need anything else, come knock on our door. Krissa or myself will run down for it. It's...." His face heated. "We made a pact, you know. To make these rest days truly restorative for him. Try not to wear him out."

Taern waited until his hand was on the doorknob, damn him, to say, "Thank you, scientist. The dinner was appreciated. The humanness too, if you want to know the truth."

Areau stomped down on his pride and his instinct to say something cutting. "Well, I suppose dinner is always in the house, but don't count on the humanity all that often. I practiced being a rank bastard for ten years. Some habits are hard to break."

"Whoring wasn't," Taern said quickly before Areau could make the grand exit.

Areau was relieved enough to look over his shoulder and nod gratefully.

"Thank you," he said quietly. "Believe it or not, I would have worried."

He hurried down the stairs with the dishes before Taern could say anything else. His heart was pounding and he was sweating as though he were craving a stripe across his back, although that wasn't the thing his blood wanted, not anymore. He got down to the empty kitchen and dropped the dishes in the sink with a clatter, then remembered he was trying not to be a git anymore and started to wash them, his hands shaking. He'd just stacked the last of them into the rack and was wondering desperately if there wasn't any pie, or cream, or some cookies or squash bread and butter, when Krissa walked quietly into the kitchen.

"So?" she said softly, offering a drying cloth for his hands. "How did it go?"

Areau tried for an insouciant smile. "Dorjan may still love me, and Taern might not hate me quite as much," he said, his voice firm in spite of what was happening in his heart.

But Krissa knew. Areau still wasn't sure what nisket of luck had led Dorjan to her, inspired him to take her home and give her like a gift to Areau, but Areau wanted to do more than thank it. He wanted to prostrate himself before it and weep at its feet. Even more so when she walked into his arms without flinching back from the scars on his face, his shoulder, the strips he'd torn from his own arms or the ones she knew lay beneath his breeches, and wrapped her arms around his waist and laid her head on his shoulder. He stood there for a moment, scenting the flower oils that she used to rinse her hair, before encircling her shoulders and letting the tension fall from his own.

"I'm proud of you, Areau," she said softly. "You've done well for your friend tonight."

Areau swallowed hard and closed his eyes against the stinging. "Thank you, my lady Krissa," he said honestly. "I could not have done so well without you."

Nyx and Cricket

OH, IT was a relief to no longer be injured or ill or hovered over like a dying hexacow being circled by vultures in the meadow!

Well, maybe not that bad, but when Dorjan returned from the Forum on the first day after rest, he felt good enough to take a gentle pass around the courtyard and had found himself in the unlikely position of having to defend himself from every member of his household, including the housekeeper, who all told him that if he opened even one stitch they'd never speak to him, cook for him, or (this from Taern) suck his cock again.

Dorjan had gaped at all four of them and scowled. "Very well, then," he told them with dignity. "I'm going for a walk around the block. Might I do that, or does someone need to hold my hand to keep me from stumbling on the monorail as I go?"

"I volunteer," Taern said smugly. "But first put on your gloves, Dorjan. It's damned near winter."

They had not held hands (because what was the point in thick-lined gloves, for one), but they had walked shoulder to shoulder until Dorjan had needed to stop to catch his breath. Taern wasn't winded at all, and Dorjan felt a pang of disappointment.

"What, Nyx?" Taern asked. They were standing in the graveyard, since it was a pretty place for all its grim intent, and Taern had stretched up and leapt to grab hold of a bare tree limb a foot or two over his head.

Dorjan tried to hold on to his sigh. "You... you move well," he admitted, embarrassed. "I was looking forward to running with you on the street again, as silly as that sounds, and, well...." He shrugged, holding his hands out at his shoulders.

"You get winded walking around the block?" Taern asked, stating the obvious while swinging from the tree. He adjusted his grip on the way back so he could swing farther without ripping his skin or his gloves and then did the same as he flew forward, releasing his hand at the apex of the swing and landing quite a few feet beyond the tree. He turned and grinned at Dorjan, and Dorjan had to laugh because he was not only gleeful, he was charming as well.

"Yes, brat! I do. But I'm not sleeping through my Forum sessions, so *that's* an improvement."

Taern stopped, his quick mind missing nothing, and came up alongside him. "You looked like seven hills of shite last week. Did anybody notice?"

Dorjan sighed. "I told them I was ill, but yes, it was noticed. I lost my temper, when I never lose my temper, and some of the older gentlemen started taking it upon themselves to elbow me through the bloody meetings in order to keep me awake."

Taern swore, wide-eyed. "I *thought* those were fresh bruises! Wanking fuckers. I'll slit their throats in their sleep!"

Dorjan rolled his eyes. "If you did that to everyone who displeased you, Taern, there'd be more blood in our bedrooms than there is on our streets!"

Taern chuckled, the evil sound warming Dorjan to his chilled toes. "Aye," he said, breathing out dreamily, and Dorjan laughed outright, feeling less winded.

Taern wasn't distracted for long, though. "The wankers on the Forum, some of them suspect me, don't they?"

Dorjan swore to himself. "It was my fault. I shouldn't have fallen aslee—"

"Balls," Taern snapped. "Don't say it. You weren't taking a bloody nap, you were lucky to be walking the halls in the first place. They suspect me."

Dorjan nodded, kicking at a tree root moodily. "Some of them do, but it's more than that."

There was a stone bench in the cemetery, dedicated to a long-dead Triari, and Dorjan sank down on it pensively, lost in a fruitless yearning for more strength.

"What is it?" Taern asked, coming to sit by him. He was close enough that their shoulders touched, and Dorjan was forcibly reminded of their weekend, their time spent skin-to-skin, private and sublime. His whole body strengthened from the touch of their shoulders alone.

"There is an undercurrent in the Forum," Dorjan said, trying to think it through. "The riots didn't sit well with many of the members, and the use of the military against civilians seems to be smacking a great lot of them in the face with what Thenis was supposed to be and what it has become. They've been asking hard questions—things I've been begging them to ask for years, but suddenly it's fashionable to wonder why we're spending our best and our brightest and all of our resources on a war that brings nobody anything but heartache." Dorjan didn't try to keep the bitterness from his voice here, not in front of Taern, who knew every secret already.

"So?" Taern asked, leaning against him subtly. "Isn't that a good thing?"

Dorjan suddenly realized they would be together tonight, when darkness fell, after dinner. There might be civilized things in the way— Lady Krissa and Areau certainly deserved some of his time, and now that both he and Areau were in fighting form again, he had much to say in the way of strategy, but that was not the point. The point was, there would be a time, a private time, when it was Dorjan and Taern and the touch of their skin and the beat of their hearts. The tingling started in his groin and spread, stomach, spine, chest, throat, eyes—Taern. Oh yes. Taern.

"Yes," Dorjan replied, getting his mind on track with difficulty. "It's a good thing. But they're bringing up my name in the process, and given I spent those days looking sickly and unthrifty…." He looked at Taern meaningfully, and Taern groaned.

"Then people who are Septra's, body and soul, are now looking at you very suspiciously, aren't they?"

"Indeed," Dorjan said. "And they will be looking for some way to discredit me, which means that—"

"It's only a matter of time before someone starts to question your young, pretty page that has never been seen again," Taern finished glumly, and Dorjan nodded.

"It's true. But Colny can't do it—you lead right back to him and he knows it, and perhaps two other people saw you in the Forum that night. So that buys us some time, but not much. The Forum has a… an odd feel to it. It's as though the monster has escaped their control—the death of all of those soldiers from a weapon we ourselves make, that has shaken people. The wise ones are asking the hard questions, but the shriller voices are asking the silly ones. The size of a market bag, the right of the poor to have free public transportation, whether the country should pay their doctors as well as their military men—hell, the right of the sly to even exist—these are important matters, but they're secondary ones to the big frightening question, and so they concentrate on these things."

"The size of a market bag is important?" Taern asked dubiously, and Dorjan rubbed his knuckle against his forehead, a gesture Areau might have recognized from their schoolroom days.

"It's important because it allows our conservative element, the side that doesn't like change, to take power. It makes them feel powerful, and that keeps them from feeling that they've been used and manipulated. If they can maintain that they are right on the ridiculous smaller matters—"

"My right to exist is small?" Taern asked indignantly, and Dorjan glared at him.

"No, it's bloody well incontrovertible! That's why the damned arguments are so much shite! Like I said, it gives people an excuse. If they can argue on this and someone can give way because they're bloody-minded wankers, that means they don't have to worry about feeding their country or saving the lives of their citizens. They can sleep at night feeling good about themselves because—"

"Because they've argued over stupid things and taken away the rights of people who haven't so much as looked at them cross-eyed?" Taern snarled indignantly, and Dorjan snapped back.

"But don't you see? You're doing it too!"

"I'm what?" Taern asked, suddenly drawing up short.

"You're distracted. There could be men digging into my past as we speak, looking for you, looking for Areau, finding things that could ruin all my work over the last ten years, and you are—"

"Being an arse," Taern said glumly, and Dorjan nodded.

"But I don't blame you. It's hard to watch someone argue for something so wrongheaded. It makes you violent—I know it makes *me* violent." And unlike most of the Forum members, Dorjan actually knew violence as a lover, intimate and close enough to cause an ecstasy of destruction if he needed to. "I'm terrified that if we give up even one right, the conservatives will take that as a sign of weakness. But while they're arguing over stupid, obvious things, children are starving in our streets, and everyone is missing the point. We are going to have to do something—something drastic—to change the face of the Forum before it comes to a head."

Taern grunted and stood up and then offered Dorjan a hand up, which he took gladly. His arse was frozen and stiff thanks to the damned marble bench and the breath-smoking cold.

Together they turned and walked from the cemetery, drawing their scarves closely about their ears and jamming their stocking caps more tightly over their heads.

"So," Taern asked when they'd walked past the cemetery gate, "what did you have in mind? Assassination?"

Dorjan had to laugh again. "Oh, I wish. But no. Assassination leads to anarchy, and we'll have played right into Septra's hands. We simply need to change their minds, but it's easier said than done."

"Take them on a tour of a dust house!" Taern said brightly. "Or maybe bring an orphanage into the Forum to lunch!"

Dorjan longed for that arm around his shoulder. Taern was precious, and Dorjan adored him. "Alas, no. It takes a truly great man to see that he's been wrong and to apologize for it, even in the face of the obvious."

Taern hmmed in his throat and scuffed idly at a rock as they passed it. "True, true. So what did you have in mind?"

Dorjan grinned fiercely, because this had been shaping in his head since the run-in with Colny, but he was finally well enough to give it voice. "How about a little old-fashioned breaking and entering, followed by blackmail," he said, enjoying this idea very much.

Taern laughed, his breath fogging whitely into the brittle chill of the darkness. "Most excellent!" he crowed. "Wonderful! I want details! When do we start?"

Dorjan felt a bit of fatigue in his leg muscles, and some behind his eyes as well. "Give me another fortnight," he apologized, and he must have sounded wearier than he meant to, because Taern stopped dancing down the walkway. Instead, he turned to Dorjan soberly, walking backward so he could keep an eye on him as they returned to the house.

"It's just as well," Taern said moodily as they made their way through the stables so they could come in the back way through the kitchen.

"What's just as well?"

"That it's going to be a while before we start."

"Why is that?"

"Well," Taern said, unwrapping his scarf in the warmth of the stable and stuffing his hat into the pocket of the wool peacoat he'd ordered from the tailor, "for one thing, you need to be in top form, or nobody will let you go."

"True enough. And for another?"

Taern grimaced. "It's that thing you said, about it taking a great man to admit that he was wrong after all this time, and to turn around his thinking."

Dorjan's eyes widened. "You actually went a little deeper than what I said, but yes. What about it?"

"Well, I think I'm going to have to apologize to Areau before we start our endgame, and it's going to take a fortnight at the very least for me to get that out without choking on it and falling down dead."

They had stripped off enough of their outerwear to have bare hands now, and Dorjan seized Taern's while they navigated the narrow hallway to the kitchen. In the quiet privacy, he brought Taern's knuckles to his lips and kissed softly, and Taern turned to him, pale skin flushing, a pleased expression in his midnight-blue eyes.

"That was sweet," he said. "What was that for?"

"For telling me what he said when I was sleeping. For apologizing to him for anything at all," Dorjan said, meaning it. Having Areau care about his well-being that evening had made his chest swell with all sorts of emotions he didn't think he'd ever have again.

"Well," Taern sniffed, "if you're going to be that way about it, I may be able to choke it out sooner. A seven-day at the most."

"Oh my." Dorjan smiled. "Submit to me some more!"

"You like that, Nyx?" Taern asked, reaching down to squeeze Dorjan through his trousers. He was, to Taern's surprise, growing hard from the closeness of the hallway alone. "Oh my," he purred in return. "Perhaps I *shall* submit to you! I like where that thought takes us!"

"Hush," Dorjan murmured, because their conversation had taken them to the kitchen, and they would need to wait for after dinner to see where the other would lead this night.

THEY ate dinner with Krissa and Areau, waited upon by Mrs. Wrinkle and her two new charges in the kitchen. When Mrs. Wrinkle mentioned how tickled she was to have the girls to keep her company, Dorjan told Taern quietly to send word to Madame M that they would take any other innocents or refugees from the dangers of the streets, should M feel she could not shelter them all. When he said this, he saw a moment of regret cross Taern's delicate features.

"What's wrong?"

"The last time I saw her was that night I'd gone looking for you. We've exchanged letters since, but...."

"Taern?" He still wriggled like a schoolboy when he got caught acting less than the gentleman.

"I was not kind," Taern said shortly. "I was worried."

"Have you apologized in your missives?"

"Of course. But...." Taern grimaced, and Dorjan filled in the blank.

"You miss your friend and you want a chance to make it right face-to-face."

"Quit reading my mind," Taern growled. "It's rude."

"Visit her tomorrow, if you like," Dorjan told him gently, and they turned their attention to Krissa and Areau—and to Areau's long-neglected strategy meeting.

The strategy meeting was actually pleasant. It was, in fact, most unlike the days when Areau ranted and screamed, demanding more from Dorjan, more, stronger, faster, more painful, simply more, and Dorjan, well, Dorjan had been pitifully willing to do anything he asked.

This was different. This time they simply talked, pushing back their plates and discussing the state of the world through dessert, getting input from Taern and Krissa as they put together a likely list of their first blackmail victims.

Taern and Krissa turned out to be invaluable. Not only did they have a working knowledge of Forum members who were sly, unfaithful, or embarrassingly insatiable, but they also told Dorjan how to watch for things like too much drink or an abuse of a drug besides dust. When they were done speaking, he had an entirely new list of members to at least consider flipping over to his side. It was invigorating talking to them, making a plan, but he must have yawned once too often, because suddenly the others pushed their seats back from the table.

"Time for good boys to go to bed," Areau said meaningfully, and Dorjan knew his cheeks heated from the implication.

Taern simply laughed. "Bad boys too," he said smugly. "Come along, Dorjan, and don't dwell too long on which one you are. It will only spoil your dreams."

But as Taern closed their bedroom door behind them and kissed Dorjan voraciously, Dorjan pondered that nothing could spoil that dream of having Taern in his arms. The moment alone was too perfect for even dreams to destroy.

IN A fortnight he was running his regimen again, and it was time. He and Taern suited up the evening before the two rest days, and Areau helped them, walking them through improvements in the armor itself.

"What's this?" Dorjan asked, grimacing at the black thing that was supposed to cover his mouth. He put it on and spoke, grimacing at the growling sound it gave him. "Seriously, Ari, what in the bloody hell is this?"

"Protection," Areau said shortly. "You're going to sneak into the hornets' nest and whomp about that thing with a shillelagh. It would be good if the hornets didn't have any more of a way to find you. Taern, here's yours; it's affixed to your mask. Don't lose them, either of you, and don't converse without them, especially when your mark can hear you, you understand?"

"Oh," Taern spoke up, his mask held over his head for a moment. "That reminds me. *You're* Nyx—what am I?"

Dorjan laughed. "Would you believe I gave this some thought?" he said, and Taern raised raven's wing eyebrows, waiting for his answer.

"I'm breathless with suspense."

"Cricket!" Dorjan said, grinning with the aptness of it.

"Oh, I like!" Areau approved. "Speedy, can leap, versatile, noisy, and a colossal pain in the arse in its true form."

Taern crossed his eyes and stuck his tongue out at Areau, who did the same in return. They weren't exactly sweet to each other, but Taern's apology must have settled something in Areau the same way that Areau's had settled something in Taern.

Which was good—and reassuring to know, because they had a job to do.

As they set out, whispering through the shadows, Dorjan was more than a little chagrined to realize that he knew the stews of Thenis better than he knew his own neighborhood.

"Are you sure this is it?" Taern's distorted voice hissed from the hexagonal mouthpiece, since it was their third look into a house on this particular block.

Dorjan risked a look inside and saw the luxury rabbit, shining chrome exterior and all. "Yes, dammit," he hissed back, unused to the garble of his own voice. "Yes, it's him. I'm sorry!"

Taern's chuckle was distinctive, even through the distortion. "Well, remind me of this the next time we want to walk in this neighborhood—it would be best if we didn't hold hands in front of a hated enemy!"

"Oh hells." Dorjan closed his eyes and took a deep breath. It was all very good to lay out this plan on a table, with friends, over dessert, but he was used to dealing with thugs and criminals. Even when they rose up in the streets because they had innate intelligence denied by the world around them, they still didn't have the same advantages of weaponry, strategy, and basic education he'd had. Even when grossly outnumbered, Dorjan very rarely felt at risk.

But not this time. This time he was both robbing and accosting a member of the Forum, and if he and Taern couldn't be smart about it, there was no place on the planet—none—where the two of them could expect to find haven.

"Remember," he whispered, his voice low enough not to trigger the voice disguise, "beware of trip wires, buttons, and traps. He has servants, security, bodyguards—if these people are innocent, we don't want them harmed. Hit his study first, the books in his library, cubbies in his desk. He's obsessive about paperwork—he *will* have proof of those girls. I don't doubt it."

"I know, Nyx. We've done this before."

"Be careful. There's a bell at the entranceway, probably a tocsin button from his room, and as far as I know, some sort of bloody loud noisemaking thing at every threshold, and—"

"Nyx!"

Dorjan took a deep breath. "Ready, Cricket?"

"Chirp-fucking-chirp."

Dorjan swung his head slowly so Taern's impassive mask appeared in his goggles. Taern's mask was much the same as his own, only rounder in the head, and his goggles were flatter and wider to the faceplate, but Dorjan didn't need to see his expression. The tilt of the boy's head said it all.

"You bloody sphincter. Can we go now?"

Dorjan didn't need to see his irreverent grin, either, but as they ghosted along the side of the stable to the back entrance very much like the one to their own home, he was damned sure it was there.

It went flawlessly at first. Eaumond was their first target precisely because he *was* such a compulsive record keeper. He kept a filing cabinet, of all things, wooden, massive, perfectly organized and, even in the dim light of the moons coming through the window of the darkened study, clearly labeled.

They struck gold in the file labeled simply "Transactions."

"Glory," murmured Taern, sub-voice box, as he looked over Dorjan's shoulder. "This is enough to...."

"To implicate everybody," Dorjan murmured. "This is Septra's entire roster of cronies. That force in the universe again—it loves us, just a little."

"Why would he just leave this here—"

"In a locked filing cabinet in a locked house in his personal study?" Dorjan whispered dryly, and he didn't have to see Taern's eyes to know they were narrow.

"Don't be smart."

"Arrogance," Dorjan murmured. "He thinks he can't be caught."

"Apparently we have something in common!"

Dorjan looked up at the indignant voice to see Forum Master Eaumond at his doorway, two healthy-looking guards, dressed for bed, at his back. Dorjan's heart raced for a moment and then continued to beat strongly in his chest.

"Oh thank Bimuit," he said evenly. "I was really starting to worry this was too easy."

And then Eaumond rang the tocsin bell at his entryway, and Dorjan didn't think it was easy at all.

"Don't kill them, Cricket!" Dorjan ordered, tucking the rather thick file in his satchel.

Taern didn't say anything—he just launched himself at Eaumond, but while young and fairly fit, apparently the Forum Master didn't believe in fighting for his honor, because he simply stepped aside. Taern crashed into the two bodyguards, knocking one backward and unconscious against the doorframe by pure accident, and kicking the other in the shin. The guard's bone gave way in the face of the armor, and the man screamed and crumpled to the floor.

"Hells!" Taern swore, but he didn't pause, and Dorjan was right on his heels.

"Left!" Dorjan shouted as they fled through the front door. There would be soldiers streaming toward the house that way, but they'd already discussed it: go toward the stews, fight their way through the soldiers, circle around on the other side of the graveyard that marked the center square of the upper classes. The run would be considerable, but there would be no soldiers that way, and hopefully the blood that had so concerned the lokogos the morning after the riots would be considered a fluke, given the Nyx's latest flight pattern.

Taern didn't even bother to reply as he went sprinting down the stairs and down the street, Dorjan hot on his heels.

The tocsin wailed above the neighborhood, loud enough to be heard from the Forum hall and the military barracks beyond, and several of the neighbors came out of their houses to see what was going on. Dorjan ignored them, and when they came to a gap between houses, he shouted, "Left!" again.

Taern took his word for it, both of them dodging far behind the courtyard in the back to the narrow grass-lined alley wedged at the back of every house on the block. Yes, the soldiers could easily be directed after them—but first they would have to communicate with the people standing on their stoops, and Dorjan had been doing this long enough to know that folks weren't always excited about getting involved when a battalion of men invaded their neighborhoods.

So they heard the soldiers entering the good quarter from the barracks side of Thenis, and kept running. They hid in the shadows at the cross street, waiting for the battalion to clear out. When it did, they ghosted across the street and ran perpendicular, keeping to the side streets, avoiding the main thoroughfares where the soldiers would begin their concentration, before spreading out. They ran steadily and quietly, not getting winded (much—Dorjan was dismayed at how much recovering he still had to do!) and not making any noise. They dodged in the shadows every two blocks or so and listened breathlessly to see if they'd been followed.

The sound of the tocsin faded once they passed the graveyard. It was barely discernible over the street sounds emanating off of the hells of

Thenis, deeper toward the center. As it was, they didn't even garner a shout of recognition or a soldier in their quarter as they cleared the other side of the graveyard and slunk along the shadows to their home.

They were in the stables, stripping their armor off, when they heard the heavy sound of knocking on their front door. Dorjan dropped his boots and his long-sleeved undershirt on the straw for Taern to pick up, and slid into the kitchen silently. Krissa was there waiting for him with a dressing gown, which he put over his smallclothes, and together they opened the door to the same lokogos who had visited them the morning after the riots.

"Good evening, Officer," Krissa purred. She was wearing a winter-weight black velvet dressing gown with white flannel lining and delicate little fur-lined slippers, but her demeanor was no less sultry than it had been earlier.

The lokogos didn't even try to hide his delight in seeing her again, and Dorjan wrapped his arm protectively around her waist.

"Lokogos," Dorjan said worriedly. They could hear the tocsin when they opened the doors, and Dorjan thought he looked sufficiently concerned about the alarm. "I trust it's nothing serious!"

"There's been a break-in of a gennelman's house nearby, wot was it!" the lokogos told them earnestly. "We're hoping you've seen something. Has he been in here?"

Dorjan tried not to raise his eyebrows at that, but the look of disbelief Krissa shot him didn't help.

"Has who been in here, sir?" Dorjan asked politely.

"The Nyx! Bloody giant lout in armor! Has himself a trained chimp this time, a real hell-raiser! Word is he throws his shite at you an' your bones break by themselves!"

Dorjan felt his jaw drop, and Krissa had to reply or he would have found himself giggling, much like Taern probably would when they told him.

"Well, sir, he certainly sounds impudent! We should definitely report to you if we ever see a shite-throwing chimp!"

"Oh, aye!" The lokogos nodded, then smiled shyly. He was, Dorjan noted, missing some teeth. "And I'll protect you real gennelmen-like, miss." His voice dropped, and he darted a covert glance toward Dorjan, although Dorjan hadn't moved an inch from where he'd stood during the rest of the conversation. "An unlike some of yer dandies and soforth, I'll keep yer virtue unspoiled, right?"

Krissa nodded gravely. "You're a brave man, Lokogos. We'll sleep better knowing your sort is wandering the street, looking for bloody giant louts and their shite-throwing chimpanzees!"

The lokogos smiled again and edged his way out, and Krissa closed the door behind him before leaning against it in relief. She blew out a breath and then glared sternly at Dorjan, who was bravely trying to hold a straight face.

"Don't you start!" she admonished, although her own smile was trying to break out. "Let's get that information to Areau, and *then* we can—"

The piercing sound of Taern's cackle interrupted her, and she closed her eyes. "Bimuit!"

When they got to the kitchen, they found Taern collapsed behind the door, howling with laughter and gasping "shite-throwing chimp!" whenever breath allowed. Dorjan found his own hysteria fading and a true, warm laughter taking over. He bent down and pulled up the satchel Taern was clutching, then handed it to Lady Krissa with a bow.

"I'll be up early to see what Areau thinks, but tell him I've got some ideas of my own," he said soberly. Krissa took it and bowed, then left the two of them—Taern still giggling—and walked out of the kitchen toward the stairs.

Dorjan looked down and laughed outright, then squatted and hoisted the boy over his shoulder, wriggling with laughter and all.

"Dorjan!" Taern objected, still giggling, and Dorjan slid his hand under Taern's smallclothes and squeezed his bare backside just to hear him yelp.

"Has it occurred to you," Dorjan asked reasonably, "how amazing it would feel to have you laugh like that while I was inside you?"

It was not his imagination—he felt Taern hardening against his shoulder as he traversed the stairs, and Taern's wriggle became decidedly sexual.

"I would *never* laugh while you were inside me," Taern breathed, and Dorjan squeezed the boy's arse harder, allowing his finger to slide down his crease and graze his puckered little entrance. Taern groaned and Dorjan kept walking.

"You'd never throw shite at an enemy," Dorjan said smugly, "but that doesn't mean it wouldn't be amazing too."

They had reached his door by then, and he opened it and deposited Taern on his feet. Taern dropped promptly to his knees on the carpet, burrowed beneath Dorjan's dressing gown, and dropped his knitted pants and his briefs. Dorjan gasped as the boy took his barely lengthening cock into a hot mouth and suckled, *hard.* He was burgeoning and erect so quickly he saw stars, and Taern clamped his lips around Dorjan in his mouth.

Dorjan leaned back against the door because his knees weren't going to do the job, and Taern started pumping him in a tight fist. "If I grease myself up," Taern whispered, "and bend over so you can fuck me, I promise I won't laugh."

Dorjan groaned when Taern added his other hand to Dorjan's balls and began to massage those too. "And I promise it will be amazing," he breathed. Taern broke away from him to shimmy out of his clothes and reach for the vial of scented oil he'd started keeping on the end table without the electric lamp.

Dorjan dropped his clothes as well, and when Taern bent over, fingering his rim, his swollen bollocks, his hard, surprisingly large cock, Dorjan was on him so quickly he felt armor enhanced. The young man's body was tight and muscled under Dorjan's own, and as Dorjan slid into him, Taern muffled a cry of pleasure on his arm. Dorjan stilled for a moment, leaned over his shoulder, and whispered, "Good, right?" because his wounds were still there, and his need to know that it really *was* pleasure overran his need to drive himself into Taern mindlessly.

"Amazing!" Taern breathed. "Now faster! Harder! Oh, Karanos, Dorjan, *now!*"

Dorjan did, thrusting hard, pounding, while Taern buried his face in the mattress and held on with one hand and pumped his own cock frantically with the other. Dorjan's climax burst upon him, and he cried out, biting Taern's shoulder as the white-red of orgasm rushed his spine and burst behind his eyes, and Taern groaned beneath him and spurted all over his fist.

Taern collapsed on the bed and Dorjan fell on top of him, the two of them panting and half laughing with the explosion of lust and sex and completion that left them breathless and still aroused.

"Here," Dorjan said after a moment. "I'm going to go get a cloth, but don't move when I pull out."

"Why not?" Taern asked, although he didn't seem inclined to move at all either.

"I want to see," Dorjan murmured and eased his way from Taern's body and stood back.

Taern was dilated, his entrance loose and messy, awash in Dorjan's spend, which was trickling down the crease of his backside to his upper thighs.

Tentatively, Dorjan reached out a finger and traced the curve of Taern's plump, muscular cheeks, then allowed his finger to dip into that dark recess. Taern moaned softly when Dorjan touched his rim, and Dorjan jerked his finger away.

"No," Taern said harshly. "I like it. Keep touching."

Dorjan did, then wrapped his arm under Taern's middle, hoisted Taern's arse in the air again, and reached out a tentative tongue to trace the pattern of spend on the bottoms of his thighs.

Taern groaned and spread his legs and begged. "Grab me, Dorjan. Stroke!"

Dorjan did and found that he was aroused again as well. He plied his tongue once, just to watch Taern shudder, and then sat up and positioned himself and thrust again. This time they were slower. Dorjan reached across Taern's chest and rubbed it, tweaked his nipples, palmed his softly skinned, tightly muscled stomach, and then stroked his cock, slow and easy, even as he pumped inside.

This time Taern turned his head sideways and they met in an awkward, hungry kiss. Taern spasmed first, and Dorjan watched, his chin buried in the hollow of Taern's neck and shoulder, as Taern's spend shot across the bed and spattered on the sheets. This time Dorjan felt Taern in his arms as he buried his whole face in that hollow and came again. They didn't speak for a very long time, and Taern was the one who got up to get the washcloth, and who cleaned Dorjan off with a reverence Dorjan had never seen before.

THE next day they met over an early breakfast, after Dorjan and Taern's conditioning and before their customary run through the stews to the Forum.

"What's your plan?" Areau asked Dorjan, and Dorjan was relieved, because he had one, and he'd been afraid of what Areau would come up with, given the massive quantities of information they'd garnered in one short grab.

"The plan is much the same," Dorjan said soberly, between taking bites of his boiled oats and sugar with relish. "The plan is, I take the information that implicates Eaumond and slip it on an honest man's desk. There is a vote tomorrow in which Eaumond figures large—let's see if the information discredits him enough for the vote to swing my way."

Areau nodded. "And if the information doesn't make the rounds?"

Dorjan shrugged. "Then we try another honest man, because my first choice was obviously not honest enough."

Areau nodded again. "The bastard was generous—made laborious notarized hand copies of everything. I hope his secretary gets paid a fortune, because the man or woman has earned it. So, what if it works?"

Dorjan felt in his gut that it would work. "We keep going. I know of two more drug-brokering meetings happening in this next week. If Taern and I could interrupt those and rob Septra of his bribe silver, we can also give people in the Forum the information they need to make honest decisions, and not ones tainted by blood money. If we can swing the Forum our way, we can pull the troops within the end of the month."

"And then what?" Taern asked seriously. "Ending the wars will not make things all better—you know that!"

Dorjan nodded sadly. "Then we start rebuilding," he said, looking Taern evenly in the eyes. "And when our world is stable again, we go to our keep and make that perfect too."

Taern nodded. "What will we be at your keep?" he asked, his gaze flickering to Krissa, and Dorjan and Areau met eyes. Areau's eyes were beautiful, blue, and for the moment, unshadowed by sadness.

"You shall be besieged by our mothers," Areau said lightly. "My mother shall try to cook for you, and Dorjan's mother shall try to sew you new sheets and bed quilts, and both of them will pepper you with questions about how happy you plan to make their sons."

Dorjan laughed softly, because it was true. His mother and Areau's mother were great friends. "And we shall write to Dre's keep," he said seriously, "and you shall see your sisters again."

Taern shook his head and looked studiously down.

"You don't want to meet your sisters again?"

Taern looked up and wiped his eyes. "It's a beautiful fantasy, Nyx, but… but I've got a feeling in the pit of my stomach that it was never meant to be."

Dorjan and Areau met eyes again. "It's going to be hard and long," Dorjan said quietly, and then he leaned over and kissed Taern softly, trying to reassure him. "But that doesn't mean it's not something to strive for."

Taern smiled at him hopefully, and Dorjan kissed him again before running upstairs to change.

HE ARRIVED at the Forum a wee bit early and slid into the unlocked office of Emon Keely, one of his father's oldest friends. He knew the man had been disappointed in Kyon's less-than-spectacular son, and he'd been earnest about trying to change the destructive course of the country.

Dorjan left a copy of the business transaction—three young girls from Eaumond's keep given to another Forum Master in trade for his vote. There was no note as to what the girls were for, but they'd been sold like chattel, and Dorjan and Taern were paying the other Forum Master a visit that night to see if the girls needed help. The receipt was damning, and since there was a debate that morning at to whether or not the government should forcibly conscript able-bodied men from the middle-class families into the war effort, Dorjan could only hope it would make a difference.

He was still hoping as he sat in the crowded conference room, listening to Eaumond make what sounded like a closing argument before asking for a vote. Keely had arrived late, pale and concerned, and was sitting through Eaumond's argument clutching what looked to be a few sheets of parchment with shaking fingers. Dorjan sat in his customary "don't look at me" position—his arms crossed, his jaw dropped to his chest, almost as though he was about to fall asleep, but he couldn't keep from studying Keely during the course of Eaumond's speech.

The man had the look of someone on a precipice, wondering if he had the courage to jump.

Dorjan realized that he was going to have to put himself out just a little if he wanted this to work. He caught Keely's eyes then and regarded him steadily, soberly, without the customary idiot smile on his face. Keely clung to their gaze like a drowning man, and Dorjan allowed his eyes to flicker down to the papers and back. Keely's own eyes widened, and Dorjan nodded. Yes. Yes, he knew *exactly* what was on that parchment, why do you ask?

Eaumond's argument drew to a close, the majority of the room applauding his speech, and Keely got deliberately to his feet. He turned to the Forum Master next to him and said, "Juame, could you possibly read this aloud for me?"

The details of a human slavery transaction took the assembly by surprise, and Dorjan watched with great pleasure as Eaumond's complexion—normally ruddy under his thick mustache and the fall of curls across his brow—waned until his lips were a cold, shocky blue.

"What exactly are you implying?" Eaumond asked at the end after a moment of stunned silence.

"I'm simply asking the assembly if they want to put the decision as to whether or not to auction off our country's sons to warfare into the hands of a man who thinks of humans as no more than hexacows as it is."

The vote wasn't held until the next day—and it was almost overwhelmingly against.

IN THE interim, Nyx and Cricket visited the Forum Master whose name had been on the receipt. The man had laid waste to his entire household with a butcher knife before his servants had overwhelmed him, killed him, and fled. Grimly Nyx and Cricket noted three young girls in a small, carefully made boudoir. They'd apparently been the man's first victims.

The two of them surveyed the blood, the vicious carnage, and retreated to the kitchen, shuddering.

"What are you doing?" Taern asked as Dorjan started rooting around for the kerosene for the emergency lamps.

Dorjan didn't reply, but he came back with two tin drums of kerosene and looked grimly at Taern through the goggles of his mask.

"They're going to blame it on us anyway," he said quietly. "Wouldn't you rather not have their families know about this?"

Taern paused for a moment. "Right," he said roughly.

They were long down the block before the tocsin for the fire sounded. They would have gone home and bathed to get the stench of kerosene out of their clothes, but there was a sale of dust pending that evening, and they had other things to do before they slept.

THERE were three hundred Forum Masters, two Triari, and Alum Septra, who was nominally a Triari but whom everyone acknowledged as the country's figurehead. In order to overturn the rulings of the Triari, the Forum needed a two-thirds majority vote.

Nyx and Cricket had discredited six Forum members, broken up two protection rackets, and stolen three loads of dust by the time solstice threatened to plunge them into deepest winter, and they were still two votes short of overturning the Triari in their stand to continue to expand the army for the next year. That might have been encouraging—in a previous year it would have been an embarrassment of victory—but one month after they'd broken into Eaumond's home and hit the mother lode of discovery and blackmail, Dorjan was called into the Forum for a special vote.

Septra introduced the bill, and Dorjan paid special attention to the things he introduced personally. It didn't matter—this announcement would have hauled him from the grave by the armpits.

"I regret to pose this to the Forum," Septra said, looking appropriately regretful. It was the same expression he'd worn when he announced the death of the eight thousand good men, and those carefully arched brows and compressed lips made Dorjan fantasize about sitting on the man's chest in armor and beating him until he heard his jaw crunch and his cheekbones shatter beneath gauntleted fists.

"I have, alas, spoken to the Forum Master in charge of this venture, and he is reluctant to listen to reason and increase the revenue of this important resource. I find his reasons noble but his refusal to bow to practicality to be ignorant in the extreme, and that is why I am here asking the Forum to seize Kyon's Keep from its heir and to appropriate the mines for our province's use."

"Excuse me," Dorjan said into the shocked silence, "did you just call me ignorant? You're offering to exploit a natural resource to the point where our planet self-destructs, and you called *me* ignorant?"

"I… *we* find your concerns to be the overwrought rantings of a man too close to his own land to draw rational conclusions," Septra said, his voice not even rising in pitch.

Dorjan grinned then, angry and aware that his guise of cheerful, simple git was not going to get him through this next challenge. "It's interesting that you mention how close my father was to the mines," Dorjan said, keeping the politeness there out of habit. "He worked the mines when he was young. In fact, we *all* worked the mines as children. Not in as extreme a state as the convicts who originally harnessed the asteroids to the planet and worked them, but we all spent a fortnight a year getting to know the ins and the outs, investing our sweat and our *blood* to those mines."

He looked carefully to see if Septra understood what he was up against, and saw a careful consideration in the older man's eyes. Septra didn't *know*, Dorjan concluded. He did not have concrete information of how the families of Kyon's Keep had tied themselves to the indigenous population of their planet, but he *had* heard some of the stories of the niskets and their appetites.

"As interesting as that is—"

"It's more than interesting, Triari Septra. It's crucial. Do you understand how the asteroids are mined?"

Septra tried a thin smile. "It's hardly nece—"

"No, sir. It's very necessary. The asteroids are blood locked to my family and to the people loyal to my keep. Not only would it be immoral to compel us to deepen the mines, it would be impossible."

There was a collective gasp from the assembly, and Dorjan kept his cheerful smile in place.

"Explain, please," Septra demanded, a muscle twitching in his cheek.

Dorjan's smile was all teeth. "No," he said with a happy grin. "I'm afraid *that* is a secret bound to my keep and my keep alone." He'd told Taern that one night over dinner, because he trusted the boy with his life. He had from the first. It wasn't until this moment, in front of the assembly of his peers, the cream of his province, that he realized how deeply that trust truly ran.

"Well I'm sure *somebody* at your keep—"

"Can be compelled, blackmailed, threatened, or tortured into doing your bidding?" Dorjan asked, not allowing his voice to harden. He didn't need to: the Triari flinched from the baldness of the words as it was.

"I'm sorry you think so ill of us," Septra said with a faint smile.

"Well, you can hardly blame me for thinking otherwise," Dorjan said, feeling as predatory as a hieter. "You just threatened to take my family home by force. Given how many of your supporters have been lately found to have moral compasses that are either broken, warped, or absent, you can't blame me for doubting that any action so counter to our province's charter is either misguided or sinister."

Septra's face washed red and then white, leaving two high spots of color on his cheeks. "Those instances are regrettable—"

"And proof that perhaps we here in Thenis need to improve our province's moral center instead of seeking to make war on our neighbors. Make no mistake about it, Triari, making war on your own keeps would be as regrettable a move, both in cost and consequence, as making an unjust, unsolicited war upon the innocent souls on this planet."

"I will *have* those resources!" Septra barked, out of patience and apparently out of words. "If I have to set the might of every soldier in the province upon you and yours like a comet on a crash course!"

"Except you can't do that alone, can you, Triari?" Dorjan asked. His heart was thundering and he was sweating like a man in battle, but he kept his voice light, never thinking how much courage it took to pretend they weren't arguing total global destruction in a room full of old men so foolish they couldn't see how wrongly they'd been led. "You need two-thirds of the Forum to slaughter the people of my keep, and even if you did, you *still* wouldn't have the secret to mining the asteroids. You. Couldn't. Do. It."

The niskets would never allow it. The bond that had existed at Kyon's Keep since the first Kyon, over twelve generations before, had been fostered of love and respect. The nisket Dorjan wore at his throat had been Kyon's, and his father's before him. Dorjan felt its fear and its exultation—the night they'd avenged Dorjan's father, it had been all triumph. Right now, humming inside the locket at Dorjan's throat, what Dorjan was feeling was fury. Flox had been angry enough at Kyon's death. This threat against *all* of the humans in Kyon's Keep? Was enough to make the locket grow red and hot against Dorjan's skin, and Dorjan was so angry himself, he hoped it scarred and burnt there, the pain a reminder of why he'd sacrificed ten years of his life to stop this man.

Dorjan was barely aware that a space around him had opened up as the Forum Masters around him sensed the danger in either affiliating with him or opposing him. He didn't care. He stood alone on the floor and kept on the idiot smile that had sustained him for ten years, and wondered if maybe his peers were starting to wonder how much of an idiot he really was.

Septra swallowed, and for a moment he looked cowed. Then he gave a particular cavalier shake of his head and his own insouciant smile. "Try. And. Stop. Me."

And the most divisive Forum argument in history began.

"WE NEED Colny," Taern said for the millionth time.

Dorjan stalked the sitting room where they all sat—even Mrs. Wrinkle—and looked at the cards and notes Dorjan had meticulously kept on his fellow Forum members.

"No," Dorjan said for the millionth time in response. "He *knew* you, Taern. He knew where you'd worked. Hitting him would be putting all of you in danger—you, Krissa, Madame M. There's got to be somebody else—"

"No," Krissa said quietly. "Nobody else. We've looked, Dorjan. You've looked hardest of all. None of the other Forum members has enough heft to get the other six Masters to swing our way. Colny— discredited or changing his mind—would be enough to do it, but nobody else. Not with the vote coming next week."

Dorjan sank to the couch and scrubbed at his face with his hands. "You two could leave," he said hollowly. "I'd send you to my keep, but obviously that's dangerous. I can send you to the one with Taern's sisters—Areau too."

"Why Areau?" Taern asked, and Dorjan and Areau met wry glances.

"Do you think anybody at the Forum knows he's alive and living here?" Dorjan asked him. "We rescued him from the asylum and my father died. The asylum never advertised his loss, and I never advertised his gain. As far as they're concerned he's either dead or—"

"Crazier than a nisket's shite," Areau said dryly, and Dorjan managed a small smile. Oh, the past month had been fraught with danger and worry, with violence and the eternal heart-pounding, palm-sweating fear of getting caught.

But it had also been the first time in nearly ten years a secret part of Dorjan hadn't yearned to do just that, to surrender to execution or fall on a guard's sword because anything, anything, would be better than what he'd been living.

These past weeks with Taern, with Ari and Krissa, had been as close to happy as he'd been since he was a child, and he was reluctant to put any part of that in danger.

Selfishly reluctant, as the people in his life were reminding him now.

"I just found you all," he said softly, feeling foolish and afraid. "How am I supposed to risk you?"

Taern suddenly stood at his side, and Dorjan looked down into his midnight-blue eyes. "You're so short," he said absurdly. "I just always expect there to be so much more of you."

Taern smirked. "You're looking in the wrong place!" He waggled his sleek black eyebrows, and Dorjan blushed.

"Maybe I am!"

"Of a certainty, your balls are made of solid rock."

This from Areau, and Taern and Dorjan both looked up and groaned. "Please don't think about my balls!" Taern begged, and there was reluctant laughter.

"We have to," Krissa said softly. "And I don't mean think about your balls, Taern. Dorjan, I've only been here a short time, but even I can see what you and Taern and Areau—"

"And you," Areau said, his voice ringing with sincerity. "You have done this too!"

Krissa's look was so liquid it hurt. She reached out and touched his cheek—his scarred cheek—with tenderness, and Dorjan swallowed. He had wrought so much better than he'd known. "The most important thing I did was help you become well enough to participate," she said firmly, and then, because she was Krissa and stayed straight to her purpose, she continued. "This is important. That night we saw you take care of the man killing girls—I thought that was impressive. The scope of what you've truly been doing here—it's terrifying, and very necessary. I've lived on the streets—I can survive again. I am more than willing to risk my identity or my sweet little place here to see this through."

"You don't have to ask me," Taern said, looking at him seriously. "You never do, but I'd be furious if you bollixed this up because you were worried about one person. My parents died for this. So did your father. It needs to be done."

Dorjan nodded and then looked helplessly at Areau.

"How long has it been since we've been home, Dori?"

Dorjan looked away. "Half a year," he said quietly. "We usually go back at each solstice."

"You kept the visits short, I know." Areau nodded. "Because I was a git, and because you didn't want anyone at home to know what… what I'd made of us. We spent part of that time in the mines so the niskets would stay bonded." He smiled then, a sort of ecstasy, and Dorjan remembered too. The niskets swarmed them, saying hello, sampling their blood, and the sensation was… sensual. It was called nisket madness, and everyone was susceptible. Women conceived children with men who weren't their husbands; men rutted with anyone nearby, regardless of gender. Dorjan and Areau, locked inside their painful dance, were twice as vulnerable to it, but nobody thought twice about the two of them, friends almost since birth, lost inside the spell of those tiny mouths, lapping away at their blood. Those trancelike times inside the mines had been for the two of them, perhaps the only times they'd ever touched each other without recrimination.

Dorjan looked away. "I offered to have us go in separate," he said apologetically, and Areau shook his head.

"I shan't bore you with why I wouldn't take you up on that. But for all of that, home is a good place, a kind place, and frankly, I miss my sisters and their children and our mum. For that alone, I'd be willing to risk my life. But it's more than that—it's the key to the health of the province, of the whole planet. That's the one thing I never lost track of in all my insanity—that we were fighting for something more. Colny, Dorjan. You have to hit him."

"He's not in the handy little folder we discovered at Eaumond's," Dorjan reminded him. "I shall have to leave notes to tip off Keely and anyone else who cares to listen."

"Excellent," said Areau, winking. "Turns out, you're not the only one here who can read and write. We could possibly help you with that."

"Bimuit, you're a pain in the arse!" Dorjan muttered, falling back into the davenport. He felt a breath at his ear, and when he looked up, Taern was right there, close enough to kiss, but his eyes were open and too sober for that at the moment.

"How's it feel, Nyx, knowing other people are taking risks for you?"

"Shut up," Dorjan snapped, because his stomach was upset and his chest was tight and his hands were sweating, all in reaction to the potential disaster he could practically smell in the air.

"Yes, my liege. Any time, my liege. At your leisure, my—"

Dorjan grabbed the cravat from his natty suit and hauled him in for a half-angry kiss. Taern melted into him, boneless and fluid, and Dorjan pulled the boy against his chest and wrapped him up in powerful arms, then simply sat there while Areau and Krissa carefully worded the blackmail note.

When they were done, Dorjan pushed Taern away to stand over their shoulders. He read the letter, gnawing his lip. "I hate this," he said. "You do realize that in this matter, I'm no better than he is, right?"

Taern sat abruptly on the davenport. "Dorjan," he said sweetly, "come over here."

Dorjan eyed him suspiciously. "Why?"

"So I can kick your arse. You're nothing like he is!"

"Taern?" he said reasonably.

"What?"

"You're full of shite. I am as sly as Colny, and I have actively led the world to believe otherwise—"

"Have you voted against that thing we do every night?"

Dorjan cleared his throat, embarrassed, and looked at Taern significantly and then to where Krissa, Areau, and Mrs. Wrinkle sat, watching with great interest.

"Almost every night," Taern amended, and Dorjan squeezed his eyes shut.

"No, Taern, I have not voted against what happens in our bedroom almost every night—"

"Did you hear that?" Taern said, pleased. "*Our* bedroom. Two months ago, I was hard-pressed to get him to let me sleep innocently in his bed."

It was Mrs. Wrinkle who broke his momentum. "Upon my word, Master Taern, you may have been naked as a newborn baby, but you were as far from innocent as a nisket is from a hexacow. Now stop embarrassing him!"

Dorjan gaped at her in surprise, and she stood up and started to clear up the detritus of tea and cookies she'd brought to them as they'd discussed strategy.

"Master Dorjan, you're a good man. Keeping your family lands isn't just good for the people on them, it's good for all the people here. You're right. What you or the other Forum Masters do on your own time, that should be yours to own up to—but you're not the one who made it impossible to do that, are you? You've fought for the rights of people to be human. If you need to expose this man for doing what he's telling other people not to, well, that's a child's lesson right there." Her eyes twinkled for a moment. "That man ought not be making pies he can't eat, am I right?"

Oh dear. Dorjan's grin made it to his eyes and stretched his face wide. "I'd forgotten you were there when that happened," he said, managing to evade *everyone's* eyes.

"Well, I was. You perpetrated the crime, you little mastermind, and then you owned up to it and didn't get anyone in trouble but yourself. Young Taern here is right about one thing. You're nothing like the people you're fighting. Who you want to bed isn't the whole of who you are. In your case, Master Dorjan, it's not even close."

And with that she bustled out with a tray full of tea and silence in her wake.

Areau grinned at him then and winked. "And it was a glorious crime too," he said softly, and Dorjan inclined his head.

"I would have done anything to make you think I was worth playing with," he confessed.

Areau's smile was as breathtaking and as clean and beautiful as Dorjan remembered it being when he was as a child.

"It worked!" Areau stood and clapped him on the shoulder. "And this will too. Now go to bed, Dorjan, and take your obnoxious brat with you. It's a good night to retire early."

Taern made sure it was.

FORUM Master Keely was not there that morning, but it was no matter. Dorjan had left Areau's carefully worded, plainly stated letter that said the male streetwalkers along the brothel stroll would have good reason to remember Forum Master Colny, and to be sure to ask him why before they followed him into any endeavor.

Dorjan left hours earlier than he usually did, and flitted through the corridors of the Forum wearing his white robe and disappearing into the sunshine spaces of the white marble building with the same grace he'd used in the shadows for ten years.

When it came time to debate the motions before the floor, Colny arrived looking pompous and self-important as always, and was surprised when the mutters began. When it was his turn to stand up and debate, a Forum Master who, until very recently, had followed everything Septra and his cronies had stood for, was the first person to stand up and challenge him.

"Before you begin, Master Colny, is there any way you can answer to the allegations we've all been exposed to?"

Colny stopped for a moment. "Allegations?"

"Yes sir. That you're sly—which, honestly, I'm not interested in, except for the fact that you've been pushing some sort of twisted bill to make that illegal. That's blatant hypocrisy, sir, and I'd like to know if you're guilty of it."

Dorjan had to give Colny credit: the man practically turned purple, but he did try to power through. "I… I don't know if that has any bearing on the subject at hand," he stammered, and Forum Master Kevet raised ginger brows over a broad freckled face made great by the wide, bushy ginger beard.

"The bearing is, we're voting as to whether or not to take a man's land from him, and you're one of the people pushing that vote. If you can't be honest with the world about who you are, how are we supposed to trust your integrity on this?"

Colny simply turned and walked away.

Dorjan and the rest of the Forum watched him do it, and Dorjan would have thought he was on the run, but on his way out, Colny sent Dorjan such a look—a fulminating, threatening glare—and Dorjan had to pause before he turned back and launched into a sincere defense of his home.

But Dorjan didn't sleep well that night, in spite of the fact that he and Taern had both run a mission into the stews. They returned to what was becoming their usual amazing moment of sensuality after a successful mission. He had Taern tucked in his arms and unconscious to the world; he should have slept like the dead, but whenever he closed his eyes, he saw Colny gloating as he turned away in what should have been disgrace.

He wondered what the man had planned.

Particles of Dust

"JUST be careful today," Dorjan said nervously.

Taern packed his satchel, making sure there was a simple lunch in there. Dorjan freely admitted he refused to eat at the Forum canteen.

"I promise I shall keep to the back ways and that I shan't linger at M's." Madame M had answered the seven-day before, saying two more of her employees had children she'd feel safer located at a Forum Master's home than a brothel keeper's—and she'd expressed her thanks. Taern had answered her back at length, and Dorjan had chided him gently about the two pages of incriminating missive Taern had asked Dorjan to run by in the morning while Taern worked his regimen.

Madame M had been embarrassingly grateful of his offer when he'd dropped off the letter.

"You are like our guardian nisket," she'd said archly, and Dorjan had blushed.

"I have much to thank you for," he said formally, and she'd laughed and patted his cheek.

"Oh, my dear. Taern? Taern blew in like a volunteer strawberry—sweet, productive, and temporary. One evening in your company and he was perfectly willing to go put down real roots in another garden."

Dorjan blushed harder. "You provide good earth here in the stews, Madame. This business is going to be—you make it safe and shame free. You treat them fairly, and they love you for it. When times are better and your brothel is a shining place of elegance and refinement in a clean city, you will know that much of the hope this city had in the darkness, they gleaned from you."

"Oh my." M dabbed at her eyes carefully so as not to smear her thick kohl or the powder that made her skin porcelain and smooth over the stubble.

When Dorjan had left, he'd placed a careful, sensual kiss on the back of her hand, and she fanned herself semiseriously.

"Oh, Forum Master—if I were your type!"

But of course she wasn't. Dorjan preferred men.

M's return letter was dropped off by a sallow-cheeked boy who had been taken into Mrs. Wrinkle's kitchen and fed soup until he fell asleep. The letter asked that they take in another child—this one an orphan M simply didn't have the room for—and, if Dorjan could, send the girl to his keep. Dorjan agreed and told her Taern would come to fetch them.

He chose this day for a reason.

Colny would need to return to the floor today or they would lose the opportunity to vote on Dorjan's lands. Dorjan feared. His fear was an amorphous thing, but it was all encompassing—he feared for Taern, he feared for his household, he feared for Madame M. He'd told her to be careful on the day Taern came to visit. He'd told Taern to wear armor under his clothes and cloak. He'd warned Krissa about opening the door to strangers. He'd told Mrs. Wrinkle that the children were to hide in the stables—in the rabbit if necessary—should anybody ask to search the house.

And still he had the nagging feeling he had forgotten to do something.

He affected his cheerful demeanor on the floor, but judging by the speculative looks he got from allies and opposition alike, he was reasonably certain nobody was fooled anymore. Well, good for them. Let them keep guessing, because he was fighting for so much more than the good opinion of foolish old men.

So he was apprehensive but not surprised when Colny stalked onto the main debate floor and eyed Dorjan with wicked intent.

"Gentlemen, some of you are aware of the meeting of the Triari this morning—they passed a resolution you may be interested to hear."

Oh hells. Dorjan knew what was coming before he said it.

"We have determined that Forum Master Dorjan, son of Kyon, is no longer able to carry out his duties of Forum Master, and that his lands are forfeit to the Biemansland Forum. If Master Dorjan wishes to contest this, he will find his city home forfeit and all the people in his environs subject to the penalties of the state. This ruling was issued by Triari Septra, with the divine voice of Bimuit to all of his loyal followers."

Dorjan's bowels iced cold and brittle, and his spine straightened and his shoulders threw back almost of their own accord. Suddenly he was unafraid, because the worst had happened, and this person, this thing that he'd become over the past ten years, was finally allowed to fly free.

"Well, then," he said, his face fell and grim, much like it was when he flew through the city as the Nyx, "this Forum has things to do. The first order of business would be to decide if the Forum acknowledges the founder of our province as a force of divinity, and wants to call the shitehole you've allowed Thenis to become declared the city of the gods. You go ahead and do that, Biemansland. I shall not stop you. But when you've decided that we have the divine right to destroy our planet, I cannot wait to watch you try to use my land with which to do it. I look forward to seeing you try—but I warn you, this ruling body has a habit of sending other people to execute their foulest orders. Should the entire army of Biemansland actually triumph—and don't for a moment think that's a given—the man who pries the key to my father's legacy from my cold, dead hand is the man who shall inherit it. Lokargo, lokogos, errant child—*this* key, gentleman"—and he held aloft the nisket flower his father had given him—"*this* key shall belong to the next living man to touch it. And it's the *only* way you'll have the power of the mines. So send your worst—politician, army"—he looked directly at Septra—"knife in the night. I've spent ten years learning to defend myself from the likes of you, and don't think I'll go down easy."

Dorjan turned around then, prepared to push his way past the milling Forum Masters, many of whom were muttering encouraging things such as "Hells, *divinity?*" and "Violates our charter!" in clear, unafraid voices. He realized that those who had begun to support him had pushed back the others and were bowing as he staged his exit.

"Don't you threaten us, Dorjan, son of Kyon!" Colny shouted from the podium. "Who says your precious little street boy is safe! Threaten *me* with exposure, will you? I *know* where that boy came from!"

Something about the venom in his voice snapped Dorjan's head around. "And how would you know if my page was a street boy or not, sir?" he asked carefully.

"I *know* where that boy comes from!" Colny snarled. "Measures are being taken even now—"

Dorjan felt the blood pounding in his throat. "You *think* you know where that boy comes from?" he snarled back. "The truth is he's the heir to what's left of Kiamath Keep, and the boy who kept innocent blood off my hands ten years ago. Chew on *that* while you plot to kill a boy this country has already betrayed, and don't ask me to clean up the blood you vomit on your own shoes."

And he could no longer stand there another moment. Colny hadn't threatened his home—not in that last diatribe. He'd threatened *Taern's* home, the place Colny knew Taern to have lived. He'd threatened *Taern*, and he'd threatened Madame M, and Dorjan might just be able to get there before his world exploded.

Taern had been running late. He'd been trying to honor Dorjan's request to put his armor on under his cloak before he went running down the streets of Thenis to visit Madame M's, and he had difficulty with the catches. Damn Areau—he liked things so complicated, and he liked to harp on it too. *But Taern, if we skipped the three hook and eyes there, the armor wouldn't have the silky rippling like a fish!* Oh, the man was a wonder with mechanical tricks, there was no denying it, but Karanos if he didn't give himself a lot of credit in that department!

So Taern was in the stables, grumbling to himself, wanting desperately to talk to Madame M about *everything*, including his complete attachment to and adoration of one shy, not-so-virginal-anymore Forum Master, when there was a thump at the front door—a loud, threatening thump, the kind that sent the two girls and the young man who had been in Mrs. Wrinkle's kitchen scurrying back through the passageway to the stables.

Taern looked at them in surprise and then sent them back toward the rabbit. With his attention focused on something else, the catch in his armor closed without fuss, and he ushered the girls into the conveyance and under the layers of blankets on the back couch.

Then he slid his hood and his mask over his head and crept along the passageway.

Krissa was back behind the kitchen door, and he joined her, both of them quieter than breath as they listened to Areau open the door.

Oh, wonderful. It was their friend the lokogos, the one who had such a flaming hard-on for Krissa.

He was not pleased to see Areau.

"Who in the fuzzy name of Bimuit are you?" he snarled, and Areau's voice was equally pissy.

"Someone who lives here. What gives you the right to come pounding down this door in the middle of the day? What have the occupants of this house ever done to you?"

That garnered a puzzled silence. "Why, nothin' that I can factor. The lady of the house wot's been real kind to me, if you take my meaning."

Taern could only imagine the icy arch to Areau's eyebrows implied in his glacial "Indeed."

"Oh, right," the lokogos said, seeming to recover himself. "Well, some order, that's what. It's come down from the Forum Masters, not like *they* knew what they were doing, but there's some boy here, some page, that they wanted brought in. And I thought I'd ask the lady of the house if she could hand him over real friendly like."

Taern and Krissa met eyes then, horrified ones, and Taern realized Dorjan's worst fears, the ones Taern honestly thought wouldn't come to pass, were there, banging on their door with a grime-crusted fist and speaking with missing teeth.

"Yes, well, even if the lady of the house were here, she'd tell you that no such boy lives here. If the Forum Master has a page, he must live somewhere else, and you'll have to look for him there."

"Somewhere else, you say?" the lokogos asked eagerly, and Taern could imagine Areau's irritated shrug.

"Well, since he's not here, I would imagine the only place he could be is somewhere else!"

"Someplace in the stews, maybe? 'Cause we've got leave to search a brothel wot's run by some freak with a cock and a dress. I've always wanted to see some bloke trying on a dress—think that would be right funny, it would be. So, could that be the place?"

Taern thought urgently to himself, *Please say no, please say no, please say no!* But he should have known better. Areau might have accepted Taern and Krissa into his household and might even harbor some affection for them (well, maybe more than affection for Krissa), but there was no doubt about it: Areau's scope of the world was too small to protect anyone outside his immediate circle. He signed Madame M's death sentence without really knowing who she was or what he had done.

"Right, sure, whatever. If I tell you that's the place, *then* can you leave me alone to my studies? The Forum Master doesn't employ me to talk to people who bother me for naught!"

"Alright, alright—don't get snippy! And don't get too comfortable, either! The word's come down, you know. Your man may not be so high an' mighty come time soon." There was an uncomfortable pause. "An, you know, should tha' happen, you wouldn't think the lady of the house, she'd fancy a bloke like me?"

"I highly doubt it," Areau snapped before slamming the door shut in the man's face.

Krissa and Taern stayed back behind the kitchen door, sweating in fear, until Areau's harried tread echoed in the hallway to the kitchen.

"He's gone," Areau muttered, "but I'm not sure for how long. Krissa, you and Mrs. Wrinkle need to pack and make your way to the train station—"

"Dammit, Areau!" Taern muttered. "You can think about trains now, when you've just sicced those men on a friend of ours?"

Areau blinked at him, at a loss. "Who?" he asked, legitimately puzzled.

"Madame M!" Taern snapped. "The woman who gave us a fucking job and a place to sleep for years. What, did you think Dorjan just plucked us from the whore tree and dropped us at your dinner table?"

Areau's expression then actually twisted something in Taern's heart. "Oh, dammit," he muttered. "I was… I thought I was doing well!" He turned to Krissa. "I'm sorry. Oh, I'm sorry, my lady. I was trying to be Dorjan, I was! I thought I was protecting you!"

To Taern's disgust, Krissa moved into his arms and smoothed her palms across his cheeks, scars and all. "I know you did, Ari. You did really well. Taern and I," she said significantly, looking over her shoulder at Taern, "haven't spoken much of Madame M to you—we weren't sure how accepting you would have been. You seemed to have a distressing prejudice against whores when we first arrived, you do recall?"

Areau nodded, accepting her hands against his face. "I do," he whispered. "I'm sorry. I'm so sorry. But that doesn't change that we need to get you all to the train station—"

"Not me," Taern said, forgiving Areau because he had no choice. "You may not have meant to cause any harm, but M doesn't know what's about to hit her. She's got a couple of children there that she was going to send to safety *here*—we need to make sure they're cared for, just like Alla and Evvy and that new boy, whoever he is."

"Who?" Areau asked, obviously puzzled, and Krissa gave a half laugh and patted his cheek.

"Dearest, sometimes human beings really do need as much attention as all your strange fixings in that workshop of yours. Here—here's what we'll do. Taern, you're right. Go to Madam M's and get her safe."

"Send her to the keep—not Kyon's Keep," Areau said quickly, looking distressed. "There could be trouble there. But Dre's keep, the one with your sisters there—send your friends there. They've been taking in Dorjan's refugees and finding them places in the countryside to live since we've started this."

Taern nodded, understanding. "I can do that," he said, fixing his helmet and blinking through the goggles. "I can do that. Then I'll go wait for Dorjan at the entrance to the stews. He always comes that way—I can warn him, and we can make our way to the keep too."

"What about us here?" Krissa asked, and Areau pinched the bridge of his nose, hard. Watching him, Taern realized that injured or not, Areau was not the person who gave orders. He and Dorjan must have worked so well because Dorjan did.

"You need to go too," Areau muttered. "You, Mrs. Wrinkle, the girls, whoever they are—Dre's keep. Within the hour. Clear out. Pack lightly, move quickly. They'll be back." He looked up, thinking hard. "They *will* be back. That lout at the door practically warned me."

"What are you going to do?" Krissa asked, all concern. Taern had to admit he was worried himself—Dorjan cared for this git. It was best he didn't put himself at too much risk.

"That thing I've been working on," Areau muttered. "My workshop. It's an antidote, mind you. Something serious. They make their money on dust. I know how to stop dust from working. There goes their money, there goes the addicts, the pain—a gift, as Dorjan would say. A thing to help Thenis, to help Biemansland."

Taern took a breath and reevaluated Areau altogether. "Good job, Areau—you *are* capable of thinking outside yourself. I'm impressed."

Areau scowled at him. "They addicted me to pain by addicting me to watered-down dust first, brat. It's *revenge*, not philanthropy! Now run! Run if you don't want your friend to be hurt! I'll meet you at the brothel and travel with you and Dorjan. I'll have silver too, so we can take the trains. *Run!*"

Taern didn't even take his leave. He turned on his heel and darted through the hallway and then out of the stables, sprinting like he was being pursued by a magnesium fire.

OH HELLS. Areau had fucked up. He had. He *knew* how small his world had become, how small it *had* to have been over the last few years, but he'd never realized how destructive that sort of smallness could be. Krissa—he'd threatened someone close to Krissa, and Krissa had become all that was good in Areau's world. The pain giver, the pleasure giver, the civilized voice in his head.

Areau had to fix it. Taern disappeared and Areau took a deep breath.

"I'm sorry," he said, half panicked that she'd forget she'd forgiven him. "I'm sorry. I didn't want to hurt you or someone you loved. It's such a mess, you see? I was trying to protect you, trying to—"

"I forgive you," she said firmly, and Areau nodded, swallowing.

"Look, I'm sorry—I... I know you probably don't feel the same way for me. It's... I'm a miserable pain in the arse, I'm an addict, and I wasn't that nice a man in the first place, but, you know. Should we not meet again, I just think you should know."

Krissa had been about to bustle out of the kitchen—ah, gods, she was so efficient! Had such purpose. Was that the youth? The profession? Or maybe it was just her. But now she turned to him, her efficiency draining from her in a cloud.

"Areau?" She came forward and put her hand on his cheek. "Areau." She tried one of her crisp smiles, but it faded, became bitterly sweet. "Do you think... these weeks, working by your side, helping you in your workshop"—she blushed faintly—"sharing your bed consensually... do you think all of that was for my contract?"

Areau swallowed hard and felt, to his shame, a rather watery smile stretching his cheeks. "I hoped not," he said, feeling like a child. "I truly hoped not."

She framed his scarred face in her soft hands and stood on her toes to press her lips to hers. She came back down flat-footed and whispered into his ear.

He jerked back, startled, and she kissed him on the cheek again.

"You have no idea how much I care about you," she whispered, and he closed his eyes and held her close.

"If I can, for just a moment, be worthy of that," he whispered back, "I shall count myself the luckiest man in the world." He buried his nose in her hair then and lingered a moment, and one moment more, and then they separated.

"Here," she said, assuming that efficient grace he'd come to know as hers and taking the short way to the study under the stairs. "I'm writing the address and basic directions to M's." She finished scratching an address and a brief map on a piece of parchment she found on Dorjan's desk, and then thrust it into his hand. He kissed her then, in the way he hadn't dared to before, possessive, needy, and open. They broke apart, and she wiped her lipstick from his lips and smiled. "Be safe, Areau."

"You too," he murmured and placed a tentative hand on her flat stomach.

She pressed it there for a moment and then firmed up her shoulders and jaw with purpose, and they broke apart.

He ran past her to his workshop and gathered his work, and then went to the stables, where he threw all of Dorjan's armor in a satchel over his back. He took a good look around the stables and one more after he walked out of them. Ten years they'd lived in the city. Dorjan had taken him to the train station via the rabbit twice a year, and three times he'd run away to the stews to find someone who would beat and fuck him when Dorjan refused.

Lately he'd been venturing to the market with Mrs. Wrinkle and Krissa.

Not once had he left the grounds alone in his right mind, and here he was, possibly leaving forever. He looked behind him once—at the great two-story mansion, a forbidding façade, the sloped gray slate roof, the dark-gray paint and white trim—and thought that he might miss his workshop, the careful, painstaking mobiles he'd hung when he'd been his most desperate, and that he would miss knowing where every last beaker and chemical sat.

But really, of all of it, the only things he'd really miss, should he never see them again, were his mistress and his friend, and he had the sudden shattering notion that *those* two things could never, ever be replaced.

Krissa's directions were concise and clear, and it was a damned good thing, because Areau wouldn't have been able to make it otherwise. Still, he recognized the graceful, freshly painted white town house she'd described from down the block—and he recognized the panicked flood of people running from it too. He started to hurry through them, hesitating when he saw the bodies—big muscular ones lying unconscious in the streets. There was a tortured scream—a man's, from the sound of it—and then Taern's unmistakable shriek.

"No, you *fucker!*" followed by more sounds of violence issuing from the front door.

Areau approached the house carefully, stepping gingerly over a man who looked like his skull had been caved in, probably by Taern's armored fist.

Areau had a hand on the doorframe, embarrassed by how uncertain he was. Go inside? Break Taern's concentration? He had no weapon, only Dorjan's armor in a satchel. What was he supposed to do in that room?

Dorjan whispered by him so quickly, Areau wasn't even aware that his friend—dressed in his black underclothes—had come up behind him, no mask, no armor, no hesitation.

Areau was emboldened enough to follow him in. What he saw there froze his blood.

A woman—a tall, broad-shouldered woman with red hair and no breasts—was splayed on the ground, her arms akimbo and the wound at her throat still bleeding. Dorjan had just felled the man who had slit her throat, judging by the knife that went clattering to the ground when the man went down, and he was going after one of the men behind Taern. Taern was outfitted in full armor, struggling to get to the woman on the ground. Even his augmented strength wasn't enough to fight off the three men holding his arms and propping his legs. The one in the middle had an arm wrapped around Taern's neck.

"*Hold him!*" the man barked. He was fumbling with something in his pocket, and what he held up gingerly made the world spin. He had in his hand a syringe with a corked needle.

Taern was strengthened by the armor and determined, and he threw back an arm and caught one man in the jaw. The man went down, and Taern almost had the upper hand again. Dorjan was rushing in to his side when the man with the syringe flicked the cork off the end and held it against Taern's throat.

"*Stop!*" he roared, and Areau's heart froze and Dorjan became a solid form instead of the battling shadow.

"What is that?" Dorjan asked. Considering what was at stake, his voice was calm, pleasant, almost innocent.

"It's dust, guv'nor. You take one step closer and it'll be in him."

"Why are you here?" Dorjan asked, and again, Areau looked at his friend, at his amazing self-possession, and marveled.

"We had orders to rough up the place. This one"—and he jerked his arm cruelly around Taern's throat—"'e got in the way."

Taern's face was angled up, and Areau wondered distantly how much he could even see of Areau and Dorjan from that angle. Was it important?

"Well, you have him under control now, don't you?" Dorjan asked, managing to make his voice flip and charming. Areau watched him clench his fist by his side and then unclench it, and wondered if he was the only one who could see how much danger these three men really were in.

"We do!" snarled the man. He wasn't tall but he was brawny, and he'd shaved his head. Areau detected a pattern of long scars on his scalp and realized that this one had taken ripping to a whole new level.

"So, you have two choices," Dorjan said, his voice still even. "You can drop him now, and let him go, and leave here. We've got bigger game to hunt today, and you may even escape our wrath."

"Who the hell're you?" the man snarled, his hand suddenly not nearly as steady on the syringe at Taern's neck as Areau would have liked.

"I am of no consequence," Dorjan murmured. "But I will tell you that should you inject that substance or hurt him in any way, who I am will be the last question you ever ask, and the one that will never be answered."

"It's no good," Taern muttered, his body deceptively limp in the grasp of his enemies. He wasn't wearing his voice distorter, and Areau was grateful. "Nyx, one way or the other, I'm going to kill the fuckers who killed Madame M."

Areau actually heard Dorjan swallow, and the tension in the room became an electric current, lifting the hairs on Areau's arms and causing him to shiver uncontrollably.

"Nyx?" said the man with the syringe. "*Nyx?*"

And Dorjan shouted, "*No!*" as the man plunged the syringe into Taern's neck and pushed.

Areau was never certain of what happened next, even though he saw it with his own eyes. Taern slid limply to the floor, but he went unnoticed, because at the same time Dorjan crouched, rolled, and came up throwing the knife lying by the dead woman's throat. It hit the man who'd been holding Taern square in the throat. While the two men on either side were gaping at him, Dorjan drove his palm squarely into one's nose, shoving it up into his brain and spattering blood everywhere. The other man watched his friends fall in horror, and was begging, taking a step back, when Dorjan grasped the knife from the dead man's throat, yanked it, and threw it again. It caught the last man squarely in the eye.

He went down and was then forgotten as Dorjan sank to the ground and pulled Taern's head into his lap. Taern was murmuring, delirious, happy, eternally happy, as long as in a couple of hours, he could get just one more hit.

Dorjan ripped off Taern's mask and slapped his cheeks, trying to get the boy to look him in the eyes. "Taern? Taern? Boy, you've got to look at me. Can you look at me? Just look... just look...."

But Taern was murmuring, the wordless sounds of a man trapped deeply inside his skull.

Dorjan looked up then, his self-possession gone, his eyes moving wildly until they locked with Areau's.

"Ari?" he asked helplessly. "Ari—can you help him? Please, Ari. Please. Ari... they're going to ride on our home! They're going to ride on Kyon's Keep, and the world can shake itself to powder if he's not here with me. Please, Ari. I can't... I can't keep fighting them, not without him. I can't... I have no strength, not without him."

Areau found himself nodding, grasping at straws, spewing hope and half-formed thoughts he never knew he'd had.

"Here," he said, sinking to the floor. It was bloody, he thought, but he managed to find the one clean space in the room. He rooted through the satchel and pulled out the kit he'd brought from his lab. "In about five hours—before you get to the keep by train—he's going to want more. Give him this instead." He tucked a corked syringe, much like the one that had been thrust into Taern's neck, into Dorjan's hand. "I don't have much. It's ten hours by train to the station, you know that, another two hours on foot to the keep. Give him half in five hours, half when you get there. He'll be hurting, but it won't be horrible, not yet."

"And then what?" Dorjan asked, his voice cracking in desperation. "Then what? Ari, that's ten hours. You and I both know you were months away from—"

"I should be dead," Areau said clearly. It was something he'd never told Dorjan before, something personal and almost shameful. "I should be dead. Why do you think they didn't kill me in the asylum, Dori? They thought I should be dead—they rubbed dust in my wounds, you see?"

"I thought it was weakened," Dorjan said, his words tripping over themselves, and Areau shook his head.

"No. No, I mean, it was, but dust is dust, right? That's why we've had such trouble with it. But I'm alive. Why is that?"

Dorjan shook his head, looking lost. All those years of killing each other inside, and Dorjan had always had a purpose, had a way. Finally, finally, Areau could give him something. Areau could give him a way.

"Because I grew up in Kyon's Keep," Areau whispered, his voice ringing with conviction. It hadn't occurred to him until they'd talked about returning home the night they went after Colny. Areau had gone back for a good visit after his stay in the asylum, and he'd returned addicted to the pain he'd been given with the dust, but not the dust.

"The niskets—they clean us out, Dori. They take our blood in great quantities when we're in the mines, and we drink nectar to recover. The nectar is our blood, isn't it? Cleaned? The dust, it's their element—blood and chemicals. They can live with it. So my blood, it was different to begin with, which is why it didn't kill me. And then they cleaned me out—"

Dorjan's eyes brightened, tracked, registered. "So the addiction didn't stick," he breathed.

Areau nodded and then began to empty the satchel. "You're going to need the armor," he said apologetically. "You're going to need to run, and I think you'll have to stow away on the millipede and…."

Dorjan stopped him with a hand on his shoulder. "Thank you, Ari. I understand that I need the armor. But I cannot thank you enough for the hope."

Oh… oh… Areau wanted to cry then, because Dorjan was thanking him, was blessing him for hope, for giving something that only Areau could, and for a bright, shining moment, Areau saw himself through his friend's eyes like he had in their childhood, and he was perfect and good.

But Areau had been selfish enough already, and Dorjan had things he needed to attend to.

"Did you mean what you said?" he asked. "About them riding toward our home?"

Dorjan nodded. He kissed Taern on the forehead and lowered him gently to the floor. Then he stood up and started fitting his armor over his legs, greaves first as Areau had showed him when he'd first made the stuff.

"The Forum Masters—the Triari, Septra included, and his particular friends—are taking a special conveyance to Kyon's Keep." He looked around the brothel, and his eyes fell on the woman in the dress, sprawled out on the floor. "They were trying to find reasons to stop me, I think," he said sadly. In spite of their press for time, he walked toward the woman and lowered her hands toward her flat, broad chest, then closed her open eyes. "I'm sorry, M," he said softly and then bent and kissed her forehead. "When this is over, I'll try to see that we take care of yours."

He stood up and turned away from her reluctantly, but Areau could see tears in his eyes, and he cursed himself again. "It's my fault," he confessed, hoping Dorjan could forgive him. "I clued the lokogos in on where to go. I didn't realize he—she—was a friend."

"She was," Dorjan said. "But this—this was set in motion without you, Ari. Don't take this for yours."

"What are we going to do?" Areau asked, accepting Dorjan's forgiveness as he'd always accepted his love. "About them coming to Kyon's Keep?"

Dorjan girded his loins then and fastened the attached breastplate. "You're going to take the first train out," Dorjan said, his hands moving quickly in accustomed paths. "When they arrive—it'll be close, make no mistake. I'll be sending a cricket out for you to get you there—when they arrive, you're going to tell them you know the secret to the mines, the ones I refused to tell them."

Areau's eyes widened. "You're not going to tell them—"

"I'm only unhinged, Ari, not deranged!" Dorjan snapped. "No. You're going to tell them they have to go into a mine and see. Then you're going to take them to the northernmost asteroid and let them all go inside."

Areau scowled at him. "And what's that going to—"

"The niskets, Ari. The niskets control the gas mixture so we can breathe in the mines, remember?"

Areau blinked. "Yes...."

"Do you remember anything about how we tether the things to the earth?"

"From north to south—I grew up there too!"

"Right. Which means the asteroid to the north...." Dorjan trailed off, and Areau suddenly found his way.

"Has the thinnest hull," Areau said, understanding completely.

"And is the most susceptible to volatile gases," Dorjan finished for him. He was almost done with the armor—all he had left was the knit mask and then the metal one. He grimaced then and went to put it down.

"Dori—"

"Why do I need it?" Dorjan asked, his voice gruff. "All the Nyx fought for, it came to nothing—"

"It gave people hope," Areau said, believing it. "I felt it when I saw you walk through the door, because I knew who you were, what you could do. Imagine living on these streets, knowing the world for one long misery, and having but one thing that might step in. Wear it, Dori. Taern needs you to be larger than life now. He needs you to be the Nyx."

Dorjan nodded and sank to his knees again. He bent down so his face was close to Taern's, and whispered, "I'm going to disappear, Taern, and the Nyx is going to take my place. Don't despair, right? Just because you can't see my eyes."

"Like Nyx," Taern mumbled. "Nyx. Nyx is a hero."

Dorjan breathed hard through his nose then and pulled on his hood and his mask. He looked at Areau through the alien insect goggles and nodded. "Run for the millipede station, Ari. We'll be gone before you get there. Mrs. Wrinkle and Krissa...?"

"Have already left for Dre's. Here, don't forget his mask," Areau said, retrieving it from the wreckage of what must have once been a fine green-and-white-striped davenport. "He hates it when you get to be a hero without him."

Nyx nodded then and whispered, "Good-bye, Ari. I'll see you at home." He took the small packet Areau had given him, with months of Areau's hard work bottled in a glass syringe, and tucked it in the satchel, which Areau had stocked with water and a little bit of bread and cheese, not knowing what he'd need.

"There's silver in there," Areau said abruptly, and Dorjan fumbled for it, then pressed it into Areau's hands.

"The next millipede," Dorjan cautioned. "Ari, it's going to be close."

"I swear," Areau vowed, "for once, I won't let you down."

Dorjan looked away before squatting to hoist Taern into his arms. "You never let me down, Ari. It was I who disappointed you."

"Never!" Areau cried, but Dorjan had taken off running, his steam armor-enhanced movements nearly too quick for the naked eye.

Ecstasy and Home

TAERN heard Dorjan's voice, and suddenly his grief over Madame M was not quite so overwhelming. He'd gotten there in time to hear a woman scream, had seen the thugs all over the brothel, and had set about to kill.

Dorjan had no compunctions about killing but no thirst for it either. He would as soon thump a man on the head and knock him out than slit his throat, but Taern had always been certain the man he let go was the git who was going to stick a knife in his back. Taern had no hesitation about killing either, none whatsoever, and so as he'd set upon the men who were threatening his one sanctuary growing up, he hadn't worried if the armor propelled his fist through a skull, a spine, or a once healthy set of teeth. He wanted the men to stop. Death was one way for them to stop, disability was another, and them running away saved him a swing, thank you very much.

And that was how he made it into Madame M's sitting room in time to watch M kick the bald fucker who had one of the girls up against the wall with his hand on her throat, right behind the calf. The man went down on one knee, and Taern grabbed the girl's hand to pull her away and send her running down the street. When he turned around, one of the other men had grabbed M by her hair and hauled her hair back.

"I'll fucking kill you!" Taern snarled, and M looked up at him and smiled.

"That's my boy!" she crowed, and the fucker slit her throat.

"M!" Taern cried, sitting up in Dorjan's arms, and Dorjan whispered to him.

"I'm sorry, Taern. I'm sorry. She's gone."

"I tried, Dorjan! I tried. I'm so sorry. M, I tried. M—"

"Sh, baby. Sh. You can weep for her, it's horrible."

"I'm sorry… I'm… oh, Dorjan… why? Why do I feel…. My skin feels prickly, like spiders and ants… make them stop, Dorjan, make them stop!"

"Not yet, baby." Dorjan's voice was breaking, thin, and Taern hadn't heard it breaking and thin since that first night in the alleyway.

"Someone's got to take care of you, Dorjan," Taern said sincerely. "Someone has to take care. You need someone. I knew it that first night. How come nobody's taking care of you?"

"'Cause you're sick, baby, and it's my turn to take care of you."

"Dorjan, what's that sound? It's all the time, and it's humming in my belly. It's making me shiver. What's that sound?"

"It's the train, Taern. We're in the luggage compartment, yes?"

"You're not sending me away. You can't send me away. I want to see my sisters someday, but you have to come with me. You can't send me out of the city without you, right? We're a team, right? I put on the armor so we'd be a team. You can't send me away!"

He was pounding on Dorjan's chest plate with his armored gauntlets. It had to have hurt, but Dorjan simply captured Taern's hands in his own gauntleted hands and held them still. "How can I send you away?" he asked, his voice calm and very Dorjan-like. "You're indispensable, you obnoxious brat!"

Taern relaxed for a moment, and then the awful, insistent shivering took over, his skin twitching like a millipede's legs. "Feel so strange. Help me… make it stop. Make it stop. Oh, help… help me, Nyx, it's getting me. It's getting me. It's… oh… I'm going to… I'm going to be sick…."

He barely remembered actually heaving his stomach contents, but he knew he had because his muscles felt abused, and there was cool water being poured in his mouth and some more sponged on his brow.

"Sorry, Nyx," he muttered. "Sorry. What's… what's wrong? My muscles… they're… they're so tight… why can't I…. My chest… my chest… *my chest!*" He screamed then, or he thought he screamed, and there was a prickle in his arm when he didn't remember taking his armor off. He must have, though—someone must have! Because he was naked, wrapped in a strange blanket, in the dark place with the clickety clatter and the constant rocking.

He didn't feel perfect then. He didn't. He still felt jittery, and sometimes he was talking to Dorjan and sometimes to Nyx, and sometimes to Areau or Krissa, but not as often. He talked to Madame M some and told her to forgive him, and she told him she was proud of him and there was nothing to forgive.

The ride was interminable, and the crawling sensation, the pain—oh, the pain in every limb, in every ligament, in every joint. It got worse and then worse and then worse and then—*oh Dorjan, make it stop!*

And Dorjan did. Taern managed to focus then, and Dorjan looked at him from deadened, exhausted brown eyes.

"You should sleep, love," Taern said quietly. "You need to be taken care of. Why aren't you sleeping?"

"I'm caring for a sick friend."

"I hope he's sufficiently grateful," Taern sniped. "You look bloody awful."

"I think he'll be grateful enough when he's done," Dorjan said, and Taern grunted.

"Couldn't be as grateful as I am that you love me."

Dorjan caught his breath. "You cued in to that, did you?"

"Well, you have to! Did you think I didn't love you?"

"I give thanks every day that you seem to," Dorjan said softly before kissing his brow.

"Careful, Dorjan. Someone in your bloody province will see!"

"I don't give a fuck," Dorjan said quietly. "My bloody province can do without me, and I don't need its approval. Not for you."

Taern smiled. "Mm... lovely thing to say. If my mouth didn't smell and taste like puke right now, I'd kiss you."

"You're ever considerate," Dorjan said softly, and Taern got to babble over that compliment for who knows how long before his stomach cramped and the semipleasant time, the time in which he remembered some of what he was saying, retreated back to the golden-toned memories of his childhood. What surfaced was the red time, the time his skin crawled and the pain came back, and Dorjan wept over him and looked at the clock and the countryside and anywhere other than Taern's eyes as he repeatedly denied Taern some relief, oh, please, something to take the edge off the sword carving him up like poultry.

"I have to wait," Dorjan said, looking at the timepiece on his wrist. "I can't give it to you too early," he murmured. "We're not close enough to home!"

Taern had begged then, cried, pleaded, and to his shame, screamed at Dorjan, abused him, called him names that were horrible, that wounded him as sure as physical blows. Taern called him a baby-killer once, looked him in the face as he said it, and watched Dorjan's features etch with a stonelike stillness against the direct hit.

"Call me what you need to," Dorjan said. "Call me what you need to. If it helps you stretch just another hour, Taern, just one more hour, so we can get you to the mines."

"Putting me to work in the fucking mines, you bastard?" Taern cried out, and to his surprise, Dorjan laughed, the sound brittle and joyless in the noise of the jouncing train car.

"Oh, Taern, if only it was all a plot to make you work!"

Taern screamed at him until something stoppered his mouth, and beat at him until his hands grew raw and bloody, but still the fucker refused to... refused... finally conceded...

Ahhhhh... bliss.

But not real bliss. Partial, edgy bliss again, and Taern tossed about some more in pain.

The train had stopped and started several times, and Taern had been peripherally aware of it. He was not prepared, therefore, when, before one of the stops, Dorjan stood, pulled his mask on, threw Taern over a strong shoulder, and waited. As the train started to slow down, Dorjan kicked open the door leading to the outside, and Taern was aware of cold whooshing air around his—oh, was he naked? No, he was covered in a blanket, and it wasn't enough, and the wind hurt his skin, and oh hells, was Dorjan *jumping* from the back of the train?

There was a dip and a whirl and a tilt to the world and Taern was suddenly not hanging over Nyx's back, he was being cradled in his arms, and Nyx was *running* full-out, with every enhancement the armor had to give, running so fast the wind blew through the wool blanket like a knife and not even Dorjan's wide shoulders could shield Taern from the cold. Taern's skin felt like it was being flayed open by rusty knives in that cold, and he opened his mouth to scream...

And couldn't stop.

HE MUST have passed out—must have. He was aware of being over Dorjan's shoulder again, of being jostled, squeezed, and carried up a liquid ladder, of vertigo and wind and then warmth and darkness.

The warmth and darkness didn't last long. Suddenly there was a whirling, a glowing, a clattering, and then that beautiful, frenetic mess was around *him*, and then it *was* him, and he was being made light and beautiful, his body becoming thin, transparent, as tiny metal flowers alit on his flesh and fanned him until his skin stopped hurting and his shivers stopped shaking his teeth from his head. They flurried around him, a confusing cloud, and then Dorjan held something to his lips, forcing him to drink. It tasted rank and coppery, but Dorjan wouldn't leave him alone.

"Fruit juice?" he begged, and he got some of that too, but then he got more of the pink stuff Dorjan called nectar, and then he was surrounded by that glittering cloud of metal flowers again, and he grew lighter, lighter, lighter, until he was going to float away.

HE WOKE up aching, his stomach sore and cramping. He felt brittle, like maple candy in the snow.

He was on a bed in a small room, surrounded by white gauze curtains. The surrounding building was... black, was the impression he got. He looked up, and there was a cavernous space above him, above the curtains, with what looked to be raw crags of rock embedded in the...

Wait. Not embedded in the ceiling. The raw crags of rock *were* the ceiling. Taern squinted at them and then looked around his little gauze enclosure again, and saw Dorjan to his left, wearing only his stretchy black knits, asleep as he sat.

"You're pale," Taern said crossly. His throat was dry and his voice was raw, but that didn't stop the charge of temper that zinged through him. "Why do you look like death?"

"Because you worried me that way," Dorjan snapped, opening his eyes and sitting up. "It didn't occur to you to wait for me before you confronted a street gang in a brothel?"

Taern glared. "I had no idea you'd be there!" he protested, and he saw the hurt on Dorjan's face and regretted it.

"Stupid prat," Dorjan grumbled. He held out a flask of fruit juice with a straw, and Taern drank appreciatively. "I'll *always* be there!"

"What happened to me?" Taern asked, returning the flask. He tried to sit up, but his body just *hurt* too much to think about it. "Why do I feel like the bottom of a sidewalk in a piss alley?"

"Because that's the shite they shoved in your veins," Dorjan grunted. He sat up too, and Taern thought again that his eyes looked sunken and his lips were near blue. "What you're feeling right now is the cost of cleaning it out of you."

"Mm... I get that. Right. That's why I feel like hexashite. Why do *you* look worse than I feel?"

Dorjan's chest shook for a moment. "We had to bond you to the niskets to clean out your blood," he said, changing the subject.

That *did* make Taern sit up. "Really?" he asked, excited. "I'm bonded to the niskets? Like you and Areau?"

Dorjan smiled faintly. "Yes, you are bonded to the niskets, like me and Areau. That pleases you?"

"Well, yes! Doesn't that make *you* happy?"

Dorjan nodded, his movements slow and old. "You have no idea."

"What do you mean?"

"Well, we actually use it as sort of a wedding ceremony, when someone new moves to the keep. The niskets feed off both parties, and then they swap nectar." Dorjan's eyes wandered. "There is usually a great deal of sex when that happens. I think we've been deprived."

Taern looked at him uncertainly. "So, we'll have the sex later. We're married now?"

Dorjan's smile grew deeper, more real. "If you want to be, nothing would make me happier."

Taern nodded, still uncertain. "What's wrong, Dorjan?"

Dorjan swallowed. "I'm just a little low on protein, I think," he said, and Taern's eyes widened.

"Wait—we exchanged blood?"

"Sort of. I think the exchange was a little more one-sided than that. The niskets couldn't clean yours out fast enough. Mine didn't need to be chemically cleansed when turned into plasma. Mine came a little faster, that's all."

Taern reached out a leaden hand and clasped his hand. "Dorjan?" he asked, squeezing that hand with all his strength. "How close was it?"

Dorjan tilted back his head and closed his eyes. "Close, love. Too close to fathom."

"Come here," Taern murmured. "Come here and put your head on my pillow. Come here and rest."

Dorjan shook his head. "I can't."

"Not even for a moment?"

"They're coming. They're coming to take my lands, Taern, and I can't allow that to happen. Areau and I have a plan, but they'll be here soon—"

"Is Areau coming?"

"Yes."

"Can he find us?"

Dorjan's mouth quirked. "The niskets will show him."

"Then come. A second, Dorjan. A minute. An hour. Please? You of all people know how precious the smallest moment is."

Dorjan nodded then and squeezed his eyes tight. He grunted as he shoved himself over and flopped gracelessly on the bed.

Taern lay on his side and looked into those shadowed dark eyes and cupped a hand to a stubbled cheek. "We're really married?" he asked, and he felt that smile—that small quirk of hope—under his hand.

"Just don't come into the mines with anyone but me," Dorjan mumbled, and Taern tucked himself against him and swore that he would not.

Soon—far too soon—there was a voice calling up from what seemed to be the floor.

"Dori? Dori? The niskets think you're in here. Dori?"

Dorjan shot upright and snapped out, "I'm up! I'll come down!"

"Did it work? Did he make it, Dori?"

Areau was apparently ignoring him, because the voice was getting closer, and behind the gauze, against a source of ambient light Taern hadn't fathomed the last time he'd looked, Areau emerged from the floor, silhouetted against the dark. As Dorjan was standing up, Areau pushed his way into Taern's curtained enclosure, his scarred face pale against his black travelling clothes and the dark of the asteroid around him.

"It worked!" Areau crowed, looking at Taern with a really sort of wonderful smile on his face. "Oh, I'm so glad it worked. He would have been lost without you!"

"It almost killed him," Taern said quietly, and Areau's eyes flickered to Dorjan.

"Well, your death would have too," he said frankly. "It's like the niskets and the mines. One of you cannot exist without the other. The asteroids need their gases and their chemical exchanges to not explode or come crashing to earth, and the niskets need their minerals to live. And our whole bloody planet needs that to happen or it will fall to shite!" Areau beamed, obviously pleased with himself, and Dorjan let out a rusty laugh.

"Proud of yourself?" he asked, stretching and looking like a man desperately trying to wake up. "That was an out*standing* conceit right there. Should we ever revive arts programs in Thenis, I think you've found your calling."

"Don't be snide, Dori," Areau said, all smugness. "It doesn't become you."

"I was serious!" Dorjan protested, laughing. "You have a flair for the dramatic." He turned to Taern, and Taern sat up fully and held out his arms. Dorjan hugged him—but not satisfactorily enough. He was trying to be strong, Taern could tell. He was keeping distance between them as though they were brothers or friends, perhaps to keep pressure off of Taern's tender, sensitized body.

"Not good enough, you git!" he snapped, and Dorjan put one knee on the bed and *hugged* him, his bones and muscles melting into Taern's like Taern was strong enough to hold him up.

Taern *was* strong enough to hold him up.

"You take care of yourself, Nyx. I don't know what you're planning, but if I'm not there, it can't possibly be sensible."

Dorjan broke away from the hug and turned to leave. He winked before he threw open the curtains and led Areau back through wherever he'd come from. "Don't worry, Cricket. I've got Areau for backup. We'll be fine."

"Speaking of which," Areau was saying as their voices grew fainter, "I'm worried about the gas to solid ratio…."

His voice went away, and Taern fell back against the pillows.

He must have closed his eyes and slept for a while before what felt to be a sudden change in air pressure woke him up. He lay there, eyes wide open in the faintly lit black of the asteroid mine, his heart pounding and sweat slowly soaking through his hair, sliding down his chest, saturating the sheets at his back.

A deafening roar rocked the floor beneath the bed and shook the entire room Taern was in, and that alone sent Taern to his feet. He grabbed the sheet to wrap around his naked waist before pattering barefoot along the hard, stony ground in search of wherever Areau had come from and Dorjan had disappeared down.

He found what appeared to be a tube, with a ladder in the middle. He bent down and pushed tentatively on the sides of the tube, deciding it appeared to be some sort of vegetable matter. The air coming through it seemed to be heated somehow, and the explosive roar of something burning hot and fast could be heard as well. Taern was too tired and achy to hop, but he could still climb a ladder, especially one like this one. Although it was held together with ropes, it was made with side slats and silken cords, including a sort of corded handrail that made lowering himself through the tube to the ground almost as easy as lying in bed, worrying himself to death.

The tube was fairly long, and he was leaning a lot on the handrails at the end, but finally he hopped into the snow beneath the opening and ducked, emerging from the womblike atmosphere of the asteroid and blinking hard to accustom himself to the gray daylight and the cold. And then the giant orange ball of fire about half a league away stole all of his attention—and all of his breath.

Standing halfway between Taern and the ball of orange, which was slowly collapsing on itself in a jagged black implosion of burning gas and matter, was a lone figure in black. As Taern watched, the figure sank slowly to his knees, his face in his hands, his shoulders shaking as though he were sobbing his life away.

Taern found himself running, heedless of the soreness of his body and his bare feet on the snow and the cold, and ignoring the burning ash stinging the air and the acrid smell of combusting gas.

The Glorious Redemption

THE train ride was interminable. First Areau worried about Krissa and then about Taern, and then about Dorjan because if Taern didn't make it, Dorjan's heart couldn't take it.

Then he remembered why Dorjan was so fragile, why Taern was his last hope, why so much of the world's future rested on the shoulders of one strong, worn battling man.

And then he worried some more. He worried about his experiments and he worried about what Krissa had told him before he left and if he could become the man she would need. He worried about how sad his people would be with the loss of their friend. He was driving himself to distraction with worry, his breath coming in pants, his body craving some sort of violence to it to calm him down. When he realized he'd used his nails to score the back of his hands bloody, he laced his fingers together and took a deep breath.

He needed to think about something else.

He thought about science. He thought about the science of the mines. He thought about the gases present in the air humans breathed and he thought about the incremental changes in those gases that made them volatile and susceptible to flame.

He thought of the stability of the asteroids and how even the most hollowed-out orbs had walls a good six hands thick, and about how combustible the gas would have to be to have the smallest thing—a boot heel striking off a hard granite or slate surface—in order to ignite it.

He busied himself doing calculations on the window of the millipede, ignoring the clackety clack of the legs rising and falling with the torque bars across the iron wheels, and every calculation he did led him to the same conclusion:

Broken, not dead; destroyed, not annihilated; no certainty of success, only certainty of failure.

What would happen to Kyon's Keep if the wrong people survived what they planned?

He practically ran out of the train station, looking around wildly for the cricket Dorjan had promised. It was there, driven by his father, and Areau had a moment of disorientation. What was Coreau doing there, driving a cricket?

It wasn't until he went to haul himself up that he saw his father had lowered himself off the machine and was standing, his weathered face hopeful, his arms open. Areau realized that his father was waiting for a proper greeting.

How many years had they arrived home, and Areau had ignored his father to rush back to his rooms and sulk? He'd hated visits home—he and Dorjan would bond in the asteroids, and he would have to admit that Dorjan's flesh was not hateful, and he'd have to give over his body to something pleasant, and he'd have to admit the abomination of what he'd been doing to Dorjan in his unspoken addiction.

He'd taken it out on everybody, hadn't he?

He took a moment and embraced his father, clutching him tightly and not fearing, not this time, for the disappointment he must have been. Krissa loved him. He *would* be worthy.

He pulled back and smiled, putting his heart in it. "I take it Dorjan preceded me?"

Coreau nodded. "His young man—it's touch and go. The niskets are all aflutter—I think they like him very much, and you know how they worry over Dorjan."

Areau nodded. "Well, we managed to beat the Forum here," he said thoughtfully. "Dorjan and I have a plan."

Coreau grimaced. "You're both too quick for me, son. I'm afraid to even ask."

Areau smiled brightly. "Oh, it's easy enough, father!" He shrugged. "Put all their eggs in one basket, and then step on it!"

Areau had forgotten how wonderful his father's laugh was, how deep and resonant, how it made children want to laugh too, and put adults at ease. Spontaneously, he embraced Coreau again, gratified when his father returned it. He pulled away suddenly, not embarrassed but hurried.

"I need to stop home," he said, and then felt bad. "Not to see Mum, although that will be a plus, but I need something there from my lab."

Coreau nodded. "Well, your mum will be happy to see you." He smiled, and it was Areau's smile, plus a few years and a lot more practice.

It was even teeth in tanned skin, and blond hair that had gone white and black with age. It was Areau's blue-eyed gaze, the one he thought he'd never be able to look in a mirror again, looking out at him with affection and hope.

Areau thought the hope was what hurt the worst. *Oh, Da, can I earn that? Please, give me time to earn it!*

The trip home had never been so long.

His mother embraced him, and his pregnant sister too, although he gave her a hard time about not having enough room in her lap to hug anybody, much less him. His other sisters were at Dre's keep, and had been, he learned, since Dorjan's message to them after he had beaten a leather punching bag to powder, distraught at the loss of so many good men. Kyon's Keep had sent as many people and supplies as they could ship out, because so very many of the soldiers who had died, betrayed by their country, had come from either Dre's keep or Kyon's, and Kyon's had help to spare.

The cricket was set on leap, and as they soared over full grain silos and storehouses stocked with preserved vegetables, Areau found a moment to be grateful for the farsightedness of Dorjan and of the hale, intelligent man at the controls. As he'd done his calculations in the millipede on the way over, he'd seen fields lying fallow that should have been made ready for the spring. He'd seen hexacows, gaunt, unfed, untethered, wandering around on six legs that were not all sound, rooting in the snow for grain or any source of sustenance, and they would surely not produce meat nor milk come spring. Suddenly all of Dorjan's anxiety over food, and how much the keep had, and how many of the civilians had been conscripted into the military, began to filter into Areau's thick head. None of those soldiers were able to help produce food—what would people eat when the snows melted?

Areau's friend and father had been part of making sure that at least their family and friends would be able to answer that question, and Areau was proud.

After the cricket made its final leap and landed in the courtyard of the sprawling villa of Kyon's Keep, Areau scrambled down the side of the thing and ran to the kitchen for his greeting, and then he sprinted to his room for the tiny instant flame he'd used to light his burners and candles as well as the bundle of fuses he hoped was still good. He ran back and hugged everybody again, harder, regretful because he didn't have time to talk, which was a shame. He was *longing* to sing happiness about Krissa, about her news, about finally being a brother and a son and a true lover and not just a pitiful addict dragging his family down to worry.

He hopped back on the cricket still smelling vanilla and flour from his mother's kitchen, and giving his father last-minute instructions.

"They'll arrive here—don't let them settle down. Tell them if they're planning on taking over, they need to visit the mines first. They have their own conveyances—like rabbits, but autonomously powered. They make a horrific stink; I saw them exiting the city. Direct them to the northernmost mine. I'll be there to direct them inside."

"Then what?"

Areau grimaced. "Well, there will be miners coming in through the hexacow fields—get them under cover as quickly as possible. I, uhm, whatever happens next, it's not going to be safe."

Coreau's eyes widened. "Be careful, son! Take good care of our keeper, as well!"

Areau nodded, shame stinging him. "For once, I can promise that with a whole heart." And with that he waved one more time and engaged.

He asked the niskets to guide him to Dorjan, somehow just needing to think of his friend to see the tiny line of flickering lights that led to the southernmost asteroid. It was the one with the smallest cavern, Areau thought, and it was the one the farthest from where they were going to lead the threescore Forum Masters and Triari who had taken to vehicles and gone off to conquer their own province.

He had a moment, when the cricket was in midleap, to think of what a glorious sight the asteroids were. They were black-brown-and-gray rocks, which matched the bright winter-gray sky in a way, and snow crusted over their craggy asymmetrical surfaces. They looked like winter flowers bobbing slightly with the wind, snow coating their odd-shaped tops, as they clung to the earth by the umbilicals Areau's mother used to say the niskets spun out of dreams and wishes.

It was still daylight, but not for long, and in one of his leaps, Areau saw an exhaust cloud over the horizon and knew that he might have gotten there in time but that it was still going to be close.

He was sincerely glad to see Taern alive, that spun-sugar nonsense about them needing each other sounding substantial and true when he spilled it out, and Dorjan's half smile was well worth the effort. But as they scrambled down the umbilical to earth, Areau knew he needed to bounce his newest idea off of Dorjan to see if there was something they could do.

"The gas ratio?" Dorjan asked, squinting. He did look terrible. Areau thought he might have been bled nearly to death in an attempt to save Taern, not that he'd admit it.

"Yes—if the asteroid's not ready to just float away on its own, we need a way to make it combust."

Dorjan grunted. "Slow, slow—why must I always be so slow!"

Areau grimaced. Dorjan was only slow compared to Areau himself. "Science was not your strong point," he admitted, "but that doesn't mean you don't have good ideas."

Dorjan's gimlet eyes glaring in his direction told him he hadn't made things better, but then Dorjan grunted and got back to thinking.

"We would need to pump the asteroid with more than just its share, then," Dorjan said thoughtfully. "Gas compresses, right?"

Areau nodded. "Yes—that's the blessing. If we have the niskets swarm the entrance after the gits have gone up into the cavern, we can compress the gas. But how do we make sure it will explode once they cut the umbilical? Compressed gas doesn't float, Dorjan—it sinks, becomes liquid. It may freeze them all to death or even asphyxiate them, but not in the time it's going to take that thing to crash to the ground, and there's no guarantee it's going to crash with enough momentum to do more than rattle them around like marbles in a cookie tin. And then we'd *really* be cooked, wouldn't we, because they'd be alive and pissed, and we'd have to give them the secret just to keep the family alive, and—"

"We will *never* give the secret," Dorjan said, striding to the cricket.

The crickets used here no longer needed steam armor to power them. It was an innovation Areau had programmed. Even when he'd been at his worst, he'd been able to imagine an independent steam power source. He'd sent the specs to his father, and he reckoned that Kyon's Keep had the only civilian crickets on the planet.

Dorjan put one foot in the stirrup and wrapped his hand in the pull strap, then went to push himself up—

And fell back down, swearing and clinging to the strap at the pommel. Before Areau could ask him if he needed help, he tried again and this time succeeded before offering Areau a hand up.

Areau put his feet in the stirrups and wrapped his arms around his friend's waist when he didn't have to. "How close was it?" he asked, near Dorjan's ear, no longer afraid of the intimacy or what it would mean to his manhood if he enjoyed the closeness, enjoyed giving his friend the strength Areau had not had to give in so very long.

"It was damned close," Dorjan breathed, relaxing into his arms for a moment. "The niskets flat-out refused to take any more blood from me." The breath of bitter laughter shook them both. "Little bastards. Seemed to think I was being impatient."

"You were, you git!" Areau said gently. "Now come along. Let's clear out the mines before those bloody awful fossil fuel conveyances get here!"

They did, leaping the cricket from mine to mine, telling the workers (there were only a few per mine because the niskets liked space to work, and they could be dangerous when they clouded) to jump on the crickets, paddle-cycles, or electric sleds gathered at the root of the umbilicals and hurry back to the keep as fast as they could. Areau directed them to go around the building proper and take the back gate, the one that led through the hexacow fields—yes, even though that meant tracking shite to the keep, it was worth it. At each mine, as they powered the cricket for another leap, they saw a gratifying trail of men crawling down the ladders like ants down a flower stem, getting ready to flee to the safety of the keep.

Finally, at the last mine, the men were scurrying away behind them, and Areau hopped off the cricket. "I'll conduct them inside," he said, gesturing nervously to the line of exhaust trailing the big buses that were heading their way. "You climb up and hide in this one." He gestured to the asteroid next to the last one.

Dorjan nodded, then said, "Wait, Ari—your hair. Pull it in front of your face there. If they don't see the scars, they won't wonder."

Areau blinked and then grimaced. "Hells, for a minute, I'd forgotten they were there!"

"I never see them," Dorjan said, smiling weakly. "I was just worried about you, and I remembered."

Areau looked at him, hanging on to the cricket by force of will. "Well, I'm worried about you! Climb up—hurry."

"Are you sure you have a long enough fuse?" Dorjan asked.

Areau nodded, but inwardly he was worried. The fuse was left over from his days experimenting with steam versus combustion propulsion. He and Dorjan had launched countless rockets, and part of each launch had been painstakingly wrapping sulfur and saltpeter in laboriously measured quantities into thin strips of resin-soaked cloth in order to make the fuse. He'd had some left—enough to launch a rocket from a safe distance away, but not, he feared, enough to launch an asteroid.

"I'll call you down when we need to get the niskets," he shouted and then hopped down and took the cricket to the last asteroid mine.

The Forum Masters were a rude lot, he decided as they all pushed past him imperiously, yammering about how they would have to find a more convenient way to access the mines were they to make visits a regular occurrence. The rudeness included Septra himself, whom even Areau could recognize after seeing him so often as a cadet. Dorjan was right. The fucker had aged damned well. Areau kept his eyes averted and introduced himself as a mining foreman, and nobody looked twice at him.

"They said we'd learn the secrets to mining in here," Septra said, surprising him as they waited for the last of the other Masters to go up.

"Aye, Forum Master," Areau muttered, keeping his eyes down.

"I'm a Triari, you simpleton. Do you not know what it is?"

Areau looked up the umbilical to where the last Forum Master was disappearing into the center of the cavern. Then he looked Septra directly in the eyes, his hand playing with the long knife he'd palmed from his room when he'd needed to cut the last of the fuse off the spool. "I know exactly who you are, you nutless fucker," he said, thinking he owed Taern a debt of thanks. Swearing had never been so fun. "You're the man who sicced an army on a defenseless keep and let untried boys massacre innocent people in the name of your own greed."

Septra's eyes widened, and he sneered. "I see even the peasants are educated in Kyon's Keep—how very egalitarian of them. Shall be the first thing I change."

"I invented your cricket, you arse-reaming git. I powered your entire army, and I spent ten years paying for the sin of believing a... a *bureaucrat* had the honor of a soldier. Go ahead. Go up and learn the secret of the bloody mines. Don't think you don't have your own lessons to learn."

Septra wasn't stupid. His eyes widened and he gaped. "Areau? Dorjan's little pet? I ordered them to *break* you!"

Areau grinned unpleasantly, suddenly knowing what he was going to do. Well, he'd been planning murder, hadn't he? Wasn't this just so much more personal a plan? The thing that had made him a bloody bastard hadn't *died* when his addiction to pain had been broken. He'd just been able to make better choices for the people around him. Well, he didn't *want* another choice for this rank fucker. He wanted the *wrong* choice for him. Areau *owed* Septra the wrong bloody choice, and he didn't think even Dorjan would deny him that.

"You did order them to do that," he said gruffly, sliding the knife out of his pocket. He and Septra were eye to eye now, and Septra didn't even blink. "You broke me and then turned me loose on the person I loved the most, and I *almost* broke him. But every drop of blood I tapped from his heart, he tapped from your streets. Haven't you wondered, Triari Alum Septra, why the Nyx was so hell-bent on destroying your income?"

Septra's eyes bulged. "You?" he hissed, and Areau rolled his eyes.

"I don't have that much class, guv'nor." He laid the accent on thick, channeling the lokogos who had made himself so free with his and Dorjan's home. "In fact, I'm just a common street murderer, myself!"

And with that, he thrust the blade he'd been toying with so deeply into Septra's chest that the haft ground up against his ribs.

He'd aimed carefully—he punctured a lung as well as Septra's heart. The man didn't even get out a cry for help as he fell, spasming, at the base of the mine he never lived to claim. Areau looked detachedly at Septra as he vomited blood and blinked stupidly, his last breaths rattling in his chest, and wondered if there shouldn't be more hoopla around this man's death. But then, wasn't that a beautiful thing about death? Everybody got one, right? The difference was, nobody would mourn this one. For all he'd been trying to rule the world—and destroy it too—the fact was, at the end, he was just a cooling body in the snow. Areau thought there was a bit of beauty to that idea. He knew for certain that when *he* died, people, *good* people, would mourn him. When his beloved friend died, the entire province would fall to its knees and grieve.

But not this git. This git was a carcass on the ground. Areau kicked him hard in the ribs, and while the body yielded, it didn't move. Yup. A carcass. Exactly as it should be.

Areau hopped on the cricket then to get Dorjan, calling the niskets as he did. They came, appearing in a whirling metallic rainbow cloud, hovering right at the mouth of the umbilical, which was about man high.

As the cricket launched, he heard the last Forum Master up the umbilical call down, "I say, Septra, are you coming? Oh my—what in Bimuit's name is that?"

"Dorjan!" Areau called, landing at the foot of the mine.

Dorjan slid down just like they had as kids, holding on to the handrails as he landed, and walked out from under the tube canopy. "Hells, Ari—you're covered in blood!"

"Not mine!" Areau grinned fiercely. "I had a little conversation with Alum Septra before he climbed up. I'm afraid he won't make it to see the secret of Kyon's Keep."

Dorjan staggered a little as he reached out to grab the strap of the cricket. "You what?"

"I stepped up, Dori," Areau said, keeping his eyes level with his friend's. "All this time, you've been going out and getting the blood on your hands. Well, I've got some myself. And I'm not sorry. Not this time."

Dorjan's smile wasn't condemning. "I'm not either. Was it horrible, the way he died?"

Areau nodded. "I stabbed him with a lower-class accent," he said, the thought making him giggle, and Dorjan squinted at him.

"A *what*?"

"''Ave a knife in the ribs, guv'nor?" Areau mimicked. "Aye, wot's all yer fancy gennelmens need!"

Dorjan laughed a little, looking bemused. "Well, Ari, I'm pleased that you're pleased with yourself," he said, shaking his head. He grasped the strap and gave a painful haul, his body sagging a bit once he was aboard.

"Oh, I am," Areau said, nodding. "What's the use in being a bloody git bastard if you can't take out the villain when you've got the chance!"

Dorjan was laughing as they leapt.

When they landed, Areau scrambled down and sprinted to the mouth of the umbilical, where the nisket swarm had grown in proportion to their combined call. He could hear the exclamations of the Forum Masters over the clatter of the niskets' wings; they were looking down from the portal in the asteroid to the cloud of the niskets, and they seemed enchanted. They were still enchanted when they began to cough as the niskets discharged the gases they absorbed while mining into the umbilical leading to the asteroid. Even as Areau ducked beneath them and tied off the fuse at the bottom of the rope ladder, more niskets joined the original number. Dorjan continued his inward call to the creatures who had shared their blood since they were children. Areau cleared the nisket cloud and ran the fuse as far as he could—a scant twenty yards—before stopping.

Dorjan came to meet him there, shaking his head. "Oh, Ari—I don't know—that doesn't look safe at all. Septra's dead—"

"We need them gone," Areau said, conviction in his voice. "It needs to happen. They cheerfully aided and abetted in the destruction of their entire province, and they did it for what? Greed? Lumium? I have no idea. All of this, and I still don't. Our families will do *anything* to help a family in need, and these people waged war against innocent lives for no reason but their own ends. If they didn't want to go out this way, they shouldn't have created us. If you create monsters, Dori, you die by them. Remember all those books we read as kids? The adventure ones? Those books knew this was the truth—if these old men don't know it, it's about time someone taught them!"

"But not at the expense of your life!"

Areau shrugged and grinned, feeling free and happy and strong. "I may live!" he said. "You start running first, and I'll light it!"

Dorjan's jaw got stony. "We'll light it together," he said, and Areau nodded. Dorjan was still gripping the cricket's strap like it was bearing him up.

"Right," Areau said and then held out his arms. Dorjan looked surprised, but he accepted the embrace.

"I lied," Areau whispered in his ear.

"About what?"

"Two things. One—your touch never disgusted me, my friend. Even if it wasn't from who I wanted, it was never anything but human, and I craved it as much as I craved the pain."

Dorjan's embrace tightened around his shoulders, and Dorjan whispered, "What was the other thing?"

"You're going to be far away when I light that fuse." And with a few swift movements, Areau shoved Dorjan onboard the cricket and tightened the strap around his waist before hitting the button for a short jump. He never could have done it if Dorjan hadn't been weakened. He probably couldn't have done it if Dorjan had had even an hour's more rest, or perhaps even a dinner to replace some of the blood he'd given. But Dorjan had given everything to Taern, and that was as it should be, and Areau, for once, was the strongest one.

"I love you, my friend," he murmured, stepping back as the cricket launched, and then he turned to the fuse.

First he asked the niskets about the gas content and got a rather happy affirmative from them—they'd apparently had the nisket fart of the century over by the umbilical, and all of that lovely gas was making the Forum Masters loopy, coughing and unhappy, but too disoriented to climb back down the ladder. Excellent.

Areau went to the fuse as it lay in the snow and pulled out his little portable flame and lit it.

And nothing happened. Oh hells. Areau walked down a yard and tried again, and again, and again. The nisket cloud was clearing, and Areau looked up to see a number of men with their heads shoved in the umbilical opening, trying to breathe fresh air. The umbilical itself was buckling as the compressed gases did what he'd told Dorjan they'd do: weighed the thing down instead of bearing it up. Oh hells, the fuse wasn't working. The only thing that would work was—

Areau ran toward the umbilical, thinking about pain. He still craved it. Krissa had only broken its thrall over him and replaced it with a fully consensual one that bowed to her. He didn't just crave her, he *loved* her, and she loved him. She was going to have his child.

But that didn't mean that pain didn't still have a fascination for him. He still remembered the dark ecstasy he'd given himself when he'd stripped the skin from his arms, or when he'd goaded and pled with Dorjan enough to be taken roughly, screaming for Dorjan to hurt him more, hurt him better.

Pain had been his first real lover, but as he looked up into the umbilical and saw that one of the Forum Masters was making a halfhearted attempt to climb back down, he didn't feel disloyal to Krissa at all. This was pain for her sake, and pain for the sake of their baby. This was pain for his father and his mother and his sisters and their children. This was pain for Dorjan, to whom he owed so much and could only pay but a little.

He felt almost serene as he pushed the portable flame up into the umbilical, although that could be the gases affecting his judgment too. It didn't matter, because the flame whooshed up and over him, through the tube, where he could dimly hear the Forum Master's scream over his own.

The flame engulfed him, the pain agonizing, destroying every nerve in his body before the flames charred his lungs, burnt him blood and brains and bones.

It was glorious.

THE cricket landed, and Dorjan tried to turn the damned thing around, but it refused to go. Areau had wrought better than he knew when he'd slammed his hand on the jump button, because he'd jammed the steering gears too. Dorjan hammered at them futilely, and when that didn't work, he feverishly unhooked the belt from around his waist and untangled his hand from the hold strap on the side, then slid down the damned contraption and turned to run toward the last asteroid.

He turned just in time to watch the flame whoosh up the tube, and even from where he stood, half a league away, he could hear Areau screaming—but not for long.

As soon as the flame traveled up, he heard a terrible rumbling sound and then a roaring explosion, but a deeply muffled one, as the walls of the asteroid held and then fractured, black and orange seams appearing as the gas inside ignited. The sheet of flame escaped the fractures and then the walls began to collapse in on themselves, even as the great floating cavern toppled slowly to earth.

Dorjan knelt in the snow, weeping, until Taern came out and wrapped arms around his shoulders.

"I'm so sorry," he whispered, and Dorjan turned into him and buried his face against Taern's bare stomach and sobbed, until it occurred to him to bring Taern in from the cold.

Not Quite a Year

Two Days Later

"WHAT do you mean you have to go?" Taern demanded, looking at Dorjan in worry.

Dorjan hadn't slept in two days. He'd had to reassure the keep, that was part of it, and he'd had to deliver his condolences to Areau's family. Krissa had arrived the next day, and Dorjan had met her as the cricket touched down. Taern had seen their exchange through the window from his bed in Dorjan's room, and he didn't think Dorjan even had to say anything. She simply read the expression on his face and crumpled to the ground.

Dorjan had caught her, of course, and carried her in. He ensconced her in Areau's room and sicced his mother and Areau's mother on her. True to the predictions made in a winter sitting room, the two women waited on her hand and foot, as though royalty was a thing on this planet and Krissa was it.

The treatment got even more intense when they discovered she was carrying Areau's child, and at one point she snuck into Taern's room so she could talk to somebody who didn't treat her as though she was bathed in the blood of Biemansland's newest martyr.

Taern talked to her like she was a human being—that seemed to be all she wanted—and then, when she was ready, he held her when she fell apart.

Dorjan came in bearing a tray for Taern and found Krissa asleep on his side of the bed.

Taern glared at him. "Oh, of course you're happy to see this. Her asleep here means you have an excuse not to go to sleep, doesn't it?"

Dorjan graced him with one of those bitter excuses for smiles Taern remembered from their first meeting. "Haven't I been weak enough already?"

He bowed faintly and left, and Taern was stuck setting the tray down and stumbling after him. His sojourn in the snow had left him sick as well as weakened, but that didn't stop him from coughing and weaving his way down the corridor of Dorjan's bloody great and confusing house, and yelling at him before he disappeared down the stairs.

"Nyx, you bloody great nisket shite, his death was *not* your fault, and if you don't get your stupid arse back here in this bed and get some bloody sleep, I'm going to climb in the first mine I can find with some big lummox who thinks I've got tits!"

This threat was followed by a bout of coughing, of course, and Dorjan strode down the corridor, swinging Taern into his arms as he passed. He deposited Taern, furious and weak and trying to keep helpless, frustrated tears from running down his cheeks, back in what was supposed to be their bed.

"That was entertaining," Dorjan said, pulling the blankets up around Taern's chin with stern intent. "Would you like to do it again before breakfast? My mother needs a good laugh—she's so busy trying to parse out the food we've got stored so the keeps, at least, don't go hungry that she's forgotten how."

Taern scowled. "I know you have big important things happening, you arse. But your heart is screaming, and the only reason nobody here can hear it is that they've got other things to drown it out."

"So do you." Dorjan's voice dropped, and he raised his hand to smooth Taern's black curls off his forehead.

"Name one thing I'm responsible for here," Taern snapped—but he did rub his face up to meet more of Dorjan's hand.

"Getting well," Dorjan whispered. "You need to get well. I cannot do the responsible hero thing without you."

"Well, you can't do it if you make yourself sick either."

Dorjan nodded. "Point taken." He stood and kissed Taern's forehead and then turned to leave. "I'll make it a point to rest as soon as I can."

But he hadn't. He'd had meeting after meeting with Coreau and his mother (who was a swimmingly lovely person, actually, and who couldn't spoil Taern enough) and with the widow who was running Dre's keep. And in the middle of this, he'd said loudly and often that someone needed to go back and alert the Forum that 12 percent of its ruling body had just exploded in a ball of flame.

So now, two days after Areau, who had been the center of his entire world before Taern came along, had died with that 12 percent, Dorjan was leaving Taern bedridden and helpless.

"You know, you're damned close to needing to be sedated!" Taern snapped—and then sniffled. Dammit! Dorjan had bags under his eyes that could be shipped to Kiamath Keep, but Taern couldn't seem to kick a lousy head cold.

"Five minutes on the millipede and I'll be out like a light," Dorjan confessed. He sat in the stuffed chair he'd put next to the bed just so they could have these little chats, and Taern smacked his knee and snarled.

"When do you leave, prat!"

"Two hours," Dorjan said, and Taern could tell he was fighting to keep his eyes open.

"Then lie down next to me and sleep for one of them, and I'll *consider* not being such a colossal pain in the arse."

Dorjan had sighed then, and since Krissa had gone back to her bed and back to being spoiled by everybody's mother (well, the really pregnant woman with the thick, curly blonde hair might have been Areau's sister, but she was obviously *somebody's* mother), Taern could scoot over and make room for him.

Taern tucked himself into Dorjan's arms and nestled his head against Dorjan's chest.

"I love you, you dumb git," Taern muttered irritably. Dorjan's response was a long-drawn-out snore.

Taern fell asleep against him, and when he awakened, Dorjan was gone.

One month later

"ARE you sure he won't object to us being here?" Mrs. Wrinkle asked for what must have been the hundredth time. She'd asked when he'd proposed the trip to her, writing her from Kyon's Keep to Dre's, and she'd asked when they'd met to board the train, and then she'd asked every hour on the hour on their way back. He'd managed to keep his temper and his perspective for most of that and had managed to lie his skinny, still recovering arse off.

But now that they were faced with their home, dusty and disused, with only a few dishes in the sink and some of Dorjan's smallclothes hanging on the line in the laundry room, Taern allowed his real opinion to show.

"He'll be furious with me," he said honestly, "but he's never mad at you. And look at this place. He *needs* us, Mrs. Wrinkle, don't you think so?"

Their housekeeper looked around, and Taern watched a ripple of grief cross her weathered face.

"Are you sure Lady Krissa won't come until after the baby?" Mrs. Wrinkle asked, and Taern moved to help her sweep open the drapes.

"I think she'd *love* to come here before that," he said, speaking the truth. "But Areau's mother—well...."

"Aye," Mrs. Wrinkle said. "Mrs. Coreau, she needed someone to fret over. But...." She looked around unhappily. "Oh, Master Taern. It's so sad in here," she confessed, and Taern had known it was coming. He wrapped his arms around her plump, comfortable figure and let her cry on him.

Mrs. Wrinkle was tough, though—you wouldn't think it, but she had been serving Nyx and his mad scientist albatross for ten years, and she was accordingly strong. In a moment she straightened up. "This place is a mess," she said briskly, and then she fought against crumpling again. "I hate to think of Master Dorjan here alone. For a while he was surrounded by family, that's all."

Taern grimaced and shrugged. "Well, for the moment, he has us. We shall have to do. You'll eat dinner with us in the kitchen?"

She nodded. "But first I have to scare the spiders out of the stove. I don't even want to think about what he's been eating."

Taern would wager not much of anything. In the month since he'd left, Dorjan had sent regular missives, a packet about every four days. The bulk of the packets was political in nature—important things about recalling the military and reassigning the troops to rebuilding the areas they had just ravaged. Dorjan had insisted on rotating troops in and out of this duty—he was pretty sure the bitterness of the recently besieged provinces would be demoralizing for the men, even as they strove to repair the harm they'd recently inflicted.

He'd also put the military to work distributing food among the poor and rebuilding some of the dilapidated housing of the poorer quarters, as well as shoring up the burned-out schools and making them havens for women and children who had been living on the streets. When the Forum Masters complained about the cost, Dorjan pointed out how much less expensive it was to provide for the children than build the machines used for war, and they shut up, mortified. (Or at least that's how he explained it to Taern. Taern was reasonably sure his missives to his mother were a bit more restrained.)

There had been personal things in the missives to Taern, as well—small, almost coded, but enough to sustain Taern as he strove to make himself useful during the day and lay in a strange and empty bed at night.

> *The stews of Thenis have changed face a bit—although I look forward to running them with you again and showing you how much.*
>
> *It's quiet here at night. I lie in bed and wonder what Areau is doing in his workshop, and then I remember.*
>
> *The Forum canteen can't make bread. It seems like such a simple thing. Tell Mrs. Wrinkle she's missed.*
>
> *They want to make me a Triari. I don't want to be a bloody Triari, Taern. I want a life with you. I want to raise Areau's child, and I want to spend time at Kyon's Keep, and I don't want to be a fucking Triari, and nothing they say can make me!*

That last one had alarmed Taern enough, but the one after that broke his heart.

> *I'm forced to pay attention to everything now—no more sleeping, no more feigning idiocy, everybody needs to know my opinion and every motion must be fought for. I've taken to sketching your likeness when I'm struggling to stay awake or stay focused. They're not good, but then, love letters aren't my specialty either.*

The sketches had been decent—not fine art, but Taern had been particularly struck by the one that placed him in bed, a sheet over his backside, while Taern looked over a naked shoulder. He'd looked into his own eyes as Dorjan saw him, and was belted in the stomach with a terrible longing. He'd stared at the picture all that night, listening to Dorjan's mother giving orders (Mrs. Kyon was particularly good at that—Taern thought he knew where Dorjan had gotten it from), and wondered what he was still doing there. His cold had gone away, and he was more than fit to travel. Perhaps for a little while, he'd stayed because he thought he could help. Krissa had been placed in charge of the children of the keep, and she was smashing at it—she joked quietly to Taern that all of her time spent disciplining errant men had made her a shoo-in. But while Taern could help at the mines or the kitchens or even with Krissa, he was rootless and unfocused, willing to be blown in any direction, unless he was at Dorjan's side.

He emerged from Dorjan's old bedroom the next day wearing only his smallclothes and found Mrs. Kyon, who had probably been up for hours, organizing her little corner of the world. Her name was Abella, and she was a gorgeous, comfortably sized woman in her early fifties, with Dorjan's thick brown hair and expressive brown eyes, but for some reason Taern couldn't call her by her given name. She needed an honorific, just like Mrs. Wrinkle.

"Mrs. Ky—"

"Taern?" she corrected, and he sighed.

"Mrs. Abella?" he tried, and she arched her eyebrows, conceding.

"Close enough. What can I do for you?"

"Is Mrs. Wrinkle still at Dre's keep?"

"Aye." He'd found her in the kitchens, and as they spoke, she cut a new loaf of bread into four quarters and smeared a thick coat of honey butter on two of them.

"Can I send for her?" he asked, and she handed him a quarter and took one for himself, and Taern smiled as they both took a blissful bite of warm bread and honey butter.

"Why? What do you have in mind?"

Taern grimaced, hoping she didn't take offense. "He's alone," Taern said, feeling his eyes burn at the thought of it. "He was alone for so long, and then he had me, and now he's more alone than ever—"

"So you're going to go to him?"

Taern shrugged. "Of course. It's what I do."

She nodded and took another bite. "It's about time. But do me a favor, if you could," she added, looking sad. "Leave Krissa, could you? Areau's mother…." Mrs. Abella shook her head. "His father too. They… they knew things weren't right with Areau, for the longest time. They need to hear about him as a hero. It eases their grief, and so does the promise of the child."

So matter-of-fact—much like her son. Taern remembered moments when Dorjan's extremity had sanded away his tact—*You're so short!* And *Have you any idea how long it's been since I've slept?* This sounded much like that.

"I'll leave her now," he said, although it pained him. "But"—he grimaced—"after the child—she may want to come to the city. She'll visit, of course, but we had a life there, Mrs. Abella. We—" Oh hells. Madame M was dead. "We had friends. And Dorjan misses people. He'd never confess it in so many words, but it pains him that all of his people are here, and he's in Thenis."

Abella nodded. "His father used to worry, you know. Even when he was full of mischief, the boy was still all about doing the right thing. Kyon used to say that no man was ever great unless he doubted the difference. I think our son is a great man. But that being said, I wouldn't mind if he was an ordinary man who spent a little more time at home."

Taern nodded and swallowed hard. "I miss him," he said baldly. They'd never talked about Taern's place in Dorjan's bed. "I miss him. I'm content to be ordinary, and I'm certainly small, but I can't even be functional unless I'm by his side."

He got a brilliant smile in return, warm in the center with eyes crinkled at the corners, and then a strong embrace. "Are you sure you won't wait for your sisters?" she asked, and Taern grimaced.

"Can they be here tomorrow? I can leave two days later."

She nodded, and because she was Mrs. Abella, she made it so.

The meeting with his sisters had been… warm and awkward at first. Abella had put them in her nicest sitting room, the one with the furniture with the long legs carved of dark wood. They'd stood in the middle for a moment, after brief bows and curtseys, and looked at each other, trying to find the children they remembered in the adults and teens facing them now. They were *definitely* his sisters—they had Mum's curly black hair and both Mum and Da's blue eyes, just like him—but he seemed to remember them wearing his breeches, and certainly not the fine sober-hued dresses they were tightly laced into at the moment.

The silence dragged out, and for once Taern couldn't think of a thing to say until the oldest, Brina, looked him up and down with their mother's customary skepticism and said, "Are you as sly as you look, or was nature just cruel to you?"

Taern looked up into her face—damn her for being nearly as tall as Dorjan!—and grinned. "Yes I'm as sly as I look, and if nature wasn't a bitch, you wouldn't have a face like a cricket's arse!"

Brina (who actually had the same elegant oval to her face as Taern, along with fuller lips and ripe curves, all at seventeen) laughed richly and hugged him then, and they spent hours tumbling words and experiences and memories over each other. Abella came in with dinner and sat with them, and when Taern spoke of his first meeting with Dorjan, her eyes widened.

"You're the boy!" she breathed, and Taern flushed.

"Yes," he acknowledged. "I'm the git under the rushes who ruined his life!"

Abella shook her head. "Ruined it? You're the boy who made him step out of line! You made him different. You made him *great*!"

Taern snorted and looked at his sisters while soberly shaking his head. "He made himself great," Taern assured them. "I just made him smile."

They laughed at that, but he knew it was the truth. And now, as he and Mrs. Wrinkle aired out their home, replaced the sheets (which looked hardly slept on), and shopped for food at the market, Taern thought about that moment in the sitting room a scant two days ago. That was what he wanted to do—make Dorjan smile. He didn't have to run about the city as the Cricket as long as he could look after the man in other ways. Of course, Taern assumed he would find things to keep him busy. Schools, orphanages, shelters—those things needed tending, and Taern found he longed for a project that he could be proud of, but at the end of the day, what he truly wanted, the culmination of his misspent youth, was to make Dorjan smile.

But as he and Mrs. Wrinkle made dinner, ate dinner, cleaned up the dinner dishes, and then retired unhappily to bed, all without seeing Dorjan, he realized he'd have his work cut out for him if Dorjan never came home.

Taern was fast asleep, curled into a miserable ball of missing Dorjan, when the electric lamp by the door snapped on and he startled, sitting up and blinking blearily as Dorjan came in from the cold.

"What in the hell?" Dorjan sounded truly shocked.

"Hey, Nyx. What, is sleep illegal now? How about eating? I knew it. You look like hell. Karanos, can't you even take care of yourself, you bloody great git?"

Dorjan stood in the doorway, gaping, and then he seemed to compose himself and started to take off his clothes. He was wearing his running kit—warm smallclothes, specially made boots, and a warm coat over the top since it was still the dead of winter. He took off his gloves and his hat, and Taern pulled back the covers, shivering in the chill in spite of the fact that he and Mrs. Wrinkle had primed the furnace when they'd aired out the house.

"You're naked," Dorjan said in wonder. "It's cold enough to drop a hieter dead, and you're *naked*?"

"You've got a talent for understatement, Nyx, do you know that?" Taern stood up, hoping his nakedness did a little tap dance on Dorjan's equilibrium. Just seeing the man again was enough to send the blood galloping under Taern's skin. "Now give over the coat—you couldn't leave this in the mudroom by the courtyard?"

"I didn't *think* there'd be anyone home to be offended by my lack of manners!" Dorjan protested, and Taern tried not to whimper when the black wool coat slid from Dorjan's shoulders and Taern saw how thin he'd grown.

"Are you objecting?" Taern asked, hanging the coat over the back of the chair by the desk. He squatted down and gestured imperiously for Dorjan's boots. When Dorjan was slow to comply, Taern looked up and saw that Dorjan was sitting on the bed with all of his attention focused on Taern's naked body. In particular his gaze rested on Taern's privates, which were on display from his position on the floor. Taern watched as Dorjan swallowed, his gaunt face growing suddenly slack with an obvious hunger.

Taern yanked off one boot and then the other, swinging his hips a little to make sure his equipment bobbed ripely between his legs.

"Nyx?" Taern asked slyly, setting the boots in the corner by the armoire and standing up straight. He reached his hands to the ceiling and stretched, showing off the line of his chest and stomach and making sure his semierect cock was clearly visible, peeking out from its nest of hair. Dorjan grunted, and Taern moved a little closer, taking Dorjan's hands as they rested in his lap and pulling them to his backside, where they commenced kneading in a highly satisfactory manner.

"Nyx?" Taern asked again, thrusting his hips so his cock—more erect than halfway so now—bobbed against his thigh. "Was there something you wanted?"

"Crave," Dorjan whispered before opening his mouth and sucking Taern's erection all the way down his throat. Taern threw his head back and cried out, and Dorjan pulled back and engulfed him again, swallowing, the heat and the wet of his mouth gripping Taern like he hadn't been stroked since…

Oh hells. The last time Taern had been touched like this, *Dorjan* had done the touching, and that had been too, too long ago.

Dorjan couldn't seem to get enough of his skin—was, in fact, running his hand up and down Taern's backside, the backs of his thighs, and then curving them inward. Taern let out a cry when Dorjan's thumb brushed his balls from behind, and Dorjan took his cue, pulling his hand forward and cupping them, massaging them, squeezing them gently while his mouth kept up that incessant, insanely satisfying suck.

Dorjan's hair had grown long, was shaggy in his face, and Taern knotted his fingers in it, not guiding or holding, just touching, shivering at the sensuality of a part of Dorjan against his fingers.

Taern shuddered, torn between riding this out, letting Dorjan bring him to orgasm, and simply doubling up, holding him close, and being a part of him when they'd been denied for so long. At his backside, the hand not teasing Taern's balls was reaching, parting Taern's buttocks, playing with his pucker. Dorjan let some spit trickle on his fingers and then prodded gently, entering a little, massaging his rim, and Taern had no choice. He clutched Dorjan to him and gasped, thrusting, spilling, gratified when Dorjan swallowed, and when his climax subsided, he jerked his hips back, to pull his cock out of Dorjan's mouth, and clutched Dorjan's head to his stomach, shaking with the force of his orgasm and the wave of things not said.

The skin under Dorjan's cheek grew wet, and Taern slid down to his knees so he could wrap his arms around Dorjan's waist and bury his face in the crook of his shoulder.

"Miss me, Nyx?" he asked, and Dorjan's hand went to the back of his head and stroked his hair.

"Did you think I wouldn't?" Dorjan asked, and Taern could hear the effort in keeping his voice light. He tilted his head back and looked into

Dorjan's face, then moved a hand up to wipe the wetness away with a thumb.

"Then why didn't you send for me?"

Dorjan looked away and told maybe the first real lie Taern had ever heard him utter. "I wanted to make it a home for you. It's not a good home."

"*Shite!*" Taern snapped, and he seized Dorjan's jaw in the cup of his hand and forced his head back. Dorjan's misery was too naked for him to hold a grudge. "You can mourn him," Taern said, hurting everywhere. "You can grieve. You won't offend me, you know. He was a part of your life, even if he was in the wrong part of your life for a while. What did you think? I wouldn't understand mourning a friend?"

He closed his eyes against the thought of Madame Matiya, her arms akimbo, blood spilling down her throat and onto her most comfortable day dress.

"You had your own mourning to do," Dorjan rasped, and Taern scowled.

"Yes, you git bastard, and I've had to do it all on my own thanks to you. Now shut up—anything you say is going to be a lie. I didn't come here for that." He sat up and started tunneling under Dorjan's knit shirt, pulling it from his body and then thumping Dorjan on the shoulder in honest anger. "*Dammit*, Nyx! You are *not* taking good care of what's mine! I may have leased you to your bloody mourning, but I did *not* agree that you could savage my fucking property, do you hear me?"

Dorjan scowled at him and made an attempt to push him away. "Bimuit, but you're pushy! I'm starting to rethink missing you!"

Taern shook his head, not willing to be mollified by banter. "You," he said, poking a finger at Dorjan's scarred and thin chest, "will never, ever, leave me behind again, do you hear me? You will *never* not have me by your side. There will *never* be a time in our lives when you have to be here and I have to be some other bloody place, because look at you! You must have lost two stone! You can't be trusted with yourself, and that's that! Do you hear me?"

He scowled down at Dorjan and saw that even though the man was still wiping tears from his cheeks with the heel of his hand, he was chuckling a little and nodding his head in agreement. "I hear you," he said soberly. "Don't leave you behind, don't abuse your property—any other strictures before we crawl into this bed together? I'm dying to hold you, you know."

Taern grunted, not completely placated. "Don't grieve without me. He was your friend, Dorjan. Do you think I wouldn't respect that? If nothing else, he was your friend."

Dorjan nodded. "Done," he said, sounding hoarse and lost. "I accept your terms of surrender. I'm yours."

"You were never, ever anyone else's." Taern was deadly serious, and Dorjan nodded.

Taern let him up then, and he stripped and didn't make any asinine protests about underwear or nightgowns, and they slid into bed together. Taern tucked in against his shoulder, smoothing his palm against the mockery of a chest Dorjan was sporting at the moment.

"Would you like to talk about him?" Taern asked hesitantly, and Dorjan made a sound in his throat that wasn't encouraging at first.

Then he sighed and said, his voice still thick with pain, "He was beautiful as a child—so bright and quick, I was always running after his shadow. I was so afraid he'd never want to be my friend, even though we'd been raised together since we were in nappies. Did I tell you that I once stole a pie just so I could share it with him and he'd like me?"

"You did," Taern murmured. "Did it work?" He was fascinated.

"Oh yes," Dorjan said, nodding. "From that moment on, until we joined the military, he never left my side."

On and on into the night, Dorjan talked, and when he finally closed his eyes, midsentence, talking about giving Areau advice about girls of all things, Taern lay there in the dark, weeping quietly against Dorjan's chest without sobbing. He'd truly listened to Dorjan and had heard love and longing in Dorjan's voice, and for the first time had seen the life of a fine and clever mind, of a stalwart friend, of a noble, *good* man, who was worthy to be mourned.

Ten Months After

DORJAN'S room at Kyon's Keep had been redone after Taern left the first time. When Taern had seen it, it had a bed barely big enough for the both of them and muted wood paneling, the kind easily sanded when, say, a rambunctious child rammed his metal bed frame against the molding. (Dorjan had not yet confessed what he'd been doing when that happened, which made Taern even more curious.)

Now, ten months after the death of Areau, son of Coreau, Dorjan's mother had painted the walls white and added a bare navy trim. She'd also moved in a bed big enough for the two of them—although not quite as big as Dorjan's back at the town house, which was a relief. Dorjan still had nights where he slept curled in a ball, and Taern enjoyed a reprieve from chasing him over to the other side of the bed.

She had also added a mirror so that two gentlemen might ready themselves for a formal family gathering without squinting into a shaving mirror, which is what Dorjan claimed he'd been doing since his teens.

Triari Dorjan had claimed privilege and had taken an extended leave at the birth of Krissa's child. He'd communicated with the Forum almost daily, and there was always a soldier—one of the ones who hadn't left the military as soon as the farming and food situations stabilized somewhat—running a packet of parchment to the door of Kyon's Keep, but Taern refused to let him spend more than an hour per day at his desk.

"Holiday, Dorjan. You made it more than clear, remember? I was there. You told them you took the mantle reluctantly and that you needed to rest. They said, 'Oh Forum Master Dorjan, we're so impressed by your ability to see right and wrong and blah blah blah blah blah we'll bend over and suck your arse if only you don't make us think for ourselves!'"

Dorjan had quill to paper at that moment, and at Taern's rather rude (and dead on) impression of the Forum Master who had, indeed, told Dorjan he'd be a nominal leader only, he arched an eyebrow. "I don't believe those were Chamber's exact words."

Taern shrugged. "They were close." He made Dorjan smile, and Dorjan allowed Taern to seize the sheaf of papers from his grasp, and that was that. A one-hour limit on work for the entire three-fortnight stay.

They had visited the outer keeps, discussed how to farm next spring, and assessed their stores to see if they could send some to Karanos and Gretzky, as both provinces were struggling to recoup their losses from the war.

And, of course, Dorjan had taken Taern to the mines to bond with the niskets some more.

Taern was reasonably sure they fucked like rabbits—when the nisket cloud finally receded, they'd both been sore in all the appropriate muscles and covered in each other—but that's not what he remembered. What he remembered was the feeling of well-being, of freedom, of joy. After he and Dorjan cleaned up and made it down the umbilical, he looked around Kyon's Keep and realized he could, at any moment, think of a place and know which tiny metal creature was there, and what it was doing. He looked at Dorjan in wonder and then looked at the giant rock pile of wreckage they'd already started to mine.

"No wonder," he said, thinking hard about Areau's sacrifice. "No wonder he died to protect this. This... this feeling, being part of your land—it makes me whole!"

Dorjan looked out at the rubble pile too. "That's not what they would have felt," he said, his voice hollow, and Taern knew he was right. The feeling of the niskets in his blood was powerful—in the best way. To people who wanted power so that other people wouldn't have it? It could be deadly. Taern understood, now, why Kyon's Keep kept the niskets on the level of fairy tale for the rest of the world. It was a very important secret to keep.

But that had been their first week back, before Krissa had given birth and before Taern had seen the effect that fresh air, *moderate* exercise, and happiness had on Dorjan.

His chest had finally filled out enough to showcase his muscles, and his ribs were finally not able to be counted under his skin, and his smile, though still guarded with almost everyone but Taern, Krissa, and her newborn son, was becoming more and more whole. This day, as Taern tied his cravat—a bright lime green, in spite of the somber month and the sober occasion—Taern thought he had never looked more beautiful.

"What?" Dorjan asked, checking his cheeks in the mirror. He had shaved in the morning as he'd overseen the preparation, and come back in to bathe and shave before dinner. Taern had cut his hair for him the day before, and he looked every inch the young Forum Master and gentleman.

"What nothing," Taern replied evenly, settling him back square again so Taern could finish his cravat.

"You're looking at me strangely. I thought my hair was crooked or there was something on my—"

"Hush," Taern said, holding his hand to Dorjan's lean mouth. "I'm thinking good thoughts about us being this child's guardians with Krissa, and about how you are too beautiful for words. Don't ruin it by self-deprecation, not today."

Faint red crescents appeared on Dorjan's cheeks, and Taern finished tying his cravat and rubbed a thumb over them.

"Remember once, we talked about the provinces and how you thought there was a power beyond the founders?"

Dorjan grimaced. "Yes—a divinity, a guiding force. Yes, I still believe it."

"So do I. You could have died a thousand times between the first time I met you and the second, but you didn't. I think that divinity must have saved you until I could take over."

Dorjan's blush deepened. "I think you would be happy living at Madame M's and enjoying the hell out of yourself without me," he said, obviously embarrassed, and Taern smacked his cheek lightly.

"Don't make me get serious with you, Nyx. This thing I'm feeling right now, before we go take custody of our son with Krissa, in front of your mother and Areau's parents and your keep and my sisters? That's a tremendous thing."

Dorjan laughed a little and looked at Taern with that shyness that could still peek out from time to time, and which dazzled Taern whenever it did. "I'm terrified," he confided. "Taern, that's Areau's child—I have such a debt to that tiny person, to his mother—"

"So do I," Taern said soberly. "You're not in this alone, Nyx. I'm there too. You think Krissa's not frightened to death? She's got a task planned when we get to the city as well, and she's depending on us to help pick up the slack!"

Madame M's brothel hadn't just been a whorehouse, it had been a sanctuary and a place where sex was not just practiced for a fee but celebrated, and where differences in sex weren't abhorred, they were welcome. Yes, all cities *had* whores—it was a fact of humanity. Very few cities had a celebration of sexuality, and Krissa thought that sort of business was necessary too. She'd asked Dorjan for the start-up money to go back to work—in an administrative capacity only—to build the brothel back up. Dorjan had agreed, with the caveat that she make sure the ones who truly wanted to were the only ones who were trained up, and the ones who simply wanted shelter be referred to the schools and shelters instead.

It was an amicable bargain, and Taern thought that in its own small way, the new Madame's, as Krissa planned to call it, would be a necessary part of building Thenis back up to a city in its prime. Hell, they'd already cleaned out the monorail so the rabbits could continue to run; Taern was optimistic about anything at this point.

Dorjan nodded and took Taern's hand from his cravat—Taern was just fussing with it now anyway—and held it up to his cheek.

"Beloved?" Dorjan said softly, and Taern knew that all of his briskness and business-as-usual drained from his spine like starch from a wet shirt.

"Yes?"

"You need to know—I mean, I can't think of words to tell you, but I think I should before we go out there. Every good thing in my heart right now, every joy, every hope for the future, every pleasant memory of a very dismal past—I owe those to you. You're their keeper. You're the one who makes them real. This moment here, this joy, this celebration, it would not be possible, it would not be possible for *me*, if you had not seen something in me in that back alley of Thenis and set about to show me that I was good too. I just thought I should tell you, since we're in this together." Dorjan smiled shyly when he finished, and bobbed his head like a nervous boy, then bent and planted a quick kiss on Taern's slightly open mouth.

"Shall we go, then?" he asked, heading toward the door and pausing to look behind him as though he hadn't just decimated Taern, annihilated him, destroyed the boy he'd been and remade him into the man who could stand by Dorjan's side, all in one casually delivered sentence.

"You git," Taern said, his voice unapologetically thick. He wiped his cheeks with the back of one hand and then put the hand in Dorjan's as he stood waiting. "I can't even believe you'd tell me something like that now."

Dorjan chuckled then and bent down to whisper in Taern's ear. "Well, when we're alone, Cricket, I seem to find better things to do."

Taern beamed up at him, thrilled and happy, and then followed him out the door. Their future was waiting, chubby fists, wrinkled little toes, furious temper, and all, and Taern couldn't wait to hold him again.

AMY LANE is a mother of four and a compulsive knitter who writes because she can't silence the voices in her head. She adores cats, knitting socks, and hawt menz, and she dislikes moths, cat boxes, and knuckle-headed macspazzmatrons. She is rarely found cooking, cleaning, or doing domestic chores, but she has been known to knit up an emergency hat/blanket/pair of socks for any occasion whatsoever or sometimes for no reason at all. She writes in the shower, while commuting, while taxiing children to soccer/dance/karate/oh my! and has learned from necessity to type like the wind. She lives in a spider-infested, crumbling house in a shoddy suburb and counts on her beloved Mate, Mack, to keep her tethered to reality—which he does while keeping her cell phone charged as a bonus. She's been married for twenty-plus years and still believes in Twu Wuv, with a capital Twu and a capital Wuv, and she doesn't see any reason at all for that to change.

Visit Amy's website at http://www.greenshill.com. You can e-mail her at amylane@greenshill.com.

Romance from AMY LANE

KEEPING PROMISE ROCK

http://www.dreamspinnerpress.com

GREEN'S HILL

http://www.dreamspinnerpress.com

Romance from AMY LANE

http://www.dreamspinnerpress.com

Romance from AMY LANE

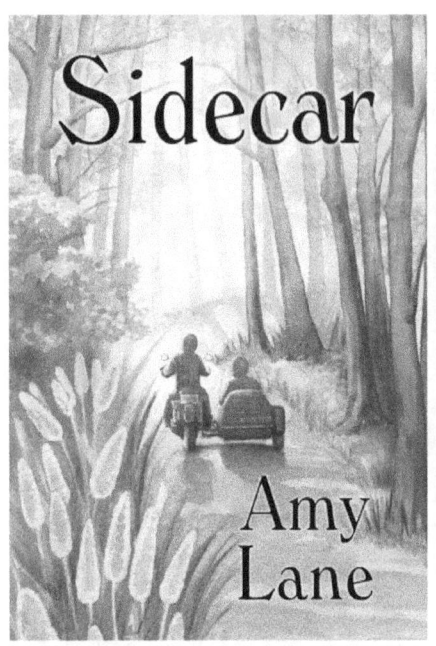

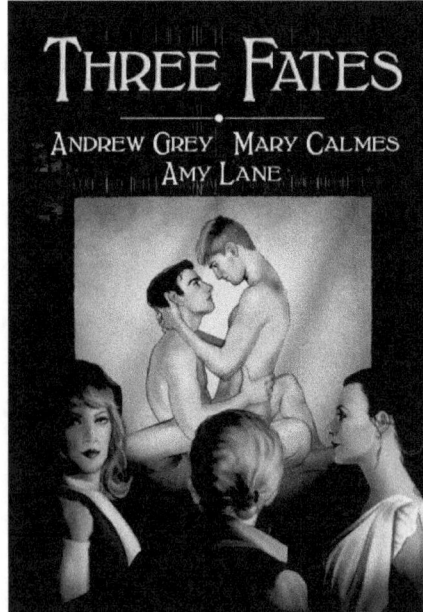

http://www.dreamspinnerpress.com

Romance & Knitting from AMY LANE

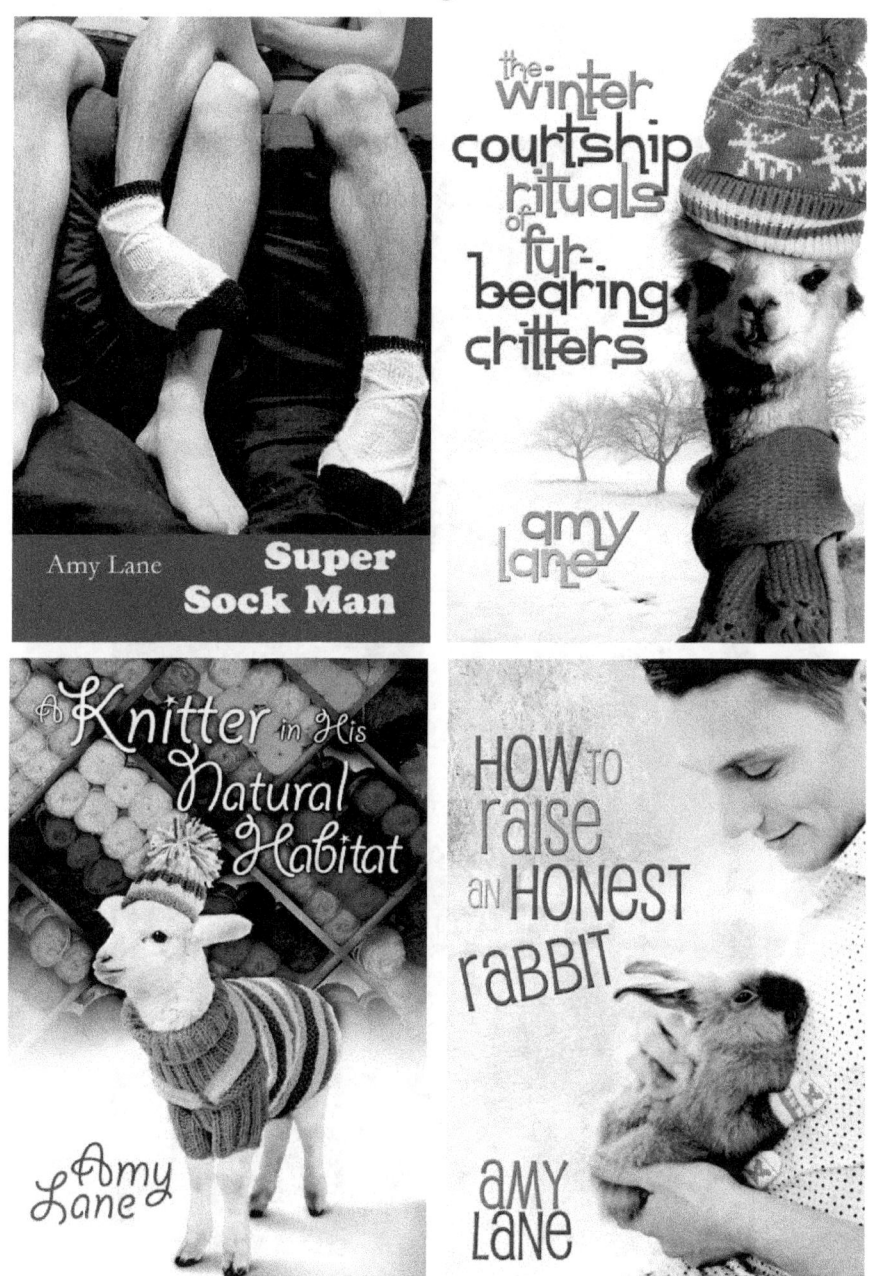